B1 Hawk

CHLOE TURNER

Deixis Press

First published in 2024 by Deixis Press
www.deixis.press

ISBN 978-1-917090-04-9 (HB)
ISBN 978-1-917090-05-6 (PB)

Typeset using Adobe Caslon Pro by
Palimpsest Book Production Ltd, Falkirk, Stirlingshire

Cover design by Deividas Jablonskis

Blue Hawk

CHLOE TURNER

Part One

–

YELLOW

Chapter One

1663

Joan found the stile in the hedge at the top of the meadow, heart thudding as she pulled herself over.

Across the valley, the grassy slopes of Rack Hill were striped today: garlanded with great lengths of drying broadcloth. Between white rows of undyed felt were hung fat stretches of the buttery yellow that Berkeley was known for, of Uley Blue and of red that would one day become Stroud Scarlet – these colours that stained the streams of her valley.

But Joan hadn't run up the hillside to admire the dyer's handiwork; she turned her back on the distant tenter racks and ran on, hoping she would not be too late to catch him.

Smoke was already drifting from the chimney of both the cottages on the upper edge of this field; she'd have to move quickly across the open ground. The fulling mills were silent for the Sabbath but there would be plenty rising early to finish their chores before the walk to church. Joan wasn't trespassing as such – this was common land – but she wouldn't want to be seen. So she quickened her step over the wet grass and across the next stile into the woods that topped the hill. The warmth of the sun on the skin above her neckline was a reminder of the dwindling minutes before the church bell began its toll.

In the woods, the great oaks and coppiced hazel offered welcome shadows. It wouldn't be wise to follow the donkey track up through the trees; she scrambled through the undergrowth instead, cursing as last season's brambles snared at her dress, until she found a clearing that looked over the path down from the highest cottages. Here, she could hover unseen. She squatted, picking at the thorns and burrs in her hem as her pulse began to slow. In the strange absence of the thump and thunder of the fulling stocks, she waited, listening for the first crunch of his tread on the stones of the track.

The minutes passed. A tree-creeper fluttered to the bottom of a birch and began to slink up its silvery bark in a spiral. Little Climber. Bark Crawler. Tree Mouse. Joan recalled the shape of the words which had sat alongside the drawing in the primer at the Dame School on the hill, how carefully she'd copied them onto her slate – the new girl, on borrowed time, desperate to catch up with the rest. *Tsree-tsree-tsree* the little bird called now as it wound its way up the trunk, its song pitched high enough that in a few years she might no longer hear it.

Joan tucked a curl back behind her ear, regretting that she had never thought to look in the shard of mirror glass her sister Alice had propped on the shelf above their bed. No doubt she was red-faced and grimy; probably she was mad to think he'd even look her way. But there was something between her and Daniel. She'd felt it when he caught her eye across the pews as they were leaving church last week, and before, at the horse fair up at the fields near the Blue Boys' Inn last Whitsun, when the herdsman had slipped on some dung and she was sure Daniel had winked at her across the pens.

Surely, soon. She fidgeted, legs cramping. The marshy ground was starting to weigh down her petticoat and she wished she'd tucked it up into her stays. This valley-side bled spring water, spilling it down to the hard-working channel of the river Frome at its base. Behind her, the Black Gutter – largest of the springs – gurgled and spat from its fissure in the clay, sustaining lush growth all around. Joan crushed the fine green spear of a young ramsons leaf between finger and thumb, admired the vivid stain it left on the scroll of her fingerprint: green so bright you could taste it. She smelt the garlic on her fingertips and her stomach rumbled; she should have brought a trug to fill while she waited.

She could see the pitched roof of Daniel's father's cottage through the trees, above a cleared line where another donkey path pushed horizontally. She'd heard the men talking about Richard Randall some weeks back. Waiting to collect a chain of yarn from the workshop, it was a discussion she'd only half understood: that he had cut loose from the congregation at Bisley he'd grown up with; that he no longer dressed like the rest; that he had drifted in with men who spoke outside the established Church.

But whatever Daniel's father thought and did, Daniel was still in the habit of making the journey down and up the valley-sides to the church every Sunday, just as his late mother had. And there was still time, if he came now, for Joan to stand as if caught in the act of picking a skirt-full of wild garlic, to accept his offer of company across the valley in time for the service to start.

A laugh now, from above. But it was a girl's laugh, and the skittering footsteps that followed sounded like a child at play. Joan shrank back. There were two figures coming down the track, and she recognised both. There was Daniel at last, with a jacket over his breeches. A fold of yellow felt in his palm: his Sunday hat, with its feather – a new one for every season – tucked out of sight. And there was Rockwood, the hunting dog he'd rescued from a trap. The dog trotted alongside him with his lopsided gait, snapping at the hat as if it were a chicken for roasting. But next to Daniel, walking backwards down the path as if drawing him on, was an even more familiar silhouette. Joan's older sister Alice wore her dresses pulled in very tight, and when she pinned her hair up as she had done today, from a distance you might take her for a gentleman's daughter. *Alice, what is the meaning of this?*

'They were touting for military men at the market last week,' Joan heard her sister say, as they passed close to where Joan was hidden. 'France, or the Dutch . . . if the King and his brother can't decide which is the greater danger, perhaps they'll take them both on.'

How had Alice had time to arrive here? When Joan had crept from their cot in the twilight an hour back, her sister had been just a tangle of bedclothes on the far side.

'I've not got the sea legs for the navy. My stomach turned taking the fishing skiff out on the millpond.' Daniel kicked a stone off the path.

'Army then,' Alice said, skipping round again to face him. 'If war's declared, they'll need soldiers.'

Daniel shook his head. 'I've not got it in me to kill a man.'

Joan's stomach chose this moment to rumble again, impossibly loudly, and she clutched at herself, desperate to muffle the sound. But Daniel, on the far side of the track, was perhaps too removed to hear it, and Alice, nearer, was apparently far too engaged for any such distraction. Instead, Joan watched her pout back at him. 'A shame. When you'd look ever so fine in a uniform.'

Daniel pulled himself up a little at this and Joan rocked back on her heels, making a twig crack beneath her foot. This time, the sound carried; Daniel's head snapped round at it. Then he stood a moment, staring over towards the trees where Joan was hidden, frowning, with a hand lifted against the low sun. She tried to make herself small, cursing the long limbs that never seemed to stop growing, feeling the prickle of a nettle as it pressed against her shin. But then Alice grabbed Daniel's sleeve, pulling him back around, making as if they should skip together. He laughed and shook his head again, but the frown did not quite leave him.

There would be an empty seat in the pew beside Joan's father this morning, and questions would be asked. She might even be beaten, but her father's heart would not be in it. Since her mother's passing, many things had been allowed to slide.

Joan stayed crouched in the scrub until long after the footsteps had faded, nursing the nettle's icy-hot sting and relishing its distraction. Even after, she did not rush home – little point now, when the three-mile walk to Bisley and back would keep her father and sister gone for hours. Instead, she criss-crossed the streams on the way down the hillside, squatting to look for shells where they crumbled from the bedrock. Through blurred eyes, she rubbed a perfect cockle shell between her fingertips, dipping it back into the stream to rinse away the loose mud, wondering for the hundredth time how it might have found its way up onto this hillside. It would look pretty on her shelf. But then she remembered the other trinkets there: that bright-blue jay feather Daniel had tucked in her bonnet once, a button she'd found beside his kneeler as they left the church some weeks back, and (most shaming) a crumb of honey cake that he had left on his plate at the wake for his mother's funeral, secreted under half a walnut shell to keep off the mice. Joan sniffed, wiping her nose with the cuff of her Sunday dress.

Her face flushed hot now to think of her stupidity; the cake crumb, of course, but even the thought that Daniel might have favoured her. How could he? She was all knees and elbows, without a penny to her name, and so many others for him to choose from. But hadn't he seemed to find her eye often enough to make her think, and hadn't he smiled often enough when he caught her gaze?

And Alice – since their mother's death, her sister had made little secret of how tiresome she found it to be tasked with Joan's care. But surely there must be some loyalty there? Anger, now, burnt Joan's cheeks, that her sister could have so little regard for her. She could only hope that Daniel had not spotted her in the bushes before Alice had pulled him round. Joan splashed freezing spring water on her cheeks to excise the memory of it all.

Perhaps it was these things a mother taught. Joan had only just turned twelve when Hannah Browning had died. Three years ago now: it had been a stray nail on the loom, just a raised pink weal, but her mother's arm had turned bad so quickly, the grey, pus-filled wound had had to be hidden under the forgiving weave of her burial shroud. The passing bell had chimed for all of her thirty-nine years; Joan had been at the Dame School only a few months back then, and could count only just high enough to hear her mother's years rung out over the valley.

But Alice . . . just a young girl herself when their mother was taken, but there were things Joan's sister seemed to have been born knowing. Two years older than Joan, but it might as well have been a lifetime. Joan shook her head; there was little point raging, questioning why Alice would do such a thing, even though she knew full well that Joan was sweet on Daniel. It was just how Alice's blood ran.

Joan cursed the rare kindness some months back – a shared embrace when Alice had found her sobbing under the quilt – which had led to her confiding in her sister. It had been the third anniversary of their mother's passing; a winter night, and in the bitter cold she and Alice had been wrapped close together. The warm feeling in her belly when she thought about Daniel had seemed to Joan like a treasure to show off: a pebble, worn shiny, or a perfect acorn, sprung from its cup.

But still, she should have known better. Alice took whatever she wanted, and knowing that someone else had need of it only made the attraction stronger. No, if there was a question, it was only in how Joan's sister had made it up onto the hillside so soon. She hurled the cockle shell back into the stream and turned to run down into the valley.

Joan had reached the first of the mills – little more than a cottage, you wouldn't know it for a place of work if you weren't from round here – when the breeze from the north brought the distant chime of the church bells at Bisley. Following the stream up the valley, she ducked her head through the reeds to peer into the channel for the sleek bodies of trout – anything to distract herself from the nagging toll of that bell. When the ringing finally fell silent, her shoulders slumped. Her father would be looking about for her, holding the space in the pew with his hat until the last possible moment, ignoring the fussing of the curate and the dogwhipper with his tongs and switch. But it was out of her hands now.

She'd walked on to cross the little bridge over the mill's tail-race, ready to climb the lynch terraces towards her father's cottage, when she heard a sound from behind the low hedge on the far side of the stream. A woman there was pushing herself up to standing, leaning on the shaft of a spade. When she caught Joan's eye, the woman started to turn away, as if she might return to her digging. Her face was familiar, but Joan couldn't recall her name. There were few strangers in this valley, but some kept themselves to themselves; Joan's mother had been one of them.

Keen to know her suddenly, Joan spoke quickly, before the woman could disappear beneath the hedge: 'Good morning, Mrs . . .'

There was silence for a moment, then the woman turned slowly back around. Joan hoped it was stiffness from her labour and not irritation which caused her to blow the air from her cheeks before she spoke. 'Freme. Widow Freme.'

Widow; wasn't the word like a dried husk? And to be saddled with it forever after, as if the loss of a loved one were not enough.

But Mrs Freme wore the title as well as you could. There was a seam of blue, like that jay feather on Joan's trinket shelf, at the hem of her sackcloth apron, and though her bonnet was grey from washing, it too was hemmed with a bright blue.

It was difficult to put an age to her – her hair was only a little whitened at the temples where her bonnet had slipped. But now, looking more closely, Joan did know her. In happier times, a few years back, there'd been Mrs Freme dancing to a fiddle – May Day, perhaps, in the shadow of the maypole, or Lammastide, celebrating the blessing of the loaf from the first grain of the year. She'd looked young enough to bear children then, though there were none wheeling around her today. Still, she'd likely be younger than Joan's own mother.

Then Joan swallowed, remembering. Freme: there was more to that name. There'd been a Sam Freme die at the big mill at the head of the valley, a few months after her mother's passing. The memory would probably have been lost in the desperate sadness of that time were it not for an unforgotten dismay at Alice's relish in the telling of it: a terrible accident, the fuller dragged into the wheel he was tending, his waistcoat snagged around the shaft and his body was crushed in the mechanism. There had been talk of grown men spewing up their midday repast at the sight of it, and the clothier forced to put the whole fulling operation to rest for the afternoon on account of what the millsman and his crew had witnessed. But perhaps Alice's callousness had been most disturbing of all.

'That's right. That was my Samuel,' Mrs Freme said, watching Joan's expression change. 'Crushed in the wheel like a cobnut in a grinder.'

'I'm sorry, madam.'

But the woman shook her head, wiping her forehead with the back of her hand. 'What will be . . . God's will, and all that.'

Joan fidgeted from one foot to the other. It was enough to have to tend the garden alone, and now – thanks to her – the woman must revisit the harrowing circumstances of her husband's death. She took a step along the path, thinking to make her excuses and leave before she could do more damage.

'But there are some small comforts in being alone,' Mrs Freme said loudly, in a way that had Joan pause mid-step. 'Between you and me, Samuel Freme wasn't always the kindest man.' She put her head on one side. 'While God's concerning himself with his chapel folk, I'll tell you: I doubt there are many missing him.'

Joan felt her cheeks pinking. She wasn't used to this frank talk; even Alice confined her more scandalous chatter to the ears of family members. And it was not done to speak ill of the dead, even the very worst of them. Joan tried to recall the sharp cool of the spring water as she'd splashed it earlier, as if that might stem the blush.

'Now, it's no real concern of mine,' Mrs Freme went on, 'but are your kinfolk not good church people?' Joan felt the heat rise up her cheeks. 'What is it that keeps you from the Bisley pew?'

'I, I . . .'

Mrs Freme laughed. 'I'm teasing you. You'll see I'm a long way from my Sunday best myself. I've not seen the inside of the church since the day we buried Samuel – you'd probably see the holy water churn in the font if I were to venture that way now. But you look like a lost soul, Joan. It is Joan, isn't it? Can I show you something? Come see my garden, if you're at a loose end.'

Joan hesitated, thinking of all the work that waited for her at the cottage. They'd have sung two psalms by now, and even Father Britton could only talk for so long. But she was curious, about this woman with her candid speech, and what lay behind the hedge. 'I'll make it worth your while,' Mrs Freme murmured. 'A morsel of something when we're done.'

The promise of food settled the matter; Joan had eaten nothing since the previous afternoon. In fact, there'd been little more than scraps and dripping in the house for weeks. Every spare farthing had been channelled into new yarn and the cost of putting out the cloth for finishing. It was not that Joan didn't admire her father's attempts to step up to the rank of clothier, to sell the cloth they wove on his own account rather than for the betterment of the mill owner, but so far the profits had been meagre. What had started well enough – a pile of wrapped cloth accumulated beside the doorway of the cramped cottage they shared, and him off on the road in good spirits, choosing to accompany these first packages to London – had quickly turned sour. Falling against the door many days later, he'd come home dirty, drunk and glum. He'd complained as long as the girls would listen: of the critical eye of the Blackwell Hall factor, of the size of his commission, and of the measly export price the man had predicted for the pieces. Alice had quickly found reasons to absent herself, so it had been left to Joan to comfort their father, but he'd had little energy left for gratitude. Instead, he'd snapped at Joan for the height of the fire in the grate, for the loose warp on the loom, for an uneven weave in a finished piece of felt.

'I'll be needed at home when the bell rings again,' she said to Mrs Freme now, remembering how she'd found him later that night, staring at the fire's embers with damp eyes, begging her to forgive him for the way he'd spoken in anger.

'I'm sure. You're John Browning's girl, aren't you? I know better than most what it's like to grow up without a mother – I dare say your stove and looms won't lie idle today, even though it's the Sabbath – so I'll not keep you long. Just a minute then, see what I've been growing here.' Mrs Freme pulled the gate wider, so that the extent of the garden was revealed. She ushered Joan in, nudging her boot against the gatepost to loosen some of the thick mud from its sole.

Joan glanced around the plot, half afraid to trespass even though she'd been invited over the threshold.

'They settled the cottage on me when Samuel died, by way of compensation,' she heard Mrs Freme say behind her. 'A lifetime lease, but I only have need of the back rooms, so there's a dye-man who rents the big room at the front and the rest of the plot, save that far bed at the back. He pays me a few shillings for tending his plants. I'd not let him know it, of course, but there's pleasure in it,' she said, lifting her spade to wave it at the beds around her. 'All these plants, and the colours that'll come from them. I only know the half of it, but there's such a joy in the growing.'

Joan was still staring. She'd never seen such a garden. Not huge, perhaps eighty paces by forty, but every space was made use of, the plot divided into neat beds with paths and rows of stones running between them. It was the plants that were most intriguing, though even the recognisable shrubs seemed to grow in different ways, and so many of the beds held unfamiliar blooms.

The process of dyeing was not entirely alien to her, of course. Joan's mother, Hannah, had sometimes gathered from the woods to add some colour to the coarse plaincloth she used for their clothes; simple boils, in colours that were not far from the earth. Dock for yellow, oak galls for ashen grey, berries for a dull pink-brown. Nettles, in springtime, for a soft grey-green that matched Hannah Browning's own eyes. As a young child, it had usually fallen to Joan to collect the new nettle stands: the leaves had nagged at her ankles while she cut the stems, leaving a rash of white, but even then, there'd been a magic in the process. She'd watched her mother steep the leaves and pummel the cloth in the liquid. And whenever her mother's glance was elsewhere, Joan would take the chance to dip the ladle and pour the steep back into the dye pot, observing over days the gradual shift from yellow to green to that soft sage grey, a tint that stayed in the fleece and would always remind her of her mother.

But that was years ago. Her father's cloth was sold white in the main, and there was no dyeing to be seen at the fulling mill where Joan waited so often for his packages of new yarn or finished cloth – the owner was accustomed to sending his own pieces out to a Dudbridge mill famous for its woad. And while the valley's biggest clothiers, Mr Iles, Mr Tayloe, and old Mr Webb, were said to colour their cloth with the finest foreign dye-wares – vermillion for red and sometimes even indigo for blue – she had only ever seen the finished results drying on the hillside.

'I can see from your face that you're already taken with it. And you're not even witnessing it at its best,' Mrs Freme said. 'In a few months, it'll be full of colour. Yellow flowers, mostly, for dye plants – yarrow and dyer's broom and camomile and all the rest. It's a strange thing, how many different magics can blossom from a yellow bud. But come summer, there'll be pink from the hollyhocks and purple heather down the middle here too. You could dye a gown like a rainbow from this garden, if the urge took you. You'll know this one, I expect?' she said, pointing down to the first of the beds.

They were little more than flat rosettes of leaves, but now Joan recalled seeing the same plant up in the barley fields after harvest. She leant down to press the leaves between her fingers.

'Weld,' said Mrs Freme, leaning her spade against the cottage's side wall. 'My father used to say that the Romans used it for the robes of the Vestal Virgins. Golden maidens to tend the goddess of the hearth . . . imagine that! You'll see it'll shoot up as the months go on: tall, flowering stems that we'll harvest when the sun's high. He gets a good yellow from the dried straw, he tells me.'

She walked on a few steps.

'How about this one?' It was a round ball of a shrub, dusted with the first of its yellow bloom. 'You've seen this before, I'm sure.'

Joan shook her head. 'That one neither.'

'This here is woad. It only flowers every other year, but that doesn't matter – the dye's in the leaves. This whole side of the garden is already full of it, but now he wants another two beds dug at the back. I'll probably have to lose my beans and cabbages. Even then, he'll still be short and will have to buy in from the Wotton growers. We've no more space here, and it takes bushels of the stuff to get that rich blue. Stinks like a drunkard's privy while you're at it, may I tell you, but those navy uniforms won't dye themselves.'

'What's this one?' Joan pointed to the first shoot coming up through a web of dead stalks. 'Reckon I've seen this in the woods round here.' Her dress was damp at the knees as well as the hem now, where she had been kneeling on the grass between the beds – she would pay for it later, when there were more stains to be bleached in the pot – but she was reluctant to move.

'Now, that's madder. When the leaves fan out, you'll see they're like prickly stars. Stings a little, like nettle, if you handle it wrong. But it doesn't favour this soil, so we have to treat it like royalty. Weed regularly and fight the slugs off.' Mrs Freme knelt down beside her. 'Here, help me pull this couch grass from out of the roots. Look, you can see the red, at the base of the plant – that's where the colour comes from. Wriggly red roots. Madder gives the best red you'll get without travelling halfway across the world for it. They say gentlemen even feed it to their hawks to make their beaks and talons richer.'

Joan leant in to rub the earth from the stem where it met the ground. The deep red of the jagged roots was shocking, as if they were alive against the soil. She wondered whether the colour ran right through them, how they smelt, how they might taste on her tongue.

'There's an alchemy to it,' she heard Mrs Freme say, 'and something tells me you've got the taste for it. But the bell tolls for you, little Miss Browning.' Mrs Freme was shaking the mud off a dandelion root, and Joan realised that she had been completely absorbed in the madder, imagining the process that might take this alien stem to the hearty russet she had seen on the tenter racks. There *was* an alchemy to it – even the miserable recollection of the events of the morning had been displaced for some minutes by its magic. But her head was clearing now and the church bell was indeed ringing, and she would have to run if she was to set and light the fire and have some food on the table by the time the churchgoers returned, her best chance of avoiding a beating.

'Here.' Mrs Freme grabbed Joan's arm as she turned to run. 'Before you go . . . I promised you food. Why don't you take a cabbage and some turnip tops back for your mo . . .' she started, then corrected herself, '. . . your father. You'll have the makings of a pottage before they're halfway down the donkey track.'

'Thank you, ma'am.' Joan ducked her head and waited, treading on one foot and then the other, while Mrs Freme tipped the vegetables into her skirts. The cabbage was a fine, white globe of a thing and the turnip tops would fill out the pot, at least.

'No need to thank me. I promised you more but that bell's got your name on it,' Mrs Freme said, leaning back against the gatepost. 'Come back sometime, if you will. There's plenty more to see.'

But Joan was distracted now by the burden of the chores ahead of her, and she said her goodbye quickly. She felt the older woman's eyes on her as she crossed the river, clutching at the bundle in her skirts, but she didn't look back as she ran up the stepped slope of the hillside towards home.

Chapter Two

The cockerel was crowing when Joan came up the path to the cottage. The bird had found its way up to the top bar of an ancient, broken loom that lay beside the front door, waiting to be split for firewood. Their cockerel was no fine specimen – dirty-white and scrawny after a long, thin winter, and short of feathers on its far wing after an encounter with a fox – but that didn't stop it proclaiming its territory across the valley all day long.

On the ground below, their sole remaining hen (red-brown and small) picked at something in the dirt. There'd been no sign of her when Joan had left this morning; and now she thought of it, it must have been while she was searching across the fields, fearing that the fox had taken the hen too, that Alice had stolen a march on her to reach the far side of the valley. Joan shook her head, bending to lift the hinged lid of the wooden crate where the hen liked to lay. One perfect egg, speckled at the top, rested at the back of the crate. It was something. In the coldest weeks, the hen had rarely laid, and times had been hardest then. Joan blew off some stray strands of straw, dropped the egg gently into the nest of her skirts with the vegetables, and stepped over the threshold into the dark.

As always, it took a moment to get used to the shadows – there were only two small windows in the main room and this deep valley caught little sun even in high summer. But she could see that their father had left in haste, having slept late perhaps, with both girls gone and the cottage quiet around him. A tangle of undergarments lay across the floor between his bed and the threshold, and his bedclothes had not been rolled away into the corner. Joan tucked them back and then turned her attention to the hearth.

The cockerel began crowing again as Joan laboured, making quick work of the fire and then tidying the loom room at the rear of the cottage where she and Alice slept, except when the distance from the hearth became too much and they joined their father beside it. When the floors were swept and the night soil carried out to the stream, she started on the vegetables for the pot. They didn't have a garden of their own; the cottage was built on a stray corner of common land, with no permission, and by rights should not be here at all. Others might have planted a few onions on the field edge, but the building of the back room into the hollow of the old quarry behind was a further imposition, and Joan's father had no wish to invite attention. Besides, it hadn't always been like this – when their mother had been alive and their father had still worked at the mill, there'd been money enough to put food on the table. But John Browning was a dreamer; without Hannah to steady his hand, he'd thrown everything at the chance of quick riches and a different life.

Joan was stirring a full pot when she heard the sound of boots on the path. Full of cabbage and thickened with the egg, the pottage looked tastier than anything they'd had in weeks. But if her father noticed the smell as he crossed the threshold, he showed no sign of it. He dropped his stick in the corner, tossed his cap onto the dresser, and ripped the curtain aside to go through to the back room.

'It's always worse when you have to wait for a hiding.' Coming in a few steps behind, Alice was smirking as she set aside her gloves. They'd been a gift, those gloves, from the vicar's wife. Payment in kind for sitting prettily for a series of portraits, Alice a proxy for the gentleman's daughter whose face would be painted in later. The soft pigskin on the palms was thinning now, and some of the stitching needed tidying, but Alice always wore the gloves as if the Queen had nothing finer.

Joan continued to stir the pot and Alice frowned.

'He kept Mrs Abell waiting for a seat, saying you were coming. She was huffing and puffing like a cow in calf. And when the vicar had us stand and Father had to move aside for her, I saw her plant her foot on his boot where the leather's come away. His nose was red with the effort of not making a sound.'

'That's between me and Father.'

Alice snorted. 'Makes an ugly girl, jealousy.'

It's unkindness that makes for an ugly girl, thought Joan, looking at the sneer on Alice's face. For all her raven hair and rosy cheeks (and the long list of other attributes Alice liked to recite in bed at night), surely it counted for nothing if you didn't have a drop of kindness? She turned away; Alice's eyes had that grey-green tint of their mother's, and it unsettled Joan to look at them when her sister was being like this.

'I don't know what you mean,' Joan said into the steam.

'I saw you there, squatting in the nettles, looking like you were relieving yourself.'

Joan shrank into her shoulders.

'Don't worry, I didn't tell him. Wouldn't want him thinking I was related to such a peculiar strip of bark.' Alice was rubbing at the fabric at her waist, licking her thumb to scrub away some mark on the weave there.

'Why did you do it?' Joan said it quietly, pushing a bunch of ramsons leaves against the side of the pot so that they bruised.

'What's that?' Alice continued to fiddle with her gown.

'Why did you do it? Daniel. When you knew.'

'Knew what? What did I know, Joan? What is it about your feelings for Daniel that I should have known?'

Joan's face was burning now, even though the fire she'd set was small. She couldn't say it. Not now, in broad daylight, with Alice like this and their father clattering about in the looms just beyond the curtain.

Alice laughed like the water slipping through a sluice gate. Then she bent down to whisper near Joan's ear. 'You just stir your pot. If *your* Daniel is sweet on me, I can hardly be blamed for it. You running round the hills with bare legs like a shepherd boy, and Daniel not far off a man these days . . . what were you expecting, that his head would be turned by the sight of a girl with burrs in her hair, a head full of school words, and a palm full of some shiny beetle she's come across in the hedgerow? It's a woman he'll be wanting, and how can I help it if he's got an eye for me?'

At that moment the curtain was pulled back across. Alice was quick to spring up and busy herself with the pile of bowls in the corner, but John Browning watched her for a moment, steadily, before he turned to Joan.

'You were missed at church, as I'm sure you realise.'

'I'm sorry, Father.'

'Where were you? Not that it matters now.'

'With Mrs Freme, at the dye house on the Millswood stream. She was showing me the garden she tends for the dyer who rents her rooms.' There was no good answer, so she might as well tell the truth. Joan stirred the cooking pot as she spoke, dreading the rise of anger in her father's voice.

But he just shook his head, rubbing at his brow. 'I was shamed to have to explain your absence,' he said. 'Don't let it happen again.'

'Yes, Father.' Joan stirred the pot harder. Through the steam she saw Alice's eyebrows shoot up – no doubt her sister had expected to see the belt fly. Perhaps she was disappointed, because when she turned from the crockery stack with a bowl in her hand, Alice's smile was not kind.

'Mrs Freme, eh? There's something strange about that woman,' Alice said then, running a finger around the edge of a bowl. 'No one ever saw her shed a tear for her husband.'

'By which you mean?' Now the anger snapped. Mr Browning's jaw was knotted as he spoke, turning towards his older daughter. Joan gripped the ladle a little tighter.

Alice laughed, but uncertainly. Her fingers twitched on the bowl's rim. 'Oh nothing, Father. I meant nothing.'

'I'm waiting.'

Alice glanced across to Joan, her mouth twisting before she spoke. 'Some of the women at the mill have a little joke at Mrs Freme's expense, that's all. That she might be growing all sorts in that garden, between the woad and the dyer's broom.' John Browning stared and Alice's voice wavered, but she kept going. 'That she's not quite right in the head, or that she's deserted the Lord and made a pact with Old Nick. Even that she should be swum in the millpond as a wit...'

Alice hadn't finished the word before their father had crossed the cramped room in a single pace, striking down on the bowl in her hand with a closed fist. It hit the earth floor and split in two with an ugly crack.

'Don't let me hear you speak like that again. Scold's bridles for the lot of you would be no more than you deserve. It shames me to hear it in my own home.'

Alice glared at the floor, her mouth still working angrily. When their father turned away to pour beer from a jug on the dresser, Joan watched her sister kick the nearest half of the bowl towards the fire.

'Go for water from the spring, Alice,' he said, without turning round.

'But that's Joan's . . .'

'Now,' he interrupted.

Alice snatched up the water pitcher and left; Joan watched her stride towards the broken gate at the end of the path, lashing out at nettle stands, and wrenching twigs from the lower branches of a beech. She would not hurry back. Joan let the ladle slide back into the cooking pot.

'No, serve up now,' her father said. 'You and I will eat together, and Alice can attend to herself when she troubles to return.'

So Joan ladled pottage into two bowls and John Browning eased himself into the chair at the head of the table to watch as she carried them across, wincing at the heat in them. She went to sit to his left but he gestured towards his right. The rumble from her stomach was insistent now, but only when he had whispered a grace and passed his spoon through the broth, nodding his approval at the thickness and the plentiful vegetables that ran through it, did she pick up her own.

'A girl so close to womanhood has grave need of a mother,' he said after some minutes. 'We must try and make allowances for her.'

'Yes, Father,' Joan replied. But she thought of the way Alice had skipped and flirted with Daniel on the hillside, and had to bite down hard on the bowl of her spoon to stop herself from saying more.

'You are a good girl, Joan, today notwithstanding.' Her father put down his spoon a moment to lay his hand over hers on the table. It had been months since he had worked the machines himself, but he still had the ragged skin of a millman: palms pricked from teasels and red and raw from the braying; fingers blistered from the machinery's grind. 'When your mother was still with us, you and Alice were like clove and orange, barely apart; how is it that you have grown so far apart?' He lifted a hand to his forehead, not waiting for an answer. 'You have talents that Alice lacks – your mother's sharp mind – and I expect that troubles her. When the priest took notice of you, intrigued enough by your interest in the letters in your Bible to pay for your schooling, you must see that it was hard for Alice. An opportunity she could not share in, and I think it pained her.'

'Yes, Father,' Joan repeated, trying not to think of the many nights when Alice had taunted her for her diligence with her school books; the times when her sister had taken advantage of the darkness to say darker things, even going as far as to suggest lewd reasons for the priest's special treatment.

'Alice spoke out of turn today,' her father went on, 'but we must make room for her to have her share of the limelight. We must celebrate the ways in which your sister shines.'

Joan stifled a laugh. As if Alice needed more room to show off – every young man from here to Brimscombe had been treated to a smile and a wave over the pews at some point. But her father did not notice; he was scooping up the last of his pottage. Only when the bowl was clean and he had wiped his mouth on his sleeve did he turn to Joan again.

'On the subject of your schooling, the time has come for that investment to reap dividends. I'd hoped to get to Stroud for the market this week, but I must ride out to Gloucester now, and I won't return before Friday afternoon. Your sister will take the cart with old Robert Parker in my place, but you'll need to ride with her. Last time, she came home with eight untouched fleeces that were priced as if they had been scoured: every one of them was sticky with oil, and even then the computation of the account was riddled with errors.'

'Of course, Father.'

'Alice will get you there alright, but you'll know my wool factor anyway, by the colour of his hat: a bright pea green. A Mr Ridler. He sets up a little way from the market house, on the west side of the Pitching. Now I don't take Ridler for a dishonest man, but he drives a hard bargain and his grasp of figures is little better than your sister's. So it will be down to you to check the computation, Joan. To verify the cleanliness of the fleece, and to confirm that it has been properly dried – I'm not paying good money for spring water and oil. As for colour, I have asked the man to set aside eight fleeces for my account, and in the mix of one white for every three coloured or dark wool.'

'Yes, Father.' Joan smiled into her bowl. It had been months since she had even left the valley – not since the start of winter certainly, perhaps as long ago as the Hampton sheep fair the October before. It was a consequence of there being so few of them in the household – too many jobs to go round – and it always seemed to fall to her to be left behind. To tend the fire, to keep the chickens from the fox . . . she had not been as far afield as Stroud since the previous summer, and had only visited the market there a bare handful of times.

'I know you won't let me down. And now here comes Alice with the water. Jump up, love, and pour a bowl for her,' he said to Joan, wiping the froth from the beer from his lip. As usual, his quarrel with Alice had been quickly forgotten; he was never able to stay angry with either of them for long. And now he lifted his cup to them: 'To a new start. May this be the day our luck changes.' John Browning drained his mug of beer – his second – and poured another, fuller, from the pitcher. When he had such a thirst, good things rarely followed. At the hearth, Joan crossed her fingers under the warmth of the full bowl.

Chapter Three

The cart-man Robert Parker pulled up his reins at The Cross at the top of the town. Neither of the mules was sprightly, and the older animal with the crooked ear hung its head while Alice and then Joan climbed down from the cart. Robert Parker, not young himself, was hard of hearing, but that hadn't stopped Alice prattling on to him all the way along the pitted road from the fingerpost at Blackness just an hour after dawn. To Joan, she'd barely spoken a word, and as the sisters straightened their petticoats on the road's edge, Joan was relieved to be freed from the discomfort of the cart and the awkwardness of their close proximity.

'I'll be seeing you back here later then, 'bout midday,' Mr Parker said, as he picked up the reins.

'Off to the George for a pitcher taller than your own leg, no doubt.' Alice hardly troubled to lower her voice as she turned away.

'We'll be here,' Joan said quickly, flushing for her sister's rudeness. Though the old man seemed happy enough as he pulled the cart around, so perhaps Alice was right and he was even deafer than the old mule.

The two of them stood together a moment at the crossing then, where Long Street met Hocker Hill, to run down towards the

Pitching. The roadside here was full of unlicensed traders peddling their beer, hard bread and livestock from rickety wagons, one eye always out for the bailiff's black hat. Amongst them, musicians – brass and reed and strings – competed for air and coins. The loudest were the two lads with shiny sackbuts on the step of the basket shop, serenading the crowd with a cap at their feet. A man was standing in front of them, shaking his fist, and though the brass trombones drowned out his words, his gestures towards the bank of cages on the far side of the crossing could not be clearer. His chickens, in cages piled across a rudimentary stall of hay bales and apple crates, were cringing against the wicker struts, despite the efforts of the young lad poking through vegetable scraps to distract them.

After the open fields and stillness of the Frome valley, the commotion at The Cross always came as a shock to Joan. It was not the noise: she was used to the thudding racket of the fulling hammers when the mills were at work, but that was a constant, not like the clatter and catcall of market day. A group of lads – millboys, from the blue of their hands, and drunk ones, from their stagger – pushed past now, and Joan almost lost her footing as they lurched against her. She reached for her sister, thinking to join hands against the pull of the crowd, but saw that Alice's attention was already elsewhere. The chicken farmer had resigned himself to the music, and now he was tipping his cap to Alice, grandly motioning to his display of scraggy birds as if they were rare thrushes fresh off the boat from the New World. And Alice was doing little to dissuade him, lifting a hand to her cheek as she laughed.

And when the shawm player aimed his elaborate solo in their direction, just as the handsome young bread man arrived in front of them with a basket of aniseed biscuits, Joan let her hand drop back to her side. How she longed for one of those crumbling biscuits, but Alice had already waved the bread man away with a grin; Joan didn't know how she could resist (the basket, not the boy). Yet again, her belly was empty as a dry well, and Joan's head felt light with it.

'Should we not make our way towards the factor?' Joan tried to keep her voice sweet, but loud enough to be heard over the clamour. 'We mustn't keep old Mr Parker waiting.'

But Alice just smiled while she pinched Joan's wrist. 'We have hours yet. Parker'll have his nose deep in egg pie.' Alice leaned in close, and Joan could smell the clove spice her sister must have rubbed on her neck this morning; who knew where she found the money for such things? 'Don't be a damp rag,' she hissed.

'Shall I go on ahead, then? Father told me what was needed.'

This, now, did attract Alice's attention; her head turned and she looked at Joan properly for the first time since they'd arrived. Alice would not like to be excluded from the matters of business which brought them here, Joan knew. Her sister was already opening her mouth for a sneering response, but just then the shawm player stepped up his reedy tune to a jig, and the bread man put down his basket and came back with hands held out as if to take her for a dance. Alice rearranged her expression into a smile.

'Go then,' she muttered, without looking at Joan again. 'Don't hurry back.'

'Shall I meet you round the back of the market house, out of the crowd?'

But Alice had already accepted the bread man's offer and allowed herself to be twirled out into the roadway, leaving the poultry man frowning at his chickens. The dancers swung out wide across the crossing, forcing a milk cart to swerve sharply, sending its churns rattling. As Joan turned away, swallowing at the size of the crowd that filled the street, her last glimpse of Alice was of her sister's laughing face as the bread man took an elaborate bow, pulling a flower fashioned from cooked dough from the satchel at his belt, already pleading for the next dance.

'Mr Ridler? My father, John Browning, has sent me on his account.' She'd been rehearsing her introduction all the way in the cart from Blackness, not wanting to look a fool, turning her face away from Alice so that her sister wouldn't see her mouthing the words. And she'd got them out, even if there had been a quaver in her voice which must have been obvious to the man. Now she must just endure his amused inspection while she waited for his reply.

The wool factor was standing behind a trestle piled high with fleeces, gnawing at a thumb-piece of cheese and dumpling while he looked her up and down. His waistcoat buttons were straining at their holes; this wasn't his first bite of the day. The pea-green hat Joan had been told to look for cast a shadow over his face, but she could still see the black in his teeth as he chewed with open mouth.

'Ah, you're the young 'un, are you?' he said eventually. When he smiled it was worse – Joan could see the dark craters left by extracted teeth right the way to the back of his jaw – but her stomach still rumbled at the sight of the crumbs that spilled down his front. 'I knows your sister already, and he told me he had another,' the merchant went on. 'Shame he's got no boys to do this dirty work.'

'Do you have the fleeces my father ordered, Mr Ridler?'

But the man was still talking, and he would not be put off. 'Must be awful quiet in your house, just the two chicks in the coop. My wife's got seven round her knees, and another on the way. Half the time, I feel like a rabbit in a nest of harvest mice – not a place to put my boot without some little fingers finding their way under.'

Perhaps the man didn't know about her mother; or perhaps he did, and this was his clumsy way of acknowledging it. Joan didn't know how to reply without sounding like she was after sympathy.

She straightened up instead, recalling the expression of the curate as he handed out the communion wafer, setting her own expression to something she hoped looked just as serious-minded. She held that face, even as she spotted the dirty pink stream that ran from the butcher's stall next door to the drainage channel in the centre of the street, and had to snatch up her skirt from it.

'The fleeces, Mr Ridler?'

His eyebrows shot up at her tone – she'd hoped to sound grown up but perhaps it had come out high-pitched and even haughty. She expected him to laugh, or worse, but he just swallowed the last of his dumpling and turned round to the handcart behind him where more wool was stacked.

'Ah. Eight, weren't it? And there was summat about the colour.'

'One white for every three coloured.'

Mr Ridler was nodding and muttering as he flopped one bundled fleece after another over the cart's back axle. Eventually he gathered them up in a pile that reached his bulbous nose, and turned round to slap the lot down on the empty end of the trestle. Joan swallowed; the mountain of wool probably weighed little less than she did, and why had she put no thought to how she would carry it all away?

'You wanting to look through them?'

Joan nodded, conscious of his eyes on her as she lifted one bundle after another, turning it over on the table, rubbing the wool between her fingers and prising it apart to see how it had been treated. She hoped she was doing it right; the urge just to accept the order and escape this scrutiny was strong. But she made herself think of her father, riding the long road to turn their fortunes around, and took her time working through the great stack of wool. As she progressed through the fleeces, she began to find a rhythm.

It was well skirted, she could see that much; there were no tag ends clotted with manure. She dug deeper into the pile. The worst of the grease seemed to have been well stripped by the first scouring. The two white fleeces – golden really, from the long-haired, leggy breed of sheep which were prevalent around these parts – were well-dried and ready for picking. But one of the darker bundles seemed damp, and still claggy with the natural oils in the wool.

'I'll have another for this one, please, Mr Ridler,' she said quickly, not giving herself time to think too hard on it.

He laughed, a great bellow that drew the eyes of the pigman and the herb-seller beyond him. Even the bailiff looked over from where he stood beside the weighing beam, rolling his eyes as Mr Ridler slapped his stomach in mirth.

'She'll have another. Watch yourselves, fellows. Got an eye like a blue hawk, has this one.'

At this, even the bailiff snorted, as he helped a boy heave a corn sack onto the pan. But Mr Ridler still tossed the dark fleece back onto the cart behind him and pulled another bundle from the table to replace it.

'This one more to your liking?' he said. Joan flushed. Enough for today. She dared not give it more than a cursory glance before she nodded her agreement.

Afterwards, it took some minutes for the factor and the bailiff to weigh the wool between them, and while she waited, she pinched her fingers behind her back to hold her nerve. At last the factor pulled out his pocket book and began drawing up the account.

'There you are. Ninety pounds of fine wool at twelve pence a pound. That's four pounds and ten shillings to you.'

Joan worked through the numbers in her head. The factor hadn't made it easy – he held the book at a distance, and his script was tight and cramped – but she found the total to be correct.

'Thank you, sir. He'll be here next week to settle the account.'

The man's brow dipped, and Joan saw his fingers dig hard into the fleece in front of him. He was a short man, a bare few inches taller than Joan herself, but by the time he spoke, he seemed to have pulled himself up by his bootstraps. 'I don't remembering offering credit,' he said. He leant closer over the fleeces, as if reasserting his ownership.

Joan resisted the urge to back away. She took a breath instead, forcing herself to take a moment. But there was a flash of yellow in her peripheral vision and her shoulders sank: Daniel, in his Sunday hat, head bent in conversation with the herb-seller. And then Daniel turning in her direction, holding a bunch of something leafy in his fist. Daniel: as if the situation could be worsened. *I saw you there, squatting in the nettles, looking like you were relieving yourself* – Joan tried to put her sister's words from her mind. Alice's words, her mocking laugh, the thought of Daniel on the path, frowning towards the trees where Joan had been hidden. It was not as if she could have avoided him forever, but did it have to be here, now? Joan looked back at Mr Ridler, whose nose was pink and his jaw champing as if that dumpling were not long gone.

'Forgive me, sir, I should have asked. With you being a factor, I assumed . . .'

'Credit, young lady, has to be earned,' he interrupted, wagging a finger close to her cheek. 'And I don't give it to any Jack-a-dandy as walks up here.'

'Of course not, Mr Ridler. Still, by virtue of my father's honest account to date, would you consider a note of credit on this occasion?'

He snorted. 'Speaks like a haberdasher of nouns and pronouns, does this one,' he called out, looking around to find his former audience, some of his earlier good humour recovered. 'Have they taken to educating the womenfolk of Chalford, these days?'

But the bailiff was busy with another farmer's boy, and the pigman and the herb-seller both had customers taking their attention. There was only Daniel, who was leaning against the market-hall archway now, watching the factor without a smile. Eventually Mr Ridler sighed and leant on the table to scribble something in his book.

'There, credit given,' he said, holding it out to Joan. '£4 10s, payable by Friday week. But woe betide your father if he's not here with the money I'm owed. I'm not a man who enjoys travelling, and if I'm forced to venture out to the arse end of the Frome valley in search of him, there'll be no fancy words as can save him.'

'Thank you, Mr Ridler.'

He raised his eyebrows. 'Dare say you earned it, Miss Browning. Not many little girls would have stood there and fought their corner. But how you going to get this lot away with you, now? Didn't think of that, did you? Don't know it all yet, after all.'

'Where are we taking them?' It was Daniel, at Joan's side suddenly, relieving the factor of an armful of the fleeces. Mr Ridler looked as if he might have some smart comment to make, but a well-dressed gentleman was drifting towards the stall and he turned aside to greet the man. Her cheeks pinking, Joan grabbed the rest of her stack of wool and followed Daniel away from the stall.

'Up to The Cross. Old Mr Parker's meeting us there with the cart at noon,' she called to his back.

He stopped to wait for her. 'Who's we?'

'Me and my sister.' They'd reached the far side of the Pitching and turned up the street.

'Ah, Alice.' Even hearing him say her name was like a dagger in Joan's side. But she must get used to this; if Daniel and Alice were courting, they would be together all the time. There would be no avoiding it. 'And where is your sister now?'

Dancing, with some young man, she wanted to say. Earning fancy breads for her trouble. 'She was going to catch me up. Probably some friend has waylaid her to talk.'

'Or she's still turning a jig with the bread boy.' Joan looked at him sharply and he laughed. 'I saw her earlier – the boy was quite the dancer.'

Daniel said it so easily, as if he didn't mind at all. But surely he must be fuming? Joan hoisted the bundle of wool a little higher on her hip and ran a few steps to catch up with him. Her arms were burning and her chest was tight, but she wouldn't ask Daniel to slow.

They were close to The Cross now, walking up past the potter's workshop and a butcher and the old ironmonger who sold elegant birdcages among his hammers and buckets and latches. Up ahead was the basket shop, but there was no sign of the sackbut players now; perhaps they had been shooed away by the shop owner, who had built a fortress of wicker on each side of the door to show off his many wares.

'Don't you mind, with you and Alice . . .?' Joan started. *With you two sweet on each other*, she had meant to say. But she was fully out of breath all of a sudden, and the light-headedness of earlier had returned. She was not feeling herself, she would tell him that, just as soon as she recovered. But her nostrils were full of the stench of the wool, still reeking of the urine it had been scoured with, and she could still smell the blood on that butcher's floor and the grassy stench of the horse manure freshly dropped in the road way ahead of them. She was flushed from the climb and the shame and her head was beginning to spin. By the time her legs gave way, she had already begun to apologise for her question and the impertinence of it, but the words came out mangled and she heard only a shushing as she felt herself being lowered to the ground.

When she came round, Joan was propped up in the shadow of the mounting block at the edge of The Cross, with one of the poultry man's chickens pecking at her fingers through the struts of its wicker cage. Daniel was sitting on the dirt beside her, resting his head on the stone of the upper step with his eyes closed on the sun. His arm on the far side rested on the great mound of wool. Joan's legs cramped and she shifted her weight a little; Daniel's eyes opened at once and he turned to her.

'You gave me a scare, Joan. When did you last eat?' he asked.

Her head was still full of clouds but she tried to think back. They had slept with full bellies after the pottage made with Mrs Freme's cabbages, but there'd been three long days of weaving since, and little more than milked crusts at the end of them. When she'd gone to collect the yarn her father had put out to Mrs Bellows up at Bussage for spinning – it was Alice's job, but with their father away, who else was going to make her? – the old woman had made her stay for a small beer and a mouthful of bread and dripping. But even that would be more than two days gone now.

'We've not had much this week,' she said. She stared down at the hem of her dress, always grimy but now pinked with the market's gore. When her mother had been alive, there had always been something. Something scrumped from the hedgerows or left on the doorstep by a neighbour, perhaps, but rarely had she and Alice gone to sleep hungry.

'Here.' Daniel pulled some pennies from the purse at his belt into his palm. 'I earned some extra, running errands for one of the Hampton men this week. First thing we're doing is getting something to fill your belly.'

She shook her head. 'I should find Mr Parker.'

'Look at the dial,' he said, pointing up at the sundial on the side of the waypost. 'You've got an hour at least, I'd say, before he'll be back.'

'But the wool?'

Daniel pushed himself upright with a hand on the mounting step. 'Here, boy,' he called, and the young lad on the far side of the chicken cages turned about. 'A farthing if you'll sit on these fleeces a while.'

The boy nodded, skipping across to them between the poultry cages as if jumping the stones across a river. When he reached them, he giggled as he rolled backwards on the soft pile.

'He's a good lad,' the poultry man called over. 'And I'll keep an eye.'

Daniel thanked the poultry man and held his hand out. Joan allowed herself to be pulled up to standing.

'Happy enough?' he said. It wasn't ideal, to leave so much wool with strangers, but perhaps if they were quick. Joan looked about for her sister but there was no sign of Alice. No sign of the bread man either, but she shouldn't jump to conclusions; perhaps it was the threat of the bailiff and the pillory that had sent him on his way.

'What did you mean, about me and Alice?' Daniel was still holding her hand, but then it occurred to her that perhaps she was grasping his. She dropped her fingers to her side. Her armpits were damp and she wished she could start this day all over.

'Nothing,' she mumbled, as they started back down Long Street towards the market. He was walking slowly, glancing at her every few steps to check his pace.

'I think you were there, last Sunday,' he said. 'I think you were there in the woods?' The shame of it, to have been caught peeping. Her cheeks burned. But he went on: 'I wanted to talk to you. When Alice knocked on my door, I couldn't refuse to accompany her across the valley, but it was you I wanted to see.'

It was a feeling like a bubbling up inside her, as if a spring had sprung inside her middle. *It was her he'd wanted to see.* But there was no time to probe the feeling further, because by then they had turned back into the Pitching, reaching the baker's stall at the southern edge of the marketplace, and her vision was full of honey cakes and caraway bread, baked pudding and jumballs. She breathed deeply into its warm sweetness, holding a hand to her belly to cover the rumble.

'Pick anything you like,' he said, and his voice was close to her ear.

She smiled, too shy suddenly even to thank him. She could feel his hand close to hers at her side, brushing her fingers as they stood there. She let her eye wander over the baker's display.

It was almost too much. The cake-bread slices were the biggest, and perhaps that would look greedy, but it was so tempting. Prettiest were the little fruit tarts, delicately baked with their fruit laid out in a spiral across their custard base. The baker swayed from one foot to the other, but Joan was dazzled by the choice. Eventually, she pointed to the small plain loaves at the back of the stall; fresh-baked, they would still be delicious, and that way Daniel's money would go furthest.

While the baker wrapped the parcel, she closed her eyes a moment, losing herself in the smell. A memory of her mother's bran cakes cooking on the hearth edge began to creep in.

'Slip one of those in the bag too,' she heard Daniel say from her side.

Later, she found it was a cowslip tart, the yellow trumpets perfectly preserved in the shiny sugar glaze. Too good to eat, almost, and she was reminded of that cake crumb on her shelf. She ate the plain loaf instead, in the market-hall arches, trying not to gobble it. She offered half to Daniel but he shook his head. He was still frowning and she tried to chew more delicately in case it was her manners that offended him. But then he lifted the tart to her, and the sweetness of it . . . it made her eyes crinkle and her mouth water. Daniel was grinning to watch her eat it. Afterwards she realised she should have saved some, should probably have kept half for Alice at least, but the regret was eclipsed by the remembered joy of the thing.

'Thank you,' she said, and he squeezed her hand. That feeling again, that bubbling spring. This time it tickled her throat so that she feared it might escape in a squeak. She patted the corners of her mouth, as if for crumbs, but really it was to cover the corners of her smile.

'I should get back to The Cross,' she said.

'Can you stay a minute? I have to buy something for the clothier, and then I can walk and wait with you.'

She wanted to. But then there was that pile of wool up the hill. The memory of the factor's pocketbook, and that huge sum owed on her father's account. But hadn't the poultry man's boy seemed genuine enough, and Mr Parker was probably still in his cups, so perhaps a few more minutes wouldn't hurt.

'Over here,' Daniel said, and he led her to a quiet stall on the edge of the church wall. The man behind it stood out from the crowd: tall, with a white collar under his black doublet, and a black, wide-brimmed hat so lofty, it put her in mind of a church steeple. It was the way she'd heard her father describe a Dutchman, though this man had come a long way from Holland if that was so, and with talk of another war, perhaps he would be better getting back to the quay at Bristol rather than hawking whatever his table held to the good folk of Stroud.

But then Joan saw what lay across the man's trestle and he had her full attention at once. Corked urns and cloth wraps, tied with bright-blue thread. Leather boxes unfastened to reveal powders, grits, lozenges. Tiny, stoppered glass flasks. And in front of every compartment, a slip of tight script with instructions and a broadcloth swatch in the colour the dye-ware might be expected to obtain.

'I thought you'd like it,' Daniel said, and Joan lifted a hand to her face, realising she'd been staring open-mouthed. Her fingers itched to touch the trays of bark peelings, gums and waxes, dried mosses and lichen scrapes. To sniff the heaped piles that sat on paper squares, and to tip the corked bottles and watch the crystals pour and reshape like sand in a clock. To peer closer at this and that, and who knew what might come of it.

And the colour swatches: she could have rested her eyes on those all day. From the hedgerow shades of yellow and brown and green; the blues, of sea and sky and stone; russets and purples, and black, good and deep, like the man's attire. She imagined the patches all stitched together: a fool's coat of every colour; a rainbow, captured and spun in the washing pail.

'Do you know them?' Daniel said. 'What they do, where they come from?'

'A few, only. Some of the herbs that come from round these parts.' The ones her mother had taught her. There was dyer's broom and camomile and five colours of lichen. Some wilted woad, and the red madder roots she recognised from the dyer's garden.

'Mr Willemzoon here has colourants and mordants from all over the world. In Rotterdam, he trades with merchants from the Mediterranean, the Far East and the New World, then he visits our wool towns twice a year, when it is safe to do so, with the dye goods he has to sell. Mr Watts, the Hampton man, says Willemzoon's stock is as good as any he's bought from the Broad Quay traders in Bristol.'

Joan looked at the merchant, who ducked his chin and passed a white-gloved hand over his stock as if to welcome her.

'He hasn't much English,' Daniel went on, 'but you'll see that it is not difficult to conduct a trade. See now, Watts is after this new dye-stuff he's heard talk of, that they call grain. They're dried beetles, would you believe it? Though to me they are more like a berry. Cochineal, that's the proper name. You'd think they were made of gold for the cost of them, but they've come halfway 'cross the world, and Watts has a mind to make good use of them. He likes the corpses to be plump and dark, with no white dust or mottling. He's very particular. And I'm to shake the glass to check that there is no grit or clay mixed in with the creatures.'

Daniel leant over, selecting three of the vials and bringing each close to his face to check the contents.

'Here, see what you think,' he said, holding one out to Joan. 'They look well enough to me.'

She turned the glass so that the mound of beetles churned and she could see that no filler bulked them out. Wrinkled red carapaces, like haw berries dried in the sun. She shook and turned the vial again: no sign of any dust or blemish.

When she looked up, Daniel was watching her, and she had to clench her jaw again to hide a smile.

'Yes, they look fine.' She handed it back.

'Watts is after a sample, he says, then he'll have Willemzoon deliver the bulk of the order when he's tested the gravity and the true colour of the dye. Watts is a *master of the tinctorial arts*, so he says, and will take no dye substance which gives results less than perfect in shade and permanence.' Daniel sounded like he was reading from a book, and Joan imagined a waist-coated gentleman giving these instructions from the door of his carriage.

'And what's the colour?' she asked. 'What do they call it, from these beetles that have come so far?'

'Scarlet, I've heard it called. Look, here it is,' he said, pulling a red swatch from the table, vivid as a ladybird's wing. 'I'm sure it'll be all the clothiers ask for, soon enough.' He turned to the merchant now: 'These three – will you wrap them?'

The man nodded, writing the price on a slate, before turning to find rags to bind up the vials. Probably more than her father had earned this week, Joan thought, and for little more than a fistful of beetles. But if they had the power to transform . . . Scarlet – in her head, she played with the sound of the word, while Daniel pulled the coins from his waist to settle the account.

And while the two men exchanged final pleasantries, she let her eye drift over the other colour swatches one last time. Never mind this new scarlet, here were colours that had only ever existed for her as slender flashes in the spring meadow: magenta, pink, cornflower blue, and yet here they were captured on pocket squares of broadcloth. That deep black: rich and dark, as if you might lose yourself in it. Truly there is something magical in it, she thought, that these humble scraps of bark and herb and beetle can be coaxed to perform in this way.

And that last blue, perse: the colour as rich and strange as if ancient lavender had been spun together with the blue of a bottomless pool. Found from the marriage of woad on white wool, mordanted with ashes; her mother had requested something like it for her funeral shroud.

She had only mentioned it in jest, of course – never one to ask for anything for herself – though John Browning would have bought a burial cloth fit for a queen if he could. But he could not. Hannah Browning had gone to the grave wrapped in a plain white broadcloth, a patch in its corner to cover a stain. Joan had seen him crying over it, too broken even to hide his sobs. It was before the small inheritance came his way last year, which had got him out of the mill and set him up as a weaver, and in Hannah's last days every last farthing had gone to Mrs Munden for herbs with any chance of healing. He'd have sold the chickens for the Hocker Hill physician to visit if there'd been time, but Hannah Browning had died before nightfall on the day a black vein crept up her arm.

Joan felt the touch of fingers in her palm and she started. Daniel laughed.

'I've paid the man,' he said. 'Shall we head back to the wool?'

They walked there side by side, but both were a little quiet, as if a shyness had inserted itself between them. At The Cross, they found that the poultry man and his boy had been as good as their word, and Mr Parker, with more than a whiff of the alehouse about him, helped them load the fleeces on the back of his cart. Not long after, Alice arrived on the arm of a girlfriend, to whom she paid an extravagant farewell as if the two might never meet again. Daniel slipped away into the crowd then, lifting his hand to Joan, and she wished she could snare the fleeting colours of that moment in the way that fleece caught a dye: she would capture the smile on his face, his yarrow-yellow cap, the hues and pigments of market day all around.

Robert Parker's cart tipped and jolted them back towards Bisley. Even Alice seemed to have exhausted herself, and the girls sat in silence. The reins hung slack in Parker's hands as his head lolled, and Joan was grateful that it was the man and not the sure-footed old mules who had visited the tavern.

The five miles offered plenty of opportunity to challenge Alice for her treachery, but Joan found she was content to leave the words unsaid, preferring to think back on the day just gone, and finding that the journey passed quickly. Even the walk back down across the common to the cleft in which their father's cottage sat did not seem so long, though Alice huffed and stamped her displeasure from a few steps behind.

Later, in their cot, Joan dozed on the memory of every one of the merchant's swatches, stitched in a circle like the rays of the sun. The red of ripe haws, deepest perse, and jay-feather blue. But when sleep came, it took her to the riverbank: to reams of crumpled wet wool, all of it rich in that uncommon grey-green of her mother's eyes, as it was lifted hand-over-hand from the Frome.

Chapter Four

It was Whitsun, and the fulling hammers would hang silent while the whole valley took a day away from the mills to celebrate.

Daniel had knocked for Joan mid-morning. Last night John Browning had come in late and staggering, and this morning her father only grunted his assent from a tangle of bedclothes at the fireside, so she was able to slip away. She and Daniel climbed back up Daniel's side of the valley together to the long, flat plateau above his father's cottage, to the wayside inn at the place called Blue Boys, where the stock fair was always held. When they reached it, the patch of common ground had been marked out with red flags which rippled in the breeze, and although it was early still, most of the stock pens were already full, and the beginnings of a crowd had gathered.

In front of them, an old man sat on a stool beside a long-horned cow, soaping the crusted mud from its bony backside, ready for inspection. At the hiring post behind him, a group of young men stood about in their Sunday best, tassels on their lapels to advertise their trade for hire. A few of them were laughing and scuffling in the dirt, already tiring of the wait while prospective employers looked them up and down. Joan recognised some of them as boys she'd grown up with: Mrs Bellows' sons, Ralph and Benjamin, both with wisps of straw threaded in their lapels to show their wish to be considered as cowmen, and Jeremiah, one of the boys she had studied with at the Dame School, now with a dusting of dark hair on his upper lip and a carpenter's hammer tucked in his jacket pocket. Three girls, each carrying a pail to mark them out as dairy maids, fidgeted with their starched pinafores and made a show of turning their backs on the scrapping boys.

'Shall we walk around?' Daniel said. 'My father is here somewhere. He is after some ducks, if he can find them cheap enough, though I don't know how I'll keep Rockwood from their necks.'

Joan scratched the fine fur behind the dog's ears. 'Ah, Rockwood, no. I wouldn't believe it of you.' He had walked at his master's heel all the way from Joan's father's cottage, so well trained that he'd barely twitched an ear at the distant squawk of a pheasant flushed from cover. But perhaps a brace of fat ducks on his doorstep might be temptation too far.

When Joan straightened up, Daniel was smiling at her, and she couldn't meet his gaze, shy suddenly. Out of the shade of the wood now, she was conscious of the prick of sweat across her forehead, wishing that she had thought to bring a handkerchief. He always looked well turned out in his Sunday hat. She felt the mud stiffening her skirts and wished she was as smart as those dairy maids, smart enough to walk beside him.

They had begun to spend a great deal of time together since that first market day. Few Sabbaths had passed without them walking home from church together, taking a longer route than the donkey paths strictly required. On a few warm evenings, he had climbed their side of the valley to ask her father's permission to sit together by the stream a while, and even when their work kept them apart from one end of the week to the other, she had woken more than once to find a small posy of hedgerow flowers on the hen coop, where only she would find them.

'Yes, let's see what there is,' she said, when she'd recovered herself. Each time they met it became a little easier, as they found their place with each other. 'I think I can hear a piper already. Alice said it would not be long before the dancing started.'

So the two of them wound their way through the pens in that direction. All around, small groups of men stood about, listening to the garbled rant of the stock auctioneer as he offered up one beast after another for sale. But there were plenty like Joan and Daniel who were here for other forms of entertainment; animals, especially cattle, might be bought and sold by stockmen across the pens throughout the day, but many came for the merchants' stalls, for the chance to meet old friends, and for the dancing that would come later. The wranglings of crown and state rarely made their way so far west to have meaning in these valleys, but here was an exception – with the restoration of the King, the prohibitions of the protectorate had been thrown aside, and the drinking and dancing Joan remembered as a young child had been eagerly reclaimed since by the Whitsun fairgoers.

'Look, it's the Morris troupe,' Joan called out. They'd broken free of the pens at last and into a patch of grass where the crowd had cleared to make room. A bald-headed man with a drum under his arm and a tabor pipe to his lips was leading a group of rosetted men, each ringing the bells on his shins and clapping his wooden sword against his opposite number's, as the dance had them weave in and out of each other.

'And speaking of your sister . . .' Daniel replied, pointing across to the far side of the crowd. And there she was, clasping the arm of her friend Harriet, whispering something in her ear as the tight breeches of the troupe's stoutest member whirled close to them. As Joan watched, Harriet lifted her other hand to an open mouth, but Alice just laughed, withdrawing her arm a moment to clap along to the dancers' rhythm. Blushing Harriet fiddled with the daisies tucked into her dark hair, but at Alice's urging, she began to clap too. When she caught sight of Joan across the space, she waved. Alice looked over then and lifted a hand in her own sort of dismissive greeting. Joan waved back at them, forcing a broad smile and pretending not to see the flicker of a frown that darkened her sister's face when Daniel's arm then reached around her shoulder, pulling Joan closer. As the Morris men picked up their rhythm and kicked their knees higher, and Daniel leant down to place a kiss on the warm skin of her temple, Joan willed away the feeling that her sister's resentment reached across the field to prod at her.

'Don't let her spoil your morning,' he whispered. 'She will if you let her.'

'She wouldn't . . .' Joan started.

'It's alright, Joan, you can be candid with me. Alice has a temper like a skep of bees poked with a stick, and everyone can see you bear the worst of it.' But Joan was frowning herself now and Daniel went on quickly, squeezing her shoulder gently as he spoke. 'You're just like me with my father: the man drives me mad with rants against the Book and the Church, but let me hear a word said against him, and I'd be at a boy's throat for it.'

'It's not like that.' But how to explain all the things she felt about Alice? Of course her sister was infuriating, with her preening and her scorn and her lies. There was no justice in the way Alice glared at Joan so, in the way she found fault with her every move; Joan recognised that well enough. And Joan was no glutton for punishment, so why did she still feel like it was Alice's approval she was always seeking? Always Alice's bare comfort she yearned for? Part of Joan ached with pride to be here now, with Daniel's arm around her, wanting her sister to see how her scheming had been overcome. But just as much of her craved Alice's blessing for the match. Just as much of Joan longed to show her older sister how much she had grown, what she could achieve. Too often she still felt like that scrap of a girl years back, chasing

Alice's distant skirts up the hillside, begging her sister to slow enough for her to catch up.

'Joan . . .' he began, and Joan turned to him – her boy, with his kind, open face, the end of his nose peeling where the sun had caught it, a little rash on his neck where a blade had been inexpertly applied. She saw how much he wanted her to be happy, to enjoy their day together. Perhaps even how much he wanted to press his lips on hers.

So she laid her hand over his on her shoulder, smoothing her fingers over his. 'My sister will keep. Let's walk on, see what else there is to see.'

So they moved on. Past the crowds, to the far corner of the fair, where the merchants had set up their stalls. There were stove cakes frying, and girls selling salted pork crackling in milk buns, and the air was full of hot, sweet yeast and bacon fat. Joan found herself grateful again that the noise of the excited crowd covered the sound of her stomach growling.

'You'd like something, wouldn't you?' Daniel said, reaching for the purse at his belt.

'No, no,' Joan lied. He'd tire of her quickly if he had to keep feeding her, she thought, and she hated to rely on him for it. She cursed herself for coming out with nothing; perhaps she could have borrowed a farthing from Alice. But such loans never came cheap.

'It's alright. My treat. I can't bear to think of you going hungry,' he said, pressing his thumb gently into the soft flesh of her palm.

So she and Daniel shared a bun and she chewed each mouthful as slowly as she could bear to, though she was ravenous enough to eat her half in one bite. Daniel saved a last piece of brittle crackling for Rockwood; the hound took it from his fingers with delicacy, then made short work of it with those sharp, hunting-dog teeth. Afterwards, they sat in the shade of the stall for a while, watching the crowd pass by. Daniel crossed his long legs in front of him and Joan tucked her knees to the side, leaning her ear on his shoulder.

'I used to think about this,' he said, 'when we sat in church.' He took one of her hands, traced each of the fan of tendons that led from her knuckles to her wrist, and it felt as if her skin awoke in ribbons behind his fingers.

'What do you mean? About the fair?'

'About you and me, here. All those dark Sundays, with the rain hammering on the chancel roof, and Father Britton droning on about Isaiah or Ezekiel or some such, I'd be thinking of a day like this: fat lambs sleeping in their pens in the sunshine, some Cheltenham puppeteer pulling shapes from the air for the children, and you and me, most of all, sat watching it all, or dancing when the mood took us. All those times when old Seymour was hissing at some little scrap for playing with his tip-cat sticks in the pew, or Britton was browbeating the congregation for our transgressions since our last visit, I confess I was almost always occupied with thinking about how you and I might sit somewhere like this one day, with our hands woven together, and how that would be a very fine thing.'

'It is a fine thing,' she said, 'and here we are.' How strange, to think that all the time she had been dreaming of Daniel, he had sat across the pews with the same thoughts. The press of his fingers across the back of her palm was sending an accompanying fan of shivers across her back now, and she prayed that no one could see from her face how much she enjoyed it.

'Look at this little man now,' Daniel said then, suddenly lifting his hand away to point, and Joan felt the lack of it. In front of them came a boy with a cup-and-ball, grubby face split with a grin, his short legs engulfed in an older brother's red breeches. 'So pleased with his new toy. How will our children look, Joan? Sometimes I try and imagine them.'

Joan was stuck for breath for a moment, searching around for the words to respond, and they did not come at once. She could hardly admit that she had never thought of it. That in every dream of their future, every fairy tale she had constructed while the vicar droned on, she had not once thought of their children. And even when she tried to envisage it now, she could not imagine herself with a baby. It was not the grisly mechanics of the delivery that repelled her, though that frightened plenty of young women and with good reason. And it was not that Joan did not warm to children – she was charged often enough with keeping the youngest members of the congregation quiet while the adults talked among themselves after the service at Bisley, and she loved watching them fool about and play. But a child of her own? It was not something she could profess to wish for yet, even with Daniel as the father. The world was just opening – she had seen often enough how quickly a young woman's life could be changed with a child strapped to her hip.

Daniel laughed beside her. 'I've shocked you I see, Joan.' And then, when she began to protest: 'Your cheeks have turned pallid as a swan's back. My father always says I jump in too soon.'

'No, I like to think of our future,' she said, careful to steer clear of any lie. 'Sometimes I even think of the way the two of us would sit around our own hearth, what we would set up there on the shelf above the fire: pots and a griddle, and perhaps a bell-metal mortar to the side, and spare shuttles in a cabinet, and would we have a separate bread oven, and where we would put the looms, and whether we would have our own spindles or have others spin the yarn.' *I am arranging less a life, than a business*, she thought. She flushed, putting it down to awkwardness, and hoped that Daniel would not be put off by it.

But Daniel just laughed again. 'I see I will have to do the romancing for both of us, Joan. No matter. It's good to keep a man on his toes.' And he took her hand again to stroke it, and she closed her eyes. And a little afterwards they danced, joining a circle who had started turning to the music of a fiddler who had started up between the stalls. And after that they stood around for a while with Ralph Bellows – who had taken his fasten-penny by now and was set with employment as apprentice cowman to a Bisley farmer for the year – and some other young people from the valley, drinking small beer and dancing again. People came and went; Joan saw Alice pass by with Harriet and another girl, and Ralph glanced over at Harriet as if he wished he could follow, but Alice hurried her away towards the dancing.

As time passed, the warmth of the day began to wane, and Daniel laid his jacket across Joan's shoulders. Eventually, the sun started to slip towards the horizon, and the merchants began to hammer torches into the hard ground, ready for the evening revels. Joan looked about, seeing these preparations and the lengthening shadows and the first hint of copper-pink in the sky, suddenly aware of the late hour.

'Father wanted me home before dark,' Joan said to Daniel quietly, reluctant to say it at all and not wanting to sound like a child amongst these half-grown men.

He seemed to understand, making some excuse about his own father, and they made their goodbyes. He held her hand as they climbed the stile to reach the donkey track, and on down into the valley. When they passed his father's house, he had her wait a moment, while he rushed inside. Coming out, he pressed a muslin parcel into her arms.

'Open it later,' he said. 'It's nothing, but I was thinking of you yesterday when I was at the mill . . . you've done me no favours with the foreman, you know. I've two bruises on my shins where he kicked me when my attention drifted. And the Hampton man said I have the doe eyes of a dairy maid when I talk of you.' He hammed it up, acting out the scene, to lighten it, but Joan heard the sincerity below all the bluster and loved him for it.

'Thank you,' she said.

He kissed her then, with his arm flat against the back of her waist. His lips were soft and she could feel the flecks of dry skin and the prickle above his upper lip. She sank into the pleasure of it, knowing that she had wished for it since they set out this morning.

'Look,' he said at last. 'We have a witness.'

A dragonfly: stout-bodied as her finger, it had settled on a patch of soft mud around the cottage's well. Its emerald wings found light enough to glitter even in the failing sun.

'Devil's darning needle,' Joan said. 'I hope it doesn't bring ill will.'

Daniel laughed. 'How could it? What we have is all good, Joan, long may it last. We should go now, though. Your father will be stamping if I keep you out another minute.'

But he kissed her again before they walked back down and up the valley-side, and the dragonfly started up into the twilight as they left. When they reached her father's cottage, there was no sign of him or Alice, so there was time for one more long kiss, before he left her there, to watch him from the doorway as he retraced his steps for home.

Chapter Five

Joan and Mrs Freme were in the dye garden again, preparing the ground to plant new madder seedlings, a fresh harvest for two years on. As soon as she arrived, Joan had begun digging at once, keen to make use of the short time she'd been allowed: her father had only given her leave to visit if she returned within the hour. He'd returned from Gloucester that morning in good humour and with money in his pocket, though it was only a small order from the minster, and quite possibly he had already drunk the profit. Even Joan could clearly see it was the London market he must tackle if he would turn his investment into growth, but the Blackwell Hall men would spare little time on a clothier who could offer them such tiny yields.

'Drive the hoe in deep,' Mrs Freme called over to her. 'Madder likes a light soil, well tilled, so that the roots grow wide and long and deep. And a sunny spot, so it should thrive in these new beds.' She was leaning on the shaft of her hoe, a halo of grime around her forehead where she had been pushing her bonnet back from her eyes. Every visit to Mrs Freme bore some new scrap of knowledge, and Joan only wished she had the time and seclusion to put it all to the test.

So they worked alongside each other, talking now and then, as had become their custom. Mrs Freme teased Joan gently about

Daniel and she tried to put the older woman off, though she had often thought since about that last parting, on the way home from the fair, all those kisses, and that huge, emerald-winged dragonfly as witness. Joan's cheeks burned even now to remember it.

'He's running another errand for Mr Watts today,' she said quickly, when the older woman asked. 'The clothier has him riding out to Wotton for more woad.'

Mrs Freme smiled. 'Leaving you with a head like a basket full of glow-worms, frantic for him to come back to you.' Joan started to protest but Mrs Freme just sighed. 'I remember those days. Samuel might have turned mean as a cornered boar later on, but he had his moments, back then.'

Joan turned her spade in the soil. She wanted to hear more, but it was such a novelty to be spoken to with such candour, and she struggled to know how to comport herself.

'Do you know, once he spelled out my name in petals on the doorstep.' Mrs Freme seemed oblivious to her discomfort, to Joan's relief. Her eyes were on the horizon as she spoke. 'Though he must have asked for help with the spelling of it – Sebeliah is not a name for the faint of heart, and God knows Samuel was no intellectual.' The older woman laughed. 'The breeze had taken the 'H' before I came outside,' she went on, 'or so he said, but the look on his face as he watched me look down on it . . . I think I married him for that look, something I came to regret later.' She seemed to come to, then, looking across at Joan and laughing. 'But I'm embarrassing you, I see, with my tales of old courtship, and I'm sure your Daniel is not the bully my Samuel turned out to be. No doubt you are wishing you never came this morning.'

'I was glad to come,' Joan said quickly. 'I've been wanting to see the madder planted.'

Mrs Freme nodded. 'There'll be little fanfare, I'm afraid. Soil well tilled, little holes dug, and plop the seedlings in, gentle as if they were little princelings. Then it's just a question of waiting for the sun and rain to do their part.'

'Even so, I want to see every stage in the process. So that I can know how the colour is originated.'

And the older woman smiled again. 'So be it. It's my good luck that you are bewitched by the alchemy of the thing, because I am very glad of the help. The dye-man asks for more and more of me, and I'm not as strong as I was.'

When the work was done, the two of them rested for a while under the tenting branches of the willow on the garden's edge. Joan thought Mrs Freme might talk more, but the older woman just closed her eyes to the dappled sun. But when Joan came to go, she held her back a moment, pressing a small wrapped package into her hands – 'Something for the walk home,' she urged – and a fat bundle of madder roots, still crumbed with mealy soil. The wet roots left a pink trail across Mrs Freme's palm and Joan almost snatched them in her excitement; her mind was consumed at once with thoughts of how soon she might be able to put them to use.

She had to wait. One chore after another, until the light was almost gone. It was in half-darkness that Joan leant down to reach a hand into the space under the cot she shared with her sister. There it was, the little urn with the chipped lip, which she'd found on the riverbank – it was a relief to find it undisturbed. She uncorked it now and pushed in the tangle of madder roots. When she'd replaced the cork, she pushed the urn as far under the cot as it would go. The roots should be safe there, alongside the other dye-wares she'd been collecting: small piles of alder bark, oak galls, and all the lichens she could find. Bundles of dyer's broom and woad and a thistle-like plant she hoped might be saw-wort. She'd tied a length of wilting nettles with a piece of twine, and in an old nightshirt were gathered the outer skins from all the onions they'd had this season, which hadn't looked like much even caught up together.

When she'd first mentioned her collection to Daniel, he'd seemed amused, and she worried he might think her as strange as Alice seemed to. What was it her sister had found to liken her to while they last sat alongside each other at the loom? A pig, a cat . . . a heron, even, *all bandy legs and head on one side, so who knows whether you're considering the meaning of life, or where your next fish is coming from.* And heaven forbid Alice should discover what was hidden beneath the cot, and Joan had wondered after whether she should have even mentioned it. But when she'd unwrapped the parcel he'd given her after the fair, she was touched by what she found there: scraps removed by the shearers, corners and edges of woven cloth, perfect for testing dyes. These she'd kept wrapped in a bolster cover in the linen cupboard so as not to attract Alice's attention, along with a little vial of some sort of fixing powder that Daniel had swept up from the mill floor.

So they were all safely hidden, her precious dye-wares, but much good they were doing; as desperate as she was to test every one of them, the opportunity to use them never seemed to present itself. Joan considered herself ignorant of every aspect of dyeing, but she knew enough to be sure that the processes took time, that the colours would have little permanence if the dye liquor were not allowed time to ferment, if the wool were lifted from the pot too soon. She remembered the hours her mother had spent on dyeing days, hunkered over a pot on the stove.

No, she would just have to wait. It would take a fine day, an empty house, the good fortune of a period of time away from the loom to prepare the tinctures. The valley had not yet shaken off the wet days of late spring – the millsmen must be begging for a dry spell long enough to get the water from their cloth without a fire – and there were many days still when the sun did not break through at all. And while Joan's father's vision had been that much of the spinning and weaving would now be passed out to other women and children across the valley, the reality was that the scale of the orders did not justify it, even though almost every penny had been ploughed back into the business and they still went without bread more often than she cared to remember. It had been weeks since Alice had been asked to take a bundle of wool up to Mrs Bellows to spin. Instead, the burden of work fell to Joan and Alice alone, their spinning wheel and looms rarely idle, and even when they were, the cooking and sweeping and the laundry would not do themselves. Patience, she told herself now, but the hidden treasures were all she could think of, and later her father leaned over the loom and cursed the crowded warp where her mind had wandered.

Two weeks later, the opportunity came at last. A surprise of a day when the sun was high and the sky was bare of cloud. Both girls had woken early and even Alice had seemed placated by the unaccustomed warmth – between them, they made quick work of what weaving there was to be done, and soon the broad looms were still. When she came to push aside the curtain and return to the main room, Joan noticed at once the cider flagon on the mantle – usually she would watch her father swill the stuff with gritted teeth, her stomach cramping with hunger to see him drink away their supper, but today his vice might serve her well.

It didn't take long for him to drink his fill and then roll off down the hill to sleep off the excesses on the riverbank. Even less for Alice to make good her own escape, to wherever it was she went (to meet a boy, Joan imagined, by the way her sister looked in any shiny surface for her reflection, rubbing clay dust across her cheeks to make them pale as the gentlewomen who shielded their faces from the sun). And then, with Alice gone, the evening ahead of Joan was long; plenty of time to fill the buckets with spring water, to light the fire in the hearth, to crush and boil up the alder bark chips that had been soaking for days in their pot, and to pummel the madder roots against a stone before boiling them too. Into every pot must be dropped a slip of list wool, to be left as long as Joan dared before lifting it with a forked twig to dry on the hearth rack.

That was what she was doing when she heard the squeak of the gate and the skip of boots on the path. Joan barely had time to place herself between the doorway and the drying rack. With her own boot, she tipped over the last remaining boiling pot, forced to watch the dye liquor sizzle as it spilt in the dust. A red slick, the madder liquor: she bit her cheek to see the precious draught soak away, to watch a wrap of orange wool curl and blacken on the coals, to see her sister framed in the doorway.

It was difficult for Joan to make out Alice's expression against the still-bright sky. But as her sister made her way inside, Joan heard her sniff and then saw her frown at the smell of the air. She feared Alice might throw her aside to see what she was hiding. But wherever her sister had spent her evening, clearly it had pleased her; Alice only wrinkled her nose, pulled out their father's chair and then slumped against its bowed back.

'Where is he?' she asked.

'Down by the river, sleeping off a flagon.'

'And what have you been brewing, witchy?' Alice began to run her fingers through her hair, strand by strand, pulling out burrs and hay seed where she found them. And she found them. Joan wondered where her sister had been rolling to come back so covered.

'Trying to make something edible, that's all. I've had nothing all day and my belly's groaning.' Joan's mouth twisted on the lie; Mrs Freme's bun had been honey sweet and her cheeks watered to remember it. She'd saved half for Alice, but she couldn't give it to her now. It would be a guilty nibble after the candle was snuffed.

'I'd better not tell Daniel. Those in love should be able to live on air alone. What would he say if he heard you'd been boiling up leaves like a hedgerow beldam?'

Joan shook her head. 'A few dandelion leaves, that's all. I'd hoped to make the beginnings of a pottage, but there was no taste to it.'

'Brewing milk-witch like a beldam, and you admit it. That Mrs Freme has you doing her dirty work, I think. There were ravens croaking as I walked up the valley-side. And I even fancy I saw a hare cross my path as I came by the apple tree. Has my sister been possessed by the crooked widow of Millswood?'

Alice laughed then with an open mouth – she threw out these jests as if they were of no consequence, as if she had no knowledge of the Toadsmoor women drowned less than a year ago for supposedly bearing the witch's mark – and Joan closed her fists tight then forced her fingers to unfurl. This would pass, when Alice had had her fun, and she must do nothing to attract her sister's attention to the rack behind her. A braver girl might pick up the pot from the embers and hurl it across the room to her sister's taunting face. But of course, she would not; Alice might taunt and tease, but with their drunken father increasingly absent, without her Joan would be truly alone.

Alice was not done yet, though. She stood up and began to sing, in a high-pitched, mocking tone:

'To house the Hag, you must do this,
Commix with meale a little piss
Of him bewitched: then forthwith make . . .'

'Alice,' Joan begged, but her sister just sang on.

'A little wafer or a cake;
And this rawly bak't will bring
The old Hag in. No surer thing.'

It was a nasty old rhyme that their mother would have struck Alice to hear. But their father was the drunken fuddlecap down on the riverbank, and there was no one else to stop her now.

'Will you piss in the night pot for me, Joan, and let me throw the spell from you?' Alice came closer now. Her face was inches from Joan's – Joan could smell her sister's sour breath, and there was nothing she could do but clench every muscle in her body to prevent herself lashing out. Perhaps Alice sensed the wobbly stepping stones she trod. 'Have you lost your sense of humour, little sister?' She laughed again and poked Joan in the ribs. 'I am only jesting with you. You need to learn to smile, otherwise folk will think you really run errands for a shrew.'

Alice crossed back to their father's chair, slumping back into it with her legs crossed and looking Joan up and down as if she were examining a joint at the pigman's stall.

'Always so quiet. You will need to find a voice, if you are to keep Daniel's attention.' Alice twirled a length of her hair around her thumb. Joan stretched her fingers back towards the wool scraps on the rack, now warm and dry from the fire – there was no way to gather and hide them, but to be scrutinised in this way was unbearable. 'But you are not as ugly as you were,' Alice went on, scratching at a hangnail now. 'And though your height is a burden – no man wants some towering virago – still, it could be hidden if you learned to dress for it.'

Joan closed her eyes; Alice's rare kindnesses sometimes struck harder than her blows. But at that moment, there was a crash from outside, as if the gate was thrown from its hinges, and Alice leapt up from the chair. Joan's shoulders sagged with the relief of it. As her sister made for the doorway, Joan turned to snatch up the wool scraps, bundling them into the flour bag above the fireplace for want of anywhere better, and then turned to the door herself.

'I thought you said one flagon,' she heard Alice mutter. Dusk had begun to fall but Joan could see their father clearly enough: on the ground just beyond the threshold, groaning, his head next to the upturned roosting box. The little red-brown hen had been tempted from the coop to peck at his temple, and the scrawny cockerel had jumped to the roof of the upturned box to squawk his displeasure. 'It looks like he's drunk a millpond.'

'Perhaps he bought more from old Parker. I've heard he brews a sloe wine that would take your head off.'

'Here, help me lift him,' Alice said. 'Zooks, but he's like a sack of stones.'

Together they heaved their father upright, supporting him over the threshold while all the time John Browning mumbled and groaned and broke wind so extravagantly that both girls were laughing when they finally laid him down on his bundle of bedclothes in the corner.

'Lost his head alright; lost his whirligigs and all, poor man. Look at the ninny. What would our mother say to look at him now?'

Joan felt the bubble of laughter inside her turn to a twist of sadness at Alice's words. It was shaming, for them all, to see him like this. When their father had first received word of that inheritance from his uncle in Gloucester last year, it had seemed like their lives might turn around. He had spilled grand plans: of a house – a clothier's house – with grand gables and fine mullion windows, like the ones dotted all over the Bisley Hundred. A garden, laid out with a bowling green and a knot garden. A canal, even, with shaped yews in its reflection, and all to be viewed from a pavilion, like the one at the manor in Sapperton where he'd worked the garden as a boy. Windmills in the head, of course, even Joan had realised that, when in reality the money was enough to set him up as a weaver and no more. But they'd all had their own hopes. In hers, a more realistic vision: a bigger cottage, on their own land. Clear glass in the windows, room to sleep away from the looms. A proper stove, a full flock of hens and a cow to milk every morning. A little fenced plot to grow her own vegetables and herbs. How their mother would have loved that. Joan pinched the skin of her palm to drive off tears.

'It's alright, Joan. You can let them drop.' Alice touched her sleeve and Joan hunched her shoulders to smother a sob. She had so wanted to hear Alice speak kindly like this, but what was it that still made her hesitate? 'Mother wouldn't want us to dwell, though,' Alice went on, patting Joan's arm. 'Here. Let's straighten the fire and then get ourselves to bed.'

Joan nodded, sniffing and wiping her nose on her sleeve. She crouched to pull a blanket over their father while Alice took up the rake and started on the coals. Joan remembered the slip of orange wool that had fallen there – closed her eyes in dread of Alice finding it, of her turning it over with the poker – but perhaps it had burned fully away. She heard Alice's footsteps cross back behind her.

'I'll brush your hair if you'll let me.' Tears again. Joan just nodded her reply. The rhythmic stroke of the brush through her hair would be so comforting. Alice could be kind when she wanted to be.

Later, when Alice extinguished the candle, Joan stared out into the darkness. She could just make out the wooden loom frames. Alice's hand passed up and down her shoulder a few times, leaving goosebumps in its path, and then not long after, Joan heard a soft snore start up from the far side of the bed. Joan wrapped a twist of her own hair – soft and disentangled now from the brush – around her finger. Then she released the spiral and wrapped all of her hair round her neck like a scarf, imagining it to be her mother's long locks. She waited for sleep to come.

Chapter Six

When she woke, it was to an itch on the soft underside of her nose and the acrid stench of burnt wool. Joan sprang up to a crouch, her head still full of nightmares: a roof swollen with flame, and a memory of the palm-sized spiders that sometimes found shelter in the bedclothes. But it was cloth fibres that had tickled her nostril. Right across the bolster lay the list offcuts that Joan had dipped and soaked and dried. Someone had taken the trouble to arrange them in a rudimentary spectrum, and at the nearest end, where Joan's head had rested until a moment earlier, lay the sorry, charred remains of the strip of madder-dyed wool, all but lost to the fire save a twist of orange fibres at one end. Perhaps Alice had found it this morning, but more likely she had picked it up last night, planning this cruel display even as she put the brush gently through Joan's hair. Joan crushed the burnt fibres between her fingers, feeling sick at the sight of it all.

'It took me a while to find them. You had me digging through Father's wool bundles and even in the straw at the back of the hens' box.' Alice was standing in the doorway, one hand on her hip.

'So what? It's no crime to dye cloth. Our mother used to do it often enough.'

'Orange, though.' Alice stepped forward to flick the charred strip on the bolster. 'Wanting to be red. Even I know that's a madder dye, and that takes a tin mordant. Did you buy it, or have you been thieving?' Alice didn't wait for an answer. 'And what about the wool – have you been filching from your own father? The man's driven half-mad by the fear of bankruptcy, and all the time his daughter's helping herself to his profits for her little experiments.' Alice spat out the words.

'It was just Mrs Freme . . .' Joan started, but Alice snorted.

'Don't start up about that old beldam again. Don't you know what they do to witches?'

I do, Joan thought, *don't you?* Thinking of all the cruel jests Alice threw at her so easily. 'I just . . .'

'I don't want to hear another thing about it. And you'll not want Father hearing about it either, unless you want the poor man knowing he's got a thief and a potion-stirrer for a daughter. So here's what we'll be doing.' Alice straightened up with her hands at her waist. *She's imagining herself at the tailor's*, Joan thought, *even now, as she scolds me*, as Alice evened out the folds in the fabric of her skirt and stroked it flat. And when Alice spoke again, it was with the imperious tone she reserved for shopkeepers and donkey boys, as if she were far superior, and not among the poorest in the valley. 'You'll make something for me,' she said at last.

Joan pushed herself upright, her mind working. It was possible, if her sister's demands were not too steep. She still had a few scraps of white wool and some madder roots which had been too big for the pot. A crime to waste them on one so unworthy, but what choice did she have?

'What had you in mind?'

'We'll start small. A pink frill – madder, properly treated – for this Sunday dress, so that I might disguise the stains around the neckline.'

Joan leant to pull the wrap of fabric scraps from under the bed. 'This is the widest piece I have.' She held out a yard strip, as wide as her palm.

Alice frowned. 'It's very plain.'

'It will be pretty once it's taken the colour. And I could cut some holes so that it resembles lace.'

Alice snatched the piece and held it up to her neck, turning to examine herself in the glass. She crumpled the wool strip into a frill and turned this way and that, pouting and then smiling at her reflection. 'It'll have to do. You'll start this afternoon. Doubtless Father will be making the most of his Sabbath with the last flagon of cider and a long sleep after.'

Joan nodded, thinking of Daniel, of how much she had looked forward to spending the afternoon with him, and whether they might still somehow spend some time together.

'Oh, Daniel,' Alice said, as if she could read Joan's thoughts. She picked at something under her nail, tucking away a stray strand of hair as lazily as a cat grooming its fur. 'Perhaps I should have said.'

'Said what?'

Alice looked up and held Joan's eye as she yawned. 'There was a rumour they were coming for his father.'

'What do you mean?' There was something in Alice's expression that made the muscles in Joan's throat contract.

'The King's men. Four soldiers and a priest called in at the inn at Frampton Mansell yesterday. The man who saw them fancied they'd be after Daniel's father, and the six other Phanatics who meet with him.'

Joan felt as if hands were tightening around her throat. How had she heard? Alice must have woken early and gone for water, eavesdropped on the other women at the stream. All morning she'd sat on the news then, even while she issued instructions for her frill, while she preened in front of the glass.

'Phanatics – what does that mean?' Joan threw the bedcovers and jumped up, pulling her smock on over her underclothes. 'Daniel's father is a kind man, who works hard. What could the King's men want with him?'

'You know he's a dissenter, Joan. He won't take the Book of Common Prayer; the man's brought this on himself. They say he's been gathering with his cronies in the woods at Cowcombe and Westley, preaching all manner of things that the law forbids. Meeting for conventicles, hiding in the bushes like common thieves . . . no wonder the Church is bent on rounding them up. He'll be banished five miles from the parish, and a fine slapped on him. It'll only be luck that keeps him from a ship bound for His Majesty's plantations in the West Indies.'

Joan tore the fabric at her hem in her haste to get on her boots. 'Not if I warn them first. When? When did this happen?'

'Last night,' Alice said. Was it possible . . .? No, surely her sister had not known all this time. Even as they put their father to bed together, as she brushed Joan's hair, as she fell asleep alongside her, the gentle snores of an untroubled mind. But a look at Alice's triumphant face was all the answer Joan needed. 'They'll have come with torches, I dare say, ready to hunt him down in the woods,' Alice went on, picking at a hangnail.

'Daniel . . .' Joan said, as she ran from the room, but it was to herself. Nothing good came of speaking to Alice; she should never have forgotten that.

'You'll be too late,' Alice shouted after her. 'They'll have driven him out along with his father, and the King's men won't have left much for them to come back to.'

By the time Joan reached Daniel's father's cottage, she was hoarse and panting, and her Sunday dress was speckled with blood at the knee where she had tripped on a stone on the donkey path. But for all her running, she was indeed too late.

The cottage's roof timbers looked to have been splintered by an axe, and the walls, fragile anyway with mortar as old as the cottage, had been pushed out so that the masonry lay slumped in piles on all sides, spilling down the hill from the lowest facing. The thick lintel from the door-frame had landed in the hearth. It was blackened and smoking on one side where the coals still had some heat. Around it lay a cloak and breeches and other possessions as if Daniel or his father had tried to pack a bag and had it struck from them. Pages torn from a pamphlet floated about, some of them charred at the fire's edge.

Joan stood with her hand over her mouth, breathing the dust and the smoke, her heart still thundering. From the far side of the valley came the toll of the church bell; their father would surely beat her this time – but how could she care now? She glanced all around, desperate for some clue as to the men's direction, but the woods quickly closed in on all sides. She kicked the smoking lintel and watched a fresh puff of ash-dust float up around it.

And then there was another sound: it was only the tiniest yelp; she might easily have left without hearing it at all. But she did hear it, and stepped closer, round to the far end of the cottage where the roof timbers were piled steepest. She picked her way through the ruined cottage, painfully slowly, wary of trapping an ankle between loose beams. Halfway across the space she paused, wondering if she'd imagined it, but then there was the sound again: a weak whine, an animal trapped. She crouched to look closer, and glimpsed bloodied fur through a gap in the timbers.

The first beam she tried to push away wouldn't budge an inch. The second gave a little, shifting on its axis as she put her weight to it, but threatened to slip down into the gap where the animal was hidden. Joan heaved it back as best she could and tiptoed a pace backwards, looking down on the lattice of broken timbers, searching for a better strategy for the animal's release. At her feet was a criss-cross of smaller roof trusses, and she crouched to work these free instead. With this she had more success, and after some time, she had created a tunnel through the rubble, at the end of which she could see a patch of russet fur and a wet nose.

'Rockwood,' she called. 'Rockwood, come this way.'

Daniel's hunting dog whimpered but didn't move. Joan tried to whistle in the way she had heard Daniel call his pet, but the sound was not right and the dog just hunkered lower. Joan sat back to let more light down the tunnel. She looked about her; this dog barely knew her, and she could see nothing around that was likely to tempt him from his lair. Then she remembered the remaining half-bun from Mrs Freme which was still wrapped up in her satchel. She pulled it out: stale, but still tempting. A crying shame to waste it on a dog, but she had nothing else. In any case, this was Daniel's Rockwood, and she'd have given any last morsel to help him.

She crumbled the half-bun into three pieces, and reached an arm's length down the tunnel to toss the first piece as close as possible to the dog's mouth. Sitting back, she watched the wet nose twitch and then the bright flash of the animal's eyes as it moved to gnaw the crumb.

With the next piece, Joan reached only half as far, leaving it in clear view in the tunnel, and sitting back to let the sunlight in on it. For the longest while, the dog did not move, and Joan wondered whether he was capable of getting out at all, whether she was cruel in leaving him a crumb just out of reach, whether she should be running for old Robert Parker and his cudgel to put the creature out of its misery instead. But then there was a creak of timber against timber, and she watched Rockwood wriggle a foot closer, his long nose close to the ground.

'Good dog, good boy, Rockwood,' she whispered, as she watched him lift the portion of bread delicately with his teeth and swallow it. She could see the dog's back now, and a patch of dark blood as big as her hand on one side. But the wound seemed to have clotted, and there was no sign of fresh blood elsewhere on his coat. She dropped the final crumb of bun in the opening to the tunnel she'd created, and watched Rockwood inch forward towards it, until his nose emerged from under the last timber and he was free.

If Joan had expected some emotional celebration, some display of gratitude, it was not to be. Rockwood got to his feet at once, shaking off a slick of ash and dust. He licked twice at the dark patch on his side, and then hurried away with his characteristic lopsided lope, without so much as a glance towards Joan. She watched him nose around every side of the ruined cottage, urgent in his search, and then all around the small yard that surrounded it. He lapped at a bowl of water in passing, its surface dark with ash, and then, with nose returned to the ground, he started out through the trees up the hillside.

Joan began to follow him, recognising the madness in chasing after thugs who had left such carnage in their wake. Reckless, and futile too: the men could have marched miles ahead already, even if Rockwood had found the right trail. She could think only of Daniel, though – where he had been taken, the dreadful prospect that the King's men might have hurt him. So for one mile, maybe two, she tramped after the dog. But Rockwood's skinny frame slipped easily through the low scrub, and he moved fast despite his wound. It was not long before she lost him. Then, for a long moment, she was alone in the woods. Sagging after the urgency of the rescue, she was left only with Alice's betrayal and the bald fact of Daniel's expulsion. It was all she could do to keep to her feet.

Then, bursting from a patch of nettles, the dog was back. Whining, snapping at the bloody mess on his thigh, he loped past her and led her back towards the ruined cottage. The air was full of burning and the last of the flowering garlic was still pungent underfoot; he'd had no chance of following a scent far. Joan could only follow him.

Back at the cottage, Rockwood began nosing at once at something under a broken chair. Joan walked over to see what the dog had found; Daniel's felt hat hung limp in its mouth, its feather gone and the ribbon torn loose from its stitching. She knelt down and patted Rockwood over his long ears, wary of the sharp teeth which marked him out as a hunter. Holding out a hand, she waited until the dog dropped the hat into her palm, scorched from the fire and ripped on one hem.

'Thank you, Rockwood.' She folded the yellow felt and tucked it into the neckline of her dress. Daniel was gone and she couldn't go after him. This hat would be all she had of him until he felt able to return.

Chapter Seven

From the moment John Browning stamped in, the hinges on the front door crunching as it was thrown wide, it was obvious that he was a man with anger to spare. He didn't wait for an explanation and Joan took the beating she was given in silence, though the force of it seemed disproportionate: through eyes blurred with tears, she saw that even Alice paled at the strength of their father's blows, and Joan wanted to scream out for the injustice of it. But after several minutes with the belt, their father slumped back into his chair, his own eyes wet and his shoulders shaking. Joan crept to the hearth and knelt there, trying not to hate him for it, determined not to show her pain. There was a long silence; Joan heard Alice begin to shuffle pots on the shelf behind, but she kept her eyes on the floor.

'Forgive me, Joan. The punishment outreached the crime,' their father said at last.

Joan nodded, not yet able to speak. When she tried to straighten up, she felt the seam in her bodice press against the abrasions beneath. She winced but did not make a sound; she would not let Alice see how much it hurt. Though it was the betrayal that hurt most of all, and she could only hope that Daniel was not in worse pain.

'What is wrong with the world,' John Browning went on, 'that an honest man cannot make a good living, nor even keep his family in check.' Neither girl replied, and he shook his head. 'This morning I have heard that we are driving good, godly men out of the valley for no bigger crime than worshipping the Lord. Hen-hearted King's men bullying young boys out of their own homes. And I dare say that had something to do with your absence in my pew this morning, Joan, but let that be the last time I have to apologise to Mrs Abell for keeping her backside from the seat in vain.' John Browning dropped his face into his hands.

Joan shifted on her knees, wondering whether it was the seep of blood or a draught from the door that cooled the raw skin on her back. 'Where have they gone, Father?' It was a risk to ask, so soon after the beating, but she had to know.

Her father was silent for a moment, hunched as though the strength had gone from him. When he looked up at Joan, his face was vague as if he'd thought himself alone.

'Ciren' way, according to Parker,' he said at last. 'The King's men chased them over the parish boundary. Perhaps they'll have found shelter in Sapperton. I know Richard Randall has associates there.'

'And are they well, do you know?'

Her father's shoulders dropped an inch more. 'As to their state of mind and body, that I do not know. The King's men are not known for their gentle treatment of those who disrespect the rule of law.'

Joan shook her head, unable to bear the thought of it.

Alice spoke up from the other side of the fire. 'They'll not have touched Daniel.' Did she say so to reassure herself?

John Browning looked over, holding Alice's gaze till she looked away, and Joan watched her sister blush. Perhaps she did have some shame. But then John Browning seemed to notice the dog at the hearth for the first time.

'Whose is the hound?'

'Daniel's.'

'We've got enough mouths to feed in this house,' her father replied, as she'd known he would.

'Daniel'll be back for him soon enough, and the creature's taken a wound in its side. Let me nurse him till he can fend for himself at least.'

'I'll not see it in the house beyond next Sabbath.'

'Yes, Father.'

'Now leave me, both of you,' he said, striking a fist down on the table.

Neither girl hung around for him to change his mind; Joan was on her feet before she remembered the sting of her scored skin and they almost collided in the narrow doorway in their effort to get away. Outside, in the warm gloom of the day, Joan stepped out of Alice's path; she hovered a moment by the hens' coop, just far enough away from her father's fist, watching the cockerel dance across the dust in pursuit of a fly. She'd expected her sister to run away down the valley at once – had wanted her to – but instead Alice hung awkwardly beside her, worrying at a pebble with the toe of her boot.

'It would have been too late, you know. You couldn't have warned them,' Alice said eventually.

'You don't know that.'

'The sun was already at its highest when the King's men were at the Crown. There was nothing to be done by the time I heard.'

Joan wanted to believe it. 'Still, you could have let me try. Given me fair warning. Who knows how long they searched the woods before they tried the cottage.'

'If I thought there'd have been a chance, I'd have told you.'

Joan snorted, thinking of the look on her sister's face as Alice had preened in front of the mirror with the frill she would have forced Joan to stitch. 'Forget it, Alice. Run off to your gentleman friend.'

'I have no such thing.'

'Who is it you meet in the valley then?'

'Harriet. And some of Mrs Culham's daughters. They like to meet to play loggits by the river. It's only you with the fancy man.'

Joan sighed. Was that it? Was that what lay behind all this: simple jealousy? How could her sister ever find peace when someone would always have more?

'You should be happy now, then – I'll not be seeing Daniel before the seasons change, and if then.'

But Alice didn't answer; she'd said her piece and now she'd be gone. With no surprise, Joan watched the neat silhouette of her sister's back shrink as Alice chased the brook down the valley-side. She should be angry, but Alice hadn't even turned the corner at the field edge before Joan started to regret the way they'd left it. It was the closest she'd get to an apology from Alice, and she'd driven her away. But her sister was out of sight now, and Joan wouldn't stoop to running after her. Instead, she made her own way more slowly into the valley, unsure at first of her destination and wary of her wounds, then walking with more purpose as her feet trod the path towards Mrs Freme. She didn't know whether she could even lift a hoe, but just the sight of the garden might take her mind from Daniel's fate for an hour or two.

'Your father is an unhappy man, Joan, and today you've taken the brunt of that.' Mrs Freme picked a worm from the soil and dropped it out of the way of her hoe. 'Even the kindest men can lose their way when they're being made to look small. Look out for some plantain on the way home. Crush up the leaves and press the juice with a little spittle on your back.'

Joan nodded, clenching her jaw against the pain. She was glad to have come, but a minute with the shovel had caused her bodice to rub sorely against the broken skin on her back. It had not taken long for Mrs Freme to notice her discomfort, and only a few minutes more to have the whole sorry story out of her.

'This dyeing, though, has got me thinking. I knew you'd be taken with it, first time I saw you set eyes on the garden. And the way you soak it all up, everything I tell you, when I only know the half of it myself. A boy with half your brains would be up at Mr Webb's school, maybe even at Mr Pate's Foundation School in Cheltenham, learning his grammar and rhetoric for Oxford. I wish I had more to share with you. But bring those swatches next time you come. You say they were a disaster, but there will be learning there. The madder, for example: how did you prepare the roots and treat them?'

'I rinsed them, that's all, before I put them in the pot.'

'And it gave you a colour, of sorts. But madder is a demanding mistress, and to get the best from her, we must treat her as gently as the potter turns his clay. There are factors at work before you even had the roots in your hand: the soil in which the roots are grown, the way in which they were dug; these will play their part. The water, also. You pulled water from the spring, I assume?'

Joan nodded.

'The dye-man – you know he likes to bend my ear with his secrets, as if telling an old woman is no more than whispering into the hearth – he says the clarity and consistency of this valley's springs lends itself to good dyeing. And the particles of the dye are more easily carried in mineral-rich water than the soft waters of the Frome. Not blues: for blues, we need the river water for the fermentation of the woad, but I'm getting away with myself. Did you boil it? The madder?'

'Yes, for as long as I dared.'

'You might think that would be the way. But the dye-man says the roots must be chopped and soaked cold first. And for as long as you have at your disposal. He had baths of last year's harvest soaking for weeks before he put them over the coals. Only when the water has browned all around can the roots be heated, and then only when they've been washed and dropped in clean water. This is on account of the brown and orange pigments, which must be removed so as not to taint the red. Afterwards the roots can be brought to the boil and the mordanted wool or cloth applied, but the pot should be kept at a slow simmer, so as not to tempt more brown from the madder. Then the whole should be allowed to cool and soak a while longer, before the wool is pulled from the pot to be dried at the hearth.'

Joan laughed. 'It is no surprise my first attempt fell so flat. There was less to learn at the Dame School.'

'And I'll say again, I only know the half of it. Even the dye-man always says he keeps learning. I've heard him say that when he's had enough of it, he'll up-sticks and follow his brother abroad, but he's still clomping round the back rooms each night. I have a feeling it'll come naturally to you, though, Joan. That you'll be stitching Daniel a new cap from your own dyed felt before the year is out.'

Joan's shoulders sank. 'I'd be happy just to hand back his old one.'

'Have faith.' Mrs Freme laid her hand over Joan's. 'Not in Him up there, but in what's in here.' She lifted her hand to point to Joan's chest. 'He'll come back, when he can.'

'I hope so,' Joan said. But all she could think of was the rubble the King's men had left of the cottage; what had he to come back to?

'He'll come for *you*,' said Mrs Freme, as if Joan had thought aloud. 'You keep your heart strong.'

Joan nodded, not quite trusting herself to speak.

'Ah now, you come here.' Mrs Freme pulled her into an embrace, and Joan let the tears fall at last into the rough linen of the old woman's smock. 'You've had enough for today. Go along home. Rest up. Don't go giving that father of yours cause to pull out the strap again. And here, take the smaller loaf from my table. I want to see some more flesh on those bones, otherwise that boy of yours will have nothing to come back to.'

Chapter Eight

There was a seam of dark cloud over the hilltop to the south, and the beech stands cast long shadows into the valley. When Joan stepped over the cottage's threshold, it took a moment to make out her father slumped on the tabletop; she thought he must be sleeping. She coughed, and then John Browning gave out a groan. When he lifted his head from his hands, she saw the pages of his broken-backed record book underneath.

'Father?'

'Joan, I told you to make yourself scarce.' His voice was more weary than angry.

'I've been gone hours. The fire'll need lighting, if we're to eat tonight.'

'Joan, I need . . .' His voice tailed off, and he cradled his head in his hands again.

'Is it liquor you're wanting?' she asked, dreading his reply.

'The flagons are all gone, Joan.'

'Run to Mr Parker for another?'

'The money's gone, Joan.'

'Small beer, then. He'll give us a jar for a farthing.'

'It's all gone, Joan. I've spent the lot. If we had a farthing, we'd be rich.'

There were tears on his cheeks, she saw now, and the page nearest had been defaced with an angry scrawl. There was a small part of her – she wasn't proud of it – which felt shame at the sight of her father so beaten. Pity, too: her heart was heavy to see him like this. And a curl of fear that wound its way into her chest, nestled there; he'd teetered back from the precipice before, but what if this time there was no way back? What would happen to them all?

'The factor's been slow in paying you, I'll bet.' Joan wasn't sure whether she was trying to reassure her father or herself. 'And no doubt the millsman's charged you more than he should have for the fulling.'

John Browning shook his head. 'No, sweet girl. It's all here, and no mistakes as I can find.' His deep sigh set the account book's loose pages fluttering. 'I thought I could do it. I honestly thought I could bring us a decent living. Forget all those reveries of canals and tulips, I thought I could build us a house with rooms, and keep a larder full of food. Obstinacy, that's what brought me down. Your mother always used to laugh at me, telling me I was stubborn as Robert Parker's deaf mule. I had this totty-headed scheme, not an inch of room for error, and none of the patience to make it work.'

Joan put her hand on his arm. 'Father, you were only thinking of us, of our future.'

He grabbed at her cheek, pulling her forehead to his. His eyes were pink and rheumy. 'Look at you, though. Not a scrap of flesh on you. Don't think I don't know that if it wasn't for your Mrs Freme, you'd be wrapped in a shroud yourself. And to think that you'll be of an age for marriage soon, without a penny to your name.'

Joan inched back, sickened by his sour breath. 'What will we do?'

'There is nothing to do.'

'Ask for alms?'

He shook his head and let her go, falling back against his chair. 'I'm half glad your mother's not here to see it. Yes, I suppose we'll throw ourselves on the mercy of Father Britton, let the good ladies of the parish fan us with their charity.' He spat the words; it pained her to see her father so warped by his wounded pride. When times had been good, John Browning had always stood a little too proudly, always been a little too keen to show his full purse – even Joan had seen that – and there would be those who took pleasure in being asked for alms now. He would have to find some humility though; Joan was starting to realise that soon they'd have to be glad of any scrap that came their way.

'What can I do, Father?'

He opened his eyes wide and blinked several times, as if focus eluded him. 'Nothing, child.' His face softened. 'This is no fault of yours. Perhaps you and your sister should practise your deserving looks; I dare say there are plenty in need and little enough to go round.' This was true enough; she'd seen the poor-relief line outside the vicar's house only last week: grown men with no boots, women with potato sacks for tunics. A blind boy in a cart pushed by his sister; her gown so dirty, it hung stiff around her ankles. Bow-legged boys so thin, their ankle bones bulged like wizened apples, one with a growth above his eye that forced the lid half-closed. How long till she and Alice joined that sorry line, until they stood out to be pitied no more or less than the rest?

'Can I look at the books?' She tried to keep her voice even, to keep the urgency from it.

She saw his brows tighten at that. 'Do you doubt your old father?' he snapped. But then his shoulders sank again. She realised that he was truly a beaten man, but she forced herself to wait in silence until he was ready to speak.

At last he stood up, his chair scraping across the floor. When he shoved the books roughly towards her, a last flicker of his earlier anger flared. 'Why not? There can be no harm in it. Perhaps you can see how these walls came tumbling down.' Then he stomped away across the room. 'Let me be, now though. I'll not be disturbed.'

Afterwards, she heard him crashing in the back like a dog in a cage. All of their mother's things – the few that had not yet been pawned – were hidden in the chest in the corner of the loom space. She had found him in there once, with one of Hannah's scarves held to his nose. When all went quiet at last, she wondered if he did the same now, lost in memories. At least it gave her time. She set to the chores, keen to get her eyes on the books as quickly as she could. And she was just gathering up the loose pages from the tabletop, tucking them back inside the cover, when Alice bundled in, pulling brambles from her skirts.

'Curse that path,' she said. 'It is a mischief to walk up in the dark. Where is Father?'

Joan nodded towards the back room. Alice walked over to the curtain and twitched it aside. 'Snoring like an old donkey,' she said, letting it fall. 'We'll not see him again tonight.'

Joan nodded, resting her hands across the record book to cover it as best she could, but Alice's eyes fell on it anyway.

'Well, has he lost it all?' Alice's tone was more tired than bitter.

Joan shook her head. 'I don't know yet.'

'Look, then. I'm in no hurry.'

A shrug of Alice's eyebrows showed she meant it, so Joan set a rushlight in the holder and held up the account book's first pages to the light. The mutton grease flickered and spluttered and she had to lean close to read her father's cramped script, conscious of her sister's eyes on her. She'd read accounts before – they'd been shown at the Dame School how to tot up a column of figures, and sometimes she'd looked over the yarn orders that came from the mills – but never one so detailed and yet so carelessly drawn; it was some time before she could decipher half of what was meant by all her father's ticks and balances. Alice had sat down heavily in the chair opposite and Joan was conscious of her stare.

'The margin's so fine, it's no wonder,' Joan said eventually. 'There's no economy to be found when the amounts are so small. And you can see from Father's notes here, the factor is full of excuses for the poor prices he'll pay.'

'We're done for, then,' Alice said. She thumped a fist three times on the tabletop.

Alice looked so like their mother in the rushlight, Joan swallowed before she replied, shaking her head. 'We can't give up yet. Perhaps if we worked together?' she started. A brief image, of the two of them, bargaining with the fuller over his costs, or stamping dye out in the millstream. Gone at once, of course. Idle reveries. Alice would not want to be near her for long enough to weave a handkerchief together.

Alice just gave a dull laugh. 'Joan, your head is in the clouds, as ever,' she muttered, but it was said more kindly than Joan expected. 'Us getting out, that's the only thing that'll help him. Leave him to his flagons and his misery.'

'That's not fair.' Joan's words sounded empty even to herself.

'See? You know as well as I do. We're both little more than a hindrance – two mouths to feed, a great big one, in your case – better off finding ourselves a man down the valley.' Alice pulled a pin from her hair and stuck it back in, higher up the plait. 'Not just any man, mind. It's a better life I'm after, not just moving to be someone else's skivvy. A gentleman with a coach and a stable. Even you, homely Joan, you'll find someone. Some fool who won't mind your long legs, who doesn't find it irksome to have a wife with a brain too big for its box.'

'There's only one man for me.'

'A Joan in the dark is as good as anybody, don't they say? And just the same, I'm sure any Fred or Thomas or Richard is as good as any other, come nightfall.' Even when Alice had no malice in her, she couldn't resist a dig.

'Dark or light,' Joan said. 'I'd only want Daniel.'

Alice snorted. 'Joan, you're a little girl. Daniel is not coming back. Our father is drinking himself to the grave. Grow up and find yourself a two-legged horse out of here.'

'But . . .' Joan started, but it seemed Alice had said her piece. She'd turned away towards the bundle of bedclothes in the corner, where their father usually slept. Snatching up the bulk of them for herself, Alice rolled to face the wall. Joan shook her head again. Even her sister's barbs and teasing were better than her silence. But perhaps it was no use trying with Alice; better to concentrate on what she might change.

As her sister's breathing steadied, Joan turned back to the stack of papers on the table. The rushlight was almost extinguished and she used the last of it to light another; it was a reckless extravagance, but she must go back over the accounts one last time. This time, she made notes of her own, drawing question marks where the figures did not tally or were indecipherable, noting down any bare opportunity to make changes. Whenever her eyes threatened to close, she forced herself to think of that poor-relief line, of how soon they might find themselves at the back of it.

She could read enough to see that her father was right in one thing: the pattern of losses was ugly. Here and there the factor complained of poorly scribbled wool and crowded warps, and she saw that he had increased his commission twice within a twelvemonth. Likewise, she noticed that the wool merchant's prices had risen steadily, while the costs of fulling and finishing the cloth skimmed almost all of the profit that remained. It made for grim reading, and several times Joan almost threw down the pages in despair. But she willed herself to find a way.

Not all the deals were bad, she could see that – the Iles mill seemed to charge a reasonable fee for its finishing, and the orders from a Mr Patterson of Blackwell Hall had increased steadily in size over the past few months – her father's contacts must be worth something. There were debts outstanding, and arrangements would need to be made, but if everything was just stitched a little closer, prices inched higher, costs tugged tighter . . .

Joan made some notes as she went, totting up sums and roughing out a new account on a loose leaf from the back of the ledger. Perhaps there was a hope, the barest one, that the business could be turned around. It would take a fair wind, and many small kindnesses. And then, if everything could be hauled back into line, was there a chance to make something more? To turn a repair into the creation of something new? Dyeing, it seemed to her, might be the missing piece. Without it, the economics of cloth production seemed doomed to labour on a dagger's edge. But with the addition of a dyeing business, while still precarious, there was the chance to make a proper living. It would take some doing, though, and perhaps her father would never countenance it. She held her eyelids open with her fingertips, forcing herself over the numbers one last time.

Outside, the cockerel crowed dawn, and Joan woke with her face on the last page of the record book, a few slim hours of sleep behind her. Stiff as a board, she pushed herself up to standing, splashing the last of the water jug across her face to wake herself. Beside the fire, Rockwood lifted his head from the dirt, but when he saw she was not Daniel, the dog slumped back down, nose to the hearth so that a little cloud of ash rose with each exhalation. On the other side of the room, Alice was breathing steadily still, but it was not long before their father padded through from the back room, his face smudged and wrinkled with sleep.

'I'll go there myself, today,' he began, tucking in his undershirt as he spoke.

'Father,' Joan started.

'No, Joan, listen up.' John Browning pulled himself straight, running a hand over his face and the dirty grey curls of his beard. 'I'd rather take myself to the bailiff than have him search me out.'

'I've looked at the books, Father.'

He laughed. How could he laugh? Joan bit down on the urge to shake him. 'Too late,' he said, 'but no mind. Don't mince your words then, child. Tell me what you found in them. No, on second thoughts, don't. I know there's nothing doing.'

'We have nothing left,' Joan started.

'Tell me something I don't know,' her father jumped in at once. 'Your old father's a lumpish nick-ninny who's pissed his inheritance down the Frome.' He made for the door, aiming a half-hearted kick towards the dog, who twisted away and whined.

'Father, wait, there was more.' John Browning hovered on the threshold, and Joan swallowed, knowing she would only have one chance. 'The money's gone, but I think there's a way to make it back. We could ask the wool merchant for more time, for a start.'

If I'm forced to venture out to the arse end of the Frome valley in search of him, there'll be no fancy words as can save him. Of course she remembered Mr Ridler's words, but he had seemed a kindly enough man and perhaps he spoke in jest for the crowd.

He shook his head. 'Ridler's charitable enough, but every man has his limits. He'd go down himself if he let men stretch him that way.'

'Press the London factor for an advance on the cloth he's due, then,' she blurted, frantic to find the idea which might convince him.

But at this, her father snorted. 'Patterson. That Scottish sly-boots wouldn't go for it. He's slippery as a lamprey, with a face not much prettier. I've never heard him close a deal without trying to eke out another penny on the pound.'

'The millsman, then?' Joan went on, hearing the whine of desperation in her own voice now. 'We have a few rolls of broadcloth left. If he'd let them be fulled and finished on account and for little enough, we might make enough to cover our costs and buy a fleece or two. Breaking even, that's all we're after now, and then perhaps luck might turn our way.' If I mind the books like that blue hawk the woolman likened me to, and watch every last pick across the warp, she thought, willing it to be true.

John Browning looked at her from the doorway, one hand on the frame. 'It shames me to say it, Joan – your mother would weep to hear it – I'm not welcome at the mill any longer. I'd heard they weren't minded to give my cloth back without full payment, so I went down there and tried to take it back by force. I ended up on my tail in the mill-race, of course, with the shearers leaning out of the windows to mock me, and Mr Iles himself came out to make it known that if I'm seen on the premises, they've permission to set the dogs on me.'

'When was this?'

'Yesterday.'

'Father, how can that be? I was only gone an hour or two.'

'I walked down there not far behind you. Let's just say they didn't waste any time throwing me out.'

Joan shook her head. It was like trying to hold back a stream with her bare hands.

'So you see,' he said, softly now, 'I've not left us anywhere to go save the bailiff. And if I walk there before noon, perhaps he'll take pity and leave these walls around us.'

Joan was silent for a long moment. She looked at her father: the sag of his breeches, his broken stoop, the bloom of red veins on his nose from the drinking. She listened to the steady in-and-out of Alice's gentle snore, wondering that her sister found such repose in all of this. It was all she could do not to curse the both of them and run away to the solitude of the woods. But she couldn't give up as they had. Someone had to find a way out of this. She took a deep breath, imagining her mother: how Hannah Browning would have stood now, how she might have fixed this.

'Let me try, Father. To run the business, I mean. To give it one last shot.' The idea came to Joan only moments before the words escaped. Perhaps she had just brought another beating on herself, and though she knew she did not deserve it, she wouldn't be surprised. Perhaps she was as totty-headed as he was and they'd be better off begging for the bailiff's mercy and prevailing on the benevolence of Mrs Britton and her like. But these were borrowed walls, built on land that wasn't theirs: there was no assurance in these precarious stones. And if the alternative was to rely on the charity of others, then it was worth fighting for.

Feeling emboldened by the thought, Joan imagined herself for a moment walking up to the door of the Iles mill, a roll of cloth under her arm to be finished. She brushed away an unhelpful thought of how she might be received there, of catcalls and laughter. She could only try; perhaps it would be a welcome distraction from Daniel's absence, and though she dared not hope for Alice's help, if she could turn their lives around, it might even bring them closer.

Joan couldn't see her father's face well against the daylight, so she did not know what to expect in reply. When he shook his head, she braced herself for the worst. It was a lot, for a man, but then what had he left to turn to?

'You'll have to let me think on that, Joan,' was all he said. And then he pushed himself off the door-frame and set off down into the valley.

Chapter Nine

It was Rockwood who heard the whistling first.

Early evening, days later. Joan and the dog were alone in the cottage – Alice was visiting their distant cousin in Woodchester, hoping for a hot meal no doubt, and their father had been barely seen for days. Joan was balling yarn beside the unlit grate when the hunting dog growled and pushed itself upright from where it had lain at her feet. They were in the habit of keeping the cottage shuttered at this time of year to keep out insects, which were flying high in the July heat, swarming in clouds above the streams and standing water. When Joan looked across to the dog, squinting in the dim light, she saw he was standing now, ears pushed forward, eyes fixed on the mismatched planks Joan's father had fashioned long ago into a door.

'What's that, Rockwood? What're you hearing?'

The dog made his lopsided way to the threshold and began to paw at the planks, more alert than he had been in a week. Joan walked over herself, running her hand over the animal's close-furred scalp, the bones all too apparent just beneath. She'd done her best to save him a scrap or two from her own bowl each time, but he was thin before he came and they were all living on little more than air and dew. Her father's hand would have come down hard if she was caught wasting food on an animal.

'I can't hear anything, pup. Maybe it's the wind.'

But Rockwood kept scratching, letting out a low whine. Eventually, Joan heard the whistling too – it was Light-o'-Love, not a tune sung by any breeze she'd ever known – and she lifted the latch to see who was coming.

'Daniel?'

'Joan, come here.' And then he was there in the open doorway, pulling her into his arms. His clothes were stiff with mud and he smelt of wood fire and cowhide. Rockwood pushed between their legs while he embraced her, trying to mould himself around his master's feet, so much so that Joan almost lost her footing and Daniel laughed and pulled her tighter.

'We've been hearing all sorts,' Joan said, stepping back at last. 'That you were hurt, that you'd lamed one of the King's men. That you'd joined up with all sorts: Seekers, Ranters, Muggletonians, and no one seemed to know which was worse.'

Daniel laughed. 'None of that. How people talk. We were chased from the valley, that's all. Now I know how pigs feel when the farmer drives them down the track with his staff. But they were too well fed to come close enough for a beating. They saw us over the hilltop and then shouted after us where the boundary lay.'

'And where have you been since?'

'Bedding down in a cow barn near Winstone; six of us, and a thousand rats. I don't exaggerate when I say there were rodents many, spry and vigorous enough to put on a travelling show. I swear if you had picked up a fiddle and struck up Jack Pudding, they'd have danced.'

She started to laugh, then pressed her fists and her face into his jacket. 'Daniel, how can you tease me, when we have been so afeared. But you are back. Praise the Lord.' She rested her head against his chest and he kissed the line of her parting.

'Joan, I cannot stay. If my father is caught within a whisker of the valley, he will be transported, for sure, and it would do his case no good if I were found here.'

'But you are just back, and now must go?'

Rockwood sat up and barked once, as if he liked it even less. Daniel ducked to rub his fingers over the dog's ears.

'I will stay as long as I can. Will you let me in, Joan? I mustn't be seen. But I have plans to set by you, and a question for your father.'

If you can find him, Joan thought. She had seen her father only three times since he had confessed the dire state of his affairs; twice he had been drunk, though she dreaded to think by what means, and the third time he had staggered in to lay two pennies on the table, before lurching off into the twilight. *Proceeds of poaching, probably*, Alice had muttered when Joan had asked her. *And it'd be just our luck if he lost a hand over it.* She'd sounded vague and disinterested. It was as if Alice had taken leave of the house already; her mind and loyalties seemed to have transferred elsewhere, just when Joan had need of her most. Joan would have forgiven her everything, so much did she yearn for her sister's support, but it was no use. And now even Daniel's return brought little comfort if he could not stay.

He followed Joan inside. The cupboard was bare and the night's meal, if you could call it that, had yet to heat on the stove, but she poured him a cup of water. Daniel took a seat on the bench and the dog laid himself across his master's feet and closed its eyes. Joan took the stool opposite, with the crack in its leg – it would not do to put too much weight on it, but she would not relax now anyway, not now she knew that Daniel would be leaving again and who knew when he'd be coming back.

'One day, Joan, we'll have a full pantry. Great flagons of milk and beer.' He must have been watching her glance about. He leant towards her, put his hand over hers. 'The best wine if we want it. Peacocks for supper, even, if the fancy takes us.'

'Don't you start,' Joan said. It came out more bitter than she had intended, but her heart was heavy at the thought that she would lose him again so soon. 'You sound like my father. All his grand schemes, yet here we are without even a crust to offer you.'

His eyes widened at this, but he leant further in.

'You haven't heard my plan yet. We had word from my uncle while we were in Winstone. My father's brother, that is, who works as a stonemason in Cirencester. His boys have joined the army; the King is building his troops again.'

'And what does this have to do with you?' She asked to give herself space to breathe, but she'd already guessed the worst.

'My uncle has made it known that he would put up the money for me to go too. Enough for my travel, my tunic, and all the mountings that go with it. A little set aside for food and lodging until I'm sorted. See, Joan, this could be the answer to everything.'

Joan hung her head. 'How could you think that this would make me happy?'

He pressed his hand on hers again.

'Joan, it's not what I planned.' She stared into his eyes. It's true there was sadness there, but surely there was excitement too. She watched the flush – it could only be guilt – creep up his cheeks. 'But I'll come back with money in my pockets, fit and ready to start a business here. Ready to make our future.'

'And in the meantime, will I wait, not ever knowing whether you'll come safely back?' Some mad old maid prattling about the soldier boy who said he'd return. Already she could imagine how Alice would tease.

'You must know that I will come back. Joan, I mean to spend my life with you. This is what I wanted to say. Let us be wed before I leave.'

Now she laughed. Truly he had lost his mind with all this talk of soldiering and marriage.

'A wedding! The church will not open its doors until Sunday. Would you speed up time, now?'

He shook his head. 'Look at what the church has done for me.' He held out his sleeves, ripped and dark with mud. 'We can do without the priest today.'

'What is a wedding without a priest?'

'It can be done. The Church wouldn't like it, but who will know to issue the penalty? Do you have Father Britton hiding back there in the looms? That dogwhipper Seymour is a busybody like no other, but even he can't hear the words spoken within these walls. Joan.' Daniel came round the table now, dropped to one knee beside her. Rockwood whimpered from where he'd been tipped from Daniel's feet. 'Please, take my hand. My father explained it: the marriage stands, even without a priest, if only your father will give his consent.'

Joan said nothing. It was so much. Her thoughts spiralled like the eddies at the side of the mill-race.

'Joan?' He rubbed the back of her palm. 'If it will make you happier, we can seek a church blessing on my return.'

Since they were very small, it had been Alice who talked of the wedding day she would have: the bride cakes, the rosemary boughs, the musicians paid to lead the bridal party up the valley-side to the church. Every detail of Alice's marriage feast was planned and imagined – painful sometimes when they slept on empty bellies and Alice would not stop talking of the breads and meats that would be laid out on the trestles in the church, the sweet honey pastries and quince tarts that would melt on their tongues. Joan had lived Alice's wedding day many times, but she had never conjured up her own. If she had, it would not be like this: a clandestine promise, wrong in the eyes of the Church, to a boy who would leave as soon as they were made man and wife.

But there was a clatter from the doorway now and her father appeared there. He grabbed at the door-frame, and for a moment she thought he must be drunk again, but he only steadied himself to scrape his boot on the stone.

'Mr Browning.' Daniel jumped up.

Joan's father looked up and frowned. When he recognised Daniel, his eyes widened and his frown deepened.

'You're taking a risk, aren't you?'

'It's my father they banished, sir, not me.'

'Still, from what I heard, that priest would have liked to tan the hide of the lot of you. And there are plenty in this valley who love to stir a pot. I hope you weren't seen on the way up here.'

'I kept to the hedges. And you know me, sir. There's a place in the pew for me at Bisley, just like there used to be for my mother.'

John Browning dropped his head. 'She was a good woman, your mother. My wife didn't share the confidence of many of the women in this valley, but she never had a bad word for your mother.'

'Thank you, sir.'

'So what brings you back, then? Apart from the obvious.' He gestured towards Joan, who busied herself with the cups to cover her blush.

'I came to tell Joan that I'm to join the army, sir. The Earl of Peterborough's Regiment of Foot, which is garrisoned in Surrey. Rutherford's Lambs, they are called, on account of the colonel and the regiment's insignia.'

Joan's father was lowering himself into his chair but he stopped halfway, eyebrows leaping halfway up his forehead.

'The army! What does your father think to that? He's not a man for fighting, I'm sure. The Yea and Nay men are pacifists, are they not?'

'It was his brother's idea. My father would only keep me safe – we're no longer welcome here, and when winter comes, the cow barns of the shire will seem even less tempting.'

'Keep you safe, so he'll have you trained as a soldier? That seems an ill-thought logic to me.'

'I am old enough now, sir, to make my own decisions. I'm sure he'd rather I stay close to home, but we've no war to fight, only to defend our part of the new Queen's dowry. Tangier, which is in Africa, I believe.'

'Africa! Son, I was going to ask whether you knew how distant Surrey was.'

'I envy you the chance to travel so far. Just think of the wonders you will see.' Joan knelt by the washing bucket to rinse the cups. Daniel's glance across to her was grateful. But her father sat back in his chair, folding his arms across his chest.

'It seems you have already convinced my daughter of this mad plan. So much so, she longs to join the army and roam the distant seas herself.'

'It is only that we cannot see a better way, Father.' Joan stared down at the murky water in the bucket.

'I came to ask for Joan's hand, if you'll let me,' she heard Daniel say behind her.

John Browning filled his cheeks with air and blew it out in a long whistle. 'Joan is barely of age,' he said at last.

'I am thinking of her, sir. I would not have her waiting without a promise.'

John Browning was silent for an even longer time. The cottage was so quiet that Joan could hear the spit of the coals and the hiss of the lid on the cauldron. Outside, she could make out the chunter and complaint of the hen, fending off the attentions of the cockerel again. Rockwood limped over towards Joan's father, as if the dog too would try and persuade him, but John Browning twitched his foot and the dog backed away.

'I'll not see her married yet.'

'Father . . .' Joan began.

'I'll not see her married yet,' John Browning continued, louder now. 'But a promise . . . Perhaps, that I could accept.'

'I don't understand, Father.'

'When your mother and I wed, we were too young ourselves. But our parents wanted to mark the joining of our families. To heal a long-standing rift, that bears no further explanation today. Handfasting, spousals, whatever you'd call it, but *in futuro*. That is, as children, we swore an oath to be joined in marriage when we came of age.'

'And how is it done?'

He laughed. 'I was a little boy, throwing stones at birds in the fields. I can't remember how the words were phrased. It will be enough, I think, to borrow the words from the Book, but to say them with a mind to the future.'

'And what of the rings and the other accoutrements which the priest would employ?' Joan was remembering the cloths that bound the couple's hands, the bells, the water and the communion wine and bread. She had attended enough village weddings to know how it was done.

'Don't trouble yourselves about all that trumpery,' her father said at once. 'God will see the love in your hearts, and it will suffice. Do you have a scrap of ribbon, Joan?'

There were no fancy trimmings on her dresses. Even the embellishments on Alice's smocks had long since disintegrated or been darned away; leaving her to hover wistfully at the market's ribbon stall. Joan could only think of the chest of her mother's things, of the gown at the bottom of that chest. Their father had refused Alice's every request to refashion it into something for herself.

'Nothing of my own.' She watched her father swallow, knew how much it would take for him to even suggest she touch it.

'You know where to look. Take a piece from the bodice ribbon on each side. Be careful with the shears, I'll not have the fabric rent.' Joan nodded and ran through to the back room before he could change his mind. 'And you, boy,' she heard from behind her. 'Get yourself out to the stream and wash the grime from your face. I'll not have my daughter wed to a scarecrow.'

She had a moment, then, to glance in the glass. To rub the dirt from her own forehead and wrestle the most wayward curls into a plait. She rubbed her cheeks and lips as she had seen Alice do. Even picked up the tiny pot of rouge her sister had obtained from somewhere, examined the slick of red around its rim, but decided against it. She would look like herself.

Then Joan laid her mother's gown out on the bed, using the yarn shears to take two pieces from the satin ribbon on each side. If she was Alice, she'd have begged to wear the dress in its entirety, but she'd seen the tear in her father's lashes at the mere thought of shearing the ribbon, and in any case, it would fall barely to her shins. She was taller even now than her mother had been when she died.

'Come, Joan. Your intended awaits,' she heard from the next room.

They stood in front of the hearth, every one as awkward. John Browning had pulled on his jacket, in a gesture of formality, but the heat of the day had not yet died and his hair turned damp spirals around his forehead. The door had been left ajar and the hen fussed on the threshold, pecking at a cricket that eluded her beak. Daniel reached for Joan's hand, and her father draped a length of broadcloth over their clasped fingers. He breathed out in a long sigh.

'Would that my wife were here today. A man should not have to see his daughter wed without his own wife at his side.'

Joan reached out and squeezed his hand with her other. He closed his eyes a moment, then pulled himself up straighter.

'Daniel, you start,' he said. 'Begin with: I will take thee to be my wife.'

'Joan, I will take thee to be my wife.'

'And now we have all the words in the Book.' He scrabbled to find his place in the text, reading aloud the words, as awkward as the slowest child in the Dame School. 'When the time comes, wilt thou love her, comfort her, and whatnot?'

'I will honour and keep her,' Daniel replied, 'in sickness and in health, and forsaking all others, will keep only unto her, for so long as we both shall live.'

John Browning nodded. 'Good, good. Your mother would be proud of your piety. Now you, Joan.'

'Daniel, I will take thee to be my husband.'

'And now you must promise, that when the time comes, you'll obey and serve him. Love, honour and keep him, in sickness and in health. And, forsaking all others, keep thee only unto him, so long as ye both shall live.'

'I will.'

John Browning snapped the Book shut with evident relief. 'There's plenty more words we could say, but a promise is enough for spousals. We'll leave the oaths and frills for the blessing, may it come soon. There should be a sign to bind it, though. A ring would be best, but the ribbon will suffice. Daniel, lay the tied strands on the Book here, and then tie it round the fourth finger on Joan's left hand.'

'There, it's done.'

'And a prayer now, for Daniel's safekeeping, and a blessing on these thy servants, let them come together in the estate of holy matrimony as soon as time and circumstance permit.'

They all stood in silence, heads bowed. Joan felt herself sway, curled her toes in her boots to steady herself. At last John Browning coughed, and Joan looked up. He saw her looking and swiped roughly at his face with his sleeve.

'I have an errand in the valley. I will leave you alone a while,' he said. He had slipped out of the doorway before they could answer.

'Marriage must be sealed with a kiss, surely,' Daniel said, when the thud of John Browning's boots had died away. He reached to place his hand in the small of her back, taking a step closer so that their faces were only inches apart. They had not been so close since the night of the Whitsun fair; even in the half-dark of the cottage, she could see the hazel shot through the blue of his eyes, the spider legs of his lashes. And when she closed her own eyes, she felt the dry brush of his lips on hers, cracked from the sun, and then a stronger press that made her heart thud so loud she was afraid he would laugh to hear it. His fingers traced the line of her jaw, and she leant her cheek into his palm. Then the cockerel gave out its extravagant crow, and they came apart, laughing.

'Even the birds celebrate our union,' he said, and he kissed her quickly on the lips again. 'But here, I brought something.' He fished inside his satchel, pulling out a muslin bundle. 'Nettle-wrapped cheese and a honey cake from the farmer's wife. It's no marriage feast, but at least I'll leave knowing you've something in your belly.'

'But you'll share it with me?'

'No, I must go, Joan. I'll lose the light, and I've no torch or lantern.'

'Wait, then, I've got something for you.' She ran through to the back room and pulled the yellow cap from under the cot, brushing off the dust as she came back to him. 'I found it by your cottage. It's a little scorched, though it was spared the worst. But perhaps you'll have no use for this now, with a fine new scarlet tunic coming your way.'

He turned the hat over in his hands, then handed it back. 'Would you keep it for me, Joan? I'd like to think you have something of mine.'

She thought of the row of strange little trinkets above the cot, how grateful she was that he would never know of them.

'And Rockwood?'

The dog sat up at the sound of his name. Daniel shook his head, and the dog seemed to understand, dropping his nose back over his master's foot.

'I'd love to take him, but I fear his leg would not stand it. Besides, I don't think the colonel would welcome a hound amongst the Lambs.'

The dog turned his liquid eyes back up to his master. Daniel smiled, then his face fell serious and he leaned over to kiss Joan beside her ear.

'I may be gone several summers, Joan. I don't know what I will face out there or how long it will be before my commission expires.'

She leant her forehead against his. 'Rockwood and I will be here. Though I'm not sure who will miss you more.'

He wrapped his arms around her and they stood silently together for some long minutes. Joan tried to memorise every single thing she felt: the warmth of his fingers on her neck, the scrape of the stubble on his cheek, even the crush of his boot on hers as their feet tangled together. And then, far too soon, he was gone. She watched him wind his way down the hillside until the twilight left the brown of his jacket indistinguishable from the sun-dried bracken and straw. Even then, she stood a while longer, watching swallows dip across the valley, and the smoke trail from a cottage on the far side as it was teased sideways by a vanishing breeze.

'Father?'

He was coming down the Bisley path, a saw in one hand and a stick in the other, beating back brambles. Joan watched for the familiar lurch in his walk, but it seemed he would spend the whole day sober.

'He's gone, then?' her father said.

'Yes.'

'Left that dog of his, I'll bet. As if we didn't have enough mouths to feed.' But John Browning didn't sound as cross as his words, and he laid his palm across his daughter's shoulders as he passed. Joan followed him to the woodshed, watched him slip the bag from his back and stack the logs he'd cut on the pile.

'Your sister will be fuming to have missed it,' he said, without turning. 'Little Joan on a promise, and a ribbon on her finger to prove it.' He hung the saw on its peg.

Joan hadn't even considered Alice, and now she felt pained for not having done so. They had been through so much together, and for her to miss such a thing. Mrs Freme too. It was not the wedding it should have been, but what choice had they had?

'I'll keep some of this cake back for her, and a lump of the cheese,' she said, as they walked back inside together. And the same for Mrs Freme, she thought. It would be a fine thing to be able to take some sweet morsel her friend's way, for once.

John Browning took her chin in his fingers, gently pinching her cheeks. 'Don't trouble yourself on Alice's behalf, Joan. I'm not sure a crumb of cake will make up for hearing her sister's been betrothed before her. But she'll get over it.' He laughed, bending to poke his stick into the fire so that sparks blew up. 'She's got my sister's rage in her, you know. Anne was born with bright-red hair and a furnace inside, and Alice is no different, though the blaze is better hidden.'

Joan stirred the pot while her father rinsed his hands over the bucket. Her limbs and her heart felt heavy. What was there to look forward to now? Alice returning, cross as a trapped wasp. Endless days with empty bellies. The long walk to Bisley to beg for alms. If her father was driven to poaching to keep them, how long could he keep it up before the keepers had him in the courthouse and a hand lost, or worse? Mrs Freme was a blessing, but even the widow could not save them now. And Daniel, gone – she could hardly bear to think of it. She leant in close to the pot, letting the steam scald her cheeks as if it might draw out some of the sadness.

'Shall I serve, Father?' she said at last.

'Wait a minute, Joan.' He hadn't slumped in his chair for once. Instead, he came to stand opposite her, holding her shoulders, one in each palm, and squeezing them until she stood up straight. 'I've been wanting to talk today. I've been thinking, about what you said about the business.' *Enough, not today*, she wanted to say, but he was not finished yet. 'I was minded to admit defeat, but you, girl, your spirit . . . well, if Alice has got my sister's fury, you've got your mother's mettle. And it got me thinking. Perhaps there's a sliver of life left in the venture, and maybe you're the one to revive it, if you're still of a mind to try?'

'I thought you said . . .'

'Forget what I said, Joan. I was a flagon down and my thinking was too full of pride. We've still got a little cloth and perhaps the credit can be stretched further, as you said. And I'd be right beside you. You could put me in charge of the weaving side of things. I'll be little more than a hindrance where the mill's concerned, so you'll do better alone there. And if not, there's enough other mills in this valley to take our business.'

As if we offered them a favour, with the paltry offer of our business! – her father had certainly changed his tune. Perhaps all Daniel's talk of soldiering had put back some fire in his belly.

'There'll be those who say that clothier is an unsuitable occupation for a woman,' he went on now. 'That having such aspirations is not befitting of a good Christian girl, and there'll be those who try to take you down for it. But you can read as well as any boy, and something tells me you've a knack for commerce that will stand you in good stead with the merchants. And if it takes your mind from Daniel being gone, so much the better.'

John Browning held himself taller than he had for weeks, though he stood beside a pot in which a single onion floated amongst the foraged scraps. Joan knew Alice would laugh to see it. Oh, Alice – it was difficult to imagine she would accept all this, even if it took work from her shoulders. But for Joan to have her father's confidence – that was a blessing. She could only hope to do him proud.

'Thank you, Father.'

'So you'll do it?'

She recalled the sorry state of the books, the precarious margin of profit that was on offer. Her stomach twisted, and it wasn't hunger for once. If there was anything to salvage, who was to say she could run it any better than her father? And dyeing: it was even higher hubris, surely, to have thoughts of taking on that specialist art, before she had even concluded her first sale? Mrs Freme would stand by her promise to teach her, but the widow only knew what she had gleaned herself. Dyeing was a practice that took years of study – for the expertise in the materials, and competence in the chemistry, and a deep proficiency in the minutiae of the workmanship – and Joan could not even afford the treatises which might lend her this knowledge.

Joan breathed as deeply as her bodice would allow. It was the family's livelihood she would balance in her hands. She imagined it delicate and precious as the first egg her hen had laid: a witch egg, tiny and white, like a perfectly round pebble in her palm. Their quiet life had been turned on its head in a single day by the arrival of the King's men and the priest. And who was to say what the next years might bring? – there had been talk of pestilence in London again, of children vomiting blood, of men with buboes at armpit and groin, of stricken servants cast into the streets to die in the gutter. And who knew when the King might send the country back out to war? There was so much to fear; her scalp itched to think of the responsibility. But the alternative . . . an image of her father behind the courthouse bar, begging mercy for hides caught and sold, of her and Alice with no choice but to join the poor-relief line . . . it didn't bear thinking of.

'Of course, Father. I would be honoured to try.' She would learn the trade at least, and use her every last breath in the attempt to save her father's livelihood. If time allowed, she would turn her mind to dyeing too, in case that way lay their salvation. Her thoughts ran to the Dutch merchant and his spectrum of dyed wool; how she might experiment again. Let Daniel return, proud to find his betrothed with a clothing business which had flourished from the scorched earth he left behind.

'That's my girl,' her father said. And he pulled her close, so that her nose was buried in his leather jerkin. She stayed there for a long time, until she could almost lose her fear in the stink and warmth of it.

Part Two

–

SCARLET

Chapter Ten

1666

Joan laid the length of stone-brown felt down across the millsman's worktop, forcing herself to take her time over the fold. The flutter of nerves she always felt on arriving at the mill – every moment expecting to be called out as an imposter – still lurked in her belly, but with each visit it had become easier to overcome.

'The nap has been raised well, Mr Higgins.' She spoke loudly to cover her nerves, and to be heard over the fulling hammers; even in this back room, the noise was thunderous. 'And I am pleased with the quality of the weave.'

She had kept him waiting long enough while she pored over the length of cloth. But perhaps he was becoming used to her meticulous scrutiny; he had only coughed once, and even that might have been due to the great quantity of fuller's earth-dust in the air.

'Thank you, Miss Browning.'

On her first visit, the men at the mill – Iles's, and now Tayloe's – had naturally assumed that she operated on her father's account. But, as the weeks and months had passed, they had begun to ask for her opinion directly. Mr Higgins now asked after her father only occasionally, and no longer in the context of the transactions they discussed. 'You'll be back next week to collect the rest, I suppose? We'll have the package wrapped for you,' he said now.

She patted the cloth on the fold and nodded. It was only a sample of the yardage they were finishing for her, but from previous experience, she had no reason to think that the quality of the whole order would not match it. Given the choice, she might examine every last thread – any defect was a penny less in the pot, a night without bread – but there were limits to what the millsman could be expected to endure.

'Thank you, Mr Higgins. And I'll be bringing a great quantity of wool for scouring soon.'

'We should have time for it. Mr Tayloe will have his own done first, of course, but I'm sure there'll be time enough to get yours in the river after.'

She nodded, straightening a finger of her gloves. They were Alice's cast-offs, and wouldn't bear close inspection, but there was something about the conceit of wearing them that lent a fraction of confidence. She was still so young; it would be easy to feel a fraud.

It had been almost two years since that day – miraculous and heartbreaking – when she and Daniel had handfasted and he had left for the army, a time in which she had blessed the way the business took her every hour and left bare few to miss him. There had been six months of desperate scrabbling, begging favours and treading the slenderest thread between profit and ruin. Long journeys on an empty belly, plenty of time to question the decision to try at all. If it were not for Mrs Freme, there were several times she would have given up the attempt.

But since: she had been a little more successful than perhaps either of them could have foreseen. She did seem to have a natural affinity for it, even she would admit that – but she was still the daughter of a weaver with a fondness for the flagon, masquerading as a clothier, but small touches like these gloves did something to boost her standing with the millmen and merchants she dealt with.

'Will you settle your account, Miss Browning, while you are here?'

She thought of the broadcloth order she had sent on its way to London, hitching a lift with the courier from Cirencester, and the negotiations she would have with the wool merchant for another twenty fleeces later in the week. She used a ledger, of course, but the numbers were always in her head: a running total of the amounts that washed in and out like a tide, leaving the bare margin on which they lived. The orders had grown with her confidence, but the margin only tiptoed higher. Rarely now did they sleep with rumbling bellies these days, and the cock and hen had been joined by two more birds and a knock-kneed lamb, but they were still a long way from the gentleman's life her father had dreamed of.

She shook her head. 'But before the month end, if you'll agree to that.'

The millsman pursed his lips before he nodded. She was always asking for a little more, pushing a little further. It was the only way to move forward.

'Very well. I'll have the clerk draw up the account next time.'

'She's in the lean-to round the back.' Harriet's mother was dusting flour off her hands when she answered the door to Joan's knock. There were deep lines around her eyes and her gown looked thin and untidy. 'Don't mind the dog, he's soft in the head. He's only after a bite of something, never gives up.'

Joan thanked her and followed her directions down the thin alley between their cottage and the one next door, the folded cloth from the millsman still under her arm. Harriet's dog was sitting in the lean-to doorway, and as soon as it caught sight of Joan, it came rushing forward on its short legs, the animal as squat and round as Rockwood was tall and lean. Lucky that she had not brought Daniel's dog out with her, he'd have made short work of this little fellow. Joan waited a moment while the creature sniffed around her ankles, then it decided the search was fruitless, and returned to its post with less enthusiasm.

'Harriet?' Joan called then, into the darkness of the lean-to. The door was propped half open but there were no windows and she wondered how Alice's friend could see to work in there.

There was a scrape and a thud and then Harriet came to the door, pushing a strand of dark hair back into her bun.

'Joan. Sorry, I didn't hear you come.'

'You'll spoil your eyes working in there,' Joan replied, but then how often had she and Alice woven late at night with a single rushlight between them?

'The door won't open wider. Father keeps saying he'll put a window in, but he's got too much on. But will you take something, Joan? A cup of milk or something?'

Joan shook her head, knowing how it was.

'No, I just came for the yarn.'

She'd said it warmly but Joan was surprised to see pink points flare at once in Harriet's cheeks.

'I'm a little behind, Joan,' Harriet said quickly, stumbling over her words. She folded her arms, then unfolded them, dropping them awkwardly to her sides. 'My brother was up half the night with croup, and all of us slept late this morning.'

Joan realised that she was embarrassed, sorry to have been found wanting. It was a new arrangement between them, this. Joan had suggested it some weeks back when Harriet had admitted to the scant wage she received from the mills. Harriet was a skilled spinner, and Joan always needed more yarn than she could source from the others across the valley, so she had been keen to suggest an alternative; and so far it had worked well for them both.

She put a hand out to Harriet's arm. 'Please, Harriet. It doesn't matter at all. I can wait a few more days. Until you're ready. Whenever really.' It would push out her own deadlines if there were much more delay, but she would not tell Harriet that. The lines under the girl's eyes were almost as deep as her mother's; she did not need any further pressure than she would impose on herself.

'I'm sorry, Joan. I meant to have it done for you by this morning.'

'Don't think of it again. We girls need to stick together. I will come back at the end of tomorrow, if that will give you time enough?'

Harriet nodded, her cheeks gradually losing their high colour. 'Thank you.'

'Can I see it?' Joan said, and at once Harriet seemed to tense again, the muscles in her delicate jaw visible below the skin. 'I'm not worried how far you've got,' Joan said quickly. 'I just want to see the colour.'

Harriet nodded then and pushed the lean-to door as wide as it would go, so that Joan could see the shade of the yarn as it came off the flyer and onto the bobbin.

'It's a lovely soft cream,' Joan said, pleased. She put a hand out to feel the spun wool between her fingers. 'Very clean. I could see it taking colour well.'

Harriet shook her head. 'I wouldn't know where to start with dyeing. I don't know how you learn all this stuff, Joan. Alice is always saying you've got a bigger brain than any man she's ever met, and you must have, to be knowing any of it.'

How strange, to think of Alice saying something like that. Joan knew Harriet well enough to know she would be telling the truth, but she could hardly imagine her sister talking of her in that way. Something in her face must have shown her surprise: Harriet laughed and took her hand.

'She doesn't always curse you, Joan. She's got a good word as often as the bad, and I know well enough not to listen to the unkind whispers anyway.'

Joan smiled, not knowing what to say. She straightened up, ended up saying a goodbye that was more formal than she intended, but Harriet seemed to take it well enough, waving her off from the end of the alleyway.

On the way home, Joan put her mind to the best colour for Harriet's yarn once it had been woven into cloth, but thoughts of Alice kept intruding. And when Alice lay next to her in the cot that night, Joan found herself replaying conversations they'd had in past weeks. Did she judge her sister too harshly? Their long history would suggest otherwise, but perhaps gentle Harriet saw qualities that Joan had been too close to see.

When she returned to Harriet's the following day, Joan wanted to ask more, but Harriet's mother was hanging washing in the yard and the time wasn't right. Instead, in the days that followed, on the rare occasions when Alice returned to their cottage, Joan took to watching her sister as she went about her business. Eventually, Alice seemed to sense her scrutiny, and snapped at Joan to keep her eyes to herself. Joan sighed and turned her attention back to the dyeing of the yarn. She had in mind a grand project, but it came with grave risk; it would not do to be distracted.

It was a perfect drying day: the broadcloth Joan had hung out at dawn in the upper meadow might be ready to lift. She'd set up the rack there yesterday – the frame she'd made herself in stolen moments over the past weeks, wanting to keep this experiment a secret, and though it was a little rickety, hammered together from the few parts of the old loom that had not yet been sacrificed to the fire, she had been pleased with her handiwork.

The dye preparation she'd kept to herself as well; madder, this time. A little scrumped from Mrs Freme's garden where it had overflowed the borders, some more found growing on a cleared patch of bank on the stream edge near Iles Mill. Her first attempt to dye with the plant had not looked like much more than a natural discolouration in the wool. But since, when time permitted, she had made up small batches of all the hedgerow dyes: dipping remnants, learning a little of the effects of heat, and water quality, and mordant on the action of the colourants. Nails left to rust in a bucket of vinegar and water could be a substitute for alum, she found. Certain mosses too, if boiled correctly had a similar fixative effect. Rhubarb could be mashed and soaked for its acid, which brought the colour out of berries. And while tin, when she could get it, would brighten the scraps of yellow cloth she dyed with broom or dog's mercury, the addition of iron water acted as a 'saddener', dimming the same shades as if the sun had gone in.

But this project was bigger, braver: a saleable length of wool woven from Harriet's finely spun yarn, and now the search for a rich, fine shade, befitting a gentleman's suit or an army officer's tunic. In her headier moments, Joan had imagined loading it on the cart for market, begging space on the wool merchant's trestle to sell a length of russet – even that new scarlet – to the highest bidder . . .

Joan had pressed Mrs Freme for all she knew, so at least she was prepared to soak the madder in the vat first, and for the liquor to simmer rather than boil, with time for cooling and reboiling, and cream of tartar added to help with the fixing. Yesterday, she'd tipped the mound of mashed roots into the cooking cauldron, mixed in the mortar and boiled it all up with a peck each of alum and bran. A handful of woad too, in case it helped the depth of the colour, though she regretted it when the stench of cabbage began to come off the boil. The quantities were the trouble – she had no way of knowing what was what. But she'd hunched over the mix as the brew roiled for hours, all the time dreading the arrival of her father or Alice. It was one thing to take on the bread and butter of the business, quite another to take such a risk with their profits. But how else would they get free of the debts that still snapped at their heels?

Only when the liquid had turned dark and foamy had she lifted the pot from the tripod with a stick, lowering in the length of woollen cloth and forcing it under with the stick's forked end. Three yards of plain broadcloth – a risky investment, but any shorter and the length would be of no use to a buyer. In any case, her confidence had blossomed over these months of handling the wool and transacting; who was to say that she could not have the same success with dyeing? Another wait, then, until the pot was cool, when she'd used all her weight to slide it over to the corner of the room. She'd covered it with an old rug, pulling a stool in front to hide it.

She'd had to make excuses that night when the cooking pot was not boiling above the hearth. But there was bread, a corner of cheese, and a small beer, so her father did not complain long. Alice too had been easily distracted; she had plans to travel in to the market on Friday and so was full of chatter about who she might see and which musicians would be playing at the Cross. Her sister's distraction had other advantages: Alice had slept on soundly this morning while Joan had crept from their cot to stir the pot again, lifting out the cloth and wringing it, before running it up to the rack on the hill. Even in the dim morning light, she'd seen an encouraging dark-pink stain across her fingertips; she'd be pushed to get that away with scrubbing, but Alice's old gloves had other benefits.

Joan climbed the stile again now, away from the stream and into the meadow. The glare from the sun made it difficult to make out the rack at all. Joan held her breath, imagining the cloth stolen, or brought to the ground and spoiled by some beast. But as she got closer, she saw that it did hang intact, and that the red had taken: not the rich crimson she had imagined, perhaps, but a subtler shade that was still fine. Berry red, like something ripe from the hedgerows; perhaps it was the touch of woad that had taken it there.

She folded a corner of the cloth, tested its nap against the ball of her thumb. Then she bent to sniff it, but there was no lingering stink of woad. A bubble of pride in her chest: how proud would her father be when he saw it? It had been a crazy risk, now she thought of it – a month's profit in her hands – but the gamble had been worth it.

As the wool felt dry enough to lift – the rack had done its job – Joan began to pull it free, folding it loosely over her arm. It was only then she saw where the problem lay. Her handmade frame had been too short to pin out the full length, so while the shade might be fine enough, hanging double over the rack, only half of the cloth's length had faced the sun. It seemed obvious now, but in the morning mist it had not struck her that the afternoon rays, which were so fierce today, might have so strong an effect: the south-facing portion had faded far more sharply than the half that had been folded to the back, with the effect that one end of the broadcloth was much darker than the other. It was a mistake that would cost the sale of the cloth. She let it slip from her grasp; it was all she could do not to stamp and cry.

For a long time, Joan crouched down in the tall grass, head in hands. A foolish mistake, born of ignorance and pride, when the business still rested so close to the cliff edge; she prayed she had not put their livelihood at risk. The beauty of the evening seemed insulting now: the fading sun, the last butterflies dancing across the clover, the glint of the stream far below. These picturesque meadows, but what did she really have? A mother long gone, a father who lurched between drunken sot and poacher, a sister whose only thoughts were of how she could escape this valley. A distant promise from a boy who might even now be lost to a musket in Africa. And no matter how hard she worked, the spectre of the poor line – of that ragged, starving crew at the churchyard gates, the threat that she and Alice might soon be amongst them – never quite seemed to leave the horizon. Joan wiped away tears with a corner of the felt, picking seeds and burrs from its length, running a fingernail along the transition where the cloth had hung.

She'd sat for a long time when she caught sight of something across the field: ear-tips above the seed-heads, about twenty feet away. Her mother had loved hares. Some might curse the creatures as doom-mongers and deceivers, symbols of hedgerow magic, moonlight and lust, but Hannah Browning had admired their silence, their grace, the fluid speed with which they covered a field at twilight. Sometimes, comforting the girls as they waited for sleep to visit their cot, she'd traced the outline of a running hare across their backs. Joan shivered, remembering. She'd heard it said that witches used woad for shape-shifting. Was this her mother, now? Conjured up somehow, by those few handfuls of the herb? Joan held her stained fingers up against the sun to watch the animal move: a dark shape slipping through the long grasses; a still, quivering beast at the field's edge, almost close enough to touch.

Joan wasn't one troubled by superstition – no doubt Mrs Freme would have had plenty to say on the subject – but she did feel a closeness, suddenly, to her mother, that she hadn't felt in many years. It was a feeling, a warmth, that sat at the base of her stomach, then flowed upwards, until she felt like she was supported from within. Memories played through her mind, not all of them pleasant, but she let them come: her mother pushing her hair back from her eyes, her mother pressing honey cakes between her palms before dropping them onto the hearthstone. Hannah Browning dancing at the streamside, and then, much later, rinsing bloodied babygowns in that same stream. The single bluebell stalk her father had left on her grave, one of few flowers in bloom when her mother's coffin came to be lowered: these were things Joan hadn't thought of for years.

There had been many hardships; there was only so much a person could bear. She was only seventeen, after all. And yet here she was: weaver, clothier, housewife. She had worked so hard that her fingernails were split and the blisters on her hands had long ago turned to callouses which never fully healed. If she couldn't reproduce the work of an artisan – everyone said it: that dyeing was an art, a science even, to be practised only by those practised few – then perhaps there was no shame in that. Was it time to retreat, to return to the comfort of what she understood? To leave alone what everyone said she would never fully comprehend? Was this what the hare, the mother ghost, was telling her?

Chapter Eleven

The market had brought a jostling crowd to town today: the bread and herb stalls were packed two abreast, and a jester was juggling and cavorting between the Butcher's Arms and the church house, his rapt audience making it difficult to pass. Joan had to lift her bundles above her head to press through the crush, wondering as always at her sister, who walked shielded behind and never lifted a finger to help.

They visited Mr Ridler first, where Joan made arrangements with the wool merchant for a fresh order of fleeces to be brought along the valley by donkey cart the following week, while Alice clicked her tongue behind her teeth at the wait. When Joan had done her business there, they went in search of the bailiff. They found him soon enough under the arches of the market hall, but there was a queue of traders and disgruntled customers who wanted his attention. Joan found the shade of the archways a relief, but Alice fidgeted and kicked at the loose masonry, making no secret of her impatience. Joan had done her best to keep Alice sweet these past weeks – her mood had seemed lighter, and even when Alice had spoken sharply to her, Joan had tried to recall Harriet's reassurances – but today her sister seemed unsettled as a cat with a teasel in its tail, and it would be easier all round if she was released of this burden.

Over an hour later, as Alice told anyone who would listen, the man led them to an empty trestle in the Pitching, where Joan could begin to lay out the cloth. Then, at last, the stall was ready for business. Joan shifted the piles of broadcloth on the planks – an inch here, an inch there – so that the quality would be best presented. Most of their cloth went up to London, but the Blackwell Hall factor drove a hard bargain, so Joan always kept some back for the local markets where the margins were higher. Alice stood at the table corner, fiddling with the list edge on a piece of felt and yawning.

'You seem distracted. Is there someone you need to find?' Joan asked.

'Walter is coming for me here,' Alice replied, without turning. 'I told him you'd be selling.'

Walter. That was his name, then. Alice might be testy this morning, but her sunnier disposition these past weeks had to have something behind it; it came as no surprise to hear that her sister had found an admirer. And it wasn't long before a man appeared at their stall: an unlikely customer, with polished pewter buttons down the swelling front of a rose-pink doublet, and a white ruff tight at his neck. Walter, if this was the gentleman, without doubt considered himself the smartest fellow about town that morning; he even wore a periwig over his own hair, and only the jester's coat was brighter.

'Miss Browning, fair as the sunrise as ever.' Walter ran his hands over the cloth on the trestle as he spoke, pressing fat fingers on the folds. To Joan he seemed greedy for something, and when he looked up at her sister, his gaze slid quickly from Alice's eyes down to the thin line of lace that frilled her bodice. Alice covered her mouth with her palm, as if embarrassed by the attention, but Joan could see by the way she laughed and twisted under his gaze that her sister delighted in it.

'Walter, do meet my sister Joan. Joan is the enterprising member of our family, here to flog her wares along with the rest. We'd all have succumbed to destitution long ago were it not for her efforts.' Alice laughed as she spoke, a high, unnatural tinkle. And this way of speaking: it must surely be copied from the vicar's wife. But it was the closest Alice had ever come to expressing gratitude for Joan's efforts, and Joan took heart from it.

'Ah, Miss Browning the younger. What a pleasure.' Walter leant over to grab up Joan's hand from where it lay on the table edge. A wet smudge on the back of her palm, and Joan regretted having left her gloves on the shelf in the cottage.

'Call me Joan.' She forced a smile, wishing that he did not inspect her face so keenly.

He grinned back. There was a flake of something caught between his right incisor and the molar behind it. 'Walter Smart, with father of the same name. You may have heard of our auction house?' Joan nodded: how could she not know it? They'd come close to selling all of their belongings under this man's gavel. 'I'm afraid there is little of consequence bought and sold in this town which does not cross our threshold,' he went on, 'and we are victims of our own success, rarely able to make the most of a fine morning such as this one. My father has allowed me just an hour of respite.'

This seemed unlikely – the man's physique suggested he found plenty of time for leisure and refreshment. But Joan just nodded and looked down to busy herself with the cloth on the table. She was conscious of his eyes still upon her, grateful when the bailiff's boy appeared at the side of the trestle a moment later with some change for her pot. While she spoke to the boy, she heard Alice's high laugh again behind her. When she looked back, her sister and Walter were arm-in-arm, already turning towards Long Street.

'Come and find me when it's time, Joan.'

'You'll not help here, then?' *That'll teach me to wish her away*, Joan thought. The streets were full and Joan had only one set of eyes. A light-fingered browser could make off with a month's earnings, and surely her sister could see that?

But Alice just made a face, as if Joan had suggested she lick the floor beneath the pigman's stall. 'I'll be in the Lamb Inn. Send in a boy for me if you don't have the guts for it.'

Joan couldn't help but imagine their mother's expression at that. It wasn't a question of a lack of courage; Joan had dealt with their father enough times not to fear the drunken patrons of any pub in this town. But the Lamb . . . the only women she'd seen coming out of its doors looked as if they were paid for their services.

Alice had already been swept away, though, grand as a duchess on Walter's arm, and Joan was quickly drawn into the bustle of the stall. She was too involved to think of her sister again until the bailiff rang his bell to warn that trading hours were soon ending and the crowds finally began to thin. Even then, it took a while to pack up the stall and settle up. By the time Joan turned the corner of the back lane on which the Lamb Inn stood, its cobbles were empty save for some detritus from a vegetable stall. There was the sign, hanging a little way down the lane on the right – she walked towards it, and towards a young boy on the doorstep, grappling with a broom handle longer than he was tall. As she made her way towards the inn's peeling green door, she watched him master it, and begin to sweep a tide of peelings from the inn's steps and away down the lane.

'Whoa, what we got here?' A man, suddenly rearing up from a dark stairwell on the other side, swaying in too close to her face. A dark stream was spreading across the cobbles from where he had stood, and he was fastening his breeches, fumbling, unashamed. A little way off now, Joan saw the boy with the broom glance from his work for a moment, then turn his back on them to return to his sweeping.

'What's a pretty girl like you doing up this way?' the man said, when he'd finally got the button in its hole.

'I've come to get my sister,' Joan said, then wished she'd stayed silent, because the man's eyes – pink-rimmed and swimming – slid up and down her then, and he came closer still.

'Got a sister, has ye? Not seen you two around, and I know most folks round these parts.'

Joan kept her lips tight shut this time, shifting from one foot to the other, but the man would not be put off. She glanced to the green door again, thought about the few steps it would take to run to it.

As if he'd heard her thoughts, the man shifted so that his bulk was between her and the inn. 'And what's that you got there, then, missie?' He was pointing to the cloth bundle under Joan's arm, brushing the inside of her arm as he did so, pulling back too slowly.

Joan looked past him for the broom boy again, but the lad had done his work, leaving the lane deserted. She glanced up at the buildings on each side of her, her breath tight in her throat: the clockmaker's was shuttered for the day, and the other merchants had blank panes, no sign of life: no help there. It was a matter of yards, but how to get round this man? He was difficult to age: those stippled, knotted fingers belonged to an old man, but there was that full head of hair, even if it was matted to his face, and his arms were thick as fence-posts. If she provoked him, things might turn out worse. She could smell the liquor on him but he was steady enough on his feet.

'No one here but you and me, girlie,' he said, as if he could see her mind working, and he smiled with thin lips. Joan swallowed. 'Now that looks like good cloth to me,' he went on, pointing again. His fingernail was yellowed and curled up like a claw. 'You taken that from somewhere, girl?'

Joan shook her head.

'You sure? Because if you've been thieving, we might have to punish you.' He took a step closer. Joan snatched the bundle of broadcloth up, but he reached a finger for it again, stretching too far so that his scaly nail grazed the skin of her chest. Joan took a step backwards towards the low wall behind her. She wondered whether the punters in the Lamb might hear her scream. The man smiled, scratching at a matted clump above his ear.

'I've not been thieving. I've been selling,' she said, stretching her fingers behind her to feel for the wall's crumbling stone.

'Selling? What, you're a clothier are you now?' He dropped his hand and tipped his head back to laugh. There were draped folds of skin at his neck, as if he had been shrunk from a much larger man.

Joan's bones buzzed with sudden anger. For a moment, it displaced her fear. 'What if I am?' she said. The muscles in her calves and biceps tightened as if she readied herself for a fight.

He tittered, the liquor breath spilling out of him. 'Give me strength. You're no more a clothier than I am the King's goldsmith. Daughter of some blue-fingered valley fellow, I'll own it, too lazy to run his own errands. Or the bastard girl of some loose-trousered mill owner, trying to earn some of Daddy's coin.' He laughed again, but the sound clattered dead to the cobbles of this empty lane. His hands drifted to his thighs and he wiped them against his breeches as if cleaning them for something. His eyes lost focus, then found it again on the thin lace hem at her chest. His mouth hung open, wetly.

'I came to the market to sell my cloth today,' she said, speaking slowly and as firmly as she could, though her focus was on the direction of his gaze and the position of his hands, and the fear was starting to reassert itself in her gut.

He shook his head, snorted out a lazy, unkind laugh. 'I think I like you, girlie,' he said, then took another step closer. Joan stepped back herself, but the wall was up against her now and she could go no further. Something cracked when the man brought his teeth together. 'I don't like your lies, mind – you're a weaver's daughter running an errand, no more – but you've got a sweeter face than most of the dried-up husks round these streets. I think you'll do me very well.'

'Hey!' A male voice from along the lane, beyond the Lamb. The man froze, and for a moment, it felt to Joan as if time stood still. She ducked her head to see past him to get a look at the other who'd called out. Would he help, this new man?

Sharp in her mind was the time when the Toadsmoor pond had frozen, and one of the Culham girls, Rachel, Alice's sometime friend, had slipped, trying to show off her skating to the farm boys, and had fallen right down to her knees with her petticoats about her head. One of the boys said something crude then, and none of them had stopped to help her up, just laughed in a nasty kind of way. They'd started calling to each other, saying things that should never be said aloud. And for a moment it had seemed like every man in the place had turned to an animal, jeering and pointing and taking a few steps closer like he'd like to have a go.

The girls had got Rachel Culham up and away in the end, but not before one of the farm boys had rubbed his hands up and down her, not a man in the place stepping in to stop him. And the next day they'd sat in church, the lot of them, as if nothing had happened, laying communion wafers on their tongues as if they hadn't a sin to answer for. Would he step in, this one? Hare or fox? Was he just moving closer to get a better look, come to jeer and catcall while the man did his worst?

Three things happened then. From the church's bell tower came the peals for six o'clock. The man reached for Joan with both hands, mouth gaping so that she could see the slicked mass of his swollen tongue. And the voice from along the lane, almost drowned by the bell's toll, called out again, louder this time, and with some urgency: 'Are you alright?'

'We don't need no help here,' the man said nastily, turning away from Joan only for long enough to address the voice along the lane. But a fellow in the grimed leather tunic of a blacksmith was walking towards them, only a few paces away now. It was the chance Joan needed. She slipped past her attacker and towards the blacksmith, ducking sideways, meaning to pass him too.

'Where you going?' She heard the growl from behind her. 'You come back here, missie. We weren't done.'

'She's done, even if you're not.' The blacksmith had stopped in the middle of the lane. He took a step to the side to let Joan pass him, and continued to stare down the man. 'Be off with you or I'll call for the bailiff.'

'Pfft. Steight's long gone,' Joan heard the man say, slurring now. 'Skipped off back to that ugly wife of his by now. You can call for him all you want.'

'Then I'll deal with you myself,' said the blacksmith.

From where she stood at the door of the Lamb Inn, Joan turned, saw him reach for the hammer at his belt. The man shrank away, like a weasel from a dog.

'I thought not,' the blacksmith said. He took another step forward, hammer in his fist, and he and Joan watched the man stumble to the end of the lane. As he disappeared into the darkness of the churchyard beyond, Joan felt the air gasp from her lungs.

'Are you hurt?' The blacksmith had turned; he was standing a few paces from her.

'No. Thank you, sir. I think you came just in time.' Her voice came out clipped and formal, but even under the slick of soot, his frown of concern seemed genuine enough. 'I'm grateful to you for stepping in.'

He shook his head. 'He's a wrong sort, I've seen him try similar before.'

'I'd better go.' Joan put with her palm on the Lamb Inn's door, though there was a kindness in this man's face that left a reluctance in her.

'Of course,' he said, 'though I'm not sure you'll find men much better in there.'

As if to prove his point, a girl yanked the door of the inn away from Joan's hand and bustled out past them, hoicking and twisting her corset as if trying to wrest herself back into shape. She barely glanced at Joan and the blacksmith, rushing past and back towards the Pitching, a stray ribbon flapping behind her as she hurried.

'Oh dear,' Joan said, 'I just need to join my sister.' She tried to peer in through a dusty pane beside the door, but the sun was still bright and if they had candles lit inside the inn, they were stingy with them. How Alice would laugh to think of her hesitating on the doorstep, and what was there to be afraid of, really? What a peagoose she was being. Some more drunks and their doxies, and they'd not have a moment to spare on her, she scolded herself.

The blacksmith still stood there, not watching her but not looking away either. When she looked at him, he nodded. Joan wondered if she'd even recognise him without that coating of greasy soot. For his eyes, perhaps. Like horse chestnuts, an uncommon richness to them. 'I could walk you in, if it would make you more comfortable,' he said.

I have no need of an escort, Joan would usually protest, but the offer was extended so lightly, as if she could take it or leave it, so she found herself willing to accept. Her stomach was churning with the smell of beer and sweat that had belched from the inn's doorway, and the encounter with that oaf had left her trembling. Probably it would do no harm to have someone by her side.

'Perhaps just inside the door, if you'd be so kind.'

She would not show Alice her fear though; Joan put her own shoulder to the weighty door, wondering how the girl had pulled it so easily. When it gave in, it let out a mighty shriek, so Joan felt every eye in the place must be on her as she stumbled inside. She heard laughter from more than one corner of the inn, and in the seconds before her eyes adjusted, her stomach tightened at the thought of all the grasping hands that might be out there in the gloom. She was glad of the blacksmith's tread behind.

In a moment, though, she began to make out the booths and the bar between. From the corner, amongst a group of seated figures, she heard a familiar laugh. Alice was sitting on a curved bench beside the empty hearth, with Walter Smart to her right. There were two other men in the group – dark-suited, so they were difficult to make out in this light – and another woman, near the table's single candle, who wore long black gloves and had a peacock brooch pinned to her bodice. She didn't look quite like the girls Joan had seen come in and out of this place before – coarse gigglers, all of them, with drunk-painted eyes and low-cut bodices – but she was a long road from the country girls they'd grown up with. But then Joan was struck by how grown-up Alice looked, sitting there with one of Walter's hands in hers, then plucking at something on his jerkin and leaning back when he laughed. She had a tumbler of something brown and dark in front of her, and when she took a swig of it now, her eyes held Joan's and they were hard as tacks.

'Ah, gentlemen, you are in luck,' Walter crowed. 'You'll not have to share Miss Boule after all. This is the delightful Miss Browning the younger.'

The two men laughed jovially enough, but Joan could see the other woman disliked Walter's presumption just as much as she did; she hissed like a cornered vixen. 'I am not for sharing.'

'I know that, my dear. A little game, that is all.' He reached a hand for the woman's knee.

Joan did not like it either, and she liked the way Walter's hand lingered even less. She glanced to Alice, but her sister tossed her head and picked up her glass, sinking the last of whatever it contained in one draught. Neither of them were accustomed to strong liquor – they'd seen what it could do to their father, after all – and Joan wondered that she didn't see steam coming from her sister's nostrils. How much must it be taking to hide the effect of that firewater? Walter rolled his eyes and turned back to Joan.

'But you are not alone. Walter Smart,' he said, holding out his palm to the blacksmith. Beside him, Alice stared at Joan with an eyebrow raised. Joan felt the colour rise in her cheeks.

'William Thrupp,' the man replied. He didn't take Walter's proffered hand, holding up his own palm to show the grime across it instead. Walter smiled and replaced his hand in his pocket.

'Very good,' he said. 'And will you join us, Mr Thrupp?'

'I'll be going, miss,' the blacksmith said then, turning about sharply. And then, more quietly, 'My forge is on Badbrook Lane, should you ever find yourself in town alone again. I'd be happy to escort you wherever you have need to go.' Joan nodded and muttered her thanks, too conscious of all the eyes upon her to say more.

'A gentleman, indeed,' Walter said, too loudly and in a tone that suggested he meant no such thing, before the blacksmith had closed the door behind him. 'But you're travelling home light,' he said to Joan, nodding towards the slim bundle under her arm. 'A good day's sales, I take it. If you have the gift of the gab, perhaps you should come and work for me.'

'I hardly think your father would want a woman hectoring from his lectern,' Alice snapped, no trace of amusement in her now.

'A little jest, Alice, that is all.' Walter's hand on her sister's knee now, twisting as if kneading dough. 'A little jest,' he said again. He grinned up at Joan. 'Your sister is out of sorts because my time has been divided this morning. My old friend Miss Boule is passing through town on her way to Evesham, and I could not let her tread these streets without buying her a sup of brandy to speed her journey.'

'I'm not cross . . .' Alice started, but for a moment she was a complaining brat at the supper table and Joan felt for her, next to this woman with her slender arms and boots which finished in a pointed toe, even if they were a little scuffed from the road. All the gentlemen laughed, and Miss Boule stretched the fabric of her gloves with a small smile, one finger after another.

'Quite the reverse,' Alice started again, her voice forced into an airy lightness this time. 'It has been a pleasure to make your acquaintance, Miss Boule. I hope our paths will cross again.' All those hours spent sitting for the vicar's wife had not been wasted; Alice could sound like every bit the gentleman's daughter, when the need arose.

'Charming, charming,' said Walter, smiling broadly at Alice now. Perhaps he does care for her, Joan thought. And when Alice stood up, her smile more firmly fixed now, and picked up her purse to leave, he pouted. 'You are going to deprive me of your company, I see. Let me accompany you to the door, at least.'

The two gentlemen nodded their good days and the woman inclined her head, and then Walter leant in to plant a kiss on Alice's cheek in the doorway.

He turned to Joan. 'I do hope you will bring your sister back with you next week,' he said. 'I will pine without her.' His words seemed genuine enough, but as the door squeaked slowly shut behind them, Joan saw that he was already striding across the room without a glance behind.

Three weeks went by, three market days, and Joan grew used to pushing her shoulder against the door of the Lamb Inn. Though she dreaded the sight of him, and her heart was in her mouth those first days, she did not see the man who had accosted her in the lane again. Nor the blacksmith Thrupp again. Once, when her business was finished early and Alice would be hours yet, she thought about calling at the Badbrook forge. Daniel would want her to be safe, she told herself, and not walking the streets for hours alone. But something in her knew it would not quite be right to do so, so instead Joan went early to the Lamb Inn, checking every doorway on the way as was now her habit, and tolerated Mr Watts' jests while her sister glared at her across the bar.

The woman with the brooch did not reappear either, but there was always some spirited crowd in the table over by the fireplace, more often than not striking girls amongst them. Accustomed to seeing her sister flit between boys like a damselfly, it was unsettling to watch Alice try so hard to keep a man's attention. Joan watched her pull her gown in even tighter at the waist on market days, pressing berry juices onto her cheeks, and there was no chance of Joan getting near the mirror glass in the morning.

In the most part, Alice's efforts seemed to be working – Walter's lips were often bent to her ear, Joan never saw her glass empty, and if she ever walked away, he would make a joke of keeping his hand on her waist until the last possible second, like a drowning sailor grabbing for a barrel. But more than once Joan saw his eye wander over Alice's shoulder: to the generous backside of the innkeeper's wife as she scrubbed tables, to the redhead pouring a flagon at the bar, to the long-haired Welsh girl who sang for farthings on the street corner. So it came as a surprise when Alice ran in to the cottage one afternoon, with Walter a step behind, calling for their father.

'You're sure he's the one?' Joan asked later, when the formalities were over: Walter had asked for her hand, and their father had given his consent. The two had made their promises, and Walter had left to spend the night with a cousin in Bussage, before returning to Stroud in the morning.

Alice laughed, leaning closer to the glass and tracing a finger over an eyebrow. 'Why, have you been scrying with your old widow friend? Do you see dark things ahead in the crystal?' Alice never missed an opportunity to needle at Mrs Freme; Joan wondered if it was envy that drove it. Either way, it was a blessing the witch hunters had never visited this valley, with Alice's loose tongue and short temper.

'Just that he is a little older,' Joan said carefully. Not just a little, of course: this was a man who had known two kings, perhaps even three, and all of the Commonwealth between. A man who must soon complain of gout, and short breath, and old man's things. And surely you can see how his eye roves? she wanted to say.

But Alice was like dry tinder tonight, jumping up from the cot side where she had been sitting. 'Don't you carp on. Father was in my ear even as he was clasping Walter's hand: "He's not much younger than me",' she said, mimicking their father's low growl. 'But I am done with blue-fingered burr boys and fullers who are deaf as old men. I don't want to be a weaver's wife, living on hedgerow forage and church scraps. Look at me: I wasn't made for this. Walter has one of the new houses on Butter Row, and a char who comes in on a Wednesday. He will buy me two gowns a year, none of these rags,' she said, flicking at the drab fabric of her skirt, 'and there'll be money left over for the trimmings.'

'Then I hope he brings you happiness.' And Joan did. It was a queer thing, that made her wish the best for one who often seemed to despise her. *I'll brush your hair if you'll let me.* She remembered Alice's soft words all those many months ago. Had it been just a pretence of comfort? But those grey-green eyes . . . it was as if their mother looked out from them. And perhaps they were both damaged by her passing.

'Happiness. Don't say it so, as if it were unlikely.' Alice took a step forward, furious now. Her cheeks were redder than any berry juice could make them – an unwelcome reminder of that spoiled cloth up on the hillside – even though Joan had not intended to offend. 'If you don't believe it, say your piece and don't mince the matter.'

Joan fell silent. That he is uppish, too proud of his full purse and always crowing on it. That his hand lingers too long, drawn to female flesh like an old dog to the fire. That there is something slippery about the man, almost impossible to imagine a lifetime spent together without his attention straying. Joan stared at a cobweb that hung like lace between the struts of the cot. Alice had been so much kinder these past weeks, her mood as light as summer even though the nights were drawing in; Joan regretted having started this. Her sister would react with furious denial. And what did Joan really know, anyway, when she had yet to lie with her own husband? Could not even say for sure that the boy was still alive. Perhaps there was something to be said for a more comfortable life, though the cost seemed higher than Joan thought she could bear.

Her hesitation was enough for Alice. 'See? It is jealousy that makes you nettle me so,' she snapped, tapping Joan hard on the nose and then pulling at her gown as if she would straighten out the matter. 'You could not keep your man, and now you're so desperate, it seems you're grabbing dirty farriers from the street.'

Joan's cheeks burned to think how this would sound if Daniel heard it – she could hardly bear to think that he ever might – but she held her tongue. Time would come later to refute this injustice, but for now it would be better to let Alice say her piece.

'So you begrudge me mine, do you?' her sister raged on. 'Well, stubble it! I will be Mrs Walter Smart next June, and you will be lucky to kneel at the hem of my wedding gown.'

The gown . . . now that might be the thing to salve the wound. Alice was jumpy and blazing now, but Joan might be able to quieten the fire yet, if she trod cautious ground.

'Have you thought what you will wear?' Joan asked, careful to keep her gaze down.

'Oh, now you are interested, are you? It is no concern of yours. Just a child, a lumpish tibb, trying to meddle in things that do not concern you. Leave me be.'

Joan nodded, but perched on the corner of the cot, risking a glance up. 'I only thought, if you wanted help with the stitching . . . June will come round quickly. And the cloth, of course. You would need to find the best market for the linen, and the wool: Ridler might give a good price if he knew the fleece was destined for a wedding gown.'

'It is only a matter of hours since Walter and I were betrothed. Barely time to absorb the fact of it.' Alice was sulky, but the snap had gone.

'Of course, but perhaps you have deliberated on it before?' As if Alice had not spent nineteen years on it, planning every last stitch . . .

Alice pursed her lips, as if she had to think hard to remember, but she could not keep up the pretence for long. 'The gown the younger Miss Tayloe wore was finer than most, I recall.' The corners of her mouth were still down, but as she smoothed the skin on the back of her palm, Joan could see that her sister's mind was working now.

Joan kept a smile from her face with difficulty; trust Alice to hanker after the impossibly grand. The younger daughter of the valley's richest clothier had married in the early spring the year before, and the extravagance of her brocade gown with its pinched sleeves and ribbon adornments had only been exceeded by the embroidered cape she wore over it. Thousands of tiny beads, and a headdress studded with lily of the valley: it was as if a court lady had been transported to their corner of Gloucestershire.

'The shape of the petticoat, and the conceit of the cape, I mean.' Alice had not finished. 'But not the colour. The cut of the bodice flattered her hips, and those lace cuffs slimmed her wrists, but the whey blue she chose for the brocade was ill-advised.' Alice's bad humour was entirely forgotten now, and she had turned to Joan on the cot, eyes bright. On and on she went, detailing every aspect of the gown: the shape of the beads, the depth of the bodice's 'v', the slash in the sleeve which had revealed a slim lozenge of pale arm. How long must she have discussed this with the gaggle of girls she met at the stream, how many hours had they devoted to this gown and its every detail? They had only glimpsed the wedding procession for a moment from the distance of the lych-gate, standing in the shadow of the many carriages from Gloucester and London. But it seemed that had been enough.

'Perhaps I could fashion something similar,' Joan said, when Alice fell silent at last. 'Stitched in linen and wool, but it could have the contour of Miss Tayloe's gown. And if you do not favour blue, perhaps crane, or peach, might suit. Even a light straw might sit well with your skin tone.'

Alice was nodding, childlike in her intensity.

'We could use offcuts for the ribbons . . .' Joan ventured, but knew at once she had strayed too far from the fantasy.

'It must not look cheap,' Alice interrupted. Joan shook her head. Only a few months ago they had gone to bed hungry each night, had her sister forgotten so soon? But perhaps Alice acknowledged this after all. 'I know you have Mother's touch with the needle, it is not that,' she said, laying a hand on Joan's.

Joan nodded, looking down at Alice's neat fingernails and wondering at the lack of grime beneath them. 'I will put aside what I can, and drive as hard a bargain as I can for the cloth.'

'Walter will pay, if we can't. He told me so. He wants a woman of substance beside him at the altar, not some hedgerow fairy.'

'Let him keep his money until you are wed. See what I can make. You won't be disappointed.'

Alice turned away to the glass, nodding, then tilting her head this way and that to catch the rushlight's glow. Joan was already wondering whether she had promised too much – she barely slept as it was, with the business showing the first shoots of growth – and whether Alice deserved it at all. *Just a child, a lumpish tibb,* yet old enough to be saddled with the yoke of responsibility, it seemed. *We must try and make allowances for her,* her father had urged, *a girl so close to womanhood has grave need of a mother.* But Joan knew that her mother would have stitched Alice a dress worthy of a court lady, even if the bodice was boned with reed bents for whalebone, and clipped muslin for lace. And with another bitter winter without Daniel ahead of her, Joan thought that perhaps she would be grateful for another distraction.

Chapter Twelve

Joan was crouched by the stream's edge when she heard the voices, the fingers of one hand pressed into the pitted side of a rock to steady herself, and the other hand on the long handle of a spoon with which she stirred a bucket on the stream's muddy bank.

It was only the first day of May, but the warm weather had already sent bramble tendrils criss-crossing the stream at this narrow section, and she had used their soft spring prickles as hooks to hang her dye samples after she'd rinsed them in the stream. She crouched surrounded by tiny, coloured strips of selvage, and frayed corners from an old bedsheet Mrs Freme had pressed on her. Now the scraps were dyed in every shade of yellow: from madder, used lightly, but also onion skins and apple-tree bark, boiled slowly over a small fire since dawn. A bundle of sun-dried lichen peeled from a churchyard stone, which she had hoped would produce a good gold, but had given a muddy green instead, even when fermented in urine. She had looked for corn marigold and ragwort, but found none flowering yet, though the tiny yellow-starred petals of a plant she couldn't name had given a coppery brown which might work well in a blend. Alice had her heart set on primrose, though, and while Joan hadn't quite found it yet, she'd come close when the grey-green bark of a prickly buckthorn bush had given a strong buttery cream, even if the bark had left her fingers stinging after she'd peeled and chopped it.

'Lavender's green . . .' Snatches of song came through the trees. Joan recognised Alice's high singing voice, and a song about country lovers that would have sent Father Britton twitching. She stood up, glancing about at her cloth strips – the voices were already close and no doubt they would be heading for the stepping stones that crossed the stream here. She'd not be able to gather them all in time, and besides, it was Alice's gown she was practising for – it would be rich if she teased Joan for witchery today.

Joan pulled a stray buckthorn leaf from her hair and smoothed down her skirt instead, sighing at the weight of the wet hem and the splashes of yellow where the dye liquor had spilt. No doubt that would give Alice something else to mock her for. *She's got a good word as often as the bad*, Harriet had urged. But Alice's actions sometimes made that very hard to believe.

Just as she was thinking it, her sister appeared between the hanging fronds of the willow on the far side of the stream, and seeing Joan, turned at once to address the other girls behind her. 'Look girls, the fairy folk are drying their laundry today,' she said, and she laughed her high laugh that always sounded false to Joan's ears.

Father Britton wouldn't like that either, the mention of fairies. The vicar wouldn't entertain any belief in the little people, likening such talk to an invitation to the Devil. Only this last week he had raged from the pulpit against the mention of them, 'or any other such vulgar fancies', but Alice had found reason to be absent from the pew that day, and anyway, she took little heed of Mr Britton these days. Joan couldn't help but admire her sister's boldness.

'Oh Joan, it looks so pretty.' Harriet had come out from behind Alice and stood beside her on the far bank. Behind her emerged

Rachel Culham, who had been so mistreated on the ice that time, and two of her younger sisters. All three of them winced at the mud on the stream's edge, lifting their skirts in anticipation. 'As if you've dressed the stream for May Day,' Harriet went on. 'I wish you'd decorate our cottage so.'

Alice coughed and Joan braced herself for the inevitable scorn, ready to fight her corner. But though Alice rolled her eyes, she didn't come back with any retort. Joan wondered how gentle Harriet might have counselled Alice in such a way that held her sister's tongue. *We girls need to stick together,* Joan had reassured her, when Harriet ran late with the yarn she'd come to collect, feeling every bit the clothier with her receipts book and her bundle of cloth from the millsman. Now, with muddied feet and her sister staring mutinously from the far bank, that confidence was harder to grasp. She smiled her gratitude for Harriet's support.

'Have you finished your work?' Harriet said then. She glanced sideways at Alice as she said it, but Alice was poking with a stick at the tray of cut madder roots which Joan had left on that side. 'Because we are walking up to the meadow at Avenis Lynch to sit together before the May Day celebrations at the church. Will you join us?' Harriet asked.

Joan looked about her: her hands were pink and sore from the buckthorn bark, her fingernails stained deep brown from so many different dyes – perhaps it was time to stop. Probably no one else would pass this way today, so she could safely leave the cloth strips pinned to their bramble tenter hooks, could come back later to inspect them and see how the colour had held. She had planned to return home before the May Day revels, to rinse the mud from her skirt and try to wring out the splashes of yellow dye as best she could, perhaps to visit Mrs Freme, but it was a rare treat to be invited to join the older girls, still more for Alice to tolerate her presence there.

If my sister will allow it, she felt like saying, but perhaps it was better to behave as if there was nothing strange in it. 'Yes please,' she said instead, stepping onto the near bank and standing aside so that the others could cross the stepping stones to join her. Harriet squeezed her hand as she passed. Alice sniffed, and a sharp elbow found its place amongst Joan's ribs as her sister walked past up the path without comment.

The meadow at Avenis Lynch was sweet-smelling with lady's bedstraw, camomile and wild marjoram. The first of the swifts screamed and dived in the sky above the girls as they made their way through the grasses, wood-brown butterflies fluttering up in clouds ahead of them. The air was full of the high, fluting song of the meadow pipit, and all around them were the black heads of crows stalking about on their patrol.

When they reached the middle of the meadow, the girls plumped down in a circle, spreading their skirts around them. Beside Joan, Alice twitched her gown away from her grimy hem, but she made no move to change places. Harriet and the Culham girls unwrapped small parcels and urged the others to share the bread and cheese they had brought along. Alice poured a dark liquid from a green glass vial, but only Rachel Culham consented to sip from the leather cup, and only then a single sip, the girl puffing and gasping as if she'd drunk liquid fire.

'All the more for me,' said Alice, taking back the cup and drinking a deep draught from it. Joan couldn't help thinking of those dead-eyed girls in the Lamb Inn, and of their father's bloodshot gaze when he woke from a night on the flagon. 'I don't need your approval,' Alice muttered, and Joan looked away, ashamed that her thoughts had played so obviously across her face.

'Shall we play loggits?' Harriet said brightly, gathering up her skirts to stand. The other girls jumped up at once, but Alice shook her head. 'We're too old for games, surely. I'll be a married woman in a month.' She lay back on the grass, spreading her arms and closing her eyes against the sun.

The other girls looked unsure then, looking across to Harriet and then down at Alice. But Harriet kept up her smile. 'Joan, will you come?'

'I've never played, but I . . .' she started, but Alice spoke over her.

'She's going to stay and keep me company.'

Harriet smiled and raised her eyebrows at Joan, before running up to join the others. They set up the game on a flatter patch of ground higher up the field. While Elsie Culham unpacked the stake and wood tiles from a cloth bag, Joan glanced down at Alice, whose face was still blank, eyes closed. She looked away, watched an ant climb over the closed buds of a head of marjoram.

'Will my dress be ready in time?' Alice said eventually. She lifted her ankle and slapped at it, where some invisible insect had nibbled. 'I'm concerned that it is May and you have not even begun.'

This was not true. Any spare moment over the winter, any spare penny, Joan had spent sourcing what she would need to make the dress. The fabric, of course, with the help of Mr Ridler, but all the other accoutrements that Alice demanded: ribbons, and boning, and buttons, even a hard-won scrap of Dutch lace that had cost more than the whole gown Joan wore today. And when she'd not been so employed, she'd been ankle deep in a freezing stream, testing every dye-stuff she knew of, to try and find that perfect shade. Today was just the latest in a string of experiments, each taking her a little closer to the primrose of Alice's imaginings. Joan looked down at her sister, wondering what went on behind those closed eyes. 'It'll be ready,' she said. Easiest to treat it as any other job, to treat her sister as firmly and professionally as any other client. 'I want to dye the cloth before I stitch it, so the shade must be right first.'

Perhaps her tone had satisfied Alice, because she just pursed her lips and nodded. From further up the hill there was a thunk and a cheer; the youngest of the Culham girls had struck the stake with her tile and now she pulled it from the ground triumphantly. Alice sighed, and rolled onto her front. 'Do you ever think about her?' she said, pulling a blade of grass, sucking at its end.

Joan, distracted by the girls' game, wondered if she'd heard correctly. Alice could only mean their mother, but her sister had always cut her short whenever Joan had tried to talk about her. *Mother wouldn't want us to dwell.* When she was younger, sometimes Joan had resorted to reminiscing into the mirror just for the chance to say aloud all the things she remembered about Hannah Browning, worried that otherwise she might forget them. She looked down at her sister now but Alice's eyes were on the grass stem and her expression was unreadable.

'Of course, all the time,' Joan said. Never more than when we're up here, she thought, where Hannah had loved to sit and listen to the birds, looking out for the black-tipped ears that gave away the presence of a hare in the grasses. Joan hadn't sat in this spot since before the funeral, and it was bittersweet to be back here.

Alice poked at the ground with the grass stem. 'I can't imagine how it will be to be married without her there.'

Joan reached her hand to place it over Alice's. Her sister didn't shake it off at once.

'Do you know, she talked to me once, about how she dreamed to watch us both get wed,' Alice went on. 'How everyone else would be thinking of the drinking and the dancing and the food, but that she would be there, holding us close to her heart, willing us to stay. Like a jewel, or a piece of delicate china perhaps – you're better with the words, you know what I mean.'

'An eggshell, perhaps.' That witch egg, again. Delicate and precious. Tiny and white.

'If you like. Like an eggshell, then, sitting in her palm. Whichever of us it was. And she'd be holding us there, willing us to stay close, but trusting whichever man we had chosen to take us, to keep us safe. And she talked about how difficult that would be, that she'd do it with a heavy heart. About how much she loved us . . .' Alice's voice was strangled suddenly, and she rolled again so that her back was to Joan this time. Joan could see her yanking handfuls of lady's bedstraw and pressing it to her eyes.

Joan sat quietly beside her sister while she recovered herself. 'She'll be there, watching,' she said at last.

Alice laughed, bitterly. 'Will she? How do you know? Father Britton would have none of it, not that I take much notice of that old duffer.'

'Can't you feel her, here?' Joan said. She laid her hands across the meadow flowers, pressing down gently to feel their mass under her palms. She'd said it as much for herself as for Alice, but Hannah Browning *was* here. Her scent echoed around the camomile. Her voice hung in the spaces between the meadow pipits' song. Joan's eyes were blurring but she stared at the banks of grasses, trying to see a flash of their mother's skirts in amongst them.

Alice sniffed and reached a hand back behind her, grasping for Joan's again, squeezing it and then letting it go. 'Look out for her then. On the day. Let me know if you feel her there, if you see any sign of her.'

'I will,' Joan replied.

'Father, too.' Alice sniffed loudly. She wiped her nose with another handful of bedstraw. 'You'll have to watch him for me. Put those hawk-eyes of yours to good use. I can't have him ruining the day with drunken nonsense.'

'Of course.'

Alice pushed herself back up to sitting. 'You could bring someone, you know, Joan,' she said, without meeting Joan's eye. 'If you wanted to. I expect it'll be a strange day, alone.'

'What do you mean, bring someone?'

'To the wedding.'

'Who would I bring? Almost everyone I know will be there.' Everyone but Daniel, of course.

'That blacksmith seemed keen.'

And with that Alice was back, straightening a strand of her hair, flicking grass seeds towards her toes. The real Alice, or certainly the everyday Alice, and Joan made herself take note of the adjustment. As always, Joan wondered at the way words tumbled so easily from her sister's mouth, as if she really meant nothing by them, when nothing could be further from the truth. Joan stifled a shocked laugh. 'I'd met him a moment before you did. He saw off some drunk who was bothering me.'

'Then you must have made quite an impression. I saw how William Thrupp looked at you, and I've heard since how he's asked after you.'

Only now you tell me this, Joan thought, then flushed with shame, because why would it matter, when she had Daniel to wait for?

'You've thought about it,' Alice pressed her.

Joan did not reply, unwilling to lie. There had been occasions, waiting over a simmering pot or endlessly passing the shuttle through the loom. But to say it aloud would make it true.

'It would be natural if you had,' Alice said, her voice silky. 'Daniel has been gone two years. Two years, without a word to say whether he's alive or dead.'

As if I need telling, Joan thought. She pushed herself up to standing, legs cramping from too long bent across the grass. 'I should go.' She felt dirty, suddenly. Ashamed of the grime on her hem and the stains across her skirts, desperate to get home and scrub them away. 'Let the others know, will you?'

'Joan.' Alice caught her hand before she could turn away. 'I know you think I meant to tease you a little, and perhaps I did. But what if Daniel never comes back? Have you thought of that? Really thought about it? Is it worth the risk, never letting yourself love another? Whatever you did to catch the blacksmith's eye, perhaps you'd be as well to keep doing it. William Thrupp won't wait forever, and you could do much worse.'

But Joan had pulled away from her, and was already running down the valley, hoping that Harriet and the other girls did not see her stumble on the rugged ground. Wishing that her feet would take her fast enough through the tangled grasses to escape from Alice's words.

Chapter Thirteen

'Not again, surely? The cloth will be worn thin from taking it on and off again.' Joan eased out the gown from the narrow closet she and Alice still shared.

Her sister stood in front of her, treading from foot to foot in her shift and stays, holding her arms out for the sleeves. Things had been awkward between them after they'd spoken at Avenis Lynch. Neither of them had mentioned the conversation in the meadow afterwards, and while Joan had tried to remember only the closeness she had felt when they'd spoken about their mother, it had been easier since to keep out of Alice's way. Today, though, there was no avoiding her. Complete or not, Alice was going to try on her wedding gown, and try it on again, and then again, until Joan's arms stung with the effort of lifting its full skirts and beading. She had laboured for weeks on this, squeezing hours of embroidery into late nights after long days, and every limb felt heavy with exhaustion. 'Be careful with the neckline now,' she said. 'I still have to finish the stitching there.'

But Alice was already straining to see the effect in the shard of glass. 'Hold it up for me,' she said. 'You'll need to tip it, so that I can see the skirt too.'

Joan obliged. Probably she should take exception to Alice's tone, but it was just her sister's way. Whatever Alice was seeing in the glass now seemed to have pleased her. She was patting down the folds of the skirt, turning one way and then the other, touching chin to chest better to see the detail of the embroidery. It was not Miss Tayloe's fine brocade, but there was no denying it was a handsome gown; absurdly so, in this dirt-floored cottage. The effort, then, had been worthwhile. Joan closed her eyes a moment, wishing that so much more work did not still lie between her and the night's rest.

'He'll be dazzled, won't he?' Alice hadn't noticed Joan's distraction, her eyes were still fixed on the glass. 'Hold the peeper higher, so I can see the full effect.'

Joan did as she was asked. 'I'm sure he'll be the proudest man in the Hundred.'

'I think he will.' Alice twirled on the spot, then she stroked a finger down the line of the bodice seam. 'The primrose is pretty here, though I wish you'd been bolder with the dye.' Joan ignored this – after all her efforts, the tint was just as Alice had requested, but her sister could never quite bear to leave a compliment alone. There was gratitude there, though; Joan saw it in the way her sister fanned her fingertips over the bodice's carefully stitched panels, turning again and again before her reflection. And grateful she should be: even with all the savings Joan had mustered, and with all the dye and stitching done by her own hand, the gown had still cost more than she'd dared admit even to herself.

'You don't think my waist is too wide?' Alice had turned her back now, peering round towards the small rectangle of glass.

'There can't be many narrower. And that cambric shift is thin as gossamer, so there is no extra bulk in the bodice.'

'It does look very fine. You have done a good job with the stitching. Mother would have been proud.' Alice reached out a hand to Joan's sleeve. Behind her back, Joan pinched the finger and thumb of her other hand, hard; so many times she had cursed her sister, but no one had such power to move her. Those grey-green eyes; it was as if their mother were here, trying on a new gown herself.

'I should go and light the fire,' she said quickly, not wanting Alice to see the tears that threatened.

'Wait, I have something for you. A small gift.' Alice bent to look under the cot, groaning at the pinch of the corset, leaving Joan to snatch up the hem of the gown before it was dragged in the dirt. 'Here, take this.' She straightened up, handing over a package wrapped in a russet wool scarf.

'What is it?'

'Wait and see.' But something special, to judge by the way her sister was fidgeting while Joan unwrapped the scarf's folds.

Inside, beneath a second layer of cloth wrap, she found two books: both were old, the uppermost with its calfskin cover curling back on itself from one corner. The script was dense and flowery, its title spilling over several lines. It had been more than two years now since Joan left the Dame School, and her reading since had been limited to bills of sale and accounts, so she took a moment to decipher the inscription:

"A Profitable Book declaring divers approoued Remedies . . . With diuers Colours, how to die Veluets and Silkes, Linnenn and Woollen, Fustian and Thread."

'See, a book of dyeing!' Alice pulled her down to sit on the mattress beside her. 'A book with every secret means and process for the same. It's translated from the Dutch, Walter told me. And the other is from the Italian. I have no clue what they say, but when Walter told me what they were, I knew at once that you must have them.'

Joan turned the books over in her palms and teased the pages apart, wondering at the recipes that filled them: "*a faire green clothe*", "*to dye Silke blew*", "*Another way to make wooll a faire red*". A world of chemistry and opportunity, everything she'd wished for. 'Where did they come from?' Joan said, dreading the answer even as she asked.

'A customer, does it matter? Some clothier from Cirencester: richer than Croesus, and ugly with it.'

'But how did you come by them?' Joan said, as gently as she could.

'A loan, of sorts.' Alice shrugged.

'When must they be returned?'

'Never, unless the old goat can see beyond the grave; he met his maker before Lammastide. Perhaps his family have not missed the gentleman much since his passing; it seems they could not wait a moment to unburden themselves of his possessions. And there were boxes and boxes delivered, enough to fill a library, so they won't know what was there and what was not.'

Joan hung her head. 'They are stock, then, awaiting next week's sale.' Too good to be true. 'Alice, I can't keep these.' Joan snapped the book shut, as if to settle the matter. A curve of dust fanned onto her skirt from between the pages.

Alice pouted. 'I don't see why not. They will not be missed.'

'It would be theft. Worse, embezzlement, if it is done with Walter's permission. The books will have been catalogued by now, and in any case, they are not yours or mine to take.'

'Suit yourself.' Alice had stepped back a pace, all the good humour draining from her face. 'I thought you would be pleased.'

'I am touched, sister,' Joan reached for Alice's arm, 'that you thought of me.' Touched and amazed. She opened the book again – the briefest perusal could not hurt – and her eyes roamed over the tattered pages; she could hardly conceive of all the colours that would explode from the preparations described: "a carnacion", "a purple silke", "linnen in a faire rose". She thought back to the first time she had seen the dye merchant in the market: that precious spectrum of samples fanned across his trestle, an improbable rainbow brought from the humble yarn and the roots and crumbs stored in the jars and vials behind. What would it be to be able to conjure all of those pigments and more?

'Touched? Yet you do not seem so.' Alice exhaled in an extravagant sigh.

'I only wish I had the resources to buy such volumes.'

'Then you should transcribe them. What? There is no law against it that I know of.'

Joan laughed. 'This manuscript alone must have two hundred pages.'

'And your lettering has always been fast and accurate. Besides, you need not trouble yourself with the text of every concoction, only those spells which interest you.'

'Spells! It is not witchcraft, Alice, only chemistry.' But there was a magic to it, of course there was. Just the weight of this tome in her palm; she felt heady with its potential.

'I don't know, you spend enough time with that widow.'

This now, this was more like the Alice Joan knew best, never missing a chance to goad. Joan shook her head; now the real world, with all its obligations, would inch its way back in. 'I have the meal to cook, and the cottage is thick with dust.'

'Let me do the sweeping, then. And Father will be content with bread and a corner of cheese.' But surely the world was turning on its axis now; she had never known Alice so amenable! If only she had been betrothed years ago. Joan looked hard at her sister, as if Alice's real thoughts might be divined from the twist of her mouth. She so wanted to take this chance; it would not come again. And who knew, perhaps it was offered in good faith? What was certain was that there was a sliver of impatience creeping into Alice's voice already; if Joan had any thought of accepting it, this was the moment to do so.

'Thank you. I will take down what I can in the back of my ledger. But tomorrow you should ride back to Stroud with the books before their absence is noted.'

'And you should leave me to my broom, before I change my mind.'

'This is the cloth, then? The weave is fine, and it should take the colour well,' Mrs Freme said, leaning in to run a hand over the soft cream nap. The widow's hands were mottled from the sun, with a black mole like a smudged star in the soft flesh between finger and thumb.

'Thank you,' Joan said. They were on the doorstep of Mrs Freme's rooms, a joined stool apiece, in the spot where the older woman liked to catch a corner of evening sun. The length of superior broadcloth between them was already promised to the army quartermaster at the Cirencester cloth fair. Destined for officer's tunics, though doubtless Joan could sell it twice over at next month's market as long as the pigment was as strong as the cloth was fine. She'd put every last penny towards it, but such a sale would pay for all the wedding accoutrements, with a little capital left over for the few weeks after. Walter had insisted on paying for the wedding feast himself, which was welcome, so there might even be some shillings left for a hope chest for Alice.

'But you look afeared,' Mrs Freme went on, her brow dipping in a faint frown. 'What is it that troubles you?'

'I can't fault the finish. It is almost too fine, and if I do not make the correct preparations . . .' That length of sun-bleached red still haunted her. 'I could be fined, or worse. That's if the gentleman will take the cloth at all.'

'Joan, take comfort.' Mrs Freme squeezed the back of her hand. Joan could smell the sage she chewed for her teeth as she leaned close. 'You have learned all you could from the textbooks, and no one could have practised harder. There is hardly a bush across this valley that has not been adorned with some scrap of dyed yarn or listing by your hand, and I have watched as the colours have grown ever more vivid, as if the land itself would be dyed by you.'

'No, you're right. I am as ready as I can be,' Joan said, though as much to make it true. Beside her was the ledger, where she had faithfully copied as many of the recipes as she could fit, working until there were no rushlights left to work under. There was no need to look inside for this latest recipe: between hints dropped by the Dutchman and Mrs Freme's dye-man, Joan had learned and memorised every step in the formula for scarlet.

'You *are* ready. You have your cloth, you have your method, you have your alum, you have your grain.'

Alum had been easy enough to obtain, but the grain, the cochineal: that had not come cheap. There'd been no sign of the pigment merchant these past months, so she'd had to bargain with Mrs Freme's man for a handful of the quantity he'd brought back from his last trip to Bristol. And when the negotiations were concluded, the man had tipped a few of the dark crumbs into the palm of her hand – small as the grains they were named for – and pulled a handled glass from a drawer which inflated them to the eye. Examining the tiny beetles, she'd tried to imagine them crawling on the spined plant he'd said was their home, halfway across the world. Grey and inanimate, even under the glass; it'd seemed unlikely that they'd ever lived, let alone that they might lend cloth its colour. And now they were in a jar in her knapsack, wrapped in an old petticoat, ready to be crushed for the blood-red pigment in their dessicated flesh. It would not be enough alone, but with a fat bundle of jagged madder roots, it should ensure a rich tint of this new shade.

'Choose the clearest spring,' Mrs Freme urged. 'Remember the dye-man swears by spring water, for its clarity and its salts. Then down to the river for rinsing.'

'Thank you. I will.'

Mrs Freme squeezed her shoulder. 'Go on, now. You need the rest. But let me see the finished piece before you take it to market, if you can. I know it'll be fine enough to grace any infantryman's shoulders.'

It was the work of a day, to clean the tin bath she intended to use for a dye vat and to transport it to the streamside, along with the various compounds she would need in the dyeing. Alum and some quicklime, but also a quantity of bran, a wrap of turmeric and a dish of ashes from the hearth. She upturned the bath to keep animals and the rain from it, and then returned in the morning with the grain and madder.

The cloth would be heavy when wet, and she would need help with the rinsing. Her father had ridden out to a tailor in Tewkesbury, a rare order for a length of shalloon for the lining of gentlemen's coats, and there was no chance Alice would risk colouring her hands so close to the wedding. In fact, if she thought Joan had any such plan, no doubt she'd try to put a stop to it, with no thought for the consequences. But Joan had persuaded the millsman to lend her one of his boys for the day, in exchange for a big order of yarn. A quiet lad, Michael Huggits, he climbed the hill a few paces behind her now, with the great bundle of cloth over his shoulder.

When the first immersion was ready, they lowered the cloth into the bath to soak it. There was a moment before the wool touched the liquid when Joan's chest was rigid with nerves; after this there would be no going back. But then it was in – bubbles bursting from its folds as the dye liquor worked its way into the fibres. From then, the mechanics of the process took over; there was no time for Joan to worry about how it would turn out.

She had set a fire beside the bath, and once the cloth was submerged, she and the boy lifted the vessel with some difficulty and set it across two thick logs so the flames would bring it to a simmer. Then not long after it was time to lift the cloth with a staff, steaming and heavy. Even with the boy's help, it was a struggle to keep it clear of the ground. When it was hung over the rack at last, they could prepare the next mix and run to the spring for more water, and then it was time to lower the cloth back into the bath, with pounded madder root and grain this time. Joan kept a little grain back in the jar, not knowing quite why, tucking it away in her pocket.

Three hours then, taking it in turns to stir it with a stripped rod, keeping the liquid just off the boil. The bath was as murky and bloodied as if a terrible crime had been done. And two other rinses after, each with quicklime and ashes, saying the Paternoster to keep to time as the book demanded. Then, finally, the bath held something closer to the grey of laundry water, and it was only the cloth which kept the red. The heat of the early afternoon was fading and the boy shivered as he stood up from the side of the bath.

'The colour is very fair,' he said. His face was still as red as the wool from all the lifting, but his arms were pricked with goosebumps.

Joan gave the barest nod, because it was too early to be sure. But the pigment did seem strong, and when she dared to muddle the cloth over and around in the clearer water, every side seemed to carry the same rich scarlet. *Fine enough to grace any infantryman's shoulders*, the widow had said, and Joan couldn't help imagining Daniel, in the red coat and green breeches of the Governor's Regiment, with a musket and a bandoleer full of charges, and a handkerchief at his neck to keep the sun from it.

I've not got it in me to kill a man. Her throat was tight with it, all of a sudden. She knew so little of his world, even if he was still in it; a word here and there in the Lamb Inn about the state of the Tangier colony: the heat and the recklessness that came with it, the savagery of the Moors, and a tale she hoped was exaggerated in the telling about five hundred men lured into an ambush, only thirty returning alive. What would have come of Daniel, with his gentle heart? It had been so long now; sometimes she went for days, weeks even, kept so busy, she barely thought of him. But when she had a moment to dwell on it, it hurt as much to think of him gone as the day she'd watched him walk away down the valley.

Joan realised that the boy was staring at her now, leaning his weight from one foot to the other, unsure what to do with her silence.

'Down to the river for treading then,' she said, brisk as she could. 'Or it'll never be dried by nightfall.'

They staggered down to the Frome with the sodden rope of red cloth, the boy leading and Joan directing from behind, keen to keep the length from burrs and brambles. Six feet wide and ten yards long – even with two of them, it was a struggle. In the river, they took off their boots and trod the cloth along the slatted racks there. The millboys used wooden clogs for the job, but bare feet seemed to work well enough. They stamped and trampled until the last of the dye residue leached across the water flow in a wide pink arc. Only when the water ran truly clear did they climb the hillside again, to hang the piece from the tenter hooks – properly this time – and let the breeze do its part.

It was no small job; the boy huffed and grunted at the other end as they lifted. Joan dismissed him then, leaving him to run off, patting the coin in his pocket, and she sat down on a stool beside the rack. There was a good draught up the valley. She pulled her shawl across her shoulders and let her eyelids fall. Nothing left to do now but wait.

Chapter Fourteen

'It's as fine a red as I've seen. I wouldn't mind a coat of it myself, though you could keep the musket and baldrick that comes with it.' John Browning was walking backwards across the cottage's main room, pulling the length of cloth taut between them.

It was the morning of the wedding and Alice had had them up since dawn with one thing and another. She was in the back room now, having flowers plaited into her hair, so Joan had taken the first chance she'd had to unwrap the folded felt and see how the colour had stayed. 'Are you pleased, Joan? It's a rare feat of alchemy you've achieved here.'

'I'll be pleased if the quartermaster thinks it fine enough for the regimental tailors,' Joan replied. But in truth she was elated, how could she not be? A fresh bolt of the relief she'd felt up on the hillside returned to her, when she'd been able to guess at the colour of the dried wool in the dusk, and now here, in daylight, to see its incontrovertible brightness. How far she had come since those pallid scraps of her first attempt, neither one colour nor another! This was a length of the scarlet, surely.

'I can't imagine he could find fault with it.' Her father rubbed the cloth between finger and thumb. 'The fuller's done his job well, the shearing is close and even, and no man could criticise the hue you've given it.' He walked back towards her, and they folded the cloth between them, until it was a tall stack on the table. 'Better get it away now, though.' He jerked his head towards the doorway to the loom room. 'She'll not thank us for the distraction. She hasn't forgiven you yet for your rosy hands, though every bit of it was done in her name.'

Joan nodded, lifting the heavy bundle and putting it away in the chest in the corner, ready for its journey to Cirencester the week after. She would have liked to have the money in advance – for once, to have been able to pay upfront, for the many small outlays her sister had demanded – but her father's words reassured her that at least the cloth might fetch the best price when she did get it to market. When she stood up, her father had turned away and was staring into the empty hearth.

'Father?'

He didn't turn back.

'If your mother was here . . .' She walked closer to put her hand on the sleeve of his coat, and he covered her hand with his own. 'Don't think I don't appreciate what you've done, Joan. I'd have been face down in that river if you hadn't stepped in when you did, bubbling at the fishes, and you've gone on to make a home here where there wasn't one. But there are days when I can hardly believe she's gone.'

'I know, Father. All our lives have been poorer without her.'

He patted the back of her hand, swiping at his eyes with the other. 'They have, and doubtless you're missing your Daniel on this day of all days.' He blew out the air from his cheeks. 'Perhaps we should take a drop before we set off for the church. The Smarts will turn out as fancy as their name, I have no doubt, and I'll have to shake the hand of every last one of them. Pour me a cup would you, Joan, before you go through to your sister.'

She'd seen this before, this grim light in his eyes. It had been a while since he'd felt the need to drown his sorrows, but when he took to the flagon, there was never a drop left undrunk. It'd be one, then another, his eyes turned bloodshot and woozy, then they'd be lucky if he made it to the church at all. 'You've no need of it, Father. You're as good a man as any of them.'

'And you're a kind girl, Joan, but something tells me they'll think different. Half a cup then, just to ease the stamp up the hill.'

'Why not wait until the feast? Mother would have wanted us dry . . .'

'She'd have wanted me to get through the day,' her father interrupted. 'The woman never begrudged me a cup of something on a difficult day.' A sharper note was emerging now.

'. . . And you always say Father Britton has a nose like a hunting dog,' Joan went on, thinking of her promise to Alice, praying that she could dissuade him.

'That he does, that he does.' Her father laughed and wiped his eyes again; she'd driven it off, for now. 'You've hit on something there. Go on then, Joan, you've bested me with your words as usual. I'll take nothing now, but you'll not deny me when we sit down after.'

There was no chance for Joan to answer him, because the curtain was snatched aside and Alice swept into the room.

'Well?' It was a demand, and a question, and a remonstration for daring to talk of anything other than the majesty of her gown, but then it was quite a gown. Everything her sister had asked for, conjured from the humblest of fabrics and somehow elevated to something grand; Joan could not help but feel proud of her creation.

'My dear Alice . . .' Her father's eyes were filling again; Joan moved quickly.

'You couldn't look finer,' she said to Alice. 'But let me fasten that ribbon at your back. And here, Harriet,' she called to Alice's friend, who hovered in the doorway behind, 'help me tighten these stays, would you? Father, would you see if old Robert is ready with the cart?' She watched him over Alice's shoulder and was relieved to see him turn about and shamble towards the doorway.

'Forasmuch as Walter and Alice have consented together in holy wedlock, and have witnessed the same before God and this company, and thereto have given and pledged their troth either to other, and have declared the same, by giving and receiving of a ring, and by joining of hands; I pronounce that they be man and wife together, in the Name of the Father, and of the Son, and of the Holy Ghost. Amen.'

Father Britton had released Alice and Walter's right hands, but now he pressed them together between his own palms, lifting his arms towards the crowded church. It was done. Through the gauze of her headdress, Joan could see the tendons in Alice's neck relax when the vicar had said his piece. But Walter did no more than nod, and his jaw continued to champ as if he had a piece of stringy meat between his teeth.

A murmur of appreciation around the church followed the vicar's pronouncement, whether for the fact of the marriage or more likely for the sense that the end might be in sight. A number of men were already filling their pipes, and the two youngest members of the bridal party began squabbling under the pulpit, until the elder of the two caught her mother's eye and pulled her sister down to sulk on the altar steps. Joan's father, looking as smart now as he'd ever been in the new tawny coat she'd sewed for him, made to stand, until she put a hand on his arm to keep him in his seat. He rolled his eyes but settled back amicably enough: dressed like a gentleman, she knew he felt halfway to being one. He stretched his arms along the back of the pews on each side and glanced round the church with a smile of proprietorial approval.

The murmur quietened and then died when it became apparent that Father Britton had more to say, and a whole raft of psalms and blessings to come besides. But the lengthy sermon did finally reach its end, the bell began to ring out in celebration of the marriage, and the congregation spilled gratefully into the churchyard after the bride and groom, while the tables were to be prepared for the meal.

Joan was a little cut off by the crowd, so she watched from a distance as the couple were showered with grains of wheat and presented with ribboned rosemary branches. The two little flower girls turned celebratory cartwheels around them. Surrounded by Harriet and the other girlfriends who had accompanied her to the church, all in matching headdresses, Alice was like a goddess amongst her nymphs. Even Walter seemed to tolerate the attention for a while, kissing his bride to the approval of those looking on, but after some minutes he whispered something in Alice's ear and excused himself. Alice's smile slipped for a moment, and Joan thought to go to her, but her girlfriends quickly closed the circle around her.

Afterwards, searching for her father among the tombstones, Joan found Walter instead, sharing a flask with some of the businessmen from town who had come at his invitation. Then not long after, on her way to the privy beyond the churchyard, just before the meal was due to start, a young girl she recognised from Iles Mill passed her at a run, tears on her cheeks. Then a few steps further on, Walter again, pulling brambles from his attire and muttering something about a rabbit in the bush. He greeted Joan with passable warmth, but when she glanced back, he seemed to be untucking his topcoat from where it had been caught up in his breeches, and refastening a button on his shift. She couldn't help recalling that man in the lane near the Lamb Inn: a stream of hot liquid across the cobbles and his clumsy fingers at the button at his belt, his hands reaching for her, his curled nail scraping her chest . . .

Walter was not that man, and perhaps he had only found the privy occupied, had chosen to relieve himself in the bush behind. But still, there was something in the scene – the urgent pace of the girl ahead of him, the defiant set of his face – that made her doubt him. On his wedding day? Surely not. But what was it about this man that left her with such questions?

Later, after the meal, the fiddlers started up in the meadow beside the churchyard. All around, men and woman groaned and clutched at their overfull bellies; Walter might be many things, and there was something distasteful in the way he had let it be known that he had paid every penny for the wedding feast, but no one could fault his generosity. The young men from the valley's mills, blue-fingered and lively, were the first to start the dancing, prancing and capering in front of the girls to persuade them up from blankets laid in the long grass.

Joan watched them for a while, trying to save it all for Mrs Freme, who had begged her to memorise and recount every detail, but still troubled by what she'd seen on the way to the privy. She watched friends dragged up laughing to join the set pieces, and wished that Daniel was here. It was an ache of a wish that had her biting her lip to make it pass. Girls years younger than her were holding hands with their intended, letting them braid daisies in their hair; it made her feel like a dry old maid. A fleeting thought of the chestnut-brown eyes of the blacksmith, Thrupp, came into her mind, but she banished it at once. When one boy did come close, grinning and holding out a posy of poppies and dandelions as if that might tempt her, she just shook her head and eventually he made a face and moved on.

As the dancing circle widened, Joan crossed over to join her father, who stood in a group of family members under the copse of trees on the far side of the meadow. None of the young lads would trouble her here; she had no wish to explain again her reluctance to join the jig. From this side, she had a clearer view of the bride and groom, now reunited in a bower constructed in the low branches of a willow tree.

'I hope she'll be happy enough,' John Browning was saying beside her.

'Yes. A strange union, but I dare say she'll make the best of it.' It was his imposing sister, Anne, who had travelled down from Broadway with her physician husband for the event. Her gown was matched with a lace-lined hood which partly obscured her face, but there was no missing her tone.

'After all, dear, you did.' Under Anne's answering glare, her husband Stephen lifted his cup to hide a smile.

'Entirely different,' she snapped. A coil of red hair had slipped from Anne's hood and she thrust it back in place before she turned back to Joan's father. 'I'm surprised you sanctioned it, John. He's double her age, and hardly a fine physical specimen. Were you so keen to see the back of her?'

John Browning lifted his hands in mock surrender. 'You have met my older daughter a number of times, Anne. Like you, Alice has the force of will that would meet a raging torrent and ask not how to cross it, but whether it would like to make way. She also shares your taste for expensive things. I don't think she enters this blindly.'

Anne behaved as if she hadn't heard. 'You wouldn't want to wake next to that every morning. But it'll not be long before children come along, I suppose, and she can make a case for her own bed.' If only that were the only problem; Joan thought again of the girl hurrying from the bushes, the unwelcome image of Walter pushing his shirt back down into his crotch, and hoped that her suspicions were misplaced.

But Anne turned to Joan then, and began quizzing her on the business and on Daniel, so there would be no chance to catch her sister alone. Over her aunt's shoulder, she watched Alice work to hold her new husband's attention. She couldn't help but replay the scene by the privy again and again. Simply coincidence, it must have been – the girl, the shift unbuttoned, and the topcoat caught up. Only a monster would be so cruel as to have relations with another girl today of all days. God forbid it were true, but in any case, she knew Alice well enough to know that her sister would not thank her for spoiling the day in front of such a crowd, so she must hold her tongue.

Eventually, the music began to take a new turn. A harpist joined the fiddlers and the jig became a regal march. Joan's uncle Stephen clapped along, just out of time to the music, until her aunt pressed a gloved hand on his sleeve and he dropped his hands with pursed lips. The bride and groom were urged to their feet and the other dancers formed a tunnel with their arms raised. Alice laughed and moved to run through it, but Walter let go of her hand; he was only persuaded by his fellows to follow. Joan watched her sister's smile slip again a moment as she was made to wait. Then the jig restarted and Walter broke a sweat around his hairline. With his cuffs stained with spilt beer and one button popped already on his waistcoat; it was true he was not nearly as handsome as her sister. But now he had his arm hooked firmly round his new wife's waist, or as far round as his belly would allow, and as Joan clapped along with the rest, Alice looked as happy as Joan had seen her. She even lifted a hand in greeting as the whirling dance passed by.

It was not long after that. Alice had twirled away again, and the first Joan saw of what was to come was the sudden turning of heads: it seemed to Joan as if every face turned to hers at once. She realised they were staring not at her but past her, to something on the path behind, which led down from the London road. A few girls were clapping, and the boys nearest the front were already cheering, but it was Alice's face that gave it away. That sour grimace at Joan, and she knew who would be walking down that path.

And when she saw the distant smudge of red coming down through the green, the stiff march of an army man, she realised that this gross imposition on a day dedicated to her sister would not be forgiven. But by then Daniel was waving, and the crowd was clapping and cheering, and she was running up the path ahead of them to join him.

Chapter Fifteen

It was not how she'd imagined their reunion. The shock seemed to have frozen her tongue, so when Daniel was close enough to call her name, she found herself struck mute, gurning like a trout tossed onto the riverbank. And Daniel looked tired, older, different, with his hair cropped close to his scalp and his greatcoat unbuttoned to the waist so that she could see the stained linen shift beneath. And when he got closer still, so she could recognise the boy beneath the dirt and the uniform and the smudge of beard . . . when he bent to kiss her, she moved awkwardly so that their noses crashed together so hard, her eyes watered. But then he laughed, kissing her again, and wrapped her into his coat, which smelt of dust and smoke and sweat.

It was really too warm to be comfortable bundled in wool for long, but Joan could have borne the heat for hours for the bliss of having his arms around her again. It wasn't to be, though; there was barely a moment before the crowd were all around them, wanting to be a part of Daniel's return. There were boys clapping him on the back, children pawing at his legs, grown men and women weeping at the simple joy of one of theirs recovered. Joan's father embraced him like a son. Only Walter and Alice stood a little apart, heads bent in conversation. After an exchange of words between the couple that looked bitter even from afar, Walter strode over with a wide smile, extending his hand for Daniel to take. But Alice stayed where she was, watching the two men talk, circles of rouge blooming on her cheeks just as her face grew stony pale. Beside her, Harriet reached out a hand, but Joan saw her sister bat it away.

'I'm sorry,' Joan mouthed towards Alice, because she had never meant to usurp her sister's wedding day and surely Alice would understand that. But this was a girl who had quibbled over the ribbons Joan proposed sewing to her own gown, in case it drew attention away from her own, and was only persuaded with the argument that all of the bridal party would contribute to the bride's beauty. If you knew Alice at all, the timing of Daniel's return could not be more ruinous.

And Joan's efforts failed, as she knew they must; Alice stared through her as if she were glass, then her eyes flicked back to Walter and Daniel. Perhaps it was unfortunate to see the two men lined up against each other: Walter did not fare well in the comparison. Even with the grime and exhaustion of war, it was clear that Daniel was a young man in the prime of life, while – side-on – the view of Walter's neck was too like a turkey gizzard, and the bald patch at the back of his scalp was visible where his hairpiece had slipped in the dancing.

Harriet and three other of her girlfriends formed a ring around Alice, calling on the fiddlers to restart the jig, trying to persuade her to join them in dancing. But Alice was having none of it: she turned away and stamped towards the churchyard. One of Walter's business contacts pointed to her retreating back, but Walter just rolled his eyes and took a draught from his cup.

'I should go after her,' Joan said to Daniel. 'You know what she's like.'

Daniel squeezed her hand. She saw that there were scars across his knuckles, and that a piece was missing from his ring finger, as if a bite had been taken from it. It had just been a word, Tangier, unreal despite the rumour and gossip in the inns. Perhaps it had been a way of protecting herself, rarely to have thought hard about what it might have been like, squatting in a blockhouse, fighting off the enemy at close quarters. But it was inescapable now: the heat, the boredom, the fear, the inevitable hostility of those local warriors whose land had been handed to England as part of the dowry of some Portuguese princess; suddenly, all of these were very real, and all had left their mark across Daniel's body.

'Let her cool off a minute,' Daniel urged. 'You don't stamp down a fire when the flames are still high.'

'Unless there's a haystack alongside.'

He laughed. 'A minute won't hurt. She'll come to no harm in the church, and perhaps Father Britton will have some words to calm her. And I want to talk to you. Let's take a walk, away from this crowd.'

She could hardly refuse. It wasn't easy to shake off the well-wishers who still surrounded them, but at last they found a quiet spot in the trees and sat down together on a fallen log. He put his arm around her waist and she leant her head on his shoulder.

'You can't imagine how much I've missed you,' he said.

'I wish you'd never gone at all.'

'I know. But my uncle seemed so sure it was the right thing to do. He persuaded my father it would keep me safe.' Daniel took his hand from hers a moment, and gripped the log on each side of his thigh so hard his knuckles whitened. 'I can't think why he did. There were plenty of times I didn't think I'd make it back at all. I had barely reached Dover before I learnt that his son, my cousin William, had died over in Bombay: killed by his commander for desertion. The letter from my aunt explained that my uncle had not left his bed since he heard the news.'

'Oh Daniel, I can hardly bear it.'

'They branded William a traitor, of course, but I am not surprised he ran. In Tangier, I saw things no man should have to witness – I will not share them with you, Joan, lest you lose sleep as I have – but there were plenty of occasions when I wondered if death might offer a better chance of peace.'

'It breaks my heart to hear it,' Joan said. She rubbed the grime from one of the brass buttons on his greatcoat with her cuff, wondering that war came with such glitter and such pain.

'I am here now,' he said.

'I thought it might never be so. And your father? What has become of him? I have asked any I thought might have word of him, but there has been no news for months.'

'He is well, or so I hear it. He has found work and a new congregation in a village in Somerset, where the vicar turns a blind eye to those such as him. Perhaps we will find time to visit him there, when our feet have touched the ground.'

'And you are home. I can scarce believe it.'

He took her hand again. 'I swear it was the thought of you, Joan, which brought me back safely. Those Moors were savage and wily, more than willing to lose their lives for the return of their land. They knew every inch of the hills around the fort, every rock in the bay, and sometimes it felt like we were blind fools in their hands, kept from the greatest harm only by the distraction of rivalries between the tribes. Still, so many of our own men perished, from illness if not by the musket. Every time one of those men stared down the barrel of my gun, dark eyes blazing from his turban, I thought of you, and these valleys, and how much I wanted to walk these paths again.'

'And now you can. It feels as if our lives might begin now.'

He smiled, nodding slowly. 'And you, Joan?' He looked up at her. There was a crimson thread across the white of his left eye. She would not ask now, but later she would make it her business to learn how every scratch was laid on him, every mark that war had traced and cut and burnt on his flesh. 'How have you been? I feared to leave you. Did you get the money I sent?'

She shook his head. 'Nothing came, but I have been well.'

He swore, then excused himself. 'I knew it was a risk – a ship was returning to Dover and the governor himself promised to place the package in the captain's hands, but so many palms it would need to cross after. I hoped it would reach you all the same.'

A risk that it must cross so many palms, or perhaps just one . . . Maybe it was uncharitable, but Joan could not help remember a time, around a year back, when Alice had always seemed to be wearing some new trinket. Always a shawl around her shoulders and never tarnished with darning holes. They'd been less poor by then, but only in that they did not sleep hungry; there'd been no farthing left over for treats and fripperies. Joan's shoulders sank a little. She hoped it was not so.

Daniel was watching her. He leant in to place a kiss on her cheek, and she shivered at the gentleness of his touch. 'No matter, what else would I have spent the money on? You have survived and thrived,' he said. 'And you look well, Joan. More beautiful even than when I left.'

She patted his hand, to distract from the colour in her cheeks. 'Thank you.'

'Has your father been well?'

She shook her head. 'I think you know what it is like. His cups brought him to a low ebb, and for a while I thought we might all be drowned by it. But perhaps it was also our salvation, because he let me try my hand where he had failed, and somehow the business has flourished.'

His eyebrows almost reached the brim of his hat. 'My Joan, a clothier.'

'You may mock, but I have found some success at it.'

'I have no doubt. I would buy anything you waved before me. Dazzled by your beauty, I'd buy a greatcoat stitched from soiled fence fleece and spiders' webs. But tell me, do you wear a coat and breeches while you bargain with the Blackwell Hall factor?'

'We'll be missed by now. We should probably return.' Joan half stood, cheeks burning, but he put his hand on her arm to stop her.

'Joan, I've made you cross and I only meant it in jest. Forgive me, army life is coarse and simple. Allow me a few mistakes while I adjust to being home.'

'All the same, they may be waiting for us to start to the procession down the hill.'

'A kiss, then, to seal our lives restarted.'

His open face, his smile; she couldn't deny him. 'One kiss.'

He did not waste a moment; standing up and taking her face in his fingers so quickly, she nearly lost her footing. One kiss, but one more searching than she could have imagined, and when it finished, she had held her breath so long, her head was spinning.

'There, I have waited a long time for that,' he said, and took her hand.

There was still a small group dancing when they reached the meadow, but the music was slower and most of the party had retired to blankets and stools in the shadow of the tall hedge. Sunset was still some hours off – it was not far off the longest day of the year – but some had left already to begin a long walk home. The bower in the willow tree was empty and there was no sign of Alice or Walter, but Joan's aunt and uncle came across to welcome them as Joan and Daniel made their way through the long grass and hay rattle.

'I told you they'd be back soon,' Anne said. 'I've asked the vicar, Joan. He seemed most obliging.' She was nodding, as if her meaning must be obvious.

Joan looked across at Daniel. She had only met Anne a handful of times, but recognised a gesture of her father's in the way his sister was patting her thighs through the full weight of her skirt: a job well done.

'She's only gone and asked if he'll marry you two.' Her father was red in the face from striding up the path from the church. 'I was doing my best to head her off, but there was no stopping her. Don't you dare pretend you didn't understand me, Anne! Any fool would know what I meant to convey by all my comportments.'

Under the shade of her silk hood, Joan's aunt sucked her lips in tight. '*Any fool* is precisely what you looked like, John.'

Safely out of her gaze, Daniel widened his eyes and Joan swallowed down the urge to laugh. But her aunt was not finished: 'I had no idea what your wild gesticulations were supposed to mean, any more than I used to when you did the same behind our mother's back. And besides, what harm could possibly come of it?'

John Browning sighed deeply. 'Anne, you may well boss those poor daughters of yours to kingdom come, and God keep them, but this is not your domain, and you would do well to keep your nose out of it. As you know – Zounds, I wish I'd never opened my mouth to tell you now – these two young people are already married in law but without the Church's blessing. A situation I had hoped not to bring to Father Britton's attention, because that man is a stickler for the letter of the law.'

Joan's aunt shrugged, brushing some invisible speck from the tight boning of her bodice. 'He seemed to take it well enough. He was most forthcoming about the possibility of a blessing.'

'Then we are very fortunate that the Father has been well supplied with his favourite tipple this afternoon, and is probably at his very most amenable.'

'The perfect day for it, then. You may thank me later, John.'

His cheeks puffed out with air, then he blew it all out and let his shoulders sag. 'I give up.'

'But Alice . . .' Joan said, looking around in case there was any sign yet of her sister.

'Her feathers were ruffled and she took off. She will tire of it soon and return,' Anne said.

'Her new husband may tire of it sooner,' Anne's husband added. 'What?' he said, when Anne's head spun around. 'He looked to have had enough of it already. I heard one of his business associates joke that he would need to bring his wife in line.'

'The procession won't happen without her, and she won't want to miss it. I dare say she will be back.' John Browning kissed the top of Joan's head. 'And now the damage is done, shall we visit Father Britton? Anne and Stephen can bear witness to it, and if we are quick about it, the whole business will be done before you sister gets word of it.'

'But if she does . . .'

'She will not. And how much better to start your life together with the Church's blessing. Let's waste no more time. I only wish your father were here to join us, Daniel. It is a travesty that the Church which urges union has driven so many families apart.'

They walked as a group down towards the churchyard gate, still hung with a rope of ox-eye daisies and white yarrow blooms. Joan held Daniel's hand and her father placed an approving palm on his back as they reached the open church doors. The vicar emerged from the darkness as if he'd been waiting for them.

'There has been an irregularity, I hear.' Joan opened her mouth to begin an apology, but he went on, arms wide with welcome. 'No matter. A small omission, easily corrected. Come inside, it is a matter of minutes to formalise the union in the eyes of the Church.'

So they followed him in and up to the altar, where he stood over them and read aloud a shortened version of the familiar words. 'The Lord mercifully with his favour look upon you, and so fill you with all spiritual benediction and grace,' he finished, 'that ye may so live together in this life, that in the world to come ye may have life everlasting. *Amen.*' He closed the Book with a solid thump. 'And that is that. Daniel and Joan, I do pronounce you man and wife.'

Daniel lifted a hand to her cheek and pressed a kiss on her lips. No bell ringing this time. No murmur of approval around the pews, no little girls turning cartwheels under cover of the pulpit's shadow. But it was enough that it was done, and their life together could begin on the right footing.

There was a cough from the back of the church then. 'She wanted to start the procession. We came back looking for you all.' One of Alice's girlfriends, the youngest of the company, was standing just inside the doors, fiddling with her hands. 'She's gone now, though,' she said, and her voice was flat and full of regret.

Oh Alice, what must she have thought, peering into the darkness of the church? Enough that Daniel, and therefore Joan, had ambushed her special day, but now they had been caught in the act of further imposition. A wedding of her own, when the church bells had barely stopped ringing for Alice's; Joan could just imagine how her sister would see it.

'She's gone now,' the girl said again, louder this time. Her flower garland sagged over one eye and her slippers were stained green from the dancing. 'And I'm to tell you she wants to see none of you again.'

Much later, in the darkness of the cottage, Joan and Daniel lay side by side in the marriage bed which had been laid out in the front room for Alice and Walter. When the remainder of the company heard that Alice had ridden back to Stroud with Walter, the procession back to the valley had been abandoned. The wedding party had disbanded into ragged groupings, finding their way along the donkey tracks in the twilight. Some of the younger folk were still in high spirits, but most were subdued: the end of a strange day.

When they reached the cottage, Joan, Daniel and her father had stood awkwardly in the gloom of a rushlight, looking at each other. Unable to bear it, Joan had busied herself with setting a fire, and Daniel crouched to help her. That morning – it seemed a lifetime ago now – Joan had moved her father's bedding to the loom room where she and Alice usually slept, but when she tried to move it back, he urged her to leave things as they were.

'That bed was set for a wedding, and didn't I watch you get wed today?' he said, clapping Daniel on the back. And not long after, he'd gone through to the back with the briefest of farewells, leaving Joan and Daniel eyeing each other across the hearth. Tongue-tied suddenly, they'd undressed in opposite corners of the room, Joan's fingers stumbling over her stays as she tried to unfasten them under the cover of a blanket. Daniel took longer than he could have needed to arrange his boots by the door, giving her time to tuck the sheet around her. Only when she'd coughed had he turned about, pinching out the rushlight with his fingers as he crossed over to the mattress.

Joan lifted a hand to scratch her face, finding one of the petals she'd scattered across the bolster all those hours ago, while her father had shouted from the cart for her to hurry.

'How many flowers died in the pursuit of this bower?' Daniel was laughing. 'I have breathed in half a dog rose, and a posy of poppies is crushed under my thigh.'

He was trying to be kind, but Joan was tired and suddenly low.

'It was for Alice. It was all for Alice, but probably she will never forgive me now.'

Daniel turned on his side to face her, and she felt his fingers on her forehead, tracing the line of her hair.

'Joan, my Joan. Everyone could see how much you had done for her; no Gloucester lady has been wed in a finer gown. And when she has grown fat and comfortable, she will forgive us.'

'You don't know my sister as I do.'

He shifted closer, kissed her shoulder. 'If she cannot find it in her to forgive, then you must forget.' His fingers skimmed her jaw-line. She shivered as they fanned across her bare neck.

'Daniel, how can I forget? She's my flesh and blood, and I have let her down.' That insistent image of Alice's face: the shock of the intrusion rendering her careful rouge brazen across ashen cheeks.

'You did no such thing. And if you cannot forget, I will have to find ways to distract you.'

The tiniest smile. He was always impatient to return to good cheer. And he shifted closer still, so that Joan could feel the heat of him. She swallowed. She had some idea of what would happen now, gleaned from overheard snippets between Alice and her friends, but her limbs felt ungainly and her belly fluttered. She took heart from Daniel's boldness, though. He guided her on top of him, lifting her arms to slip off her shift, then pulled her down to kiss him.

'My father . . .' Joan whispered.

'He snores like a boar already.' Daniel's hands were all over her body, and she felt dizzy with it. 'I would fill you with children,' he whispered in her ear, 'and Alice and her quibbles will be long forgotten.'

I would fill you with children – she considered this afterwards, as they lay side by side, and she remembered how he had watched that boy with the cup-and-ball at the Whitsun fair all those many months ago, the affection in his eyes. *Look at this little man now, so pleased with his new toy.* Today she had felt as old as the valley, but they were barely more than children themselves.

'We are young still, my heart,' she said, into the soft rhythm of his breath. 'You would not be too disappointed if the blessing came slowly?' *Or even that we might take steps to delay it.*

'Young enough to have many. Joan, why would we wait! I would come home each day to a houseful, like a litter of leverets.'

It was hard, to hear the joy in his voice, after so long without it, yet his words set a weight in her gut.

'But how will I visit the markets and the Blackwell Hall factor with babes in tow?'

He laughed aloud at that, so much so she had to shush him, and they waited in silence while her father snorted and shifted in his blankets.

'You jest, of course,' Daniel said at last, when the pattern of John Browning's wheeze had returned. 'But the image of you riding out to London with a crop of babes strapped to your saddle . . . it was precious.' She did not remember this teasing snigger; perhaps it came from the trenches of Tangier. It brought up the hairs on her neck.

'I spoke in all seriousness.'

'Joan, your efforts with your father's business have been valiant. All those assembled today sang your praises. But we are married now. You are my wife. You can't have thought things would continue as before.'

'But no one understands the accounts as I do, and it has taken many months to build relationships with the millsmen and the factors.' She heard herself as he must, whining like a petulant child.

'And your help will be invaluable in introducing those men to me.'

'So you plan to take charge.'

He breathed out deeply before speaking. 'Joan, my dear, don't make this strange. We have both been sorely tested, and you have shown great spirit. But the business of the clothiers is best left to the men who can handle it. You need not waste your time further; better to concern yourself with our new home. The money from your aunt and uncle will furnish us with rooms for six months, maybe a year. Time enough for you to make a comfortable nest, and for me to earn the money to keep it.'

'You will run the business alone?' Her voice was dull as lead.

'With your father's support. The discipline of work will keep him sober.'

'It was work that drove him to the flagon.'

'Then I will curb his habit.'

'And what of the dyeing? I had only just begun to learn the magic of it.'

'Joan, please. It is our first night together. I did not dream of you all those nights for this. You have beautiful hands; let them stay that way, not scarred with mordant and dye.'

She had no reply, and the silence seemed to expand between them, until she felt its presence as if it were pushing them apart in the bed.

'I love you, Joan Randall,' he said at last. 'And you love me. Let that be enough.'

Let that be enough, she thought; but the bolster was damp with her tears before she slept.

Chapter Sixteen

'It was a joint decision, to invest in the wheel. You agreed: there is little enough profit in wool, without handing the bulk of it to the fullers. You cannot blame me now if the mills upstream are stealing our water.'

Daniel was standing in the cottage doorway with Rockwood at his feet, the dog nosing at the copper leaves that had rolled in from the beech beside the stream. Daniel's grip on the doorpost was tight enough to whiten his knuckles, but John Browning took his time with his reply. Kneading dough on her father's table – there was no room to do so in the lean-to they rented down in the valley – Joan watched the lump in her husband's throat rise and fall as he stood in the doorway. She saw him seethe at her father's position, but also his fear that he had pushed it too far this time.

'If you had not spoken so highly of the stream's speed and clarity in the town's inns,' John Browning said at last, taking a step forward, then bending to stroke Rockwood's head on the doorstep, 'perhaps word would not have got around, and they would not have sought to dig the new races.' He took his time in straightening up. 'The Stephenses have managed well enough on their own small stream my whole lifetime, and it is only since you came back that they have had any thought of doing otherwise.'

They were eye to eye now, both squared as if for a fight. In the months since Daniel had returned, rarely a day had passed without her father and her husband falling out over some aspect of the business. That Daniel was too full of novelty and expensive notions; that he couldn't take direction, for all his months in the regiment; that he overrated the knowledge he'd gained in the months spent working for the Hampton clothier before his exile from the valley, and should begin his apprenticeship again at her father's right hand. These her father voiced again and again, to her husband's face and behind his back.

Daniel, in turn, made no secret of his opinion that her father was a little too fond of his riverside nook and his afternoon snooze; that he lacked the practical ambition that went with his grand ideals; that he often accepted a humble sale price rather than demean himself by bargaining. John Browning's drinking was nothing like it had been, but both decried each other equally for their time spent in the inns on market days.

The relationships and understandings Joan had carefully nurtured with merchants, millers and factors would sustain them for a while, but then... She pressed her thumbs hard into the dough, dreading to think that the tensions between them might take them all back to the dark days before her father had yielded the reins to her. Since the leftovers from the wedding feast had run out, they'd gone back to existing on a meagre pottage, and Daniel was already talking about selling the ewe she'd hand-fed as a lamb.

Joan watched him pull himself upright in the doorway now, setting his cap more firmly over his ears and fixing his gaze on John Browning. 'And if you had held your ground with the wool merchant, sir,' he said, furious pink circles at his cheekbones, 'and made all the market visits we agreed on, we would not find ourselves in such tight straits.'

John Browning blew the air from his cheeks and gripped the back of the chair beside him.

'Please, don't blame each other,' Joan said quickly, before her father could think to reply. It was a risk to intervene – she'd learnt that these past months – but how could she keep quiet when they seemed determined to sink the business with the weight of their own obstinacy? 'The millsmen up and down the valley are talking of how hard orders have been to come by these past months. How much the factors take for their hallage in London, and the difficulty of keeping good labour. There's not a family mill that hasn't been affected by the steep rise in the price of fleece and vitriol, and all the factors will say is how we must drop our prices to compete with the Dutch and the French.'

'That is little comfort, Joan, when we have no legal standing on which to fight this theft.' Her father's face was grim; he was right, of course. It was no secret that their cottage encroached on common land: if he contested the Stephenses' water rights, no court in the land would find in his favour. And Daniel and Joan's own rented rooms were little more than a lean-to at the back of the Bliss Mill cottages; no chance of moving the expensive wheel there, even if it was possible to shift the monster now that it had been installed.

So they could not fight the mills upstream. But the Stephenses had felt this latest pinch too: Mr Stephens was weak in the chest, and his only son dragged a leg behind him after falling from a horse; getting their cloth to market was difficult and much of the work had to be farmed out to the other cottage mills. Joan had seen the girls' ragged dresses in church, and the familiar dent in the younger children's cheeks which comes from night after night with no real sustenance. She had seen them digging the new channel with their own hands, not even the youngest girl excused; it was dug in desperation. It would not do to prey on others, but she could see an opportunity that might suit all parties, if only she could convince her father and Daniel of its merit.

She dropped the lump of dough back onto the board, fearing that in her frustration she had overworked it and took a deep breath. 'If they have taken our water, better that we take their mill,' she said.

The Stephenses' mill was small but had always been productive for its size, and with two able-bodied men to work it and the newly dug race to drive the wheel, a better profit was almost certain. It would be a great upheaval, and not without risk, but they could sell their own equipment, and maybe Walter would stand behind a loan to fund the rest.

Daniel laughed aloud. 'An eye for an eye. Do not anger my wife, she will take Biblical retribution.'

'I only meant that they might be prepared to sell, if the price was right. They seem desperate, and I have heard Mr Stephens talk of his wish to move from the valley because the wood smoke from the drying furnaces troubles his chest. Perhaps they could be persuaded.'

'And has a wood sprite left you a pot of gold? Because I wish that you had told me of it earlier.' At least she had raised Daniel's spirits; he seemed so tickled with his joke, his eyes were shining. She turned away before she was moved to say something sharp. Her father remained stony-faced.

'I feel sure we could raise the funds, if Walter saw fit to back us,' she said, wary of his expression.

They would have to repair that relationship first, of course. Of the many times Joan had called on Alice at her new house since the wedding day, only once had she been admitted, even then with bad grace and for a conversation even more awkward than this one. And even if she could bring her sister round – no small task, because Alice was famous for her grudges – asking the favour of Walter would be a bitter pill to swallow; the man's smugness seemed to have only increased now he walked around town with his new wife on his arm. But Joan could see no alternative.

She looked from one man to the other. If she'd hoped to mend this latest rift with her suggestion, it had worked up to a point, though not as she'd wished. Both her father and Daniel were staring her way with expressions somewhere between bemusement and distaste. Her father would never go for it, she saw that now: it was too bold, and he had lost his taste for gambling after the business's last decline. She had hoped for Daniel's support, but she realised that he could not even allow himself to consider the idea's merits. How many times had he urged her to keep her nose from the business, and she saw that now he would refuse even the best suggestions from her, with none of the deliberation they deserved.

'Perhaps we could discuss how to proceed tomorrow,' Daniel said to her father, suddenly cordial.

'Indeed. I will call on you soon after dawn.' John Browning inclined his head in polite dismissal. 'Joan will be home when the bread is baked.'

Daniel nodded and ducked his head under the lintel, lifting a hand to him in farewell. Joan could have hurled the lump of dough after him – it was as if she had not been in the room. Where was the union in this marriage? And these two men, like jostling rams! Even now, with the immediate quarrel patched between them, they seemed to realise none of the urgency in the matter. Four months since Daniel came home, and only another two until they would be left without a roof over their heads, when the money gifted by her uncle and aunt ran out.

But now he was gone, and not a word said to her in goodbye, and she was left in her father's dark cottage like a borrowed tool. They'd be back here, that's where they'd be, if he would even take them in. The space had felt cramped enough when she and Alice were young, able to squeeze into the narrow cot in the back room. Fully grown now, Daniel was taller than her father. With arms barely outstretched, he could still touch both walls at the cottage's narrower end, and he had to stoop where the ceiling was at its lowest. And the room felt cluttered enough as it was – every shelf crowded with cracked jars and unwashed pots, the floor alive with chicken feathers where the broom hadn't touched it in weeks. For now, her father made the most of the late autumn warmth and set up his bed in the back room, but when the weather turned, he would be back by the hearth, and the three of them would be falling over each other. It was impossible to imagine the two men containing their disagreements under such circumstances, unimaginable that they could all live in that way. She did not know how much longer she could hold her tongue. No, she would not hold her tongue . . .

'Father . . .' she started. But he was fussing over some tangled yarn in the far corner of the room, rubbing at the greasy windowpane to let in more light to unknot the yarn by.

'What?' he said, barely looking up. She saw by the frantic movement of his fingers and the muttered curses that he would be deaf to her.

'Nothing, it can keep.' She picked up the dough, lifted her knife to cut it for loaves, let the blade thud into the board and felt some of her anger seep away with the impact. Tomorrow, she would have it out with him. Daniel too.

But as Joan bent over the table to start shaping the bread, a strange fluttering sensation started up in her belly. It was unfamiliar, this feeling, but it was not uncomfortable, so she carried on with her work: shaping the little loaves, slicing their tops, setting them amongst the coals to bake. When she finished, and her father disappeared into the back, Joan took up her darning by the fire, but the odd sensation did not fade. She put it down to nerves, or a touch of indigestion, shifting her position in her seat in case it helped. Only later, when she bent over with the tongs to lift the loaves from the coals, did its significance strike her. Her heart dropped to her boots. Not a child, not so soon. Her life had barely begun.

Chapter Seventeen

'When did you last bleed?'

When she'd woken this morning, Joan had been resolved: she could not bear this alone. In her mother's absence, she would consult her closest friend. And now they were huddled close to Mrs Freme's fire; it was only October but an early frost had come from nowhere and the whole valley was white with its chill. The old woman peeled the paper skin from a head of garlic as she waited for Joan to answer.

'I don't keep a record of it.' Joan looked back down to the coals.

'But you must have some idea.'

Joan forced herself to look up. It was not a time to be shy. 'More than once since Daniel returned, but probably no more than twice, and now I think of it, perhaps two or three moons since.'

'And the feeling: a fluttering?' Mrs Freme's fingers danced above the flames.

'Sometimes, yes, and sometimes more like the bubbling of a spring.' Joan put her hand to her waist. The sensation was gone now, but she'd felt it again as she'd walked here down the Millswood stream. The lightest flutter in her belly, that heralded a fetter as heavy as a ball and chain.

'And your breasts, are they tender?'

Joan breathed out to keep her voice steady. These were conversations for a girl and her mother. But she had only Alice, half a day's ride away, and in any case, Mrs Freme was closer to a relative than Alice had ever been. 'Everything feels tight inside my stays, as if I am a pea pod expanding in the sun.'

The older woman nodded. 'It is a little early, I think, for this to be the quickening. But it is common, in the first months, for the stomach to expand a little; a passing indigestion, as the body adjusts. Either way, I feel sure you are with child.'

Joan hung her head.

Mrs Freme leant over to place a hand on her knee. 'You are afraid to bear a child?' She went on before Joan could reply, poking at the coals with her stick so that little eruptions of sparks spouted from the red glow. 'It is understandable, but you are young and strong. The odds are in your favour.'

'It's not that,' Joan replied, though who would not be apprehensive, when so many of the valley's children had lost their mothers that way. 'It is just so soon. And we have barely enough to keep ourselves.'

Mrs Freme nodded, setting down the garlic bulbs on the small board on her lap. 'You are not far gone. And so it would not be impossible to undo . . . especially if the child is not yet quickened, and so is as yet unsouled; then it is only a matter of bringing on your bleeding.' Joan gasped, but Mrs Freme continued, her voice quiet and steady into the fire. 'You should tell me how you really feel, Joan, and don't mince the matter. Because there are ways. There have always been ways. You must know that not every woman wants to be with child.' She set aside the board and leaned closer.

Joan was silent, swallowing and gripping the rim of her chair to steady herself. 'How would it be done?' she said at last.

Mrs Freme shrugged. 'Herbs. A tincture. There are printed herbals, lists of abortifacients. I believe madder may be amongst them, alongside laurel and savin. Blood-letting of the foot, too, is favoured by some. But I would need to find out more. It is not something I have ever needed for myself.'

Joan imagined Alice in the room. How her jaw would be working to hear Mrs Freme talk in this way. But she had to know a little more: 'And afterwards?'

Mrs Freme pursed her lips. 'I know enough to know that the act itself is not pleasant. These herbs and physicks are powerful, and indeterminate in their effect. A blunt instrument if you will, and one that is wielded blindly. You will appreciate that the body must be shocked into expelling what has lodged there. But done properly, everything afterwards would be as before.'

Some pain, then, and all would be well. It seemed too easy: a gateway back to freedom. She could not help but think of Daniel, at home now, chopping wood for their own fire. They had so many years together ahead of them, and when the time came for children, she would welcome them with open arms. If he knew, perhaps he would understand. She felt sure he would, just as she had accepted and stood by the decisions he had made on behalf of them both.

'He would not understand, and you should not tell him.' There was no room for doubt in her words. When Joan looked up, her friend was regarding her intently.

She was right, of course. Joan would not have been afraid to challenge her, even with that fierce stare – their friendship had shifted and grown in these past months, as had the respect between them, to something more equal and sisterly. But there was no need: how many times had Daniel held Joan in his arms and imagined aloud the joy of a growing family, even naming the girls and boys and envisioning their temperaments? How often had he rested a hand on her belly, as if willing it to grow and swell? How often did he watch the small ones play on the riverbank, and take her hand when she caught his eye? With his own family all but lost, Daniel had made no secret of the fact that all he could think of was to begin another. She could not expect him to fathom her desire to wait, nor could she ever tell him if she chose to take matters in her own hands. Yet what basis was that to carry on a marriage less than one year old?

'Do I have time to think it over?' she asked at last.

Mrs Freme shook her head. 'If you want to take the herbs, it would not be wise to wait. Those I know of are effective only for the first weeks after conception. Afterwards, the attempt might fail, might even harm the baby.'

'It is today or never, then?' Joan could feel the grim set of her jaw.

Mrs Freme leant over, touched Joan's cheek gently. 'I think you have your answer already.'

Joan nodded. As she stared down at the grubby folds of her gown, she felt as if a key were turning in a lock against her. For a long moment she was silent, and when she did come to speak again, her shoulders hung low. 'I must accept what has been dealt to me. If something went wrong, or the chance never came again . . .'

'Let us put the conversation aside, then, as if it never happened.' Joan could hear the forced brightness in Mrs Freme's voice, and she appreciated her friend's unflinching loyalty. 'A celebration, instead. Let me be the first to congratulate you.' She put a hand on the stool and pushed herself up to collect a jug from the shelf behind her. 'To your first child,' she said, pouring them each a cup of small beer. 'Daniel is a lucky man.'

Joan took the cup she was offered. For the first time, as she sank a deep draught of the weak liquor, she had some comprehension of her father's impotent urge to seek oblivion. Between a rock and a hard place, how good it might feel to slip, senseless, between the gap. But that would help none of them. She handed back the cup and thanked her friend.

'I'll be thinking of you,' Mrs Freme replied, as Joan lifted a hand in the doorway.

Outside, the dawn fog had barely lifted from the valley and Joan kept her shawl wrapped close about her as she ran home. When she reached their little outhouse, she was still chilled to the bone. There was a rushlight burning in the window – Daniel was back – but despite that, and the cold, she waited a moment on the threshold before pushing the door. One last chance to change her mind. But then she heard his voice inside, singing that old song again. Light-o'-Love. What a father he would make.

'I can scarcely believe it,' he said later, lowering his lips to the bare skin of her navel. 'We will be parents before summer comes.'

'All being well,' she urged, but who would begrudge him this happiness? In the low light of a dying fire, he laid his cheek across her belly, as if he would hear the heartbeat, and his smile was the smile she had fallen for all those years ago, grinning at her across the churned mud of the Whitsun fair stock pens. She lifted her chin to lean and stroke the curls from his face, wishing beyond anything that she could share his joy.

Months rolled on, Joan's belly swelled and Daniel's smile only grew wider. Her father too seemed cheered and settled by the news, and the relationship between the two men seemed to soften. They found a way to split the work between them, and the only argument of consequence between them in past weeks had concerned the names they favoured for the new arrival.

Joan was grateful for the new affability between the men, and though she could not feel the same ease, she blamed the discomfort of the pregnancy, and kept herself busy to curb the worst of her imaginings. While Daniel was away, travelling between mills and market, she often worked on the loom at her father's cottage, massaging swollen fingers and ankles between passes of the weft threads across the warp. As winter took hold of the valley, and shin-deep snow shored up the threshold, she barely felt the cold, and when her stiff back would permit it, she worked on the loom late into the night, conscious of the dwindling days and weeks until their rental account would become due. Excited by her news, her aunt and uncle had sent more money from Broadway, enough to settle the account for another six months, but that would expire just a few weeks after the baby was born.

As the time passed, Daniel grew more solicitous, voicing his concerns that any physical work might fatigue her and put the baby at risk, as if the women of this valley sat in their lying-in like so many gentlewomen. She laughed at first, but his hurt frown drained the humour from her. Then she protested: she was strong – her arms were tight as rope from all those months of carrying weighty rolls of broadcloth – and the bump did not impede her work at the loom.

When it became clear that he would persist, she withdrew into herself a little. *Have I not given up enough*, she demanded, though only inside her head. And she looked about at the other men in the valley, searching for examples to hold up to Daniel, of men whose wives kept their employment when they were with child and even after. But for every example she raised, he just expressed his pity, exhorting her to be grateful for the chance to do the best for their child. One dangerous day, Joan felt so low that her thoughts strayed to the blacksmith, William Thrupp, and whether he too would have sought to impose his will on her in this way. But then Daniel returned from the mill with a posy of the first snowdrops in his fist; and he was so earnest, and his eyes so full of love, she did put aside the loom at last, wincing at the thought of the state of the business's account book.

Instead, while the men worked, she spent her time stitching impossibly small garments from paper patterns. It was Mrs Freme who lent her these, and she couldn't help but wonder how the widow had come by them, but something in the widow's expression as she handed them over made her reluctant to ask. Sometimes, Joan dyed these tiny frocks, with whatever she had to hand – ivy berries or walnut shells, twigs and nettle prunings from the hedge outside the lean-to – ignoring Daniel's muttered complaints at the jugs and strainers around the hearth, the strange odours that rose from them, the dark stains at her cuticles. On a couple of occasions she slipped out while he was sleeping, kneeling by the streamside with her old tin bath, giving new tints to their bolster covers and an old shawl, paying for it afterwards in sore joints and Daniel's thunderous expression on her return.

Between all this, there were visits from unexpected well-wishers: Mrs Britton, the vicar's wife, and Harriet, who was herself pregnant, and whose impending delivery filled the girl with a terror that took much of Joan's remaining energy to dispel. But from Alice herself, there was no word. Joan had written to her sister with the news that the baby was expected in the spring, around the equinox if the calculations she and Mrs Freme had performed were correct, but though the boy who took the note said that he had read it aloud to her, Alice sent nothing back by return. Joan was saddened by her sister's stony obstinacy; her letter had been heartfelt and unstinting in its apology, even though the events at the wedding were scarcely within her control, and it would not have taken much to send a message of goodwill. But there was little she could do about it – she moved like a mud-caked sow these days, and it was struggle enough to lift the water from the stream and cook Daniel a meal at the end of each day.

More women began to drop by the lean-to as the impending arrival came closer, with advice and gifts. Mrs Britton returned, with a bag of swaddling bands and tail-clouts that her daughter's child no longer needed. Others brought tinctures and tonics for the worst of the discomfort, little knitted coats, and endless plates of food. Despite Daniel's new cordiality with her father and his best attempts to hide the account book, Joan could see that the business was floundering again, but with the constant procession of covered dishes left on the doorstep or lowered to sit beside the fire, during that time they ate like gentlefolk.

Mrs Freme was the most regular visitor throughout the winter. The older woman had told Joan to expect an urge to make the house right, like a robin readying its nest for the new brood. But in fact it was Daniel who seemed to be struck more keenly; knocking together a cot from old floorboards, and hammering cupboards and shelves into the lean-to's thin walls so that their few possessions could be tidied away from the small area of bare floor. It was Daniel who knelt beside the millpond, breaking the ice to bleach and rinse the swaddling bands and clouts, folding cloths and towels and readying the basin, and hanging the tiny garments, dwarfed by their pegs, from a string between their window and the mill's stove tower. And he was gentle with her; so gentle that she wanted to shake him sometimes, to tell him that she wasn't some porcelain figurine, afeared of breaking, just a little fat and out of breath. He barely left her side, though she urged him to turn his attention to the business that must sustain them all. *I have married a good man*, she thought, and tried to put aside her frustrations and prepare for the new life that was coming.

Chapter Eighteen

For all the preparation, when the moment came, she was alone on the hillside. She had woken that morning with a sudden urge to walk; the lethargy of the long winter had fallen away and she'd found a new energy in her swollen limbs. Daniel would have tried to forbid it, but he had left the house before dawn, wanting to collect parcels of spun yarn from cottages on the path to Bussage, so Joan told no one where she was going. Even she could not have honestly said she knew it was safe to stride out so close to her time, but neither Daniel nor anyone else could have stopped her.

It was April, and though spring had been slow in coming this year, the worst of the snow had melted to mounds of grey in shaded corners. The paths were slick with thawed mud, but Joan had put on her stout boots and taken a stick her father had left behind the last time he visited. Her old cloak seemed to have shrunk – perched across her shoulders, it felt little more than a handkerchief – so she'd set it aside. Besides, the weight in her belly kept off the chill, so she'd left the house with only a light shawl and a bonnet more suited to a midsummer day.

She stamped up towards her father's cottage first, thinking to stop there for a cup of something, but there was no answer to her knock. Only the old hen, which had outlived the rooster, appeared to greet her. So she trudged on up, following the path of the stream and then joining the Calfway track towards Bisley. It was uncomfortably steep and she was soon short of breath. More than once she had to pause a moment, groaning at the pain in her hips as she covered the uneven ground, and a couple of times the wet mud tried to claim her. But she staked the ground with her father's stick and kept on going.

Joan paused only when she reached the ridge of the hill, beside the long, low mound which was said to be a remnant of the Roman invasion. There, she turned to look down over the valley, her skirt heavy at her ankles, and her hair slicked to her face from the exertion.

Spider webs were glistening in the hedgerows, and a buzzard skimmed the tree-line on the far side of the valley, calling with its eerie mew. Joan fanned her fingers across her belly, expecting to feel the baby kick, but all was quiet. Now she considered it, there had been little movement since she woke this morning, as if the baby too might be making its preparations. Joan's breath settled until she was still and soundless herself, and she felt as if the air quivered with expectation.

When the first tightening came, she was prepared for its arrival, but not for the full force of its grip on her innards. She grabbed for the trunk of a slim birch, and her hands slipped across its smooth bark while she waited for the contraction to pass. A quietness, then, before the next came. So long that she had time to feel a chill, and began to think of climbing back down towards the cottage. But the tightening arrived at last, and after that second pain, the third was closer behind. By the fourth, Joan knew she would not make it down to the cottage in time. It should have been frightening, but she felt only a stoic certainty. She stamped down a hollow in the hedgerow, pushing aside the brambles and snapping what stray twigs she could, laying out the shawl to cover the worst of the rest. Her bonnet's ribbons were irritating the skin of her throat, so she stripped that off and threw it aside, pulling back her hair with a scrap of cloth instead.

She had never seen a birth – perhaps that helped – though she had seen the cattle calving on the common often enough, and heard enough of Mrs Stephens's screams some years back to understand the magnitude of it. Dropping to her hands and knees in the hollow now, looking down on her monstrous belly, she felt not unlike a beast herself. But despite her fear, she was relieved to be alone. There was a freedom here. No one to press her back against the bolster, to force her upright over a birthing stool. No one to fuss over superstition; stuffing the keyholes, untying knots and opening and shutting drawers to drive the baby out, brewing stinking caudle and pronouncing over the redemptive power of Eve's pain. Daniel, too, much as she loved him, would have been a presence hovering outside the lean-to door, coughing away his nerves and playing on hers. She was right to have broken free of the cocoon he had woven around her. She moved her knees apart now, dropping her head and groaning as another contraction passed through. A wren which had been hopping through the undergrowth took flight at it.

The tightenings came faster then, with only the briefest pauses between, and her groans were loud and deep. She wished for a cup of caudle after all, anything to help stem the pain, and she cursed aloud as each contraction reached its peak; glad, then scarcely caring that there was no one on this empty hillside to hear her coarse words. When she felt a wetness spread between her legs, she stripped off her undergarments and found them bright with splashes of fresh blood. Red cloths drying on the hillside: she thought back to that day, remembered something of the joy she'd felt to have succeeded in her ambition. She would have laughed if it weren't for the pain; what had come of all that effort? She wiped sweat from her forehead; pulled the ribbon free from her hair and shook her head like a dog. The pressure seemed to drop and what had been hot and feverish turned cold and clammy. That old curl of fear sneaked into her chest.

Mrs Freme had told her to expect it, and she tried to hold tight to that thought. 'There will be a quietness. A lull. You will have pulled the plough to the top of the hill, and all that remains is to let it carve the earth behind you as you walk home.' So she recognised that moment of calm, but even so the fear was niggling. She pushed herself up onto her knees, gripping a hawthorn branch between its long thorns to keep herself steady. May tree, fairy tree, would it bring her luck? Her thighs were wet with blood now, and her head was dizzy with the loss. What if she did not have the strength to go through with it? She could not in all honesty say that she had not expected this – the birthing – when she came up here alone today. But what if her desire for solitude and stillness had put her life and the baby's at risk?

There was no time to think beyond that. The contractions returned with new savagery, and she dropped back to her hands and knees with a grunt. Her head still spun but she clamped her jaw shut, concentrating on the pain in her hands where prickles came through the thin fabric of her shawl. It was not long before the urge to push came, and after that there was only a blur, ending with a scream as she bent between her legs to clutch at the baby who fell there.

'Joan, Joan.' Daniel's voice, a pace away then looming closer. 'Here, quick, take the baby. Have one of the women swaddle it. I don't know whether she can hear us.'

There were other voices behind. At least two women, murmuring between themselves, and then Daniel's voice again, close to her face. 'Joan, please. We need to get you home.'

'How did you find me?' She opened her eyes a crack but the torch was bright and smoky. She closed them again and turned into the shawl to breathe.

'We wouldn't have, if the light had fallen any further. You were seen, walking up the Calfway, by the lad who carries milk up to the vicar. But it was hours before I heard of it.'

Joan tried to move, then fell back groaning.

'Zounds, the blood. Can we stem it?' Daniel's hands at her thighs, pressing the damp folds of her skirt against her clammy skin as if he would mop up what had been and gone.

'Has she passed the afterburthen?' It was Mrs Wyatt, the woman who passed for the valley's midwife, but Joan would rather have heard Mrs Freme. She felt the woman drop down by Daniel's side and then a freezing draught as her skirts were prised none too gently away from her skin. Joan shivered. 'Ah yes, I see she has.'

It seemed an age while Mrs Wyatt pushed and pummelled beneath Joan's skirts, making her wince at the pain and the cold and the shame of it. If she'd had more strength in her, she might have pushed the old busybody off. But at last the woman let the sodden petticoat drop, rocking back on her heels. Joan closed her eyes again.

'Well, the girl's half frozen and she's soaked the ground with blood, but she seems well enough. She should have known not to walk out alone. And without women around her – it's not right to bear a child without a witness. Not Christian, still less correct in the eyes of the Law.' The woman would have quoted the statute, given half a chance; she was offended not to have been summoned at the due time. Joan would have laughed if she was not so weak; as if the Law would trouble itself with what went on tonight. And surely God supported childbirth in all its forms, even a lowly country girl, labouring in the shelter of a hawthorn?

'She is safe now, she will be well.' Daniel's voice was gruff and short. Joan had hurt him, she knew, by running from the preparations he'd made. She had put herself and the child at risk, but he would not show his pain here. Joan felt his hands slip under her back and then lift upwards, pulling her up and into his chest. 'She needs no witness,' he said as he got to his feet, staggering only a little, and began to walk away before the woman could say more. Joan turned her face into the damp wool of his coat, breathing the warm stink of him. She could still feel the echo of the baby's soft skin at her fingertips, and the thought comforted her. As they moved down the hillside, the rocky path lulled her to sleep a while, but when they came out of the trees, she came to again, and the absence hit her like a missing limb.

'Our girl,' she said into his chest, little more than a weak moan.

'The bairn will be fine. Harriet has her. Let's get you home.'

All the way down the path he sang to her in the half-dark: Golden Slumbers, a slow, soft song that she remembered her mother singing. She realised that in all her bravado about the birth, there had been another dread lurking: she'd feared his need for a child, afraid that it would come between them, as their marriage had come between her and the work which had brought her such fulfilment. And still now she could not yet be at peace: her mind was dizzy yet with bloodied cloths and the sagging exhaustion that followed the labour, and the baby who had been borne away by invisible arms.

But she had not anticipated the thud of love and gratitude that had come with the safe delivery of their daughter, and she heard in Daniel's voice how much he loved her. She opened her eyes a moment, saw the valley through the watery moonlight. In this place, she felt she had lived many lives already, and now it was time for the wheel to turn again. With the little girl held in her arms, safe, swaddled and warm, and Daniel's arms about them both, it should be enough. If she could let it be, then perhaps all would be well after all.

Chapter Nineteen

Joan laid the sleeping child on her back and tucked the blanket around her woollen longcoat: late autumn now, and the days were mild, but the nights already held a chill. The little girl lifted her fist to her mouth at once; Mrs Freme had said it would not be long before she cut her first tooth, and perhaps that accounted for the long nights of indignant bawling they had endured these past few days.

Joan took advantage of the peace to tidy the lean-to: everything must have its place, in a nook so small, and with Daniel running the business in amongst it all. The last curl of a strip of bacon hung from the shelf next to his yarn scales, and three small rounds of sheep cheese – bartered with a neighbour for offcuts of unfinished felt – sat on the mantle between dripping pans and a tied bundle of raw wool. Everything they owned was held in this small room, or tucked between the beams in the cramped attic above.

Drawn back to the cot by a whimper, Joan traced her finger over the downy skin of her daughter's cheek, impossibly peaceful now. How to describe the colour of her complexion? Blue veins below skin as milky pale and delicate as the fine porcelain that she'd seen on the vicar's table. But how quickly it flared to the high pink of amaranth, livid red catkins blooming across the little girl's jaw and up into the dimples beside her mouth. Joan imagined for a moment a cloth in that rich, flushed hue; where would you begin to formulate the pigment?

The child was calmer than most, or so Mrs Freme would have it, but still Joan hardly recognised herself and Daniel in the temper of a child so young. She couldn't help but think of Alice when she watched those crimson cheeks crumple in sudden outrage. It had been so long since she and her sister had spoken now and – infuriating as Alice could be – Joan felt the lack of her just as she missed their mother. Daniel had seemed to sense her sadness. He'd urged her to take her little girl into town, to introduce her to her aunt, and recently Joan had begun to think she might. But just as she had resolved to try and mend the rift, her circumstances had changed, and not even Daniel knew it yet. She sent a silent prayer for Alice's well-being now, and stroked the little girl's cheek again, winding one of her delicate curls gently around her fingertip.

Catherine, they'd called her. It had been difficult to decide on a name: both she and Daniel had nursed thoughts of naming the girl after their own mother, and though they did not debate it directly – an argument might have broken the spell which descended when she arrived in their lives – there was some unspoken agreement that neither would relent. In the end, the night before they were due up in Bisley for the churching service that would return Joan to the congregation, they'd settled on Catherine, after the Portuguese princess who had brought the Tangier colony to England as part of her dowry. Joan had been surprised Daniel had wanted to recall the horrors he'd seen in Tangier, and few had a good word to say for the foreign queen consort, but he spoke of his army days more fondly with the passage of time.

Perhaps he had sympathy, too, for one whose religion set her apart. Joan, too, had an affection for Catherine of Braganza, a woman who was known to enjoy fishing and archery, and was said to shock her pious courtiers by playing cards on a Sunday, even following the trend of sporting gentlemen's clothing that was said to be popular in court. It was ridiculous, of course, because Joan had never met the woman and never would – all this was based on the scraps of conversation she heard when taking her paddle and laundry basket down to the stream. But it was a connection of sorts, and it was a pretty enough name, she allowed, even if it only kept the peace between them.

What a journey it had been, since that night on the hillside. Joan felt she'd sunk out of sight since, like a charmed fairy-tale princess, with a small, often angry creature curled in her arms. Daniel, too, had been mesmerised by the baby, much to the further detriment of the business. But Joan had been too spellbound to care about anything but the three of them. A blissful, sleepless time, where day and night were frequently merged, and even on the warmest days, she'd sometimes seen none of the sun. These past days, though, there had been a shift; she'd felt as if she'd awoken, a sudden, ferocious awakening, as if emerging from a fog into dazzling sun.

'She is growing well.' Joan was surprised by Daniel's voice from behind her. He had been dozing by the fireside when she'd lifted the child to her breast.

'She is.' Despite all that happens around, Joan thought. Just as she'd been released from whatever strange enchantment that had overtaken her these past months, Joan had quickly realised that the business had continued its downwards spiral. There had been some lucky breaks in the early months after the birth: a large order from a London draper, and some advantageous deals, more generous than they had grown used to, with the factor who managed most of the East India Company trade. She would have liked to put it down to better management, but recently her father and Daniel had been at each other's throats again, and neither seemed to have any natural affinity for the business. It seemed more likely that luck and a temporary upturn in the overall trade had been at play. In any case, the spell of good fortune had been short-lived: their few sales since had been hard won and with tight margins, if the sparse coins in Daniel's pockets were any guide. But he still refused to show her the books, and by now their arguments were so well rehearsed, she felt she hardly needed him in the room to have them.

'Some good news came today,' he said now, coming close behind her and laying a hand on her shoulder.

She put her fingers over his. In many ways he was such a good man, with such a good heart; she must remember it. And she had been greatly moved by his tenderness with Catherine. Neither of them had been prepared for the chaos the child's arrival had wrought, but he had proved to be a gentle, generous father, just as she'd imagined. Pray that his news was something substantial; they sorely needed to raise enough to keep their rooms through the winter. If it was difficult to see how they could return to her father's cottage before, it was impossible now. Daniel's mood had been dark these past weeks and things had been tense between them, but he was smiling down into the crib: the signs were good. Perhaps it would be the opportune time to share her own news; she'd held it in for more than a week, waiting for the right occasion.

'Yes?' she said, turning to face him. It was always tempting to quiz him, but she knew from experience that he was most forthcoming when left to tell a story at his own pace.

'Last week I met a merchant in Evesham who sells cloth to the Hudson's Bay Company. They trade across Prince Rupert's land.'

'And he would trade with us?' Unable to help herself, she'd jumped in too quickly, and saw his face shut down. Impatient, and of course, she was rewarded with a frown. It was so hard to keep her own counsel.

'We got on well, but made no deal at the time. I have heard word that he visits Bisley this week, though, and has made enquiries after me in that regard.'

She shivered; it could be something, it could be everything. Sometimes she saw their livelihood as if balancing on the head of a pin, ready to be blown any way by a breath of wind. She forced herself to make light of it, kissing Daniel softly on the lips, and holding a hand to his cheek. 'Perhaps it will be the start of great things.'

He shook his head. 'Don't let us assume too much, Joan. Probably he has asked to meet all the clothiers from the valley. He will have travelled up from Bristol and there will be plenty who want to make his acquaintance. Perhaps he is a sly boots who likes to play one off against the other.'

'But you are a good judge of character, and you liked the man. I know you'll make a good impression. And our cloth speaks for itself.' Even this wasn't always true – their weavers worked hard and the fulling was almost always carried out to their specification, but her father, who took responsibility for much of the production, seemed blind to defects he would once have spotted a mile away. Sometimes Joan wondered whether his eyesight might be faltering. But Daniel would not want to be reminded of that now. It was reassurance he sought from her, not challenge, hard as that always was to accept.

He was smiling now, given the lift he needed. 'I will do my best. And pray that this man holds the key to our future.'

'Speaking of the future,' Joan took a deep breath, 'I have some news of my own.' Without thinking, her hand lifted to her belly, and so she did not have to say the words.

Daniel's mouth fell open. 'But you are still nursing.'

She nodded. 'It is not impossible, though rare.' Mrs Freme had explained.

'How long?' He grabbed for her hand, rubbed his thumb across her fingers.

'I have not bled since May Day.' She recalled the last time clearly. She had been decorating the hawthorn bushes with white ribbons, remembering blood on the white linen.

Daniel's brow dipped in a frown as he counted. 'Then we will have another in the spring.'

'I know, and how will we manage?' she started, but he was clapping his hands already, then dancing, caught up in the joy of it. In the crib, Catherine's eyes flicked open, and he quietened only long enough for the little girl's lids to droop again.

'A boy, perhaps, this time,' he whispered, his breath hot in her ear. 'Joan, we'll be a proper family. How many more shall we have, now we have started?'

And there was joy in seeing the delight on his face, as he led her over to their bed and pulled her down beside him. But for her, the wait for the quickening was little better than the dread interval before the executioner's axe fell. All those months touring the markets and fairs, touting her stock and bargaining with merchants; the dyeing, bringing colour into the cloth as if it flowed from her fingertips – it felt like a lifetime ago. What life could there be for her now?

When Joan woke later, the far side of the bed was empty and Catherine was protesting in her crib across the room, irate limbs flailing above the coarse-cut bars. Joan washed and changed the child, and then took her back to the bed, balancing a stack of bobbins on the sheet to amuse her. Daniel was gone for some hours, and the two of them fell back into a doze. When Joan woke again it was with a start. Her arm, which had lain above the covers, was chilled. She got up and had just begun to resurrect a fire with a pyramid of kindling when Daniel pushed open the door, a cloth-wrapped parcel at his elbow. Catherine squawked and lifted a chubby fist towards him, and he bent to kiss the child where her nest of downy hair formed a swirl.

'What is that you have?' Joan asked.

He shook his head, grinning. 'You'll have to wait. I've asked your father to join us.'

Joan was still teasing the fire into light when John Browning stamped in some minutes later, dropping his coat and stick and moving to warm his hands by the early flames. With the four of them inside, the room felt cramped as a hen coop, but at least it was keeping the baby entertained: Catherine's eyes were bright as she lay propped against the bolster, watching the familiar faces move in front of her.

Daniel unpacked his parcel at once. 'A celebration, sir. Come the spring, I will be a father again, God willing.'

'Another? So soon? What joy this brings!' But her father's eyes had already slid to the plate of sweetmeats Daniel was setting out, and the bottle that sat uncorked beside it. Gingerbread, sugared almonds and twists of sugared orange rind. John Browning bent low to sniff the plate, then brought the open neck of the bottle to his nose and smiled. 'Bristol Milk. Smooth and sweet.'

'Where did you get all this?' Joan began. But her father was already shifting weaving parts along the shelf to reach the cups, and Daniel had lifted a pink-shelled almond to her lips.

'Tayloe's man was down in Bristol this last week. I knew he'd have come back with a cartful, and the man can never resist an extra coin.'

But we barely have bread to last the week, she wanted to say, and the bacon curls back on itself, it runs so thin. You could have bought five cheeses for the price of those foreign sweetmeats, and Catherine needs a fresh bag of millet flour for pap, if I am not to nurse her forever. She grows so fast, and her feet poke from her long coat already. How could you be so short-sighted, to waste our last pennies on expensive sugared nuts and Spanish sherry?

But Daniel looked so happy, revealing his treasures like a trickster at the fair who pulls a tame magpie from a cloak. Part of her did warm to see it; but it made no sense to waste their money so, still less when winter and another child awaited them.

She tried to blow away her frustration, unnoticed by the two men in the hiss and spit of the now-lively fire, but it was no use: she was angry at Daniel's thoughtlessness, and the feeling would not be easily dismissed. It was too much this time. She could expect no support from her father, that was clear. 'Spoiling us, Daniel,' John Browning said, and he'd wasted no time in filling his hands with goodies. Now his nose was deep in a full cup of the liquor, and he twirled a bundle of preserved rind between his fingers.

They were gorging like kings at a banquet, but in days the shelf would be bare again. It was block-headed and it shamed her to see it. Joan turned away to busy herself with something in the corner, not trusting herself to keep silent. They kept her from the business she loved and understood, and now they would guzzle down like pigs at the trough every ounce of the goodwill and capital she had built up.

'Joan, you've barely touched anything,' Daniel said, seeming to notice her restraint at last.

'I have no appetite. The baby perhaps . . .' She held her hand to her belly again. It wasn't true, but it turned out that fury suppressed appetite as well as sickness.

'A shame, but if the baby says no, all the more for us, sir,' he said, and he chinked his cup against her father's. John Browning's mouth was stuffed full, and he grunted cheerfully in reply. Joan turned away again, sickened by their gluttony. Two simpkins, faces slick with sugar dust, and not a thought for the future between them.

Chapter Twenty

A week later, the sherry and sweets were long gone, the last of the bacon rind had been boiled up for broth, and a north wind had brought the first icy blast down into the valley. The Evesham merchant who claimed to sell cloth to the Hudson's Bay Company had turned out to be a trickster, making off with Daniel's purse and a package of first-rate broadcloth. They had barely eaten a thing for days: Joan could feel the angle of her hips jut from under her skirt, her milk ran thin and the baby cried from hunger. Now, as she knelt to put on her boots, intending to scan the hedgerows for anything worth eating, her vision spun and raced until she put a hand out to the table leg to steady herself.

She had no choice but to go out, though. Daniel wouldn't like it; she didn't have to ask him to imagine his frown of irritation, the same frown that emerged every time she put to him some small scheme to improve their position: pretty dyed handkerchiefs that she could sell amongst the women of the valley, laundry she could take in from the millsmen, baked goods that she could sell at the Michaelmas fair. All fell on deaf ears, as if there might be some disrespect in trying to make a little money, in trying to survive. Could he not see that this Arctic wind might bring snow any day, and with nothing in the larder, then they would truly starve?

But today there might be bullaces still left on the tree at Hell Corner, where Dimmel's Dale met the Frome. A high wind had brought the beech masts down all around – she could collect a skirt-full if they'd not all been harvested for the pigs. Just as she picked up the baby to dress her, though, there was a knock on the door. The visitor on the threshold was engulfed in a red wool cape. The hood fell low to hide her face, but something about her stance gave her away. Joan's mouth fell open.

'Alice?' She was almost sure it was her sister, but the hood was so deep, she could not be certain. It was fastened at the neck with a gold enamel pin, and the colour: rich as cherry flesh. Dyed with those strange beetles, perhaps, and how many of the tiny creatures must have been crushed in order to magic that rich red, not far from the livid crimson she had dreaded and admired on Catherine's cheeks. It was a shade so at odds with the fading autumn green all around, it was as if something alien had landed in the valley.

When Alice slipped the flawless felt back over her shoulders, Joan saw that for all her finery, her sister had changed little. Thinner, perhaps, and painted like a doll. Enamel drop earrings hung in her ears, to match the cloak pin. The cloak might be opulent enough for a gentlewoman, but it seemed to Joan that it sat strangely on Alice's shoulders: the colour clashed with her eyes and did little for her complexion, bringing out only the unnatural circles of rouge on each cheekbone. 'Come in. Please,' Joan urged.

Alice nodded, and followed her. Inside, Catherine was protesting at the draught from the door, thumping the wooden boat shuttle that passed for a rattle against the sides of her crib and wailing. But when the child caught sight of Alice, who bent low and put a finger out to be clasped in her fist, her mouth crinkled into a wide smile.

'It's been a long time.' Joan watched her sister making her daughter laugh. Strange how even the smallest children feel that instant connection with some and not with others; it was as if the two had known each other forever. Catherine was drumming her feet on the muslin sheet in delight at this new, exotic creature, whose earrings caught the glow of the rushlight and must have seemed like stars hung above her.

Alice said nothing for a long time. For a while she continued to make faces for the little girl, but when she tired of that, she unfastened her cloak and set it down on the bed. Even then, she paused to grimace at the untidy quilt before speaking. 'I was very hurt,' she said at last.

'At the wedding?'

'Yes, at the wedding.'

'Alice, I have apologised so many times. All those times you would not see me, and when you did, you seemed not to hear. My letters . . .' Joan started, but Alice spoke over her.

'Not content with commandeering my day with the spectacle of Daniel's return, you tarnished the sanctity of my union with Walter in order to tidy up your own sordid attachment.'

Joan gasped. 'That is unfair. Daniel had no knowledge of the wedding, and I had no knowledge of his return. And to describe it as sordid? We had not lain together . . .'

Alice made that face again, her eyes drifting back to the ruffled bed.

Joan took a deep breath. 'Daniel and I were promised to each other, and the blessing was a consecration. I wish Aunt Anne had not pressed the vicar to conduct the service there and then, but I promise you, I had no part in it. Please, Alice, understand that I wished only happiness for you in your marriage. I had no thought of usurping your celebrations.'

Alice removed one glove, and then the other. New, palest kidskin, flawless even though she must have been on the road since dawn; gloves barely more robust than the skin they protected, for hands that were never sullied with any labour more taxing than embroidery. Alice laid them across her palm with exaggerated care, looking about for somewhere to lay them and apparently finding nowhere adequate. The lean-to was a little disordered – between the darning and the carding, the laundry and the cooking, not to mention attending to the child, there rarely seemed to be a moment to tidy it, even if there had been space to put everything away – but Joan was no sloven. Alice would find no lice or vermin here, never mind that her sour expression said otherwise.

'We will never agree on it, but no matter,' Alice said at last, tucking the gloves away in a pocket hidden in her gown instead. 'I have not come to rehearse these arguments again.'

'Then why have you come?' Joan said, regretting her harsh tone at once. It would do her no favours with her sister, she knew that from long experience. 'Can I serve you something?' she added quickly. Joan scanned her shelves, desperate for anything that might find approval. Her eye found the jug above the hearth, a last cupful saved to make milk-broth for Catherine's supper. 'Milk, perhaps, or nettle tea?'

Alice made a noise that might have been a snort of laughter, and gave no other response. But she came a little further into the room, lowering herself onto a corner of the bed, wincing as the densely packed straw must have pressed through her petticoats. She lifted a hand to undo her bonnet, and now Joan saw how thin her sister's arms were, and she wondered at the marks she saw there.

There'd been some words said once, down by the stream, about Walter and how free he was with his hands, but Joan had hoped it was idle gossip. When she had visited Alice in town, even on the single occasion she had been briefly admitted to the house,

Alice had acted so proud and haughty, it had seemed ridiculous that she might be anything less than mistress of the household. But now, seeing how the nub of her forearms protruded from the flesh above her hands, at how those pink welts had found themselves around her wrists, Joan wondered at the state of her sister's marriage. It seemed impossible that Alice would tolerate such things, but then Joan thought back to that first day in the Lamb Inn – to the elegant, provocative Miss Boule, with her long black gloves and her pointed boots – at the lack of respect Walter had shown Alice then, the casual disregard he seemed to have for his intended.

'Perhaps later,' Alice said now, laying the fine lace straps of her bonnet in her lap, one over the other. She seemed hesitant all of a sudden, and so Joan kept her silence, waiting for her sister to say her piece. 'I find myself in need of a little help,' Alice said at last.

Joan's gaze drifted back to her sister's skeletal wrists, but Alice caught her eye and glared so sharply, tucking them under the cover of her bonnet, Joan understood that that subject would not be discussed. 'What is it I can do?' she asked instead, keeping her voice as light and open as possible.

'Father says you are with child again,' Alice began, staring at Joan's waist, where no doubt the thickening could be seen in the strain on the hem. Her belly had swelled so much more quickly this time. She resisted the urge to put her hands there, but there should be no shame in it.

'You have seen him then?' she said instead.

'I met him on the path from Blackness. He is looking older. I do not remember his eyes so rheumy. As well you are having children young, because it may not be long until you have an invalid to attend to.'

Joan ignored this. All conversations with Alice were the same, like freeing an injured beast from a snare. Like Rockwood, trapped under those beams, all those years ago, it was necessary to wait until the hackles were lowered and the worst of the growling was past. Poor old boy, Rockwood, now so old his eyelashes covered his eyes and he barely moved from the fire. 'It is early yet,' Joan said instead, 'too early, truth be known, to have spread the news. But my husband was unable to contain his gladness.'

There must have been some note of discontent in the way she said it, because Alice's eyebrow shot up at once. 'Don't tell me there is discord in paradise?'

Joan's patience would be tested today, she saw that already. 'What is it I can do for you, Alice?'

Alice slumped back on the bed now, staring up at the beams and mouthing as if counting the wormholes there. In her crib, Catherine stared up at the same beams, pawing at invisible shapes in the air. If nothing else, the unfamiliar voice was a welcome distraction for the child; this was the most fractious time of day.

'Is your witchy friend still living in the valley?' Alice said eventually.

Joan breathed out her irritation. 'Mrs Freme is no more a witch than you or I.' Alice had been in the room for a bare few minutes, but already it was as if they were transported back to their young days.

'But you know who I mean,' her sister said, pulling a curl in front of her eyes and examining it minutely.

'What would you want of her? The widow bears no ill will towards anyone.'

'Then surely she will want to help.'

'And what is it you need, exactly?'

Alice pushed herself upright, and arranged herself more formally on the bedside, her expression suddenly as composed as if she was calling on the vicar's wife. 'Put simply, I do not seem to have your luck in conceiving.'

Joan flushed. It was not what she had been expecting. 'And you have been trying,' she said when she had recovered her composure. 'I mean . . .'

Alice laughed. It was the teasing giggle Joan recognised from their childhood, but it sounded hollow now. Alice's heart was not in it. Perhaps her distress was genuine. 'We have been trying, as you put it, for some time,' Alice said. 'So long that Walter grows tired of waiting. He comes to me with all manner of suggestions, from his sisters and his mother, so much so that I begin to feel like a joint of meat on the Sunday table.'

'What sort of suggestions?'

'Times. Durations. Positions. Bizarre rituals to be performed before, during or after the act. Preparations to be rubbed on the neck of my womb or over his member.' Joan had been feeling pained for her sister, but the deliberate relish with which Alice said the last found its mark. Her cheeks flushed and Alice laughed again. 'Joan, you are a married woman now, and you grew up in the fields. Surely there is little about the deed of copulation that can embarrass you?'

Joan ignored this. 'And you continue to bleed?' she asked, finding some comfort in mimicking the formal voice of a physician. 'There have been no gaps in your monthlies, and they are regular in their term?'

'Since they began.'

'Have you prayed . . .?' Joan started.

'Don't, please,' Alice replied. 'I have enough from his mother about God, and how my unclean womb must have so displeased Him that he has stopped the seed in its journey from womb to stone. Rarely enough is she seen in the church, let it be known, because she dislikes the hours spent in company of the flea-ridden masses and her fat legs do not enjoy the walk back up the hill after, yet it comes easily to criticise the purity or otherwise of my organs.' The neat outline of Alice's circles of rouge bled outwards into angry crimson clouds.

'And have you seen a midwife?'

Alice snorted. 'The woman in Stroud is mad and old. She talks of bathing in ash-water, and allowing a husband to defile the bed with urine pissed through a wedding ring.'

'Another, then.'

'Mrs Freme will do. If you are to be believed, she doesn't bear the witch's mark, but I have seen and heard enough to know she has knowledge of healing herbs that may be of benefit to me.'

'Perhaps, but she professes no expertise in midwifery as far as I'm aware,' Joan said, conscious of her sister's dwindling patience but determined to understand Alice's insistence on the widow. 'Doubtless she has attended births as a gossip, along with other women of the valley, but no more than that. It is Mrs Wyatt who has the most knowledge of the practice in this valley, and a manual that she calls on, but even she has no licence from the bishop. You might be better travelling to Gloucester: certainly there will be women there – men too – who are better versed in the promotion of fertility.'

Alice threw her bonnet aside, clearly exasperated. 'How would I explain the trip to Walter? He is all too aware of our situation and I don't want to press home the idea of my redundancy as a wife. Barren. Like a lone apple tree that stands fruitless on a hilltop. His ugly sister Margaret was so bold as to say I should feel lucky he has no children elsewhere! That I could be like the queen consort, Catherine, forced to watch as her husband sires women in every corner of his kingdom. But rather that than be fat and haggard, with brats hanging off my skirts and a belly that is so distended from carrying them, it must be scooped up like a roll of dough into her stays.' Alice grimaced, as if she sucked an unripe pear.

Joan glanced across at her daughter, feeling as if she should close the child's ears. But the little girl was still content in her cot, amused by their voices and by the fan of chicken feathers that Joan had hung above her to spin in the draught. Had Alice really said all that to her sister-in-law, or had she managed to hold her tongue? If it was the latter, perhaps her sister had grown up a little after all. 'Not Gloucester then,' Joan said, 'somewhere nearer. There must be licensed midwives all over who would be well placed to help you.'

'The money, though – how would I account for it? Perhaps you don't understand: Walter likes to know my whereabouts, and while he is generous, every penny must be accounted for. No, it must be here – he thinks nothing of me coming here, puzzled only that I would choose to revisit my sorry roots – and it must cost nothing. But I'll not have that old busybody Wyatt with her scratchy nails and wormtail hair near me. It's Widow Freme or none at all.'

Joan knew the set of that jaw; better to give up now while Alice's temper was still contained. 'Shall we go now, then, if you are resolved to see her? I can make Catherine ready.'

Alice slumped back onto the bolster again. 'I would rather you went alone.'

Joan shook her head. 'But how can Mrs Freme judge your condition, if you are nowhere to be seen? She has no crystal ball, despite all your mocking.'

'You know enough to tell her. Let her mull on that. And for my part I will act on whatever she sends word to do.' Easily thrown off the tongue, but even that seemed doubtful. Alice had taken full possession of the bed now, and it occurred to Joan how rarely her sister did not get what she wanted. Little wonder then, that the events on Alice's wedding day had caused her such aggravation, and the surprise should only be that she had come round at all.

Joan glanced towards the cot, but Alice had an answer for that too: 'Leave the child with me if it is easier.'

So here was a chance to mend the bridge between them, and it would be no great hardship to walk the quarter mile along the river path to Mrs Freme's place. If it earned Joan her sister's goodwill, then it would be more than worth it.

'I will not be long,' Joan said, but she closed the door on them with some reluctance.

Chapter Twenty-One

'I am no more a midwife than you are a chemist, though if there were ever a person more suited to the understanding of the way this world's humors and particles mix and blend and spark it would be you.'

They were in Mrs Freme's back room. The widow had set up a makeshift table there – three planks between two barrels – and set a trivet for the cauldron upon it, where she was boiling up late plums to strip the stones from them, ready for jamming. She lifted a sticky finger from the pan to emphasise her point. The air was thick with the sweet flesh of the fruit and Joan tried to swallow down her hunger.

'She'll have none of it. It's you or no one.'

'And what if I say no?' Mrs Freme dropped a handful of the plum stones into a jar beside the pot, and they clattered against the sides. Joan said nothing for a moment. It was an imposition, of course, to have asked, and how could Mrs Freme understand her need to appease her sister, when all she had seen of Alice was malice and disruption? But the widow went on: 'Don't answer that. It's enough that you have come. You will have your reasons. But to offer any view, when I have not set eyes on the girl for more than a year? It seems like madness.'

'It makes no sense, I know, but she is resolved.'

'Then you must give me all that you know, and I will give in return the modicum of knowledge I can profess to hold.'

'Thank you.'

Mrs Freme shook her head. 'I can't help but feel that no good will come of this, but I will not deny you. But come on, tell me what she told you.'

Joan took a deep breath. 'Alice is slender – slighter than on her wedding day – but otherwise seems in good health. There is nothing to suggest that her humors are not in balance, and her monthly terms are regular and constant.'

'Her mood?'

'Variable.' A euphemism, of course. Volatile would be closer to the truth. 'But no more than usual,' Joan went on. But as she spoke, she found herself possessed with a concern that twisted in her belly – extreme but familiar: she felt the absence of her child like a sudden pain. Was it wise, to have left Catherine in Alice's care? Joan had been reluctant, but now she thought back, Alice had all but bundled her out of the door. She reflected with growing unease of all the things that could go wrong. Alice had no experience with babies – unlike most of the girls in the valley, the two of them had not grown up with younger siblings at their hips – and she was hardly known for her patience or her constancy. What if she tired of the child, and simply left her there alone? Daniel would not return until nightfall. But then Alice would not want to miss Joan's return – perhaps that was the only shred of comfort she could draw on.

'Her eyes: are they clear?' Mrs Freme was asking now, and Joan forced herself to concentrate. She thought back to the way Alice had fixed her gaze when her eye had drifted towards her sister's wrists. Grey-green, mother's eyes. 'Bright, yes, and not shot with blood,' she said. Perhaps she should mention the marks she'd seen, but some uncalled-for loyalty to Alice made her bite her tongue.

'And . . . forgive me but . . . she understands what is required in order to bring the seed of man and woman together?'

Jane kept her eyes on the surface of the pan, where the remaining plum stones bobbed in the syrupy juice. 'I believe she knows well what is required.'

'Good. And he – Walter – is in good health too, I assume, otherwise she would not have come to you. It sounds to me, then, that it is just a matter of the passage of time. But from my scant knowledge of your sister, I suspect that will come as little consolation.'

Joan nodded in agreement. She could only imagine the reception she would get if she returned with the advice to keep trying. Much as she wanted to get back to Catherine, she must dig a little deeper.

'Is there no remedy that may accelerate the conception?'

Mrs Freme sighed deeply. 'It is surely Mrs Wyatt Alice should be consulting, not me. I have had no children of my own.'

Joan so wanted to stop her friend there, to take this opportunity to ask her why. Joan longed to probe a little, remembering the little paper patterns Mrs Freme had lent her when she had been preparing for Catherine's arrival; they knew each other so well, but so much about the older woman remained untold. Had there been children, who had not survived, or had she and Samuel found themselves unable to conceive them? Of course, it could be that Mrs Freme had taken steps to avoid a pregnancy – she'd known enough to advise Joan back when she'd needed it – or perhaps that Samuel wouldn't countenance it. Joan had heard enough snippets about the man's temper over the years; had he been worried that he might hurt a child? But there were lines in Joan's relationship with the widow – there always had been – and she must continue to respect them. Mrs Freme was as candid as she wanted to be, and no more, and Joan could see in her expression that she had said all she wanted to say on the subject. 'So my knowledge is limited to the back pages of herbals and kitchen manuals,' Mrs Freme went on, her voice a little brisk now. 'At least Mrs Wyatt has the books to call on.'

'Alice will have none of Mrs Wyatt.'

'Then let's make a note of the little I know, though it'll scarce be worth your ink to take it down,' she said, nodding towards the paper in Joan's hand and the quill pen and pot she had set down on the table edge. 'Strange to me to think of Alice wanting a child – forgive me if that seems harsh, but she never seemed the mothering type. Still, take this down, for what it's worth.'

'Thank you.'

'Let's see then . . . the time after the monthly term is the most fertile time, as you'll know, and good use should be made of it. Remind her of that for starters. As for remedies: there's a man in Bristol – Sermon is his name – who advocates the use of all manner of eccentric elixirs: hare spittle, tryphera magna, a treacle of mouse ears, to name but a few.'

Joan's nib scratched against the page torn from her logbook as she tried to keep up. She had prepared enough ink to fill her pocket vial, but her quill would soon need sharpening and now she realised she had left her knife on the shelf back at home. 'But you'll not need those potions,' Mrs Freme went on, dismissing Joan's careful notes with a wave of her hand. 'Balderdash, the lot of it. Sermon seems like a man prone to blowing his own horn, and I am not convinced of the research he has conducted into his recommendations. Perhaps his ways will appeal to one such as your sister, but I do not favour such extreme and hard-won remedies myself. Better, simply, to eat an early supper, and be sure to obtain a good night's sleep.'

'Anything else?' Without Sermon's elixirs, the list was brief, and it would not serve her well to go back to Alice short-handed.

Mrs Freme stirred the pot, staring down as if looking for inspiration amid the steam. 'When the husband lies with her, he should take his time – you'll be aware that both partners must enjoy the act in order for the seed from both to be imparted, and he has his role to play in that.' Joan felt her cheeks begin to pink, but the widow was in full flow now and did not pause in her directions. 'The blockage, of course, may lie with Walter; such matters are rarely discussed, and perhaps she is cautious to mention it.'

Joan laughed. 'I have never known a subject on which Alice is reluctant to speak her mind.'

'You know your sister best, and I have no doubt you are right. But because women are colder than men in their constitution, and therefore more susceptible to diseases of the flesh, it is often assumed that a barren woman is thus for her own fault. Not always so. A man of choleric temperament such as Walter may need some balance in his humors if his seed is to travel as it should. If she can, Alice should keep from his diet those foods likely to worsen the imbalance: cloves, capers, rabbit and goat. She might consider foods that may induce and stir up lust, by all means: game birds, almonds, currants. Some swear by strong wines, taken in moderation.'

That was more like it; even Alice should be satisfied with instructions of such particularity.

'Ground acorns, parsnips and artichokes may all stimulate the blood in his yard. A tincture of sage may assist in the balancing of her own humors, though it must be taken in moderation: too much can have the effect of bringing on the monthly term.'

Joan scratched away with her tired nib, and when she had finished her transcription, she looked up to find the widow working at the jam pot again. Fat steam-clouds came off it as she turned the glutinous maroon liquid over with her ladle.

'That's me done, and I think I am ready,' Mrs Freme said, turning to set it back on the stove and grunting with the weight. Then she took a small jar from a row arranged along the windowsill.

'It will not be set, but will you take some home for yourself? I've half a loaf you can take with it.'

'Only if you can spare it,' Joan said, half hypnotised by the pot which had quickly recovered to a rolling boil. The sweetness in the air was so intense, she felt she could taste the jam already.

Mrs Freme nodded, tying a muslin square over the jar with a length of twine. 'Save a little in the bottom of the jar. Then a spoonful on the child's lips if she's teething. By the time she's licked it off, she'll have forgotten what it was that got her mewling.' She handed the covered jar over to Joan, along with a hunk of bread in a paper wrap. 'And as for Alice, you wish her well, but the next time that girl has you running her errands, you think twice before doing her bidding.'

As always, it was hard to argue with Mrs Freme, and it was hardly the first time Joan had rolled over when Alice had called, but she felt better for having come. She kissed the older woman on the cheek as she turned about. If it healed the breach between her and her sister, it was no great hardship to trip along the riverbank and take advice from a friend. And there was the other thing too – those marks on her wrists, and something about Alice's bearing, that told her all was not as it should be – if Joan could do her part to help her, she must. It was what their mother would have wanted. But now, she would hurry back along the valley to retrieve her daughter.

By the time Joan reached the lean-to, she had recovered some of her composure. The building was still standing, and her sister's basket still sat on the step, and even Alice would not be so foolish as to leave a child unattended. So Joan didn't walk in through the door at once, but leant a minute at the side window as she often did. The seal had come away and left room for a fierce draught she had not got round to fixing, but it made for a good listening window, and she always liked to hear Catherine's contended burble and coo before the little girl caught sight of her and began to fret. Joan had all but forgotten that Alice was there, so it was a shock when she leaned close to the window's lead frame and heard her sister's voice close by on the other side. The bed was pushed up against this wall, so she'd not moved far, but her voice was low and husky, and it was clear at once that it wasn't Catherine she was addressing.

'It's a shame, a man like you, having to scrape a living in this grubby valley.' The groan and rustle of the straw mattress then, as if Alice was turning over. 'I expect they had the greatest respect for you in the regiment. They'll have looked up to you, valued you – I can well imagine it. I'm surprised you came back at all.'

'They liked me well enough. But I was never an army man. I grew tired of it eventually.' Daniel's voice was fainter, as if from the far side of the room. Tell her you came back for me, Joan almost said aloud. She felt the casual disloyalty like a bruise. But Alice wasn't done yet.

'I remember you saying you didn't have it in you to kill a man. Did you, when the time came? I expect it came soon enough, with those dirty Moors all around. Hot and dry and angry, that's how I picture it. Did you take a man down, Daniel?'

'We all did. We had to. I'd not have come back if I hadn't.' His voice was even, impassive, and still distant. He was over by Catherine's cot, Joan assumed. There was no sound from the little girl, but perhaps she had fallen back to sleep. Joan wished she held her in her arms now, for the comfort.

'And how did it feel?' Alice's voice had dropped lower still. Syrupy as that jam in the pot. 'Did it make the blood rise up in your yard?'

There was a cough and Daniel said something inaudible. Joan felt nausea rise in her throat. She should stride in right now, but her feet seemed glued to the soil. She heard Alice's mocking laugh as if she alone was meant to.

'So shy, still, Daniel. I like that. And I like the thought of you, with your hands astride another man's throat. Is that so wrong?'

'We are all driven by base urges. I saw enough in Tangier to know that.' He sounded closer, as if he'd taken a pace towards her.

'And that's how it's done, is it, when the fighting reaches close quarters: one man's hands on another? Come here and show me, Daniel. Put your hands so around my neck, that I can feel the urgency of it.'

Joan put her hand to her own throat without thinking. There was another cough, and the sound of a chair being pulled up. '"Death, that hath suck'd the honey of thy breath".' Daniel's voice again, quoting something in an actor's intonation. Shakespeare, probably, though how strange to think he knew enough to quote the score. 'Have I remembered the lines?' he went on now. 'A travelling company came out to Tangier, commissioned by the Earl for the birth of his first child. They performed *Romeo and Juliet* on the turret walls of the fortress.' And yet he had never once mentioned it to Joan. It was as if her husband had been replaced by a stranger.

'A man such as Shakespeare can put beauty into the darkest things,' Alice said. Joan could imagine the arch of her eyebrow as she said it.

'Indeed. But I will not put my hands about your neck, Alice. I have been too close to death, I do not wish to rehearse it.'

Joan could hear Daniel's voice more clearly now, and it too was strange: wooden, strangled, as if he held himself under the tightest control. Then there was silence a moment, just the crunch of the mattress again. Alice, and what was she doing now?

'Then put your hands on me anyway, Daniel. I can see in your eyes how much you want to. Come here and show me how an army man treats his woman.'

It was enough. Joan pushed herself away from the lean-to's crumbling masonry and strode round to the door. Inside, it was as if a play had been interrupted, Alice and Daniel its frozen leads. Her sister, in the bed, lay undressed to her stays, covered only by the quilt across her lower legs. And Daniel was frozen in motion, halfway across the room, having left his chair and reaching out towards the mattress. It was he who recovered himself first, dropping his arm and bracing his limbs as if coming to attention.

'I wanted to lift the quilt to cover her,' he said.

'Only now?' His brow crumpled but she went on. 'I have been at the window these last few minutes. I heard it all.'

'It must look strange, I see that. Must have sounded stranger. But she told me her gown had been soiled by Catherine. That you had told her to rest under the covers while it dried by the fire. I was not prepared for her to throw the quilt aside.'

It was possible he was telling the truth – even in her fury she realised that – but the rage that had taken hold of her would not be dispelled so easily.

'I heard quite enough. She cast modesty aside when she begged you to put your hands on her neck the first time. Why did you not bid her to leave then? No, not bid her, why did you not compel her? Throw her across the threshold. Zooks, Daniel. How could you let the witch remain in our house?'

Joan thought how ugly she must look; anger pulsed in her temples as if the vital blood below the skin surged against the fabric of her veins. But Alice . . . Alice was uglier, surely, with her jealous thoughts and her malicious ways. Joan had no need to turn her head to know that her sister still wore only her undergarments, that she had made not the slightest attempt to cover her nakedness.

'It is not the first time your sister has made lewd suggestions. I had no thought of acting on them. I had hoped only to keep the peace until you returned.'

'Your excuses are thin as barley water. As if I would want her in my house, when she behaves in this way. You should have thrown her out at once, not waited for her to bare her breasts.'

Daniel hung his head. He took a step towards the crib.

'Don't!' He would not take comfort from their child, while her own heart was broken. 'Let her rest,' she said more gently. Catherine, at least, should sleep on.

Joan had barely glanced at Alice's face yet, but now her head was turned by a low laugh from the bed.

'The gape-seed of you, mouth gurning like a millpond carp! How Walter will hoot when I tell him. It was a jest, simply a jest. You never learned how to take a joke.' Alice rolled her eyes in a theatrical shrug. I should have never let her cross the threshold, Joan thought. *I can't help but feel that no good will come of this*, Mrs Freme had said, and she should have listened. 'Ignore her, Daniel, she was always like this.' Alice was sliding on her gloves from the floor beside the bed, fitting one finger after another, taking her time as if it was the final accessory to her outfit and that she wasn't lying back in a loosely laced corset and slip, her breasts clearly visible between the slack ribbons. 'A mulligrubs for attention, our mother used to despair.'

'You begged him to take you. Where is the comedy in that?' This was Alice all over, drawing you into an argument, when her actions were so contemptible, there should have been no discussion at all.

'Take a moment to compose yourself, little sister,' Alice said, nastily. 'You are making a show of yourself. Perhaps there was a little flirtation between us, but what can you expect, when he comes home each night to find you moaning that the shelves are still bare and the baby's bawling? And can you honestly say that your eye has never been turned yourself?'

That last did it. 'Enough. Out!' Joan shouted it with an assertion that would have had the millboys running, but Alice only smiled, easing herself upright with the pace of a vixen stretching in a patch of sun. With her elbows held close to her sides, the corset gaped more as she sat and Daniel coughed uneasily, turning halfway towards the fire. Alice laughed at his back. Joan felt a sharp twist in her belly, as if something tore; no, not that. Surely Alice could not take the unborn child too?

'Look at him,' Alice said. 'So afraid to glimpse another woman's bubbies, lest he's reminded of the poor substitute he has at home. And now even that has a question over it. Do you know your wife as well as you think, Daniel? Ask her, sometime, if she has ever caught another's eye.'

'Get out. You sicken me.' Daniel, finally, and a real anger in his voice. How had it taken so long for him to speak up? What had he been thinking? What was he thinking now, with Alice's heinous suggestions? But at last here he was, wrenching the unspoiled gown from the rack by the fire and tossing it towards the bed. He wheeled away then and stood with arms folded beside the door-frame, muscles clenching in the flesh of his jaw.

'You never told me what your witch-friend told you, Joan,' Alice said, as she lowered her gown over her head and picked up the red cloak from where it lay beside the cot. She spoke as casually as if none of the last hour had come to pass, as if they had met by chance beside the pond and paused a moment to pass the time of day. She slipped the cloak over her shoulders, taking her time with the brooch that fastened it. 'I'll be at Father's until the morning,' she said, looking up at last. 'Walter's carriage comes to Bisley at noon. Do come, we can talk then, when you've had a chance to calm yourself.'

Joan closed her eyes a moment, letting a hot wave of fury wash over her and away. She could no longer divine what was real: had there been any truth in Alice's plea for help, or had she strung Joan along from the start? Perhaps Mrs Freme had had something, when she'd spoken earlier of the male imbalance – did Alice seek from Daniel what Walter couldn't give? She wasn't sure whether it was better or worse that such a betrayal might be grounded not in passion but in the desperate urge for a child. And Daniel: was her husband true to her? She could scarcely think what might have happened if she had not burst in when she did. Broken with sleeplessness, it was more than she could bear to contemplate it all. Alice, though – her sister's betrayal was crystal clear.

Joan opened her eyes, fixing her gaze on her sister. It was wasted breath, to raise your voice to her. Better to use the silky voice of contempt that Alice favoured herself; perhaps it was all she could understand. 'Mrs Freme's no more a witch than you are,' Joan said with icy calm. 'And it wouldn't surprise me if your womb was cursed. You'll not see me tomorrow, and I hope we never speak again.'

Chapter Twenty-Two

Joan opened her eyes to a strip of clear blue between the top of the window frame and the roof of the drying house next door. She kept as quiet as she could as she rose from the bed, and Daniel didn't stir as she padded round the lean-to in stockinged feet, piling on layers and pulling boxes and rolls and parcels from shelves and corners. Catherine wriggled sleepily as Joan bundled her into a sling fashioned from a leftover strip of broadcloth. Harriet, who had safely delivered a little boy of her own, had once showed Joan how to tie it so that the baby was secure but not short of breath, and Mrs Freme had given her a pin to fasten the fabric ends on her shoulder. When Joan pushed it through the coarse fabric now, it reminded her of the pin that had fastened Alice's cloak. This simple iron ring brooch and Alice's gold enamel cameo: what different turns their lives had taken. She swallowed away the bitterness that came from thinking of her sister.

Daniel rolled onto his back and began snoring with open mouth. They'd talked until late into the night, whispering in the last glow of the rushlight, rehearsing at his insistence the events of the afternoon until she felt that she had watched it as if it was played by a company of actors and still had less sense of what was real. It was Alice, of course, who should shoulder most of the blame – that much was clear. Alice, like a hunting spider, pulling others into her funnel web. And there was no doubting Daniel's contrition, his pain for hers, his regret at a lapse in loyalty he could only half deny. She was left to bring up Alice's slanderous remarks about her own devotion – perhaps he was too contrite even to mention them – and when she did, he accepted her explanation of the encounter with William Thrupp at once, not questioning her constancy. But Joan was left with a sour taste in her mouth. Something good had been soiled. Perhaps it would pass, and time would heal. But there was a splash of bright blood on her petticoats when she dressed; if the child was displaced, ripped from her by this conflict, it was difficult to see how anything could be the same again.

When she was ready at last, Joan chipped a corner of cheese from the rind and took a crust for Catherine to suck. She pulled the door behind her, leaving Daniel unconscious on the bolster. She retraced her route of the night before, all the way along the river path along to Mrs Freme's, with the tools and tins she'd tied to her waist clanking together with each step, despite her best efforts to move soundlessly. When she got to the widow's door, there was no answer to her gentle knock, so Joan slipped into the garden through the side gate, silently begging her friend's forgiveness as she pulled a handful of madder roots from the plant at the furthest edge of the beds. She would explain later, and bring something for Mrs Freme in return.

She closed the gate behind her and took the path up towards the stepped grassy banks of the lynches. Against her chest, Catherine sighed and closed her eyes again. The child had kept Joan close to home these past months, so she was no longer as fit as she had been; as she climbed the bank now, Catherine's weight strained the muscles of Joan's lower back, even with the support of the sling. But she was determined and kept up her pace, her hair dampening around her face. Halfway up the hill she met the donkey track, and followed it on up towards her father's place.

At the fork just below the cottage, she rested a moment under the sole oak that stood there, kneeling to gather up some of the wrinkled galls that had fallen with the acorns. A sound from the other path caught her attention and she peered up through the coppices. A thin rope of smoke was rising from her father's chimney. She could just imagine Alice in there, with her stockinged feet lifted to the fire. Hands cupped around the last of her father's milk. *Do come, we can talk then.* Joan adjusted the sling on her hip, took a slug of water from her flask, and stamped on past up the hillside.

It took longer than she'd hoped – the winter sun was lifting a little steam from the grass when Joan reached her destination. She unwrapped Catherine and lifted her carefully from the sling. She spread the fabric across the ground by way of a blanket and laid the little girl down there, a few paces away from where she planned to work. The child was well-wrapped for the cold and seemed content enough, awake now and staring up at the half-bald trees, lifting one foot after the other to try and pull off her stockings. Joan watched her a minute and then straightened up, ready for the task in hand. Some of that earlier bitterness was slipping away already, with the prospect of what lay ahead. It had been far too long.

Late May she'd been here last, just before the wedding, and the grass had already been high. A year and a season on, the meadow was dying back for the winter. What had been verdant green was slumping in sickly pale drifts, clinging to Joan's boots as she waded through it. A bank of nettles had grown up in the copse of trees where she had hidden the tin bath and the other dyeing equipment, but she stamped them down and soon found what she was looking for. Not the bath, which she had dragged back down into the valley that same day, but a smaller basin, and under it a cloth-wrapped bundle with more tools: a knife, two hanging weights and a measuring cup; a pestle, for crushing roots, and the cupped stone she had heaved from the stream to serve as a mortar. She'd missed the paring knife at home since, but she had not wanted to come here before now and so she had made do with a blunter one. She turned the tools over in her hands, remembering the joy of that day and the one after: *It's as fine a red as I've seen. I wouldn't mind a coat of it myself*, her father had said, and her heart had surged to hear it. But what poison might Alice be pouring into his ears now, even as Joan crouched here?

Enough, she had not come here to mourn or grouse. Joan pulled the bundle of yarn from her pocket – no time or money for broadcloth, but this would suffice for now – and from the other, three small vials that she'd pulled from the roll of muslin under the bed before leaving: alum, turmeric and a quarter-full jar of cochineal, the last of the quantity she had bargained for so long ago. With them was wrapped the logbook. All of these she placed in a neat circle beside a bare patch of soil where she'd light the fire. She'd had no money or time to acquire lime, but perhaps there was an alternative which would serve as a fixer. Fire first, though. When her flint spark had set flames amongst the bundled leaves and kindling, she walked over to the copse and, glancing all about her first, lifted her petticoats and squatted, sending up a little cloud of steam as the stream of hot urine struck the base of the empty jar.

A wait, then, while the fire swelled. Joan set logs in a pyramid above the kindling, and when they had begun to take, she pulled three stones from the low wall by the stream and set them up around the fire to form a rough trivet for the tin basin. When the logs were glowing, she washed the basin in the stream and set it on the triangle of stones, then tracked back and forth for more water until the basin was half full. She pored over the recipe book – the proportions would never be right, she would have to make do with what she had, but at least she could follow the processes she had so faithfully copied from the dye books Alice had procured for her. Some good must come out of all this.

Soon the water was boiling and Joan began. The rest was pounding, crushing, dipping. Soaking, simmering, cooling. Rinsing, dipping again. While Catherine looked on, chewing on the boat shuttle that she loved to press against her gums, Joan toiled until her hands were red and sore, and the strands of hair at her temples had turned to ringlets in the steam.

Without all the compounds the Dutch and Italian dye-men required, or where they differed, she was obliged to guess and estimate many aspects of the processes, submerging the yarn five times in differing combinations of liquor so as to give it the best chance of taking the colour. But at last the final dip was done, and when the liquor was cool enough to pour away, she took the armful of sodden yarn and pulled rocks from the stream to leave a channel deep enough to rinse it. The quantity did not merit taking down to the Frome to be paddled on the slatted platforms in the leat there, and part of her feared to be seen there in any case, though the greater part wished Daniel were here now, to see his wife defiant, with red-raw fingers and hair clamped to her forehead, happier than she had been in months to see the fine red tint that the yarn had taken.

The stream ran clear at last and Catherine had begun to mewl behind her, so Joan wrung out the yarn as best she could. The tenter she had fashioned herself last year was nowhere to be seen; perhaps it had been taken for firewood, or perhaps it was somewhere else in the valley, hung with some millsman's cloth. Instead, Joan found a pair of ash trees with overhanging branches whose smooth bark would serve well enough. When she had finished, the tree was hung with scarlet lacing. A tiny rebellion, and one that she would surely pay for, when she came home to a cold room and a husband angered by her red fingers and the empty hearth. But looking up at the branches, as pretty as the rowan trees in summer when soft-hearted girls and boys adorned them with ribbons to better their chance in love, Joan's heart surged with a sudden, fierce joy. There was such wonder in this, how had she let herself be kept from this for so long? Probably Daniel would be too unsure of his own position to do more than grumble into his boots and wield the firewood axe with more ferocity than was required, but she would stand her ground if he thought to question her.

Reluctantly, Joan turned towards home. It had started so well; how had she and Daniel come to this so quickly? She ducked to lift the child back to her hip, and wound the muslin back around to secure the sling. Refilling her pockets with the tools she would take away, she upturned the basin in the bushes again to hide the rest. As she was straightening up again, a hand on Catherine's back to stop her slipping, she felt that familiar fluttering across her belly. The child held on, then, despite the blood in her petticoats. Daniel would have a boy, of course, but it was another girl, Joan fancied; a strong, stocky girl, not willing to give up the comfort of the womb so easily. A fighter though, to best the scheming wiles of her aunt and her mother's wretched grief. She would need that fight, to survive in this valley. Joan put a hand to her belly and said a quick prayer for the safety of the child.

'Is it not enough that I work every day for the love of my family? That I have sores from riding the cart on that jumble-gut lane to Stroud each week, and a weal across my shoulder from carrying the sacks of wool?' Daniel was puffed up with indignation; it was as if Alice's visit had never happened, and his whole being had swelled with moral righteousness at her abandonment. 'There was no yarn to send out to the broadweavers, because you had not collected it from the mill, and I have missed a trip to market worrying about your whereabouts.'

'I am here now,' Joan said, refusing to rise to his complaints. Under her skirts, her feet were planted a little apart, ready to withstand his words as if they were blows. 'And there will be more custom in Northleach tomorrow anyway. Robert Parker's son is driving out there just after dawn; I met him coming back through the valley.'

Daniel glared at her, but said nothing. Perhaps he recognised how ridiculous he sounded. But strange to say, though she had no thought of pandering to his grievances, she was glad of all this exasperation and bluster. Last night it had felt as if the spectre of her sister was still in the room, until Joan hardly knew whether she was quarrelling with her husband or the lurking shadow of the bitter woman who had laughed as she crossed the threshold. Safe to say Alice was long gone now – was it possible they would never set eyes on each other again? – and Joan felt rejuvenated, cleansed, by her day on the hillside.

'Where were you, anyway?' he said, gruffly. 'I was worried for the child. And you, of course. You should have told me you were going, at least.'

'On the common towards Bisley.' She'd had her hands behind her back, but she let them slip to her sides now, watching Daniel's eyes take in the pink tint to her fingertips, the crimson lines under her nails that would take a week or more to fade.

He put his head in his hands, rubbing the skin at his temples, tanned to a deep brown by a summer on the road. She heard him laughing through his fingertips.

'There are men who'd beat their wives for less,' he said, but he didn't move.

She planted a kiss just above his forehead, where the hair had begun to thin so that she could see through to the scalp below.

Daniel would never understand her passion for dyeing, that was clear as spring water. But perhaps this small rebellion had carved out a space in her heart, a release, large enough to forgive him, for a new child to fill. Even when Daniel was at his most ridiculous, pacing about in his patched coat and ill-fitting breeches, huffing and puffing at her disobedience, she saw through the bluster to the boy beneath. The same boy whose eyes had widened with relief when she crossed the threshold just now, a thought just glimpsed before his face reshaped itself into crossness: that fear that she might never come back. It was that boy that she still loved, through all the infuriation, and she could only hope this new child would bring yarn enough to darn the holes in their marriage.

Part Three

—

BLUE

Chapter Twenty-Three

1677

'Guide us, Lord, in all the changes and varieties of the world; that we may have evenness and tranquility of spirit: that we may not murmur in adversity nor in prosperity wax proud, but in serene faith resign our souls to thy divinest will; through Jesus Christ our Lord.'

The vicar had been in full flow for some time. Since the death of his wife, Richard Britton had become more earnest in his preaching – solemn as an undertaker, only raising the dull timbre of his voice to recall the apocalyptic scenes foretold by the Book of Revelations – and more strict in his application of the Church's laws. His sister Jane, who had kept house for him since Sarah had passed, was sitting in the front pew between the curate and the clerk, twisting the sash of her gown into a hard rope. It was difficult to imagine that there was much joy in their household, with no children between them and a cloud of grief still hanging around their grand house's draughty halls. Still more difficult – impossible, almost – to imagine that Richard Britton was the same priest who had endorsed the belated blessing of Joan's marriage to Daniel ten years ago, the man full of beer and cake, only stopping short of joining the dancing after.

It would not do to think of old grudges while the grieving vicar preached of martyrs crying out for vengeance. But the man had talked for so long and he showed no sign of reaching the end of his piece. Joan pressed her fingertips into the skin on the back of her other hand, rippling it across the delicate bones. The finest web of lines, only visible when she leaned close, had begun to creep up from her wrist. At Joan's side, Daniel muttered something, coughing away his impatience. She patted his thigh and he nodded towards her. Theirs was not a perfect life; far from it at times, when a bad deal or an order rejected could mean bare shelves for weeks, and there were matters unspoken which lurked below the surface like the dark eels that sometimes congregated in the mill leat. But what a blessing that their own small home was full of children's laughter; a distraction, if one was needed, from any discord which rumbled beneath.

Joan let her eyes slide up to the church's flat roof, allowing Father Britton's familiar words to drone over her. It was alive, this church, when you looked at it. So familiar, but always something new to find amongst all the timber and stone. In the beams, those carved bosses: York rose, Stafford knot, and the oak figures which supported them – pipers, deacons, sinister men with daggers among the folds of their coats. In the chancel too, there were dragons, bishops, queens, grape harvesters and hidden faces, peeping, mocking, from intricate foliage. What did it mean, all this? It seemed so far from the torment and hell-fire which Father Britton threatened. How did it go towards the worship of their God?

'Mama?' Esther, their younger daughter, was reaching a hand for her from Daniel's far side. Joan had tied her curled hair up with a piece of stray yarn this morning, but now she saw the bow was already undone and the yarn slipping; nothing about Esther stayed tame for long.

The black cape of the dogwhipper twitched in his side pew, and Daniel pressed a hand on their daughter's knee to quieten her. But Joan was not afraid of the tap of old Seymour's staff anymore. She leant over to her daughter, offering her ear. Daniel shifted on his seat in discomfort.

'Can we play a while after?' Esther whispered, with all the discretion of a small child. Joan could see she'd got a spinning top in her lap, made for her by Joan's father, and badly concealed by her hymnal. 'With Annie,' Esther added, and grinned. The woman in front of them clucked and fidgeted.

Annie was Harriet's younger child, and she had grown close to both of Joan and Daniel's girls. Joan could see the girl now on the far side of the aisle, round-faced and with chestnut hair just like her mother's, bound up in a neat bun. Annie was a sweet girl, just as Harriet always had been. Still so strange to think that Harriet and Alice had been so close. Perhaps they still were; it was not something Harriet and Joan ever talked about, another quiet body below the surface of the stream.

'Very well. Until your father and I are ready to leave,' Joan replied. She retied the yarn, tucking away the loose strands that fell around Esther's face. Her daughter allowed this reluctantly, bristling at the attention, and it would not be long before the strands escaped again. Long-legged, and happiest outdoors, the weekly church service was a badly concealed torment for Esther. Her feet tapped a rhythm on the kneeler throughout, as if enchanted to dance, and her fingers were always just as busy in the dust of the pew shelf above. Rarely did the service conclude without a neighbour turning round to complain of some intrusion, and it was only a matter of time before the dogwhipper was moved to act. Joan knew it pained Daniel greatly, as if Esther's unquiet mind reflected on his fatherhood, but Joan refused to be angered by it. There would be enough strictures on her daughters' lives; she knew that well enough already.

Sitting on Esther's far side, Catherine – also tall and slender, but with all the poise and patience her younger sister lacked –

kept her gaze on the vicar, watching his tormented face as he tightened his fingers in a fist, declaiming the plagues of fire, smoke and brimstone. Her eyes were wide and Joan wished the vicar would not relate the dark and strange pronouncements of Revelations with such fervour. Catherine was a sensitive girl, prone to deep thought and night-time terrors; this sermon, with its human-faced locusts and beastly menace, would come back to haunt them later.

'They are almost grown. How did it happen? Little John will begin his studies at Mr Webb's school when summer ends,' Harriet said, and Joan shook her head, smiling.

The two women were standing beside the old well, watching the children exercise their legs among the gravestones. Though it was midday, a mist still lingered around the upper branches of the tree canopy, and the air was full of tumbling copper beech leaves. On the apex of the church's broach spire, a raven seemed untroubled by the thunderous peal of the bells tolling for the service end. Its fellows pecked at the moss on one of the chest tombs at the far side of the churchyard, adding to the clamour with their strange, gurgling croaks.

Harriet's boy was called 'Little' only to distinguish him from his father, though even the difference in height seemed to diminish with each passing month. Ten now, and he reminded Joan of Daniel when she had first begun to notice him in the church pews, with his curls and his dark eyes and the knobbly knees visible through his stockings. Little John was standing a little way from the girls but not quite separate from them, and it looked as if he was torn between wanting to distance from their childish games but still hankering after a chase around the tombs.

'I'm sure you have heard that Alice is with child,' Harriet said, her voice light, her eyes still on her son.

Joan pressed a hand to her mouth, turning a splutter into a cough. She had been engrossed in the children's play, and she had no time to conceal her shock. It was not that she had forgotten her sister – how could she, when this valley heaved with their shared childhood, and every day her own girls played in the places and ways that they had done – but she had only set eyes on Alice once since that awful day: a chance meeting, at the market in Stroud, Alice suddenly there on the steps of the apothecary. She'd lifted a hand towards Joan, and opened her mouth to speak, but Joan had wheeled away before she could hear the bitter words she knew would come.

'I see you had not heard,' Harriet went on, quickly, having turned at Joan's choked cough. 'Forgive me, Joan, I was unsure whether to mention it, and now I realise I should have held my tongue.' Harriet's cheeks had flowered crimson and she was biting her lip. Joan put out a hand to her sleeve to reassure her.

'I am pleased to hear the news,' Joan said, refusing to think too deeply on it. Not here, not now. Following Harriet's example, she kept her own voice as light as if she commented on the weather. 'I wish Alice no ill. Is she well with it?'

'Well enough. Though a little ill-tempered.'

Joan laughed. Now *that* she could imagine. Harriet had flushed again. As ever, it was a puzzle and a comfort to Joan that her sister had ever had enough warmth in her heart to make and keep a friend as good as Harriet.

'Walter will be pleased, I imagine,' Joan said, to console her. And no doubt it was true; the man must have relished the news as confirmation of his virility.

Harriet brightened. 'They say he's all over town, full of it, and that he's employed a carpenter already to fashion the furniture for the nursery.'

I am surprised he has such confidence that the child is his, Joan thought, but did not say it, knowing that Harriet would be pained by such talk. It did not sit comfortably to think that way, anyway. Despite everything, when she said she meant her sister no ill will, she spoke the truth.

Joan looked across to the girls, who stood at the foot of a great oak on the far side of the churchyard. Esther was talking quickly, her head bent towards the other two girls, exhorting them to do something. And she was persuasive, because Joan watched Catherine and Annie – Catherine shaking her head as she did it – drop to their knees and form a platform with their joined hands in front of her. Before Joan could take any step to forbid it, Esther had stepped lightly into their palms and sprung from there into the lowest branches of the oak, tucking her skirt up into her bloomers and climbing so quickly that she was ten or fifteen feet above the ground before Daniel's low voice barrelled across the gravestones from where he stood with the vicar's sister, freezing Esther mid-scramble.

'Doesn't Esther remind you of her?' Harriet's voice, hesitant at Joan's side.

Joan shook her head, gave a sad little laugh. 'Yes.' Of course she did. Alice, who had no fear of heights, no fear of anything much, who – long before she'd found the looking glass and rouge – had used to pelt the boys with acorns from the top of this very oak when their parents' eyes were turned. Joan remembered suddenly the feel of her sister's grasp as if it was still around her fingers, heaving her up to sit beside her on the branch there. The graze of branch against knee. The bubble of excitement at the void below them. Alice's smile of conspiracy, as she revealed to Joan the gleaming pile of acorns, apple green in their gnarled cups, in her skirts. Joan turned away now and busied herself with the satchel at her side, unwilling to meet Harriet's eye. She swallowed away the memory; it was linked to too many more.

There was a little of her sister in Catherine – in her beauty, her poise – but far more in Joan's feisty younger daughter: never content unless she was the leader, always sure of her own position, not afraid of the dogwhipper, or the vicar's sister, or anyone else who might stand in her way. Perhaps it was best Esther had not spent time with her aunt; she needed no schooling in the art of rebellion.

A gravelly cough and then 'Those clouds': Daniel was beside them suddenly, pointing up at the darkening sky. He had Esther's reluctant hand in his grip, and Catherine a pace behind – even she, always obedient, looked glum to have been dragged from the game. 'Dark in the east and the west, so there's rain coming wherever the wind takes them. We should be going.' There was a strange energy about him; a surly sort of impatience, that surely went beyond these few minutes idling while the children played with their friends. Joan glanced about, looking for someone who might have spoiled his mood, but when she thought back, Daniel had been acting strangely all morning. He'd barely said a word on the walk up the hill, just stamped towards the distant spire, his hair slick to his temples as if the climb were much steeper.

'Is there something wrong?' she asked.

'Because I want to avoid a house-full of damp gowns and sodden cloaks?'

Never one for conflict, this was enough for Harriet. She made her excuses, kissing Joan on both cheeks and crossing the churchyard to join her children, who were walking the length of the boundary wall with arms outstretched, Little John having given up the pretence of being too old to play.

Joan knew from the deep set of Daniel's brow that any further questioning now would reap no benefit. 'Very well,' she said instead, and began to gather up the stray garments the children had shed.

They made their way towards the Calfway track which would take them home. Daniel walked hand in hand with the girls, probably holding them more firmly than Esther, at least, would have wished, and though Joan saw him smile at their jests, it seemed to her that his jaw was tight. His whole posture, in fact – shoulders slumped, boots kicking at the fallen leaves as the girls skipped through them – was that of a man with something bearing down on him.

Chapter Twenty-Four

'Will you tell me now?' she said later, when the girls were tucked up nose to tail in the low cot they shared. It was cramped, but better than it could have been – if it had not been for the death of Daniel's uncle two winters back and his generous bequest, they would still be cooped in the lean-to, and how would the four of them have survived in that one small room?

This cottage had a tiny chamber off the main room, just large enough for the girls' bed, as well as a long attic above where the looms and equipment could be kept and used. It sat in a sheltered spot on the lower slopes of Hyde Hill, not far from the Black Gutter spring, and though they would never own it, the landlord was old and kind. On the occasions when their rental account had drifted into arrears, he had accepted the late payment without complaint, nodding at the bowl of eggs Joan brought to sweeten it.

Daniel only shrugged at her question, but when he sank onto a chair, his shoulders drooped low again. They rose only when he began to cough – a rasping hack that brought something up in his throat, and he spat into the fire before slumping back again. 'Matters of business, that's all. It will be resolved,' he said eventually, kicking at the log that hung over the hearth edge.

She crossed the room to him, putting a hand on each shoulder. She'd intended to rub them, but he flinched and a knot of concern formed in her belly. 'Have you shared your troubles with my father, at least?'

Daniel breathed out a grave laugh. 'Joan, I love your father as I love my own, but he is an old man. He was never the most practical, and these days it is all he can do to put his breeches on the right way round.'

It was hard to hear, but her father's decline was undeniable. Sometimes, when she climbed up to his cottage, she found him staring out of the window, slack-jawed, his eyes as milky now as the clouded glass Daniel had fitted for him.

'Then tell me,' Joan pleaded. 'No doubt you are right and I can do little, but it might soothe you to unburden yourself of it.'

But Daniel shook his head. 'Joan, there's nothing you or I can do. We are an irrelevance. A speck. Like some tiny creature, a caterpillar or a worm, trying to keep pace with our fleet-footed insect cousins. But we will never keep up. Powered machines replace what used to earn us profit. This year it seems every mill in the valley has a gig-mill to raise their cloth, despite the prohibition, and the money to bring the finest teasels from Yorkshire too. Another slice of profit is denied us, and how long before the weaving too is taken over by some thundering contraption, and our livelihood is finally ripped from beneath our feet?'

He was right, of course. There had been change – new machines, new mills, the landscape of the valley groaned with it. But need they be left behind? Leaning his head back against the stone wall, his chest still covered in fulling dust and his eyes bloodshot and pink-rimmed; he looked so broken, she longed to cheer him. 'We can't fight the changes,' she said, gently, knowing that she trod on fragile ground. 'But perhaps we too could find a way to benefit from the new machinery?'

He leaned forward to spit into the fire again, sitting back with a low wheeze. 'There is nothing wrong with the way we do things, Joan,' he said, a tightening in his jaw, and she knew then there was no use trying. 'It is the only way we know, and I'll have it no different.'

His eyes were blank with obstinacy, and Joan sighed silently. He might try to keep it all from her, but even she had seen so many opportunities missed. Orders badly priced, or lost to competition through indecision or a lack of confidence, investment opportunities allowed to slip through their grasp because neither Daniel nor her father had the appetite for speculation. They could not look to Walter now for surety, of course, but there might be others prepared to lend on a sound venture. But Daniel had become as cautious as her father. When old Stephens had finally died, they'd had to watch the mill above John Browning's sold to a clothier from Stonehouse, who raised the weir so high afterwards, the stream down was reduced to a trickle. The wheel they'd invested so much in was sold in parts for pennies. Joan had not attended the auction herself, not wanting to risk seeing Alice, but it was difficult to understand how it could have raised so little. She tried not to imagine Walter decrying its condition so that buyers folded their arms until the price reached rock bottom.

Joan stood up, minded to leave Daniel alone a while. In this mood, he was prickly as a teasel himself, and she only seemed to make things worse. She wished Rockwood were still alive – the old dog had always soothed him when he came to lie across his feet. They'd found him peaceful beside a cooling hearth one morning many winters gone, and Joan had watched Daniel turn his back so that the girls would not see his tears. Even now, his hand hung down over the arm of his chair, palm cupped for an enquiring nose to press.

'And then there's this new weave they called Spanish cloth.' She was just leaning over the washing basin when she heard him behind her, and she turned back to listen. 'It's all that Blackwell Hall man will talk of these days – they're shipping it out by the boatload, and still the Continent is hungry for more, if he's to be believed. But the mills want too much for the dyed yarn. That way, too, the door is closed to us.'

The solution seemed very clear to Joan, but let him say it himself. She busied herself with the girls' milk cups, still rubbing at the glaze long after they were clean.

'I know what you're thinking,' he said, shaking his head. 'That you could fix up a shipment of Spanish with a few dry roots and a tin bath. You're like a child piling pebbles in the stream, who fancies herself Inigo Jones. Dyeing is a science, and it should be left to the dye-man. It's simple enough.'

She hung her head over the basin.

'Joan,' he said more gently, and she heard him turn towards her. 'We've no more right to take a part in it than to stride up the hill to Father Britton's pulpit and have a go at preaching his serm . . .' He began to cough again before he finished. She turned in time to see his face redden sharply before the fit was over. She didn't like the rattle she heard from the bottom of his lungs, but he batted away her hand when she reached for him.

'What of the Butler mill?' she said, when he had recovered himself. A conversation from the women at the stream had come back to her suddenly. 'Abigail Butler has no wish to run it herself now Henry is gone, and I hear they are looking for tenants.' It was another tiny mill, barely more than this cottage, but the stream beside it was fed by two fat springs, and no mills above to steal the water.

Daniel laughed. He took a swig of beer from his cup. 'Do not make me tell the girls that their mother has gone mad, Joan.'

She ignored the slight. 'The stream is strong and the sharp drop in the slope there must drive the wheel well.'

'And how would we pay the lease? Is it this fairy gold again?' Daniel's voice was sharp and mocking. She did not like to hear him like this.

'It would need to be a joint endeavour. My father's place to be sold, this place given up, and we would all need to live in the rooms above.'

'Like mice in a hat!' he spluttered, suddenly cheered. 'Joan, you are ridiculous now. Three adults and two young lasses, in a room little bigger than a hen coop. Would you have me cuddle your father to sleep as well? Or doze with his big toe resting up my nostril?'

When he was like this, it was all she could do to keep her own temper. She breathed out before speaking. 'It would not be comfortable, I admit, but a sacrifice worth making, and not forever. As soon as the mill turned to profit, we could look to rent another room elsewhere, or build one on the back, if Abigail Butler was amenable. Your father wrote that he would provide something for the girls' future, now that he is settled in Somerset. Perhaps he could be persuaded to invest a little in the scheme, if it were explained as a mechanism for their good health.'

'You have been making grand plans, Joan.' Daniel's voice was bitter, and she didn't like the way his eyes glittered. 'How much of my father's money have you spent, in your mind? Have you chosen silk curtains and a new gown for your new abode?' He wheezed as he spoke, and clapped his chest in anger.

'Daniel, please. That is unfair. I have thought of this only now, and I am thinking only of our collective happiness. There would be much to discuss and decide, of course, but it could be an option for the future.'

He said nothing for a moment. The air seemed to have gone out of him, as if he could no longer be bothered with her. Her shoulders dropped like his; what was the point?

'Joan, you are like a market zany tonight,' he said eventually, 'with all these mad propositions. You might as well be juggling balls and making flowers appear from a hat. My father does not have that kind of money, and who else would lend us?' But before she could answer, he aimed another lazy kick at the end of the nearest log, sending up a shower of sparks. 'We are doomed to be poor, Joan. I confess I am glad my mother is not here to see it.'

And would that mine was here to help me persuade my block-headed husband, Joan thought, shaking her head when she wished she could shake him instead. But it had been a long day, with Harriet's news of Alice too; better to turn her attention to the alchemy required to turn a hard end of cheese rind into an edible meal. She was about to turn about when Daniel's shoulders began to heave with that choking cough again. A brew of horehound would see to that, she reassured herself, though she slept uneasily, wondering whether she should have tried harder not to rile him.

Chapter Twenty-Five

'It would be far from comfortable, but a sacrifice worth making, and not forever.'

Could Joan be hearing this correctly? Her own husband, repeating back to her father the very thing he had roundly rejected? And using her very words, and without even a nod towards her to acknowledge the absurdity of the situation?

They were up in John Browning's cottage, Catherine and Esther left outside to play while they waited for the walk up to church. Joyful gales of laughter rolled in through the doorway as the girls chased the old hen's daughter around, Esther leading the charge, and even in her outrage, Joan was grateful that Daniel was too distracted to quieten them. John Browning had been lacing his good boots and he'd sat up to laugh too now, but at Daniel's words. His chest rose and fell like a pair of bellows, no more accepting of her husband's suggestion than Daniel had been when she had proposed the same last night.

'Seems to me there's a king's ransom left to find before we'd be halfway to financing it,' John Browning said, when he'd recovered himself. 'And that's if you and I were happy bedfellows, Daniel, which is something I'd have to be persuaded of.' He chuckled again, looking to Daniel to join him, but Daniel's face was all seriousness.

'I have been thinking on that too. What if Walter could be persuaded to make the investment?'

Joan gasped. Enough to steal her ideas, but to suggest such a thing without even consulting her . . . She stared across at him, knowing she must look like a bobbing pigeon as she ducked from side to side to try and catch his gaze, but he seemed determined to avoid her. Her father, though, stared back at her intently.

'And Joan would be happy with that, would she?' he said, his head on one side in question. 'Because now you mention Walter, I had a letter from the man only last week, begging me to intercede in a reconciliation between my two girls. It seems Alice's condition – I take it you know of it? – has made her think a little on family, and she has realised the error of her ways, or something like it. Stubborn as a goat, of course, but Walter seems convinced that we could broker a ceasefire, if Joan cared to consider it?'

'Well, then . . .' Daniel started.

But Joan interrupted. Her husband's disloyalty had made her feel bold. 'As if! Alice has not begun to regret her actions, only to realise that she wants something from me. Assistance with the child, probably, when I have enough on my plate here.'

'Let's not concern ourselves with your sister's motives,' Daniel said quickly. 'The effect is the same. If we can smooth the matter over, Walter may come to our aid.'

Joan watched her husband speak, feeling anger flicker up and down her frame like a blaze through a haystack. As if he were discussing a cross word over a chipped cup or an appointment missed! The woman tried to seduce you, she thought. Are you so block-headed you cannot see how that affects me? *Then put your hands on me anyway, Daniel. I can see in your eyes how much you want to. Come here and show me how an army man treats his woman.* Even if her husband had somehow forgotten Alice's words – and what man could have done? – Joan still heard them in her nightmares.

'Think a little on it, Joan. For me.' Daniel was pleading with her now, and she looked at him again, this man she had been with for so long, expecting to feel that anger rage ever more fiercely. That he stole her ideas and passed them off as his own. That he called on her, not only to recall the desperate events of Alice's last visit, but to consider picking up with her sister again. But as she looked across the dark cottage to her husband's hunched form, Joan felt the anger die down to a flicker, a sudden pity overwhelming her in its place. He was so thin, she saw now, and there were dark shadows under his eyes. None of them had slept well these past days, with the autumn winds howling and that new cough seeming to rattle the very beams of the cottage, and last night Esther too had begun to croak and splutter not long after she'd laid her head on the bolster. This morning Joan had risen early to pull a last few stands of horehound from the pasture behind the cottage and steep them over the remnants of last night's fire, but Daniel had gagged over his first sip and refused to have more. When she looked at him now, he looked ground down, far older than his years – perhaps it would do no harm to give the matter a token consideration.

Somehow, her agreement to think on the matter was taken as an acceptance. But Joan was mightily distracted in the following days by the deterioration in Esther's health, too much so to pay much attention to any thought of Alice: the little girl spiked a high fever that night, and Joan had been occupied since in sponging her down and trying to get a drop of liquid inside her, while comforting Catherine who took her sister's illness hard.

While Joan had neither time nor inclination to consider her own deceitful sister, a plan had evolved without her, it seemed. Daniel had made preparations to travel into Stroud. He came to find her kneeling by the stream, and told her that he would meet her father at the Blackness fingerpost in an hour, and that they would travel on together to meet first Walter, and then, all being well, Alice herself. Joan heard his words fall like stones across her back, but she was too exhausted to do more than hang her head over the soiled linen. When she did look up, her only thought was that Daniel did not look fit enough to step beyond the gate. His face had a greenish hue, and before he had finished bidding her farewell, he coughed into his hand and wiped it on his breeches, leaving a streak of red across the yellow wool.

It roused her enough to consider begging him to stay, but she knew he would take it for a wish to scupper his plans. They had skirted around each other since he had brought up the idea of Walter's backing with her father – her rage at his disloyalty fought with her desire to comfort him in his illness. And now, even as he said his goodbye, he was gripping the dead hedge to steady himself, and she saw in the white of his knuckles how much he needed its scaffold. She could only wish for his safe passage, and lift a hand and smile as he waved his handkerchief from the curve of the stream before he slipped from sight.

They did not make it far. Later, John Browning explained that they had not yet reached Thrupp before Daniel slumped against the carriage side, his eyes rolling back in fever, and they had to stop the cart to prop him up lest he fell over the side altogether. When he and old Robert Parker's son leaned close enough to see his complexion, it was clear Daniel was in an unfit state to go further.

'Green as a pike's back, and not much prettier,' her father had said. Her husband was struck down and in that moment, Joan had seen her father as an old man too. Teeth like yellow pegs and eyes rheumy. 'I knew then we had to bring him home,' he'd finished.

Three days since: a blur of sweat and steam and bloodied linens. Mrs Freme had come every day, with bowls of food and fresh milk and a host of herbal medicaments for Daniel and Esther – Joan accepted all of these with gratitude, but was afraid to let the older woman over the threshold in case she succumbed herself. Harriet too had visited but Joan sent her away just as quickly, afraid she might spread the affliction to her own children. Catherine had clung to her sister's side and would not be routed, but eventually the time came when Joan knew she too would need to leave.

'Go up to your grandfather's,' she said, gently as she could. Catherine nodded, her little mouth working to contain her tears. It hurt to send her away but there would be food and milk at the cottage, and nothing good would happen in this house now. Catherine bent to kiss her father's forehead, then the top of her sleeping sister's head. She reached out a hand to Joan and Joan squeezed it gently. 'I'll come for you later,' she said.

After Catherine had gone, Daniel opened his eyes briefly; the whites were yellow now, and laced with a spider web of pink. He must be so weak, but she had nothing left to give him, even if he'd take it. Somehow he found the vigour to lift her hands from her lap, bringing them to his lips.

'I'm so sorry, Joan.'

'Sorry for what, my sweet? You have nothing to be sorry for.' It was easy to forgive anything now.

'That's not true, you know it's not. I'm so sorry that I held you back,' he said. His body was wracked with a fit of coughing then, and Joan croaked a sob to see it. When his chest settled, he seemed to draw himself up in the bed. He was finding the strength for his goodbye, and she was not yet ready to hear it.

'My blue hawk,' he said, taking her hand in his. She tried not to look at the way the flesh had melted away around the bulge of his knuckles. 'It was envy, I suppose. Everything I loved in you, I wished I was worthy of. Forgive me, Joan, for all that I asked of you.'

'Be in peace, my love.' Joan lowered her forehead to his cheek so that her tears would fall unnoticed onto the bedside. If he could find the strength, then so should she. 'I have made my own mistakes, and you have been everything to me.'

He was quiet, then, for a long time, and after a while she lifted her head to check that his breathing hadn't stilled. Behind her, Esther coughed and moaned; Joan was halfway to her feet but her daughter turned on her side and started up her rasping snore again. Terrible, to be torn between them like this. It was Daniel who seemed weakest, but when she turned back to him, he had opened his eyes again.

'Will you send word to my father, in case he will come?' he asked, his voice like a scratch of nails on wood now. And she nodded, though she could see with dreadful certainty that it would be too late, and in all likelihood the poor man would arrive only to see the dirt shovelled onto his son's coffin.

'I wish Rockwood was still here,' Daniel said then, even weaker, and his eyes were drooping again already. Joan rested her fingers on the soft hair at the crown of his head. Later, as he napped fitfully, she rolled a blanket into a fat twist and laid it over his feet, so that he would feel the weight there and be comforted by the memory of his faithful old dog.

It was after nightfall when Mrs Freme came to the door. This time she refused to leave, and she held Joan against her until Joan sobbed into her shoulder. Then she built up a grand fire and sat by it, stirring a pot of something that gave off vapours both soothing and reviving, and Joan was grateful for her obstinacy and her silent companionship. One last lease of energy gifted, to take her through till sunrise.

In the event, after so many nights of pain and anguish, that last one was peaceful as the millpond before dawn. In the side room, Esther's breathing slowed so that her chest barely rose and fell. When Joan knelt to stroke the curls from her forehead, she could see only the tiniest cloud of steam each time the little girl exhaled. In the main room, Daniel's coughs had merged into a steady wheeze, as if the lowest notes of a church organ drifted in on the breeze. Mrs Freme handed Joan one dampened cloth after another, but in truth they both knew that father and daughter had gone beyond such comforts now.

Joan had planned to keep a sleepless vigil, but when dawn came, she woke to find herself kneeling at Daniel's bedside, her cheek creased with the mattress's straw. She glanced behind: Mrs Freme was still by the fireside, nursing the last embers. How could you let me sleep, she wanted to exclaim, but she knew the answer: *what was there to be done?*

Joan wheeled about to check on Esther first, but the girl was much as she had been, breathing heavily as an old man, her little body quivering with the intensity of whatever gripped her. Joan pulled up the quilt, laid a hand across Esther's pale brow; she whispered her daughter's name in vain hope, but only her eyelids flickered. So Joan turned back to her husband, straightening the sheet over his lifeless form, only then letting her eyes drift up to where his head lay on the bolster.

He was gone, she saw that at once, and she gasped 'no' but the sound that came out was mangled and alien. Daniel's complexion had lost its green sheen, and was as pale now as the alabaster busts in the church's chancel. His jaundiced eyes were fixed on the ceiling beams, and she wanted to close them, but found that her hand would not move there. In the end it was Mrs Freme who rose from her place by the fire and leant over to smooth his lids – raw with soreness, now relieved – downwards. Joan dropped her head to his chest and rested for a moment, but there was no comfort to be had there. Eventually, she staggered to her feet and the two women stood together, hand in hand, looking down at the body between them.

'We'll need to call for the searcher,' Joan said at last, taking back her hand, full of a sudden urgency. 'To register his passing. And they must ring the bell for him.'

'In good time.' Mrs Freme had moved to the windowsill. 'These formalities can wait a little.' She began to light a row of rushlights, then turned to the hearth shelf to do the same.

'You will do us out of wicks.' Joan was amazed at the lightness in her own voice, as alien as the strangled denial earlier.

Mrs Freme just continued, igniting each from the last. Only at times of celebration would they ever have so many lamps lit; a bizarre and discordant luxury to have the walls ripple with candlelight now. 'It is as well to fill the house with light at such a time,' she said, when all were lit. 'To cover the glass too, lest his spirit be held here.'

'And if I do not want him to go?'

Mrs Freme squeezed her arm. 'Daniel will do no good, trapped here. You must help him Joan, this one last time. Do you have mourning cloths somewhere?'

'Folded under the bed at my father's.' They'd draped every window for weeks after her mother's passing, even the looking glass, and Joan had so hoped never to see those dreadful cloths again. But still she picked up her cape and made for the door. She made it only as far as the threshold, arrested there by a cough from Esther that seemed to wrack the girl's whole body.

'Let me go for them,' Mrs Freme said, pulling on her own coat. 'I'll call for the searcher too, if it's your wish, and send word to the church. I won't be gone long. You stay with the girl.'

She had pushed past Joan and closed the door behind her before there could be any argument, and Joan did not hesitate in crossing the room to her daughter's bedside. Kneeling there, she found that the fever which had burned under Esther's skin for a week now had all but dropped away. It should have been a good omen, but this sickness was a devious beast: Joan knew that well enough from the progress of Daniel's illness. Esther's skin felt cold and dry; Joan threw off her shawl and slipped under the covers beside her daughter, pulling her skinny frame into her arms so as to use her own body heat to warm her, burying her face in the tangled mess of Esther's hair.

'Don't go, baby girl,' she whispered, 'please, Father, keep her for me.' And Esther's curls, still damp from the fever's grip, were further soaked by Joan's tears as she cried and prayed and sang for her daughter's salvation.

But it was not to be. Even as she held her, Joan felt Esther's breathing slow and lighten and slow and lighten until it was barely more than the thimble-breath of a bird, hardly audible above the crackle of the rushlight wicks. And as she clasped the girl to her, wary of clutching her too tight, that wracking cough reduced to a wheeze, and then to a low whistle. Eventually that too fell silent. All around, the walls flickered with the incongruous glow of the rushlights, until at last her daughter's final breath was released with the gentlest sigh. In the bed behind her, Joan pushed her cheek into the mattress's rough straw and let all of her tears fall.

She would bury them in this new scarlet: Daniel, and his daughter beside him. Scarlet for her soldier boy and scarlet for the little girl with the untameable hair. She would dye the cloth herself, Joan resolved: one single length, enough for them both, and it would be a labour of love. The finest broadcloth, woven by her own hand, then dipped and hung and dipped and hung until it took the richest, brightest pigment. Brighter than rose hips. Brighter than the ladybird's wing. Brighter than the tiny strawberries that hid under their parasol leaves like veiled jewels.

She'd have to be quick about it, even in this chill. Father Britton would not tolerate their precious bodies lying in the crypt for long. And when it was done, she would put those dye-stuffs aside, and never dye the colour again. Enough bloodshed, enough heartache. Though in her heart of hearts she knew her father would not be long behind, she had seen enough death, and never wished to be reminded of this pain again.

Chapter Twenty-Six

Joan stood at the window, watching the formation of a fat drip of snow-melt as it hung from the top of the frame, waiting for it to plough down in a channel through the banked drift on the outer sill. On the path outside the window, the white was retreating, leaving round patches of blackened mud here and there. The cushion of snow on the roof of the woodshed next door had started to slide. Joan looked behind her, to the threshold. Whoever built this cottage had not found level ground; meltwater had slipped under the door and was pooling across the dust there.

The first dusting of snow had come on the day of the funeral, along with a whistling wind, and Joan had wondered whether her older daughter had been sobbing as much for the bitter cold in her toes as for her father and sister as they tramped up the hillside towards the church's tolling bells. More fell the day after they'd buried them; three inches or more, as if God were laying a final blanket over their resting place. Peering out over the threshold, Joan had been reluctant to soil the pristine whiteness of it with boot prints, and Catherine had been too exhausted to argue, sleepless with nightmares for her sister and father's souls, tormented as she was by Father Britton's sermons of damnation. The vicar would have no prayers or communion for the departed, who were beyond human intercession now, but Joan and Catherine both kneeled each night and prayed for their safe passage to heaven – anything to help her daughter snatch a few hours of merciful rest.

And since, as the drifts piled up on the windowsills, they had huddled inside the cottage like woodland creatures in their winter den, surviving on hard cheese, breadcrumbs, and buckets of snow pulled in from the doorstep and set before the fire to melt. It had been a time of silence, of holding each other through the cold, of slow, painful release. They were both drained of emotion and wracked with a fierce tiredness. The time before the funeral had passed in a grim blur of activity. Weaving the shrouds had been no small task, even with the help of Harriet and other women she had known since childhood, but Joan had set her mind to it and would not be dissuaded.

The dyeing, too, had not come easily: the longest length of broadcloth Joan had attempted – cold, wet, and impossibly heavy, even with Catherine's assistance and that of the young man who had helped her once before. And even when Joan was finally satisfied with the intensity of the pigment, the heavens had not cooperated: sleet that chilled the bones, so the cottage was all but emptied for tenter racks and a great fire, and she and Catherine squeezed into the tiny back chamber to make room for the steaming length of broadcloth. It was fortunate that so many families had wanted to show their support by bringing gifts of food to the house; otherwise she and Catherine might not have eaten at all during those first weeks. And every minute Joan dreaded the first throat-clearing in Catherine that might herald the return of the dreadful affliction which had taken her father and sister.

Today though, with the arrival of this weak winter sun and its accompanying thaw, she felt that dread slip away a little. It was tempting, to stay cocooned here forever, or until time healed the raw pain that snagged her heart every waking. But it would not be healthy for Catherine.

'Shall we walk out today?' she called back into the room, to where Catherine was lying on her cot, squinting to see the letters she was copying onto her slate. 'The thaw has begun.'

Catherine roused at once, swinging her long legs around to stand and pulling a shawl around her. 'Can I see Grandfather?'

Joan nodded. Her father had seemed more together than the rest of them at the funeral, but who was to say how he would have spent these weeks trapped inside by the snow. It would be reassuring to hear that he was in good health, not curled around a gin bottle.

'If you're happy to go alone. I must go to Millswood. Mrs Freme . . .' Joan started, but Catherine had already laced her boots and had a foot to the door-frame, hauling the swollen door open.

'I'll be back before dark,' she said, and then she was off, striding away through the white slush with unaccustomed speed. Catherine had been cooped up too long.

Mrs Freme was nodding as she opened the door, as though Joan had sent word ahead. 'I thought you might emerge sooner, being as strong as you are, but I dare say you have had your hands full.'

Joan had not seen her old friend since the day of the funeral. They'd walked together behind the coffin cart that day, which was driven by Robert Parker's boy and the old man come out of retirement to walk alongside to keep the donkeys steady. Mrs Freme had held Catherine's other hand, and behind them walked Joan's father, with Harriet and her husband Ralph a step behind. Daniel's father had sent word that he was not well enough to make the journey, though a serious young man from his church had come in his stead. Joan had wondered whether Father Britton might make the connection between this stranger and those who had been expelled from the valley, but the young man had not been troubled by anyone during the service, and had been allowed to stand beside the coffin while the pallbearers lowered it into the ground afterwards. There had been no sign at all of Alice.

'I bring the spring with me, or the first sign of it at least.' Joan leant in to plant a kiss on the older woman's cheek. It struck her that Mrs Freme seemed to age like a woman from a painting: her skin gaining delicacy for what it lost in firmness, her hair whitening without losing its weight to frame her face. Only her old friend's hands gave her away: deep-set wrinkles that no amount of beeswax would soften. Sun-mottled patches, and the stained fingertips of a woman who knew the soil.

'You'll be bringing a draught, if you don't hurry in off the doorstep.' Mrs Freme was brisk, but her expression was full of compassion. 'Come in, come in. Let's get those wet boots in front of the fire.'

It would be a relief to be inside; one cocoon exchanged for another. Joan hoped Catherine felt as secure in her father's cottage. The two of them had barely been a moment apart since the day they'd lost Daniel and Esther, and no doubt Catherine felt as exposed and vulnerable today as Joan did, almost as raw as the day they'd lost them.

'And? How have you been?' Mrs Freme asked, when they were sat together.

'A little low.'

The old woman nodded. 'I see that.' Joan watched smoke curl from a log, as the flames flickered over its damp bark. 'But he would not want your life to end when his did. You cannot mourn forever, Joan.'

'How can I not?' Joan said, then regretted the sharpness in her voice and shook her head. 'I never thought a house so small could feel so cavernous.' And the waking, every morning, to the empty bolster beside her. To the sight of Catherine swamped in a quilt that was meant for two. A fresh agony each day.

'I can imagine.' Mrs Freme looked at her steadily. 'You feel numb. But you have taken that first, tiny step; in leaving the house, in coming here.'

Joan nodded, looking down at her hands. In the weeks since the funeral, a rim of scarlet had still clung to her fingernails, fading slowly to a high pink like the corncockles that Esther used to pick from the meadow beside Joan's father's cottage for her hair. Now though, even those last remnants of the funeral shroud's pigment had faded away. Maybe it was time, to begin to think of the future.

'Perhaps,' she said. 'I have Catherine to think of, after all.'

'Catherine, and yourself. You are still young, Joan.'

Joan smiled. 'I do not feel it.' When she looked up to meet her old friend's eyes, she noticed for the first time that the light in the room was not as she remembered. The chamber beyond the hall was less gloomy, and the side door, which led to the dye-man's rooms and was usually kept locked, hung open. Mrs Freme watched her glance about.

'I wondered when you'd take note of it.'

'What is it? What's changed?'

'Well, a strange thing, now you ask. The dye-man has retired at last, though in good health rather than ill. He always said he'd go abroad, though I never believed it, but I came home from visiting my sister in Berkeley to a note from the man, telling me that the urge to roam had struck him, as it struck his older brother at a similar age. So he has departed for Southampton, having settled funds sufficient to cover his account for a year.'

'How extraordinary.' To be able to escape like that. To voyage for pleasure, as if it were the most normal thing in the world.

'He and his brother have plans to swim in every one of the Italian lakes, if you can countenance it.'

Joan recalled a time she and Alice had swum in the millpond, so long ago, long enough that they felt no shame in stripping to their slips and leaving their gowns on the bank. Joan could still remember the silky feel of the carp-green water, the cling of her slip as she gasped and splashed at the cold. A world apart from an Italian lake, no doubt, but the memory – Alice's hair wet to her scalp, slick as an otter, her hand around Joan's under the water to keep her afloat – weighed heavily today on Joan's bruised heart. 'And what of the dye-garden?' she asked.

'I am to keep it as before, and he has left funds enough for that too. But if he finds the Continent to his satisfaction, he may not return. In that case, and in the meantime, I am instructed to do with his plants and his equipment as I see fit.'

Joan was awake, suddenly, the stupor of cold and grief banished for a moment. 'And what do you see fit, in the meantime?' The first kernel of an idea.

Mrs Freme raised an eyebrow. 'That was my first thought. A small tragedy to leave these rooms unused for half a year or more.'

'And the plants, too. Many will pass their useful best, surely, if not harvested this coming season?'

'Exactly my concern.' Mrs Freme had begun to smile.

'How would it be if someone were to use the rooms in his absence? To keep them in good shape, make use of the equipment, and return any profit to you as freeholder?'

Mrs Freme laughed. 'I had wondered just the same thing myself. Joan, your cottage will no longer be tenable with Daniel gone – it's only thanks to the kindness of old Collins that you've been able to hunker down there so long. How would it be if you and Catherine came here? Just time enough to get your feet back on the ground. It might be longer if my dye-man finds the clear lakes of Italy more to his liking than our greasy ponds.'

'Ah. Thank you, it is a happy daydream. But my father . . .' Joan started. She'd hardly seen him this last month, but in the back of her mind she realised she'd resigned herself to moving back to her father's cottage, to keeping house for him in his last days.

'. . . is more sprightly these days than you give him credit for,' Mrs Freme finished for her. 'I have heard that he would sell his cottage, pay down his debts and find somewhere more comfortable to spend his dotage. Perhaps – and I say this only to give you fair warning – not alone.'

Joan's eyes were wide at this. It was as if she had emerged into a foreign world today. 'I wish I heard this from him.'

'Joan, I'm sorry. I have little time for gossip, as you know, but you have been in hibernation so long. There has been talk – that is all – as there always is when a mill cottage may come up for sale. And something about the vicar's old cook. She and your father were friends as children, I believe – you would know better? – and have grown close again, it seems. I would have closed my ears to such prattle, but your father's name and the talk of a sale was difficult to ignore.'

Joan shook her head. 'Of course. The old place . . . I suppose it was always going to go some day. It was my mother's house as much as his, and a little of my childhood will go with it, but there we are. But if he has found a companion, I could not be happier for him.' She laughed sadly. 'With my father otherwise occupied, and Alice all but gone, I feel very alone, all of a sudden.'

'All the more reason to consider my offer. I would love the company, and you can pay your way by helping out around the place. But I'll not take your profit – any penny you make is for you and Catherine alone.' Mrs Freme took Joan's hand and smiled. 'I can see your mind working like the innards of a clock. There are many things to consider, I know. But come in, take some camomile with me. We can put the world to rights after.'

Chapter Twenty-Seven

'And here they are. The blue hawk of Chalford and her sharp-eyed daughter, come to fleece me for sport.' Mr Ridler still wore his pea-green hat, or another just like it, and though he looked older, he had lost none of his tight round belly. It took practice to understand him these days – his lips hung loose over gums all but empty of teeth – but he always looked out for Joan and Catherine when they ventured into town for the market.

'Good morning, sir. How is trade?' Joan said.

'Brisk enough for such a cold morning.' He rubbed his hands together. 'And what will the wool women of the Frome valley have today?'

Joan stepped forward at once to handle the bundles he had set out in front of him, separating the individual fleeces with practised hands in order to examine the quality of the finishing. Catherine took Joan's arm, hanging back; she was always shy on market day, alarmed by the sudden crowds and the slobber and boom of Mr Ridler's chatter.

'Come, Catherine, try this one.' Joan moved her daughter forward gently, slipping her arm free to put a hand on her back. 'Press the fibres apart so that you can feel how the fleece has been treated. See that there are no burrs or clotting caught in the strands, and that the dock wool and any sweat locks have been properly removed in the skirting.' Joan watched her daughter tease the fleece apart, tentatively at first and then leaning in to inspect it more closely.

Mr Ridler sucked on his pipe and raised his eyebrows. 'No hope for us traders, if you're training up more like yourself, Mrs Randall.'

'You'll have nothing to fear if your fleece is as well treated as that one, sir. Now I'll take ten of the white and half as many of the brown. Bob Huggits' boy will collect them at the close of trading in his cart.'

Mr Ridler nodded, laying down his pipe. 'Thank you, ma'am. I'll draw the account up now, if you'll pass by when you've finished your business.'

Joan smiled, and took up Catherine's arm again. They had moved in with Mrs Freme a year ago, and in the months since, Joan had worked hard to pick up her old contacts: Mr Ridler, but also the fullers, pickers, shearers, broadweavers, and all the other links in the chain that would take her cloth from fleece to market. The first orders had been tiny, of course – individual lengths for gowns and curtains, bedspreads and shrouds – but even on these, the dyeing added greatly to the margin in the sales.

With the dye garden on her doorstep, and with Catherine as a willing accomplice, Joan had begun to speculate with small batches: soft greys, greens and earth browns. They were popular in the market, these shades of the landscape; the rich might favour bright pigments which marked them out in the crowd, but the rest preferred these subtle, natural hues. Colours of the valley, but with the depth and permanence of a well-fixed dye. Joan loved them too, but she was always drawn to blues, and eventually the calling was too strong. Every time she readied the dye-man's deep tin vats, she felt its pull. Rich midnight blue, robin egg, periwinkle and cornflower, the dusky bloom on a sloe – she tried to capture all of them in the net of her cloth. Once, from a wrap of muslin in the back of her drawer, Joan pulled the jay feather Daniel had tucked in her bonnet so long ago, and she and Catherine spent a morning trying to recreate those vivid stripes sometimes matched by a summer sky.

It was rare that her fingernails were not stained blue these days; Catherine's too, and so often were the woad vats busy that Mrs Goodlake, her father's new companion, complained of the cabbage stink whenever she visited the house. It had been worth it though: it was not long before Joan was able to produce fine blue broadcloth in a quantity large enough to approach the wool-town markets, and eventually London. It took some months to find a carrier who would give secure passage of her cloth to Blackwell Hall, but soon after she had taken on Michael Huggits full time, and she had the young lad accompany the orders as they made their way there.

There had been challenges, of course. New competitors and the rising cost of raw materials that Daniel had so struggled with. That first visit to the Blackwell Hall factor: the man did not respond well to the sight of a woman in his warehouse, and Joan realised quickly that she would need to work doubly hard to convince him of the merit of her account. Still now, not confident he gave her the best prices, she sold her cloth locally wherever possible. She was ever more grateful to Mrs Freme, who had taken care of Catherine in those first months while she had toured the shire's 'wool churches': Northleach and Tewkesbury, Cirencester and Chipping Campden, always with a great stack of folded broadcloth at her back on the journey out, hopeful that she would be less well supported on the journey back.

'What have we left to do?' Catherine's voice brought her back. They were halfway across the Pitching, just broken free of the crowd.

Joan pulled her daughter close while an overladen cart of milk churns made its way past – half pushed by, half dragging, the boy at its handles. 'An errand or two. You could run to the apothecary for me. Your grandfather needs more of that yeast tincture for his feet.'

Catherine nodded, always glad to be useful, taking the coins Joan held out into her palm. 'Where will I see you?'

'I must catch the bailiff. See me back here, or under the arches. I'll not go far.' Joan watched Catherine go, until the crowd closed behind her.

'She's like you,' she heard from her side. Something in that lazy drawl was familiar, something that brought up the hairs on her neck. But when she turned, Joan didn't recognise the man immediately, sat at the kerbside with a floppy hat that sagged over his face. Years had passed after all. But those knotted fingers were somehow familiar, as he bent over what was left of a pie, loosening dirt from the crust with a fingernail. And when he glanced up again, lifting his hat in a mock salute, she saw that matted hair, thinner now, and those pink-rimmed eyes. She took a step back. 'Don't go running away now. You're quite safe here,' the man said, pushing himself up to standing.

'Leave me alone,' Joan said, somewhere between a hiss and a whisper, wanting a stronger voice but finding it had deserted her. She was back in that alleyway near the Lamb Inn again, so long ago. His face looming into hers, mouth hanging open wetly. The wall at her back.

The man laughed, that dirty titter she remembered, then threw the pie crust back down to the gutter it must have come from. He took another step towards her. 'Leave you alone, should I, Widow Randall?' Her shock must have shown on her face. 'Been a long time, hasn't it? And yes, I know exactly who you are. I make it my business to know everyone around these parts, you'll recall.'

He'd been a shambling figure in a doorway back then, best forgotten. A beetle-head, a loose-handed carouser, one drink away from oblivion. She'd been grateful to get away from him, and hoped never to stumble over his sorry face again, but she had put his existence from her mind long ago. It seemed he had not done the same – it nauseated Joan even to think of it – had he been watching her all this time? She wished she had his name, at least, so that she could shame this slug in front of the crowd.

'Wasn't as far gone as you thought I was,' he said, reading her expression, and it was true there was no trace of liquor about him now, even if he still wore the tattered garments of a drunk. He looked older, but leaner, a wiry strength about him that made her throat tighten with unease. 'And I never forget a face. Takes my time, but I like to know things about people. Especially women who likes to think they're better than what they are. Better than us menfolk, even.'

He jutted his chin towards her. A few heads turned at the bitter tone of his voice – the herb-seller frowned from behind his stall – but no one moved to intervene. 'I *have* been watching you, if that's what you're wondering. And I'm surprised they don't take you for a witch,' he went on. 'All that time you must spend hunkered over a stinking cauldron. Wouldn't take much to spread the word about, would it? There are men in this town spoiling for another dunking.'

Joan swallowed, wanting to look across towards the apothecary's door for a sight of Catherine, but not wanting to draw his eye there. She glanced around her instead, anxious for any familiar face, but the crowd seethed past in a disinterested mass, too distracted by the heaving stalls and the piper who had started up under the arches to notice her wild eyes.

'Expecting your blacksmith to leap out from behind the butcher's block, are you?' The man snorted. 'Thrupp's not been seen here for a year or more. Word has it, he burnt his arm so badly, he had no choice but to scuttle back to his father's farm.

Running the old man's errands round Nether Lypiatt, cos he's no good for anything more.' He put a hand out and reached for the tassels on the shawl around Joan's throat, pulling one tight until the stretched wool was pulled thin.

'Don't touch me,' she hissed, batting away his hand. A few more heads around them turned, but the man laughed again, as lightly as if they were playing loggits. Joan watched them shrug and move on.

'Think you're too good for it, do you, Widow Randall? Think your business takes you above the likes of me? Perhaps you'd rather I touched your daughter then, witchy.' He leaned in and his voice was syrupy as treacle. 'Now she's a pretty girl, isn't she? Thin as a blade of grass, but I wouldn't kick her out of the cot.'

Joan flinched, unable to hide her horror, and he laughed again. 'What are you scared of, Widow Randall? In this crowd? Surely I wouldn't dare to lay a hand on you here, would I? Wouldn't press a hand up your skirts?' But he was close enough for her to glimpse the scar that ran from his ear to where his tunic met his neck. To recognise those fingers – old man's fingers, hooked and mottled – and the thickness of his arms, that seam of muscle below his tunic, which sat at odds with the age of them. To see the yellow-marbled whites of his eyes, and their direction towards her corset and the ribbons that tied it.

You would, and you will, she thought. *I know very well you will try any moment, but I won't let you.* And just as he made a grab for her, his right hand grasping at her breast, his other at her neck, she stamped, hard, on the loose leather of the man's slipper. In the same instant, she shoved her palm against the muddied linen of his tunic. And as he yelped and fell back with the force of her thrust, Joan shrieked for the bailiff, Steight, hoping she'd be loud enough to be heard over the piper's tune. Steight looked up from where he stood at the victualler's cart;

at the sight of Joan's expression, he shouted back, a great boom across the market stalls, and began to push towards her through the crowd.

The sound of Steight's voice had the man turning about at last, and trying to wrestle his way off in the opposite direction. But the marketgoers' attention had been properly caught now. They resisted his escape through the crowd, and the man rebounded against the mass of them as if he'd fallen onto a taut skin. Some of the men in his path jostled together so that they formed a longer wall, pulling in others to widen the chain. Wives yanked on husbands' arms, calling on them to assist, and the crowd thickened.

The sun had broken through the clouds and the man was squinting into it, looking this way and that for another way out, but the crowd had formed a loose circle around him. The man was shouting obscenities now, calling Joan a witch and a whore. 'You haven't seen the last of me,' he yelled, but then someone got a strap across his mouth and silenced him. Mr Ridler called across from his stall, and Joan saw in the corner of her eye the green flash of the old merchant's hat as he began to push his own way through towards them. When the bailiff Steight broke through the ring of linked arms, he had only to grab the man by the shoulder, and Ridler was only a few steps behind. Many hands were offered to help drag the man away.

'Doesn't have many friends in this town, does Boothe,' said Mr Ridler afterwards. 'There'll be plenty to speak against him. But he didn't harm you?'

Boothe. His name seemed to speak of all the things he'd wanted of her. *Only my pride*, thought Joan, but she shook her head at the merchant's question.

'He's done similar before. They'll want him charged this time. I dare say you'll be called, for testimony,' Steight said later, after he had quizzed her and turned to go. 'But there's nothing to fear in it. A little time in the gaol will help him repent of his actions.'

'Joan, will you sit a moment?' Ridler now, with a hand to her arm. 'There is a stool behind my trestle.'

Joan had to swallow not to flinch at the touch, much as she liked the man. She shook her head. But everyone wanted to offer something, now. From beside the wool merchant, the herb-seller pressed a sprig of dried lavender into her palm, urging Joan to follow her back for something more to calm her nerves. Then the victualler offered a cup of something back at his cart. Joan forced a smile, heartened by their concern. 'Thank you. But I am quite well. Something and nothing. I must wait for my daughter here, so she knows where to find me.'

They wouldn't leave her at once, fussing around her – even the piper stopped his playing to come and ask after her health – and Joan tolerated the attention while wishing them away. But she refused every offer, with thanks, her eye still trained on the far side of the street for the first sight of Catherine's blue gown. Eventually, the well-wishers returned to their stalls one by one, some more reluctant than others to give up on such rare drama. When Catherine finally appeared through the crowd, Joan was standing alone.

'You look pale,' Catherine said at once, looking up at her. She did not have to look up far – they were almost equal in height now. 'Are you quite well, Mama?'

'Very well, thank you.' Joan would not trouble her daughter with it. Catherine had nightmares enough. Joan pinched her fingers in her pocket to keep her voice steady. 'Did they have the tincture?'

'Yes.' Catherine pulled a brown vial from her skirts. 'It smells of old stockings. I cannot imagine how it can help.'

Joan forced herself to laugh. Her legs felt unreliable, wobbly as the jelly in an eel pie. 'Your grandfather swears by it. Shall we go on?'

'A little something first?' Catherine's eye had been drawn by the baker's stall, and now she was grinning and pulling on Joan's arm. Catherine might have the height of a woman, but her daughter was not yet even the age Joan had been when she had lost her own mother, and sometimes the child in her still emerged.

'We have errands yet to run, Catherine,' Joan said. As much as anything, she was keen to get away. Some of the folk who'd watched the man dragged away still stood about, as if waiting for the next chapter.

'Something to share. Please?' A memory of Daniel came to Joan then, sharp and sweet together. That cowslip tart, those yellow trumpets, perfect in its sugar glaze. She scanned the baker's table, half-afraid to find one like it, but perhaps it was too early in the year. It seemed churlish to deny Catherine when she had change in her pocket, though, and perhaps a little something sweet would settle the thud of Joan's heart in her chest.

'Go on then. A slice of honey pudding, please sir, cut into two.' The baker moved forward with his knife to separate a piece from the dense mound of dough. Joan could taste it already; she and Catherine shared that sweet tooth.

They moved under the arched hall to eat their pudding. From its shelter Joan watched the market crowd surge and shift around the stalls, reclaiming the space as if nothing untoward had happened there. Women bartered eggs and hedgerow forage for cheese and winter greens. A stout man in a leather jerkin laid out horseshoes in a fan, calling out their quality. With the bailiff otherwise occupied, Joan saw one of the young lads from the Tayloe mill pull a limp partridge from a wicker basket, swiftly plucking its feathers before handing it to a man who waited. Beyond him, further into the shadows below the church school, some quack doctor Joan didn't recognise had set up stall, his patients waiting in line behind the stool where he would treat them. An old man with a rolled up trouser-leg held out a blackened ankle for inspection.

Perhaps it was busier now than it had been when she was a child, but in many ways nothing had changed since. The catcalling stallholders, the jester on the hall steps, the drunken millboys with their stained fingertips . . . all here, just as then. If Joan closed her eyes, she could imagine Daniel as if they were transported back, her tall young man leaning up against the market hall, or the yellow of his Sunday hat as he leant in to hear what the soft-spoken herb-seller was saying. It pained her every day that he was gone.

And then there was Alice. Impossible to think of those old days without her sister . . . in a flash of bright skirt, a dancing tune from the band, a high laugh from somewhere in a side street. There was that dread, too, of course, that the Alice of today might lurk round any corner. Joan had still not set eyes on her sister since Daniel threw her from the house so long ago. She looked down at the cobbles, slick with last night's rain and this morning's spillages, suddenly unwilling to glance around too hard in case she found her.

'Where next?' Catherine had finished her piece of pudding and was patting her cheeks for stray crumbs.

'Come with me,' Joan said. If I must be transported back there, then let us do it properly, she thought, taking Catherine's hand. She had spotted the tall black hat of the Dutch merchant as they had walked down Long Street earlier. And now they found him in the same quiet corner on the edge of the church wall, a little more stooped than he used to be, his vials and pouches and corked flasks displayed with those same swatches before them. She'd been here since, of course, many times, but never with Catherine, who turned over the scraps of dyed broadcloth now with something like the wonder Joan had once felt.

'I thought you'd like it,' Joan said. 'Your father brought me here, so long ago, when we were just beginning.'

Catherine's cheeks reddened. Any hint of romance sent her cheeks blazing. But she leant in close to see the contents of the merchant's wares, tipping up a stoppered bottle of green crystals, sniffing one of the stacked bundles of dried herbs. Joan watched her turn the label on an earthenware urn to read its contents – she and Mrs Freme had taught Catherine to read between them – and then return to the coloured swatches, testing the colour-fastness of the wool with her fingertips.

'I have been buying from Mr Willemzoon since I was not much older than you are. I want you to learn all he sells.'

'What's this, then?' Catherine held up a small glass bottle to the light; cochineal beetles, of course. 'Grain?'

'That's right, Catherine. For scarlet. They call it grain, but really they are beetles from a spiked plant from the other side of the world. Cochineal, vermillion, the creatures have many names. Do they look well?'

'I'm not sure how a dead beetle could look well. But they are plump as if full of juice.'

'Very good. Shake the glass now. We must check there's no grit or clay mixed in.'

Catherine did as she was asked. 'Nothing but the little critters themselves. It will make a fine scarlet, I think.'

Brighter than rose hips. Brighter than the ladybird's wing. Joan bit her cheek as she remembered how she had eked out the few grains she'd had left to dye Daniel's funeral cloth, having to rely on madder's lesser shade. Now she had money enough to dye a ship's sail with the stuff, but was she any the richer?

'Enough for today,' she said, already moving away from the stall. Catherine looked surprised to be dragged away so suddenly, but Joan needed to put space between herself and these memories. *Enough bloodshed, enough heartache.* Enough drama too; she felt as if she had lived ten days over since they'd left that morning at dawn. Joan muttered only the briefest farewell to the merchant as she hurried Catherine away through the crowd; she would have to make good another day.

'Mother? Mama?' Catherine had resorted to patting Joan's hand to catch her attention. When Joan met her eye, her daughter's brow was marred with a deep frown and she was clicking her tongue on her teeth.

'Sorry, my love. I was a world away.' For Joan, there was always a period of reflection when she returned from the town. It might be that she spent the day dreading any glimpse of her sister, but when she returned with no sighting of Alice, there was always a pang of regret. She put it down to the shock of the double bereavement, worsened today by the actions of that pig Boothe in the market. It was the work of a moment to recall her sister's many faults and quell the feeling; she vowed not to think of it again.

'A hare. That is what we should choose,' Catherine was saying now. 'It was Esther's favourite.'

They had been discussing the symbol for their cloth mark. It was Mr Ridler who had suggested it: that with the increasing popularity of their broadcloth, it would serve them well to use a mark to distinguish it. They had talked of trout and sheep and beech and ash, but discounted them all.

'My mother's too. And your sketch is very fine.'

When Catherine drew, the lines flowed without correction, as if the drawing already existed beneath the surface of the slate and her chalk merely drew it to the surface. Joan loved to watch her: the concentration as her daughter bent over her slate, the widening of her eyes as her ideas took shape. The hare she had sketched with the barest few lines still held all the urgent poise of the creature.

'But I fear others may not look on it as we do,' Joan went on. Catherine's shoulders sank a little at that. She had been full of enthusiasm when the conversation began, and Joan hated to dampen it like this. 'It is only that people hold such superstitions for the poor creatures. Doom-mongers and witches' familiars, that is how they think of them. It's ridiculous, I know, when we know them for the gentlest of beasts, but we must think of the sale of the cloth.'

'What then? I have exhausted my ideas.' Catherine swiped the slate with a rag as if she might prefer to throw it across the room. Joan could not help but smile at the drama in the gesture. Her daughter hovered on the tightrope between child and woman, and it both broke and warmed Joan's heart to watch her find her place.

'I have it,' Joan said, thinking again of Mr Ridler. 'He calls me the blue hawk, and he has you for one too. Could you draw something like it?'

'Yes, yes.' Catherine was caught up in it at once, and it was only a moment later before the bird was there: fan-tail and fingertip wings. Blue hawk. Spur-hawk. Stone falcon. Truly her daughter had a gift, to be able to render a creature so sparely.

'You have it. Oh Catherine, you have it.' Joan was surprised to find her eyes full of tears, and when she felt a hand on her shoulder, she started.

'Is this the one?' Mrs Freme had padded in silently on feet cushioned by several layers of stockings. She felt the cold, these days, and rarely strayed far from the fire. 'You have done a good job there, girl. There's our blue hawk, riding the breeze before the deadly stoop. Will you fashion the mould in clay for the clasps?' They could pour lead into the mould, then, again and again, and when each clasp had cooled, every piece of their broadcloth could be simply marked with a pinch each side to leave the soft metal bird-stamp behind.

'Tomorrow,' Joan said firmly, and Catherine made a face but she put down the slate and stood to bid them goodnight.

When she had slipped away to her cot, the older woman eased herself down onto the stool Catherine had left. Joan held out a hand for her to steady herself, but Mrs Freme shook her head.

'She grows quickly, your girl. And you have both come so far.'

It was true all Joan's hard work had brought them all some comfort. But it hadn't been straightforward. The dye garden was a demanding mistress, and Joan often wondered how Mrs Freme had ever kept it alone. And while the dye-man's rooms were tall and airy, they were already cluttered with his own equipment. When Joan's father had sold his cottage, the buyer had made a great deal of its imposition on common land, reflecting the irregularity in his price; there was no room for looms in the tiny Toadsmoor cottage he bought to replace it, so all of his tools and stock had been gifted to Joan. They could only be stored in a pile in a corner for now, something else to be navigated as she and Catherine spun and weaved and dyed in the cramped space. Every beam was hung with strips of dyed cloth, twenty experiments for every piece sold, and even the ironwork at the end of Catherine's cot was wound with dyed yarn.

As for her father, if Joan had feared he would waste away in old age, she could not have been be more mistaken. He seemed to have a new lease of life. When Joan had heard it said that he had taken up with the sharp-tempered cook, old Mrs Goodlake, she had hardly believed it, but then she'd seen them for herself, strolling along the Frome one evening after the fulling hammers had fallen silent, and the pair had not seemed so unlikely. Like a tattered gentleman and his lady wife, in fact, out for a promenade. These days Mrs Goodlake even smiled from time to time.

'You are becoming thin again, though,' Mrs Freme said now, leaning over to pat Joan's knee. 'It will serve no one if you fall ill from overwork.'

Joan smiled. It was a great comfort to have a friend to think of her. 'The widow', ridiculous now, Joan knew, when she was one herself, but a great part of Joan still expected Daniel to walk in at any moment, as if he might have slipped out to visit her father, and didn't instead lie six feet under the Bisley churchyard. And despite Mrs Freme's concern, Joan had thrived on the bustle and commotion, and her arms were as strong as they were slender, Catherine's too.

'Did the day go well?' Mrs Freme asked. Her bonnet had slipped back from her forehead and the hair below it was pure white now. Joan watched her old friend lean her head against the timber post beside her, knew that she would not burden her with news of what she had endured in the market today, though she would sorely love to unburden herself with the thought of it.

'We sold well. Ridler has agreed to keep us well stocked over the coming weeks, as we build up the stock for the army commission.'

Mrs Freme nodded. 'And Alice? Any sight of her?'

'Not today. Not a whisper of Alice. Not since that time Catherine saw her sister-in-law coming away from the butcher's stall with a boy loaded up with joints and sausages.'

'Forgive me for asking, but you know it will happen one of these days. What would you say if you met your sister?'

Joan took her time to answer, though she had wondered the same a hundred times. She looked down at her hands, twisted her fingers while she struggled to find the words.

'I would . . .' she began, and then she looked across at her friend and laughed. Mrs Freme's eyes had drifted closed, and though they fluttered a moment at the sound, it was not enough to rouse her. Joan leaned over to press a cushion between the timber post and her old friend's head, helped her down into a chair. It had been a long day, and Mrs Freme was long past conversation tonight.

Instead, Joan sat up alone a while, replaying what had occurred with Boothe in the market, worrying at it, in case she could have done anything to invite such attention, though she knew in her heart she had not. And then, when she had put the matter to rest, she was surprised to find herself thinking of the blacksmith a moment: Thrupp, with his burnt arm. And when she slept, she dreamt of tending to his injuries, though even as she did it, she knew what she was tending to was her own broken heart.

Chapter Twenty-Eight

Later that same year, and summer was at its end. On the hillsides, the first puffballs were cropping, incongruous snowballs in the long grass. The beeches were turning gold, the ivy flower-heads were dizzy with bees, and great, pulsing murmurations of starlings darkened the valley's skies each night.

The three women had spent the previous day grinding the first wheat for a Lammas loaf – fashioned into a hawk, of course, with salt for her eyes and the tips of her wings obligingly charred by the fire. Mrs Freme had seemed in good spirits, accompanying Joan and Catherine to the dancing which took place in the meadow after the church service, and staying up later than was her custom. On the way home she'd pulled wild celery stalks from beside the mill stream, tucking them into her belt for the following day's pottage. When Catherine insisted on crossing the river with the old stepping stones rather than using the bridge, Mrs Freme had followed, laughing and holding out her thin arms for balance. When they returned home and Catherine had slipped away to her bed, the widow was sleepy and a little breathless, but she seemed in the mood for confidences; she called Joan the daughter she'd always wished for, and showed her some of the linens from her hope chest, pressing on her a pretty lace-trimmed pillowcase which had been embroidered with her initials. But when Joan came to call for her the next morning, the old woman lay still in her bed.

Joan touched her old friend's arm where her nightgown sleeve had ridden up. She slept deeply these days, and sometimes Joan had to return several times before she was fully roused. But now her skin was cool as freshly dug earth. She had passed in her sleep, with the handful of meadow flowers Catherine had picked on a stool by her bedside table. Joan closed her eyes for a long moment, and then reached for the posy, crushing a clutch of leaves on a pennyroyal stem and bringing the peppermint scent to her nose. It was one of Mrs Freme's favourites. Perhaps she would make an oil of it, perfume the funeral shroud, send her old friend on her way with the scent of the meadows around her.

Joan took a step back from the bed. The old woman looked at perfect peace, and though her chest felt hollowed at the thought of living on without her, Joan knew already that this would not be the raw, savage mourning which had followed Daniel and Esther's deaths. A grateful sadness. Recognition of a life well lived, and a friend who would be sorely missed. For Catherine, of course, it would be different – she had known Mrs Freme her whole life, and the widow had been like the grandmother she lacked; Joan's heart was heavy with the thought of bearing the news.

'Catherine,' Joan called – there would be no comfort in waiting – and then she held her daughter while she shuddered out the first wave of her grief. Afterwards, they laid the widow out together. Catherine's tears splashed heavy on the sheets as they worked but she did not cry out and Joan did not question the decision to ask for her help. There was a slim pleasure in attending to one they had loved so much.

When they had washed and readied the old woman's body, they dressed her in her favourite lavender gown, dyed by Joan the year before, and then sat together by a low fire, sharing a cup of small beer. They took their time in calling for the searcher and sending word to the church, knowing that Mrs Freme had little time for such things. Instead, they lit every rushlight in the house, setting them on windowsills and thresholds. They went about their business around the widow for the whole of the rest of that day, reluctant to allow the world to move on.

'Mama, can I walk home with Annie?'

It was the day of Mrs Freme's funeral. The church service was over and there would be no gathering afterwards. It was not a lack of generosity on Joan's part, but something Mrs Freme had often mentioned, urging Joan to forgo the expense of the revelry and spend the money on a good flask of wine for herself and Catherine alone.

Joan had imagined that she and her daughter would spend the evening together, then, in quiet contemplation of their lost companion. Her reluctance must have shown on her face, because Harriet laid a hand on her arm. Harriet, who was looking thinner and a little pale these days with the effort of keeping her growing family. Her husband Ralph was not always able to find work in the fields, especially as cheaper, younger men came home from army commissions, so Joan always tried to keep the lightest piecework for Alice's friend – her friend, now, absurd to talk of her as anything else after all this time – paying her all she could afford.

But now Joan realised she should be doing more; Joan had work enough for all of them, Harriet could join them in the business. Work with them, not for them; it was only fair to mark their long friendship in this way. But then, weighed heavy in her gut, she remembered the fresh instability of her own position. She and Catherine would have to leave Mrs Freme's house, which had been leased to her only for the length of her lifetime. Their cosy arrangement with the dye-man and his spacious rooms was doubtless what sustained the business; who knew what would remain of it if they had to start all over again?

'I will not let Annie keep her long,' Harriet said, oblivious to Joan's reckonings. 'Not at all, if you would rather she come home with you.' Of course, Harriet understood without Joan needing to explain; Harriet had always been quick to pick up on others' pain, always keen to dispel it.

But when Joan looked at Catherine now, arm-in-arm with her best friend, her daughter's fingers scored with weaving lesions and eyes dark from rising each day before dawn, she didn't have the heart to refuse her. 'No, she can go,' she said. Catherine's childhood had been short even by the standards of this valley. She was half-woman already – the glances of the young man in the next pew had not escaped Joan's attention – and she had been through so much. Mrs Freme of all people would have understood; there would be time enough for remembrance. 'Send her home well before dark, though, will you?' Joan asked Harriet.

Harriet nodded, and ushered the girls away, their hands already clasped and the air full of their chatter. From behind, Harriet's waist was as slender as theirs, and with the lines on her face hidden, she could be just another young maid among them. Joan watched them until they had turned the corner on the path before making her own way back down into the valley.

She was alone then, when she returned to Mrs Freme's house. Now that the formalities of the funeral were concluded, perhaps the luxury of a day of rest. Once inside, though, with the windows hung with mourning cloths, Joan found the gloom oppressive. And where there should have been repose, she found herself unable to relax, unused to such leisure and all too aware of the uncertainty that filled their lives now she had gone. Where would they go? Mrs Freme had been both friend and patron. Had Joan done enough yet so that she and Catherine could stand on their own feet?

It was too early for such thoughts. Yes, the day would come when they would have to close the door of this house behind them, but she knew the legal process around property was long and tortuous, and it might grant them some respite. But Joan found she could not escape the itch of uncertainty with all the apparatus of her business around her. She needed fresh air, and the tranquillity and inspiration she had always found in the dye-garden. So she was there, alone, planting woad seedlings and pulling weeds from the roots of the established crop as she had done so many times before, when she heard the gate screech on its hinge and the crunch of footsteps on the gravel path behind her.

It would be Catherine, back after a change of heart. They would have their time together after all. 'The other pair of gloves is on the chair by the stove,' Joan called, without looking back.

But there was no response, and there was no answering tread towards the back door.

'Cat got your . . .' Joan started, kneeling up and turning her head about. But the words fell away when she saw who stood behind her.

'I was given the wrong day. I came ready for a service on the morrow.' It was Alice, and her expression of deep regret might appear genuine, but Joan disregarded it; it was sad that long experience had schooled her to be so untrusting.

Alice was garbed in full mourning: an absurdly fine black gown, with lace and frills and ribbons that made it seem gaudy and overblown despite its hue. Jet black. No small matter to dye the cloth for it, Joan could not help but imagine, requiring hard water to dissolve the lime, and a great quantity of dye-stuffs: woad and logwood, alder and maple bark, copperas and alum and blue vitriol. Joan could see the words in that old dye manual her sister had procured for her so long ago. Surely the queen consort mourned her mother in less extravagant style? Joan dropped her eyes back to the earth, to give herself time to recover her own expression.

'What nonsense is this?' she said at last. 'You barely knew the woman.'

'Can I not mourn my sister's friend? As soon as I heard, I knew I must come to offer my support.'

Again, the voice was full of remorse, and no one else would have doubted the sincerity. But Joan had built a hard wall around the place in her heart which concerned Alice, and it would not be so easily dismantled. Where had she been when Daniel and Esther died, if a funeral drew such compassion?

'Why have you come, Alice?'

'As I said . . .'

'Why, in all honesty?' Joan interrupted, her voice high and urgent. 'I implore you to tell the truth, for once in your life. Because I have no husband left to seduce, and barely a penny to my name, and I am sorely vexed to imagine what you could want from me.'

Silence then, and Joan shook her head and went back to her weeding. There was a calm to be had in feeling the grit of the earth between her fingers, as she pulled goose-grass and fat-hen from between the woad leaves. What was it to her if Alice stood there all day or left without another word? Pretend that she was no more than a gatepost, Joan would not let it trouble her.

But Alice cast a long shadow across the beds, and it became difficult to ignore. In any case, Joan's sister had never been able to keep silent for long.

'I admit it was an excuse,' Alice said at last. 'I do not pretend any great closeness to Mrs Freme. Though perhaps now, as a widow myself, I feel more appreciation of her position.'

Joan could not help but turn round at this.

'Yes, he's dead,' Alice confirmed, pulling her shawl around her. 'A month ago.' Joan wondered that she had not heard, but she had not been near the town for longer than that, and with the funeral arrangements for Mrs Freme, there had been little time for talk of anything else. Her father must have known? He could not be so much preoccupied with his new acquaintance. Could it even be that he had taken seriously Joan's request that they should never speak of Alice again?

'By the end, his skin was pitted and pustuled as a toad's back,' Alice went on. 'The physician was kind enough to record it as scurvy, as would befit an honest gentleman, but I'm afraid the cause lies with one of his long-standing proclivities. If ever there was a man who invited his own demise, it was Walter, and no amount of mercury purging could cure him.'

Joan got to her feet, brushing the dirt from her knees. This news was all no more than Alice deserved, it was true. But Joan brought her hand to her mouth, bit on the soft flesh of her finger as she regarded her sister's face.

'The irony was, he died accusing me of bearing another man's child. Indignant, as if his yard had never left his breeches in the presence of anyone but his wife. You were lucky, to have the man you did,' Alice said then, and her eyes dropped to the floor as she spoke. Joan read her features as if studying a text. The years had taken their toll on her sister; it was some time since Joan had used the looking glass. And now she saw in Alice's face how she herself must have aged. The creping around her eyelids, the slackness of the skin under her chin. No amount of fancy clothes and town living could escape the passage of time, it seemed. But when her sister looked up, Joan recognised their mother's eyes – always so damnably hard – and she saw that her sister had indeed suffered. That something, however small, had shifted. Perhaps her father had been right, reporting that the pregnancy had changed something in Alice. And it touched Joan, against her better judgment, so that she did not throw Alice out at once, as a great part of her wished to do.

'Perhaps I was lucky. You have not been afflicted yourself, I hope?' she said at last.

'Not yet, though I dread to wake every day for the first sign.'

'I am truly sorry for your loss.' Joan held Alice's gaze while she said it, but then she turned about with the intention to return to her weeding. She had done her part. The wall between them might have been taken down a brick or two, but it had been built over many years, and it endured.

'Wait, I have something to show you. Someone, rather.' Alice caught Joan's sleeve as she turned about.

'I'm not . . .' Joan started.

But Alice had already pushed the gate back open, and beyond it, on the bank of the stream, Joan could see a basket, with a cloth laid over one half to ward off the sun. She watched Alice walk out and lift the basket's handles to return with it, the wicker sides bumping against her knees.

'See?' Alice set the basket down at Joan's feet and peeled away the sun shade. 'I have called her Hannah. Walter wanted Sarah, after his ill-tempered sister, but under the circumstances he could not refuse me.'

Alice continued to prattle on but Joan hardly heard her. It was not just that she had not expected to be surprised with a child today – although to be presented with one with such peachy, unblemished skin, cushioned in such a finely spun longcoat, felt both an affront and also a blessing on this raw, painful day. But it was more than that . . . it was this child, this one, who resembled so strongly not Alice, not Walter. Not Joan, even. No one so much as their mother. Little Hannah was fat and round as a bumblebee, but her eyes, unblinking and clear as she fixed them on Joan now, were all Hannah Browning's. Grey-green as nettle-dyed wool, like a message from the past. Joan's own daughters had not been visited in this way. What did it mean that this little girl alone, the outcome of such an unfortunate union, had been blessed with her grandmother's peepers?

'I wish you well, both of you,' Joan said at last.

'You need not worry. Walter has left me a rich woman . . .' Alice started, patting at the luxuriant fabric of her gown as if reassured by its extravagance, as determined as ever of her superiority. 'Perhaps he had no time to change his will. Certainly his sisters were surprised by the generosity of it.' This was the old Alice. Joan almost laughed to see it. It would not surprise her if Alice had written that will herself. But then something in her sister's expression changed. Alice's eyes reddened and her shoulder sank a fraction, and Joan could imagine her alone suddenly, in that echoing house, with only the snide carping of her mother- and sister-in-law for company. It was not as if Joan's own future looked brighter, but she would not have the burden of enduring it alone.

'Thank you, Joan. I know I do not deserve your support, and you are kind to offer it,' Alice said, and she dropped her head in a little bow. 'I'm sorry for your many losses. You deserved far greater happiness.'

Joan nodded. Alice was not truly changed – how could she alter her nature, when it was seared down into the fabric of her bones? – and it would be wise if something of that wall in Joan's heart was never dismantled. But a rope, perhaps, could be thrown over it. Unlike Catherine, Joan was lucky enough to have a sister alive, and what a waste not to make the most of it.

'Come back, sometime,' Joan said. And then, when she saw Alice's face brighten too quickly, 'Catherine will be pleased to see the baby.'

Afterwards, Joan watched her sister go, shuffling the basket back through the gate and along the river to the little bridge there. On the far side, Joan saw now that a young girl was waiting under the willow – the child's nurse, perhaps – and when she had relieved Alice of the basket, the two disappeared together up the hillside.

Joan watched them until they were faint dots along the valley. And she stood there a while after, pressing the leaves of a stand of woad between her fingers, smelling that familiar cabbage stink and letting the stain mark her fingertips, until the last twist of the path took Alice and the young girl out of view.

Probably she would never truly understand her sister. Definitely she would never truly trust her. Now, as so often, Joan wished there was something true in the hedgerow sorcery that claimed Hannah Browning's spirit which might be conjured up with this palmful of woad. Joan had lost one mother, now she'd lost the closest thing she had to another, and she must seek to understand her sister alone. But in fact she hardly needed her mother's voice to tell her, and she knew it as she turned away: better to have Alice in her life than live without. Joan threw the crushed woad leaves in the river, watched them leach blue-green as they floated downstream, and then Catherine's familiar call drew her home.

Epilogue

Three months later, on the heels of a solicitor's letter informing her of the upcoming sale of the widow's property, Joan Randall received word that the proposed buyer was one Mrs Smart. A week after, by another legal missive, she learned that Alice had indeed bought the property, and had the intention of settling a lifetime lease of the garden, the dyehouse and the rooms on one Mrs Joan Randall and her daughter, Catherine.

From that day, Joan Randall built the business she had begun so many times. With Harriet's help, she cleared out the old equipment and whitewashed the walls of Mrs Freme's cottage. Over time, they were able to set up wider looms and some of the modern equipment which Daniel had so frowned on. Sometimes Harriet's youngest, Betty, played in amongst them, plaiting stray yarn strands and assembling rainbows from the dyed edges. Occasionally Harriet's husband Ralph would drop in, on his way home from his new job as the church's groundsman.

When Joan's father died, after five happy years on Mrs Goodlake's arm, Joan spent the small sum he left her on a lease of the Butler mill with its two fat springs, and had Catherine oversee the millsman there. Joan herself took responsibility for Mrs Freme's dye garden, which had run a little wild in her last days, but was now as thriving as it ever had been: thick beds of woad, smaller patches of madder, every hedgerow dye flower she knew of, and a small, cherished plantation of indigo, which the Bristol merchant had brought at great expense from his latest trip to the Rajput territories. The dye vats were always full, and it was not long before they produced a first shipment of the striped Spanish cloth that was so in demand abroad. Joan imagined broadcloth marked with that fierce blue hawk transported in the hulls of ships traversing every one of the seven seas, to reach lands more distant than she could ever have imagined.

The dye-man himself never returned from the Continent, though a banker's draft for the rental of his rooms continued to arrive in the spring of each year, and Joan heard once from the French tailor who visited the market in Stroud from time to time that an English dyer had set up his business in a former fort just across the Italian border from the merchant's hometown, and that he was doing a fine trade in the rich, dark colours which were popular in the region at the time. She gave the money he sent to the church for alms each time.

Boothe, the man from the market, spent some time in the town gaol. He would have returned there not long after, having stolen a basket of latches and other ironmongery, but he was understood to have accepted an order of deportation to Prince Rupert's Land, where he claimed he would make his fortune. Nothing more was heard of him, though many ships went down on that sailing and perhaps his was among them.

Joan encountered the blacksmith Thrupp in the market in Stroud one Saturday, caught off guard with her arms full of broadcloth samples and wraps of dyestuff. She saw at once that his burns extended from under his sleeve in whorls of pale scar tissue across the back of his palm, and she almost put out a hand to touch them. But they exchanged only pleasantries, as she understood him to be married by then, though it was strange that he found reason to be in the Chalford valley on more than one occasion over the years that followed.

Alice visited the valley from time to time. She'd bought a clothier's villa at Cainscross, after the sale of the Butter Row house, and she would always arrive in a smart carriage that looked out of place on the donkey path, with Hannah peeping shyly from behind her skirts. If Catherine was at home, Hannah would throw her arms around her cousin, and Joan would smile to see it, but she and her sister were more careful with each other. Their partings were tender, even if each left with some relief. It was Alice who told Joan about the blacksmith, whose wife had left him to return to her family in Cornwall, complaining that the cold winters in Gloucestershire left her longing for the relative warmth of that coast. Afterwards, as she often did after Alice's visits, Joan spent time in the dye garden, planting new seedlings, taking her time to loosen the roots and bed them in the soil, allowing herself to absorb what she had heard.

And when the great wheel of the seasons had turned ten times more, it found Joan knelt in that same garden, harvesting a bed of woad she had planted that long-ago morning. Catherine's twin boys were playing dice around her boots as she eased the plants from the soil. Behind her, pegs and twine marked out the foundation of some extra rooms she had commissioned at the back of the house, for Catherine and her family. A small concession to a new-found wealth: a clothier as good as any other, and the Blue Hawk mark had ridden the breeze to travel wide and far.

As Joan straightened up, she pressed a hand into the small of her back. Her joints might creak and curse a little these days, but she still had appetite to climb the hill to her tenter racks, and to walk along the riverbank with the blacksmith, on his regular visits to the valley. And as she knelt in that garden, old eyes still sharp, Joan saw in the dye plants all around her the many colours that could come from them – those that marked the life she had lived, and those for the years that were yet to come.

Acknowledgements

Joan's world – 17th century Gloucestershire – was one dominated by men, where women's working roles were lowly and often confined to the domestic sphere. While Joan's story is a work of fiction, I was inspired by a few, rare glimpses of real women that I found in Gloucestershire's textile industry: women who had found a way to carve something different for themselves – among them the indomitable Mrs Playne, who took over with some success the running of her husband's mill on his death (with eleven children in tow!), and a fleeting mention I came across of a female clothier from nearby Dursley. Undoubtedly such women were rare, and generally found their opportunity in unusual circumstances. A little further afield, I enjoyed the recent discovery by metal detectorists in Great Yarmouth of a trading token issued by a 17th century businesswoman in her own name.

In writing Blue Hawk, I explored and made use of historical reference books too numerous to mention. Local readers may recognise familiar surnames that belonged to families living in Chalford, Bisley and Stroud around this time, some of which survive today, or live on in the names of those mills still standing. Where I have used real names, the personalities and actions assigned to these historic characters are entirely fictional.

I'm incredibly grateful to Ian Mackintosh, local textile industry historian and founder member of both the Stroud Preservation Trust and the Stroud Textile Trust, who was kind enough to read and comment on a draft of Blue Hawk for me. While I took on the vast majority of Ian's suggestions (and am thankful to him not least for identifying a mid-novel resurrection of a dead minor character!), I have retained a couple of historical liberties and tweaked certain aspects of local geography in the interests of the story. In particular, the 'scarlet' dye from the cochineal beetle for which Stroud became famous, appears a few decades earlier in Blue Hawk than is reflected in the historical record. All mistakes are my own.

'Blue Hawk' was a real nickname around this time for someone with a sharp eye, and is also one of the traditional names for the sparrowhawk. Ornithology fans will no doubt observe that it is the male bird that has the blue-grey plumage, but I still liked it as a moniker for Joan.

Lots of people supported me in writing this book, for which I'm really grateful. I wrote much of it at Spacehoppers in Stroud, a co-working space where the excellent coffee and good company spurred me on. I'm always thankful for my network of writing friends, and in particular for the constant support of Laura Pashby, Sarah Edghill, Hannah Persaud and John Holland. And of course for my family and my husband Jon, for giving me space to write and keeping me sane.

Milton Keynes UK
Ingram Content Group UK Ltd.
UKHW042215050924
1520UKWH00006B/137

9 781917 090056